'A vivid and vital take on a space age future th~t ~ever actually hap-
pene~ ~~e, you may find yourself thinking, woul~ ~~ ~~~ ~ve'
                                                                    SFX

'A joy to read, it's yet another feather in Baxter and Reynolds' well-
adorned hats'   *SciFi Now*

'With these two titans of the genre, jaw-dropping imagination and
laser-sharp wordcraft are guaranteed. They have created a beautiful
novel, wonderful to explore'   *Sun*

'Brings the strengths of both writers - a thorough grasp of scientific
principles and the ability to present them in well-paced, engaging nar-
ratives'   *Guardian*

'Humanist, meditative, this is old-fashioned science fiction as evidenced by its sense of wonder and a positive attitude to scientific
progress but, alongside, manages to keep the thrills on overdrive and
the cosmic and planetary problems ticking along. A good read'
                                                        Lovereading.co.uk

'If I'm honest, I wasn't expecting *The Medusa Chronicles* to be much
more than a tip of the hat to Arthur C. Clarke, but Baxter and Reynolds go far farther by realising a resounding sweep of a story with rich
seams of science and speculation, some unforgettable spectacle and
not a few emotional moments'   Tor.com

ALSO BY STEPHEN BAXTER FROM GOLLANCZ:

NON-FICTION
Deep Future
The Science of
     Avatar

FICTION
Mammoth
Longtusk
Icebones

Reality Dust
Evolution

Flood
Ark

Proxima
Ultima

Obelisk

Xeelee: An Omnibus
Xeelee: Endurance
Xeelee: Vengeance

DESTINY'S CHILDREN
Coalescent
Exultant
Transcendent
Resplendent

A TIME ODYSSEY
(with Arthur C. Clarke)
Time's Eye
Sunstorm
Firstborn

TIME'S TAPESTRY
Emperor
Conqueror
Navigator
Weaver

NORTHLAND
Stone Spring
Bronze Summer
Iron Winter

ALSO BY ALASTAIR REYNOLDS FROM GOLLANCZ:

NOVELS
Revelation Space
Redemption Ark
Absolution Gap
Chasm City
Century Rain
Pushing Ice
The Prefect
House of Suns
Terminal World

Blue Remembered
     Earth
On the Steel Breeze
Poseidon's Wake

Revenger

**SHORT STORY
COLLECTIONS:**
Diamond Dogs,
     Turquoise Days
Galactic North
Zima Blue

THE
MEDUSA
CHRONICLES

STEPHEN BAXTER&
ALASTAIR REYNOLDS

First published in Great Britain in 2016 by Gollancz
an imprint of the Orion Publishing Group Ltd
Carmelite House, 50 Victoria Embankment
London EC4Y 0DZ

An Hachette UK Company

1 3 5 7 9 10 8 6 4 2

A CIP catalogue record for this book is
available from the British Library.

ISBN 978 1 473 21020 2

Typeset by Input Data Services Ltd, Bridgwater, Somerset

Printed in Great Britain by Clays Ltd,
St Ives plc

MIX
Paper from
responsible sources
FSC® C104740

www.stephen-baxter.com
www.alastairreynolds.com
www.orionbooks.co.uk
www.gollancz.co.uk

To the memory of
Sir Arthur C Clarke

A MEETING WITH MEDUSA

Arthur C Clarke, 1971.

In the 2080s Howard Falcon is left crippled by the crash of the dirigible *Queen Elizabeth IV*, of which he was Captain. His life is saved by experimental cyborg surgery.

In the 2090s Falcon pilots a solo mission in a balloon craft called *Kon-Tiki* into the upper clouds of Jupiter, where he encounters an exotic environment complete with an ecology dominated by immense 'herbivorous' beasts he calls 'medusae', which are preyed on by 'mantas'.

Falcon's cybernetic surgery left him with superhuman capabilities but isolated from mankind, for there will be no more such experiments. But Falcon 'took sombre pride in his unique loneliness – the first immortal, midway between two orders of creation. He would . . . be an ambassador . . . between the creatures of carbon and the creatures of metal who must one day supersede them. Both would have need of him in the troubled centuries that lay ahead.'

This book is the story of those troubled centuries.

PROLOGUE

Falcon would always remember the day he had started to dream of escaping into the sky.

Commander Howard Falcon, World Navy, had been just Howard back then, eleven years old, living in the family home in Yorkshire, England, part of a Federated Zone of a newly united world. And it had snowed overnight.

He smeared his dressing gown sleeve across a cluster of panes in the window, wiping away the condensation. Each little square of glass had a precise L-shaped frosting of snow on the outside, where it had gathered on the lower edge and in one corner. There had been flurries of snow over the preceding days, but nothing as heavy as this overnight fall. And it had come in right on schedule, a seasonal gift from the Global Weather Secretariat.

The garden Howard knew was transformed. It seemed wider and longer, from the hedges on either side to the sawtooth fence at the end of the gently sloping lawn, and a ridge of snow lay on the fence, neat as the decoration on a birthday cake. It all looked so cold and still, so inviting and mysterious.

And the sky above the fence and hedges was clear, cloudless, shot through at this still-early hour with a delicate pale-rose pink. Howard looked at the sky for a long time, wondering what it would be like to be above the Earth, surrounded by nothing but air. It would be cold up there, but he'd put up with that for the freedom of flight.

Yet here in the cottage's parlour it was snug and warm. Howard had come down from his bedroom to find that his mother was up already, baking bread. She liked the old ways of doing things. His father had prepared the fire in the hearth and now it was crackling and hissing. On the mantle over the hearth was a collection of ornaments and souvenirs, including a clumsily assembled model on a clear plastic stand: a hot-air balloon with a gondola open to the air, a plastic envelope above.

Howard found his favourite toy and set it on the windowsill so it

3

could see the snow too. The golden robot was a complicated thing, despite its antique radio-age appearance. It had been a gift on his eleventh birthday only a couple of months earlier. He knew that it had cost his parents dearly to buy it for him.

'It's been snowing,' Howard said to the toy.

The robot buzzed and rattled to show it was thinking. Somewhere in its maze of circuits and processors was a speech-recognition algorithm.

'We could make a snowman,' said the toy.

'Yes,' Howard agreed, with the tiniest flush of disappointment. At a given prompt the robot tended to come out with the same response, over and over; any mention of snow, and the robot would propose making a snowman. It never suggested a snowball fight, or making snow angels, or sledging. It didn't really think at all, he reflected with faint dismay. Yet he loved it.

'C'mon, Adam,' he said at last. He snatched the robot off the sill, tucking it under one arm.

He went to the cupboard under the stairs to fetch his scarf, being quiet so that his mother did not nag him to put on warmer clothes before leaving the cottage. Then he remembered a chore he'd promised to do. Scarf around his neck, he returned to the parlour and used the poker to stir up the coals. For a moment, mesmerised, Howard stared into the depths of the fire, seeing shapes and phantoms in the dance of the flames.

'Howard!' his mother called from the kitchen. 'If you're thinking of going out, put your boots on . . .'

Pretending not to hear her, Howard crept out of the cottage, closing the door quietly behind him. He crossed the unmarred whiteness of the snow-covered lawn. His slippers pressed imprints into the snow. The air was chilly enough as it was, but there was a damper, more determined cold already seeping through the soles of his footwear. He set Adam down on the stone plinth of a bird table, where he could overlook proceedings.

Howard began scooping up snow.

'That is a good start,' said Adam.

'Yes, it's coming along.'

'You will want a carrot for the nose and some buttons for the eyes.'

He worked for a while longer. After a time, Adam encouraged him again. 'A very good snowman, Howard.'

In truth, the snowman was a lumpy, misshapen form, more like an anthill than a person. Howard found some twigs and jammed them into the slumped white mass. He stood back, hands on his hips, as if

4

the half-hearted effort was about to transform itself into something creditable.

But the snowman looked even sadder with the twigs.

'Look,' Adam said, raising a rigid arm, pointing into the sky.

Howard squinted, at first not seeing anything. But there it was. A tiny sphere, elongated at the base, moving through the air, with an even tinier basket suspended under it. A flame pulsed from the apparatus over the basket, a brief spark of brilliance against the brightening sky. The sun must have crept over the horizon, at least from the altitude of the balloon, for the side of its envelope was picked out as a crescent of gold.

Howard stared and stared. He loved balloons. He had seen them in books and in movies. He'd built models. He understood how they worked, sort of. But this was the first time he'd ever seen one with his own eyes.

The balloon was passing out of sight, going around the back of the cottage. Howard had to keep tracking it. Barely looking down, he grabbed Adam and ran, scuffing his way through the failed snowman, sending it toppling to the ground.

'I want to be up there,' Howard said.

'Yes, Howard,' Adam said patiently, his head bumping along the ground.

'Up there!'

ONE
ENCOUNTER IN THE DEEP
2099

1

The waves of the midwinter ocean crashed against the hull and spat foam over the railings around the bow. They might as well have been dashing against cliffs for all the difference it made to the great ship. On deck there was not a trace of the swell, not a trace of rocking. The *Sam Shore* felt as solid and still as if it were anchored to the seabed.

So what was wrong?

Falcon's eyes swept to port and starboard.

Zoom and focus.

Machines frolicked in the grey waters, their pale white bodies easily mistaken for living things.

Track and enhance.

The sleek forms, each a few metres long and equipped with cameras, grabber arms and miniaturised sonar pods, swam gracefully alongside the tremendous hull. At times they came alarmingly close, and Falcon wondered how safe such activity could be, given the choppiness of the sea. What if they collided with the carrier's hull? The safety of President Jayasuriya was at stake . . .

'Whale watching, are we, Howard?'

Falcon turned with some reluctance, the balloon wheels of his undercarriage slipping on the damp deck. But human company, after all, was why he was here; not even Howard Falcon was reclusive enough to turn down an invitation from the World President to join her for New Year on the world's largest cruise ship. Especially not *this* New Year, the birth of the twenty-second century. And he wasn't surprised to see who had found him, with no less a figure than the Captain in tow. Both shielded their faces against the cold and the spray, eyes narrowed to squints.

'Geoff Webster,' Falcon said. 'I'm barely off the shuttle and you've already tracked me down.'

Webster grinned. 'Howard, every time you descend from space I hear celestial trumpets.'

Webster, more than sixty years old, was one of Falcon's oldest friends: one of the few he'd kept in touch with since the *Queen Elizabeth IV* accident. Webster's manner towards Falcon since his rebuilding hadn't changed one iota, being just as ornery and honest as he'd ever been. And, since Webster was Administrator of the Bureau of Long Range Planning, one of the most significant branches of the Strategic Development Secretariat, he was a useful ally. Indeed Webster had provided crucial backing for Falcon's latest, career-defining venture: his solo journey into the clouds of Jupiter, from which he'd returned only months ago.

Now Webster grinned and presented his companion. 'Howard Falcon, I want you to meet Captain Joyce Embleton.'

To her credit, Embleton didn't hesitate to stick out a hand in welcome, and she managed not to grimace when Falcon took it with what passed for his own hand. 'Very good to have you aboard, Commander Falcon.'

She was trim, upright, fashionably bald under an elaborate peaked cap that was jammed down hard against the wind and the spray. And to Falcon's surprise she sounded impeccably British, here at the helm of what had once been the pride of the US Navy. But then it had been more than sixty years, he supposed, since Britain and America had been united in the Atlantic Partnership.

'You're quite the celebrity, Commander. We all followed your jaunt into the depths of Jupiter, earlier in the year. You may find yourself pestered for autographs by some of the younger crew. Although—' She glanced at Falcon's upper body.

Falcon said dryly, 'Believe it or not, I can still sign my name.'

Webster glared at Falcon. 'Howard, we're guests. Be nice.'

Embleton walked around Falcon, inspecting him in a no-nonsense fashion. 'Well, you don't strike me as a shrinking violet. There's still something of the human in you, isn't there? That *is* the face your mother gave you, even if it's become a somewhat immobile, leathery mask.'

'They warned me you were blunt, Captain Embleton. I thought they had to be exaggerating.'

'They weren't. Bluntness is a time-saver, I find.' She cocked her head at him. 'Ah, I see you're trying to smile.'

'I promise not to scare your guests by doing that too often.'

'I have an impulse to ask if you need anything to keep you warm. Most of our guests require something in this damp Atlantic wind, though of course the worst of the weather is kept off by our sonar and electromagnetic screens.' She snapped her fingers. 'Conseil?'

A dustbin-sized robot rolled away from another clump of guests and towards the Captain. 'May I serve you?'

Falcon, surprised, found himself nostalgically charmed. 'Hello, little fellow. Are you any use at making snowmen . . .?'

Webster raised his eyebrows.

'Never mind.'

Embleton said, 'We can get you anything you need, Commander.'

'Most people in these situations ask if I'm liable to rust.'

'I did think of it. Anyhow, I'm sure you won't feel out of place here.' She leaned over and murmured discreetly, 'You aren't our only guest from outer space. Look over to starboard.'

Falcon made out a group of passengers, tall, elegant; when they moved metal glinted on their limbs, and even from here he could hear a whir of servomotors. 'Martians?'

'Third generation. Bigwigs in Port Lowell. On Earth, they can't get out of bed without their exoskeletons. And I'm told that the intensive work done to save *you* pushed that technology ahead by leaps and bounds.'

'Glad to be of service,' Falcon said.

Embleton nodded. 'You may not be very good at smiling, Commander, but you can tell a joke.' They took a step closer to the railings around the edge of the deck. 'And you seem to be taken by our sea sprites.'

'Is that what you call them . . .? Captain, my background is the World Navy, but I'm out of my depth here. Took me a while to figure out that these beasts were mechanical, rather than exotic dolphins.'

'Well, there are dolphins around, and all manner of other wildlife. The seas have rather recovered, you know, since the bad old days. No, these sprites are best thought of as wardens – and very helpful to us they are. Come, walk with me . . .'

It was a reasonable hike. The carrier's flight deck was a mile long, the passengers had been told, and quilted with hatches that had once released fighter aircraft and smart missiles. To Falcon, looking ahead from near the bow of the craft, the great superstructures and fin-shaped hydroplanes at the stern were faded grey by mist.

Embleton said, walking slowly, 'Commander, the dear old *Sam Shore* is a war veteran, ninety years old, and spends much of its time in dry dock. When at sea we use any intervals when we're not under power, like this one, to allow the sprites to tend to the hull, the engine vents – even keeping off the barnacles is a challenge.'

'The sprites are independently powered? Autonomously controlled?'

'Self-powered, yes of course, but only a small degree of autonomy. The sprites are controlled from the ship, by the Bosun—'

'The Bosun?'

'Our main computer. Which itself is essentially subordinate to the commands of the crew.' She glanced down at Conseil, which had followed them, holding an empty drinks tray in one flexible manipulator. 'Interesting to reflect that the most advanced artificial intelligence on board is actually this little chap.'

Falcon bent to read the robot's manufacturer's plaque. He learned that 'Conseil' was a General Purpose Homiform Mark 9, a product of Minsky & Good, Inc., of Urbana, Illinois, United States, Atlantic Partnership. Falcon knew the name; Minsky specialised in computing technology. They marketed the best desk-top models available, and some of their advanced minisecs were small enough to fit into a pocket.

'An experimental model, able to take the initiative to some extent. Makes his own decisions about which guest to serve next, to anticipate requests, that sort of thing. And he has some emergency-response capabilities. I'm told that in fact he's capable of a good deal more independent thought and decision-making than our Bosun. And here he is serving drinks – but that's the way we like it, of course. With people in charge.'

Webster asked, 'Conseil? Why that name?'

Falcon tutted. 'Philistine. A Jules Verne reference, of course.'

Webster wasn't impressed. 'That's rich coming from someone who looks like a *prop* from a Verne movie.'

'What about time delay?'

Embleton looked up at Falcon. 'I'm sorry?'

'In your control of the sprites. Here they are playing around within metres of what I believe are your main ballast tanks, running along the hull here.'

Embleton smiled. 'You've looked us up, I see. Given what happened with the *Queen Elizabeth*, I see why you'd be concerned about time delays and reaction times . . .'

Twelve years ago, a signalling time delay between a remotely operated camera platform and its distant human controller had been a crucial factor in the crash of the dirigible *Queen Elizabeth IV*. When the platform had hit turbulent air, the controller had been too far away to react, the platform itself too simple to respond autonomously . . . The result had been catastrophic, for the platform itself, for the airship – for its captain, Howard Falcon. He wasn't likely to forget.

Embleton went on, 'But you needn't worry about the sprites. The signal delays are minimal, we have a suite of backup options, and the sprites are tightly programmed. If they're not sure, they just shut down.'

'But the most elaborate failsafes can go wrong. Yes, as happened with the camera platform that brought down the *Q.E. IV.*'

Webster pointed up. 'A platform not unlike that one, coming towards us.'

Light flared down from a camera platform hovering silently not two metres above their heads.

And just as the light hit Falcon, a man came striding up, brisk, handsome, dressed in a crisp World Navy uniform. A small entourage trailed him, including a younger man continually glancing at the blocky minisec in his hand. The leader looked around forty, but Falcon knew that with the life-extension therapies that were becoming available, looks could be deceiving.

Falcon recognised him. He could hardly not. This was Captain Matthew Springer, conqueror of Pluto: this year's other hero of space exploration.

Springer took Falcon's artificial hand without flinching. 'Commander Howard Falcon! And Administrator Webster. Captain, forgive me for interrupting. Commander, I was so pleased to learn you'd be on this cruise . . .'

Falcon was aware of the camera platform descending, eager to capture this historic encounter, but with its multiple lenses all trained on Springer.

And Springer was staring closely at Falcon. 'Hey – you're breathing.'

'So are you,' Falcon said dryly.

Webster rolled his eyes.

But Springer seemed immune to irony. 'Makes sense, I guess. A touch of humanity. And you can speak more or less naturally. As opposed to through some kind of loudspeaker attachment, right? So what do you use for lungs?'

'I'll mail you the specifications.'

'Thanks. You know, I followed your exploits as a boy. The ballooning stunts. And I have to tell you that of the last generation of technological pioneers, you're the one I most—' His aide touched his arm, murmured something, pointed to his minisec. Springer held up his hands. 'Got to go – drinks with the World President. You jump when called, right, Commander? Catch you later – and please come to my talk about Icarus and my grandfather, which will be in the—' He pointed at Embleton.

'The Sea Lounge,' Captain Embleton said with good grace, even as Springer retreated.

'And with that he was gone,' Webster said. 'Trailed by his fan club like a comet tail, and by that damn floating platform.'

'Not that the camera spent too long looking at me,' Falcon said.

Embleton laughed. 'Well, we wouldn't want to scare the sea sprites, Commander.' They set off towards the stern again, trailed by Conseil. 'I'm sure there are plenty of people on board who'll be fascinated to meet you. We even have one of the medical team who treated you aboard. But I insist you allow me to give you the guided tour . . . The *Shore*'s keel was laid at the peak of the last period of real global tension, but the ship never bared its fangs in true anger, I'm happy to say. As a Navy officer yourself you might find elements of the design interesting. Of course, nowadays we're famous for our world-class passenger facilities.' She glanced over Falcon's seven-foot-tall body. 'I wonder how you'd fare on the ice rink?'

Webster laughed out loud. 'He could skate, if we swapped his wheels for blades. But it wouldn't be pretty.'

'Commander Howard Falcon.' The voice was a gravelly growl.

And – as a group of passengers passed them, drinks in their hands, gaudy as flowers against the Atlantic grey, all no doubt fabulously rich – Falcon stopped and found himself facing a group of chimpanzees.

There were a dozen, of whom three or four glared at the humans with undisguised hostility. The chimps wore no clothes save for loose stringed jackets heavy with pockets, even though some were evidently shivering with the cold. They huddled down on the deck, their closed fists scraping the metal surface. Their apparent leader was older, grizzled grey around the muzzle, and he stood a little taller than the rest.

Embleton stepped forward briskly. 'I should make proper introductions. You know Commander Falcon already. Commander, this is Ham 2057a, Ambassador to the World Council of the Independent Pan Nation, and another guest of President Jayasuriya.'

Falcon tried not to stare. This was the first simp – superchimp – he'd seen since the crash of the *Q.E. IV*. 'I'm glad to meet you, sir.'

'And I you, Commander.'

'Are you enjoying the cruise?'

'Missing home in Congo treetops, to tell truth . . .' The Ambassador spoke distorted but comprehensible English, evidently with some effort. One of his aides seemed to be an interpreter, relaying the speech to the others in pant-hoots and gestures. 'Know you, of course. To us, Howard Falcon famous for more than Jupiter.'

'The crash of the *Queen*.'

'Many simps died that day.'

'And many human crew—'

'Simps! Given slave names, like my own. Dressed like dolls. Made to work on cruise ship grander than this one, *Boss*.'

Falcon was aware of Webster flinching at that word. 'Well, now, Bittorn's programme was well intended,' said the Administrator. 'It was meant as a way to establish a bridge between cousin species—'

Ham snorted. 'Simps! So damn useful, clambering around space stations in zero G – climbing in airship rigging. And so funny-funny cute in little slave uniforms, serving drinks. Other animals too. Smart dogs. Smart horses ... Smart enough to know humiliation and fear. All dead now ...

'Then, ship crashed. *You* barely survived. Millions spent saving you. Some simps survived, barely. They not saved. Millions not spent. Simps *euthed*.'

Embleton stepped forward. 'Ambassador, this is hardly the time or the place—'

Ham ignored her. 'But you, Commander Falcon. Records of crash. No cameras, but forensics, word of survivors. Some simps lasted long enough to tell story. The ship, doomed. You heading *down*, down to bridge, risk life to save ship, if you could. And you found frightened simp. You stopped, Commander. Stopped, calmed him, told him go, not *down, down*, but *up, up* to observation deck. Where he would have best chance. You said, "Boss – boss – *go!*"'

Falcon looked away. 'He died anyway.'

'Did your best. His name, Baker 2079q. Eight years old. We remember, you see. All simps. Remember them, every one. They were people. Better times now.' He surprised Falcon by reaching up with one hand. Falcon had to lower his upper body to take it. 'You come visit Independent Pan Nation.'

'I'd like that very much,' Falcon said.

'Climb trees?'

'I'm always up for a challenge.'

Embleton smiled. 'Not until you've tried ice skating, Commander—'

But a voice cut across her words: '*Whale ahoy! Starboard side!*'

Falcon turned with the rest.

The whales were heading north.

Looking out over this grey ocean, under a grey sky, the great bodies looked like an armada, a fleet of ships, not like anything living at all. Of course they were dwarfed by the tremendous length of the carrier, but there was a power about them that no machine of mankind could ever match: a fitness for purpose in this environment.

Now one tremendous head lifted out of the water not thirty, forty metres from the flank of the *Shore*, misshapen to Falcon's untutored gaze, pocked and scarred like the surface of some asteroid. But a vast mouth opened, a cave from whose roof dangled the baleen plates that filtered this beast's diet of plankton from the upper levels of the sea, a thin gruel to power such a tremendous body. And then an eye opened, huge but startlingly human.

As he looked into that eye, Falcon felt a jolt of recognition.

He had travelled to Jupiter, where, in layers of cloud where conditions were temperate, almost Earthlike, he had encountered another tremendous animal: a medusa, a creature the size of the *Shore* itself, swimming in that unimaginably remote sea. This whale had been shaped by evolutionary pressures in an environment not entirely dissimilar to Jupiter's hydrogen-helium air-ocean, and surely had much in common with the medusae. And yet Falcon felt a kinship of common biology with this tremendous terrestrial mammal that he knew he could never share with any Jovian medusa.

Ham, the simp Ambassador, was at his side. 'There you are, Commander Falcon. Another Legal Person (Non-human).' And he pant-hooted with laughter.

2

During dinner, the USS *Sam Shore* discreetly submerged.

Hatches and service ports were closed and sealed silently. Ballast tanks were opened, the in-rush of water politely muffled so as not to disturb the passengers. The dive planes were set for a one-degree descent, barely noticeable even to those guests paying close attention to the level of the drinks in their glasses.

Falcon noticed, of course. He sensed the angle of the deck, the tilt from one end of a corridor to the next. Through the sensors in his undercarriage he picked up the change in the subsonic frequencies coming from the engine, signalling a decrease in the power output, possible now that the ship was moving underwater in its optimum environment.

Very few things escaped Falcon.

After dinner, and before Springer's speech, he and Webster went for a walk.

The so-called service deck of the *Shore*, beneath the immense hangar deck, was a cavern of girders and rivets and rails and cranes and rotating platforms, where once fighter planes and nuclear-tipped missiles had been fuelled, serviced, refurbished. Now this brightly lit chamber had been transformed into a combination of shopping mall and upper class hotel – and on an astounding scale, a full mile of it.

'You should feel at home here, Howard,' Webster was saying. 'After all, if the *Queen Elizabeth* hadn't crashed, you'd have ended up a cruise liner captain too, wouldn't you? Of course, nowadays you'd never get a dress uniform to fit . . .'

Falcon ignored him and inspected the fixtures. For this prestigious cruise the ship's owners, together with the World Food Secretariat, Marine Division, had used the space to mount an exhibition of the modern ocean and its uses, presumably intended to prompt well-heeled passengers to become investors. Falcon and Webster glanced over exhibits, models and holographic and animated images of various wonders natural and otherwise – although Falcon was unsure if anything about Earth's oceans could still be called natural. At the close of the twenty-first century a large proportion of mankind was still fed by tremendous plankton farms, sustained by the forced up-welling of nutrient-rich materials from the ocean floor. As land-based mineral sources had been depleted the sea bed had been extensively mined too. Of course, nowadays humanity was more than conscious of the needs of the creatures with whom it shared the world – and even, in the case of the uplifted chimps, shared political power. But the whole Earth was becoming a managed landscape, Falcon thought, like one vast park – which was one reason people like himself became hungry to leave.

They found a panel on career opportunities, and Webster bent to see, curious. 'Look at this stuff, Howard. The specialisms you can take on: seamanship, oceanography, navigation, undersea communications, marine biology . . .' He straightened up stiffly. 'You know, the Bureau of Space Resources uses some sea floor locations for simulation work. You can trial suits designed to cope with the heavy pressures we will encounter on Venus, for instance. Shame we can't go see that during this jaunt.'

'No,' Falcon said, 'this tub is strictly a shallow diver. Just enough to hide from enemy aircraft—'

'Excuse me.'

The woman stood alone in the gloom of the gallery: soberly dressed, dark, she looked to be in her mid-thirties. Falcon, at seven feet, tow-ered over her by a good foot and a half. Not surprisingly perhaps, she seemed nervous.

Webster snapped his fingers. 'I remember you. Nurse Dhoni, right? You were at the military hospital, Luke Air Force Base, Arizona, when we—'

'When Commander Falcon was brought in from the *Queen Eliza-beth*, yes.'

Those days – those *years* – of recovery still lived in Falcon's night-mares. He did his best not to recoil.

'Actually, it's Doctor now. I cross-trained. I specialised in neurosur-gery at—'

'Why are you here?' Falcon snapped.

She seemed taken aback, and Webster glared at him.

Dhoni said, 'Well, because of you, Commander. Once the Presi-dent's staff had invited you, they looked around for friends, family and such to make you welcome. And of your medical team from back then, I'm the only one still working in the field. The rest have retired, moved on, or in one case died – Doctor Bignall, if you remember him.'

'You didn't have to come.'

Webster growled, 'For God's sake, Howard.'

'No, Administrator Webster, it's OK.' She sounded as if it was anything but OK, but she held her nerve. 'I needed to see you, Commander. After your exploits on Jupiter made the news, I did some investigating. It's been an awfully long time since you had a proper check-up, let alone an overhaul.'

Suddenly Falcon was suspicious. He glared at Webster. 'Did you set this up, you old coot?'

Webster looked as if he was going to try to bluff his way out, but gave in with good grace. 'Well, now, Howard, I knew you wouldn't listen to me.' He rapped his knuckles on the shell of toughened alloy where Falcon's chest should have been. 'The outside stuff is doing fine. We can switch components in and out with no trouble. But what's inside was pretty beat up to start with, and isn't getting any younger. How old are you now, fifty-five, fifty-six . . .?'

Dhoni reached out uncertainly to Falcon, then dropped her hand. 'Let me help you. How do you sleep?'

Falcon set his jaw. 'As little as I can.'

'Even with the sleep inducers? There are new treatments now, things we can offer you—'

'Is that why you're here? To use me as a lab rat, again?'

That got through the last of her defences. Her mouth worked, and she swallowed. 'No. I'm here because I care. Just as I cared then.' She turned and stalked away.

Falcon watched her go. 'She nearly burst into tears.'

'No, she didn't, you ass. She nearly knocked your block off, and you would have deserved it. I saw you back then, Howard. I know it was a nightmare. But she was there all the way through, Hope Dhoni. Just a kid. There all the way through.' He seemed to struggle for words. '*She wiped your brow.* Oh, the hell with you. I need a drink.' He walked off, calling back, 'Enjoy Springer's ego trip. I've had enough heroes for now. But when you find that woman again you apologise, you hear?'

3

In the USS *Sam Shore*'s Sea Lounge, Matt Springer stood at a lectern beside an empty, dimly lit stage.

The room itself was extraordinary, Falcon thought, as he rolled in and discreetly took a place at the back. The Sea Lounge was probably the single most famous, or notorious, feature of the cruise ship this huge carrier had become. It was a place of curves and tangles and sweeping panels, no straight lines, all in the colours of the sea: green and blue and with a mother-of-pearl sheen. The stage itself stood under an apex where arching ribs joined, and the audience before Springer was cupped in a shallow basin. Captain Embleton – there in the front row alongside the President – had told Falcon this was experimental architecture. The same technology they used to filter-mine sea water had been put to work sculpting this room, layer by layer – the room had been *grown*, like a sea mollusc's shell, rather than built in the traditional fashion. Even the hidden service elements, the ducts and pipes and vents and cabling, had been planned into the carefully computer-controlled process.

The decor meanwhile looked high Victorian to Falcon, with polished tables, high chairs and divans. The tables were set with expensive-looking glasses, cutlery and porcelain crockery. But Falcon noticed the details – each item of cutlery marked with the motto MOBILIS IN MOBILI, the small flags on each table, black with a golden 'N' – that gave away the true inspiration behind this place. Falcon allowed himself a smile. More than two centuries since its launch in the pages of Verne's great novel, Captain Nemo's *Nautilus* still sailed seas of imagination. Falcon murmured, 'You'd have enjoyed this, Jules.'

And in this elaborate setting, dressed in a crisp Navy uniform, smiling at the passengers as they filed into their seats, Matt Springer looked at ease, welcoming, in control. Falcon envied the man for his human grace in this very human company, while Falcon himself skulked in the shadows.

But he was not alone for long. Webster soon found him.

Falcon murmured, 'Buddy, if you're looking for the water fountain, he's the good-looking fellow in the other corner.'

'Very funny.'

'You showed up in the end, then?'

'Turns out I have some residual good manners. So what do you think of the Sea Lounge? Quite something, isn't it?'

Falcon grunted. 'It's like a huge oyster shell. And Matt Springer is the big fat pearl in the middle of it.'

That made Webster laugh.

With a gracious smile, Springer settled his hands on the lectern and, speaking without notes, began the show.

'Madam President, Captain Embleton, friends. Good evening. Thanks for coming. I'm here to tell you the story of Grandpa Seth – who is the reason my family came by its notoriety in the first place, and the reason I had to go all the way to Pluto to carve out a little piece of history of my own.'

Sympathetic laughter: immediately he had them eating out of his hand. Falcon seethed.

'I do need to dispel a couple of myths about him. First of all, although my family always referred to him as "Grandpa", Seth was in fact my great-great-great-great-grandfather, and, of course, he never got to meet even his own grandchildren. But his fame extended far beyond his own lifetime, and he was always a kind of presence for the family, so "Grandpa" he will always be.

'And second, no, Sean Connery didn't play him in the 1970s movie.' More laughter. 'Connery was in the picture, but in another role. A professor from MIT. Sometimes I watch that old picture over again. Shame the science got left on the cutting room floor, but it is fun! And it was the first attempt to dramatise those extraordinary events.

'What I'm going to show you tonight is the latest attempt to tell that story. Of course, the whole drama was recorded and heavily scrutinised at the time, and later there was a slew of books, autobiographies, technical studies. So with modern processing of the contemporary imagery, and armed with the screeds of psychological analysis of the principals that followed, we can do a pretty good job of reconstruction – we can see how it was to live through those dramatic days, and even get some sense of what the principals must have been thinking and feeling at the time.

'Tonight we'll see a selection of scenes, key incidents. Just sit back and relax; the 3D should be easy on the eye. Those of you with neural jacks are welcome to try out the immersive options, though they are all restricted to passive mode.' Another smile. 'Don't try pressing any buttons in Grandpa's Apollo Command Module. And maybe you'll have some insight into how it felt, on Sunday 9th April 1967, when Seth Springer was given the bad news that he wasn't going to the Moon . . .'

An area of the wall behind Matt Springer's lectern became a glowing rectangle, filling with the deep, limitless blue of a cloudless sky. The angle panned down, taking in an expanse of blocky white buildings laid out campus-like amid neat areas of lawn and roadway. For a moment or two it could have passed as a contemporary scene, the buildings' utilitarian architecture revealing little. But as the point of view zoomed in, so vehicles and figures quickly gave the game away. Squared-off cars, men in suits and hats and ties, despite the obvious heat. And few women to be seen at all. This was a scene from a hundred and thirty years in the past – from the first faltering days of the space age.

The point of view narrowed to one building, then one window of that building. And then, with one dizzying swoop, through the glass, into an air-conditioned office. Contemporary fittings, polished wood and leather. Lots of photographs and flags, cabinets and framed documents, a desk with a calendar and a briefcase, but nothing that Falcon recognised as a computer or visual display device . . .

'*The Apollo Moon programme is cancelled. But the good news is,*' the man behind that desk was saying, '*you two good old boys are gonna get the chance to save the world.*'

'In five minutes there won't be a dry eye in the house,' Webster said. 'Save mine, of course.'

'Come on, let's duck out of here. There's only so much Springer either of us can take. Also there's someone who wants to talk to you.'

'Let me guess. Nurse Hope.'

'Wise guy. And *I* need a bathroom break. You coming, or not?'

A short walk under a roof of ribbed bulkhead led to another of the *Shore*'s advertised features, the Observation Lounge, a cafeteria-bar. Falcon estimated a quarter-acre of carpet was scattered with tables and floor cushions and even a kids' play pen, over which loomed an immense blister, a window of toughened Plexiglas. At this time of night, an hour before midnight, nothing was visible beyond the window save pitch-dark ocean.

Hope Dhoni sat alone at a table before the window. She had some kind of equipment on the table, an open case. As Webster and Falcon approached she looked around and smiled warily.

The little robot Conseil – presuming it was the same one – rolled over towards them. 'May I serve you?'

'No,' Falcon said curtly.

'He'll have iced tea with me,' Hope said firmly. 'Thank you, Conseil. You always liked iced tea, Howard.'

Webster grinned and sat down. 'And a bourbon for me. On my tab—'

'You are all guests of the President on this voyage, Administrator Webster.' Conseil had a mellifluous, almost Bostonian accent, Falcon thought. It was certainly a lot more humanlike than the buzzing monotone of Adam, that treasured toy from his childhood. The robot trundled away to a softly lit bar area at the back of the room.

And Falcon rolled away on his own balloon tyres towards that big window. It curved over his head. Cautiously he touched it with one fingertip. He thought of cottage windows, frosted by snow on a winter's morning – sensations that had been relayed to his brain through skin and nerves, rather than a network of prosthetics and implanted neural receivers.

A light swam by in the dark, a perfectly smooth, horizontal motion. One of those sea sprites, he assumed. Again, he felt uneasy about how close the automated critters came to the boat. That pilot light was all that was visible beyond the window.

Hope Dhoni came over and stood at his side. 'One of the ship's most famous features,' she murmured. 'The window itself, I mean. An engineering marvel. Rather like you, Commander Falcon.'

'Look,' he said. 'I'm sorry. The way I reacted when we met. Those days under the surgeons were difficult for me. Even remembering them—'

She slipped her hand into his. He could sense the pressure of her fingers, measure the moisture and warmth of her palm – he even had a vivid, unwelcome impression of the bone structure. He could not *feel* her hand in his, though, not by any meaningful definition of the word.

Suddenly uncomfortable, he pulled away. Too many memories. Too much pain.

For both of them.

'Come,' Hope said gently. 'Sit with us.'

4

If his recovery from the *Queen Elizabeth IV* crash twelve years earlier had been traumatic for Howard Falcon, so it had been for Hope Dhoni, at the time a twenty-one-year-old trainee nurse at the old USAF hospital in Arizona to which Falcon had been rushed. She had been by far the most junior member of the team.

When he was brought in, crushed and burned, laid out on the bed's pale green blankets, Falcon had not even looked human. Hope had spent time in inner-city emergency departments and military trauma wards, and she thought she was toughened up. She wasn't. Not for this.

But it was Doctor Bignall, second-in-command, who had helped her through. 'First of all, he's alive. Remember that. Barely, though: his heart's about to give up – you can see that from the monitor trace. Second of all, don't think about what he's lost but what he still has. His head injuries seem manageable . . .'

She could barely see the head under what remained of Falcon's right arm.

'And that arm he threw up to protect himself might even have preserved his face. Some of it.'

She watched the team work, humans and machines, as tubes snaked into Falcon's body. 'So what's the first priority?'

'To keep him alive. Look at him, he's suffered well over fifty per cent blood loss, his chest is wide open. We're replacing his blood, all of it, with a cold saline solution. That will cut brain activity, stop cellular activity—'

'Suspended animation.'

'If you like. And that will give us a chance to get on with the structural stuff. A *chance* . . . Oh, wow, he's in cardiac arrest. Crash team . . .!'

The structural stuff. When Falcon was stabilised, achieved essentially by shoving him into a room full of machinery that would emulate the functions of his broken body, it turned out that there was little left of him that was saveable but brain and spine – and some of his face, preserved by that flung-over arm. The good news was that was quite a lot to build on. Monitors already showed ongoing brain activity. Hope would soon learn how to tell if Falcon was asleep or awake, and she wondered which state was worse for him.

What followed, for Hope, was a rushed course in neuroinformatics. As the hours turned to days, the team worked as quickly as they could. They needed to establish a connection between what was left of Falcon and the equipment that would sustain him for the rest of his life. And that meant reading information from, and writing information to, what was left of his broken nervous system.

Sensors on prosthetic extensions to Falcon's surviving stump of an arm were able to use his own nervous system to communicate with the brain – but for the rest of his body, his spinal column was so badly damaged that that wasn't an option. New communication pathways had to be built. So microelectrodes were lodged within Falcon's brain – in the motor cortex area responsible for physical movement, and in the somatosensory cortex, which governed the sense of touch. More sensors were placed in the lumbosacral region of his spine with a control hub to link the brain to the lower limbs. Once it was possible to transfer digital information into and out of the nervous system, a suite of prosthetic body parts was brought in and tried, one by one, each of them riddled with microsensors that communicated continually with the devices anchored to the brain and spine.

Even hastily improvised, it was an impressive feat.

Hope was able to help with the medical side. As the recovery proceeded she flashed lights into eyes of metal and gel, and pinched sensor-loaded plastic flesh, testing for sensation. She learned later that Falcon slowly became aware of this, over the days and weeks of silence inside his own head: sparks of light, dull feelings of pressure. But the first external stimulus he'd been truly aware of was a sound, a metronomic thumping that he'd believed was his own heart, but was in fact the combined rhythm of a room full of machinery.

The team had been highly motivated. They weren't just saving a life; they were doing so using the latest techniques and technologies. Indeed, the doctors said, this case was driving the development of new techniques altogether.

Sometimes they were over-keen. One younger doctor had bragged in the canteen, 'You know, this must be the most interesting trauma case since they gave up fighting wars . . .' Doctor Bignall punched the man in the mouth. If he hadn't, Hope Dhoni would have.

And now, a dozen years later, here stood Falcon, restored.

A golden tower.

People said that in this iteration of his support gear Falcon looked a little like the old Oscar statuette. When he stood upright, there was an abstract sense of a human body rather than its literal shape: a golden, wedge-shaped torso, shapely shoulders and neck, a featureless head – featureless save for the aperture through which a partial face peered, leathery human skin exposed to the air. Artificial eyes, of course. His lower body was a single unit, shaped to suggest legs; it looked solid but was segmented to allow Falcon to bend, even to 'sit' with reasonable verisimilitude. And under the 'feet' was a kind of trolley riding on balloon tyres. At rest, Falcon kept his arms folded over his chest, to reassure onlookers; when deployed his arms moved with a mechanical whir of hydraulics, the motions stiff and inhuman, the hands like grabbing claws.

This was not the first model within which Falcon had been embedded. He liked to complain that he had made more human-looking snowmen as a boy . . .

Dhoni remembered when Falcon had first started to feel pain again.

Falcon couldn't tell them he was in pain, at the time. All he could do was flicker an eyelid. He had no mouth. His tear ducts no longer functioned. But the machines told of the pain. And Hope knew.

It took two years before he could turn the page of a book unaided, with a whir of servomotors from the single exoskeletal arm hooked up to his body. Every night of those two years, Hope Dhoni had washed Falcon's face and wiped his brow.

5

Webster called them back to the table for their drinks.

This time Falcon sat down, or at least folded down his undercarriage.

Dhoni said in a rush, 'I know there's every chance I won't see you again any time soon, Commander—'

'Howard.'

'Howard. I do recall you got out of that clinic as fast as you could – how did Doctor Bignall put it? "Like a delinquent kid who's finally old enough to steal a car."'

Webster barked laughter. 'That's you, Howard.'

'But I would urge you to come in for regular checks, refurbs and upgrades to your prosthetics – and medical attention to your human core. But while we're here,' she said doggedly, 'while I have the chance, I want to show you a new option.' She patted the box. 'This is a virtual reality extensor kit. Right now it's interfaced to the ship's Bosun and to the global net.' She took out two metal discs, each the size of a new cent. She handed one each to Webster and Falcon.

'Neural jacks,' Falcon said.

'You got it,' Webster said. His own hand hovered at the back of his neck.

'*You*, Geoff? You've got one of these sockets? Virtual reality is for kids' games or training simulators.'

'Like hell it is. I'd have no idea what my kids and grandkids spend their time doing without this hole in my neck. Besides, half the world's business is done virtually now. Even my Bureau's. And, unlike you, I always treat myself to upgrades.'

'You never told me.'

'You never asked. And you never told me *you* have an interface. Surgeons installed it while they were hacking your brain stem, did they?'

'It was a necessary component of my treatment. The destruction of my spinal cord—'

'That was twelve years ago.'

'It needs upgrading,' Dhoni said quickly. 'But this smart new kit is downward-compatible.'

Falcon stared at the bright coin. 'Virtual reality? What's the point?'

Webster leaned forward. 'Look, Howard. I think I see what the doctor's getting at. We live in a *good* age. The world's at peace. No borders, no wars, and we're driving towards our goals of eliminating hunger, want, disease—'

'So what? And why the VR jack?'

'Because, in this nascent utopia, there's no place for you,' Webster said brutally. 'That's what you think, don't you?'

'Well, it's true. I'm unique.'

'That can't be changed. The medics saved your life, Howard, but in a radically experimental way. You were a one-off. And as the Earth recovers from the depredation of the past, people are becoming more – conservative. Machinery is fine, but it has to be unobtrusive.

'If your accident happened now, you wouldn't be treated the same way. You'd be kept on ice until biological replacements could be prepared for your broken body parts. I'm talking stem-cell treatments, even whole lower brain and spinal cord transplants. They'd have made you human again. Machines are machines, to be kept separate from humanity.'

'So I'm the only true cyborg. The only living symbiosis of man and machine.'

'Hope tells me there's nothing that can be done to change that for you now, physically.'

Dhoni seemed about to reach for Falcon's hand, but she pulled back. 'But there are other options.'

'*This*, you mean? To escape into artificiality?'

Webster shook his head. 'There are whole virtual communities, Howard. And once you're in there you can be fully human again. You can do things – well, hell, all the things you can't do now. Run, laugh, cry – make love—'

'It's the real world for me, Doctor Dhoni. That, or give me an off switch.'

Hope flinched.

Webster said, 'Damn you, Falcon.'

Falcon rolled back from the table, straightened up, and left.

When he'd gone, Dhoni said, 'I suppose I should apologise. I didn't mean to spoil the evening.'

Webster's look was rueful. 'Oh, we were making a fine job of that by ourselves. But I guess a virtual substitute for life was never going to be enough for a man like Howard Falcon . . . "Some other time."'

'I'm sorry?'

'That's what he said, as he was about to leave Jupiter. He looked over at the Great Red Spot – the mission planners ensured he had stayed well away from that – and he said, "Some other time." The control team up at Jupiter V heard it clearly. It's the kind of line you stick on a T-shirt . . .

'But in a way he has a point. About Jupiter anyhow. His mission in the *Kon-Tiki* was heroic, but he only scratched the surface. Jupiter is an ocean of mystery. Literally anything might be found down there. And since he got back from Jupiter he's already been seeking funding for follow-up missions. One reason he's showing his face here, I think.'

Dhoni nodded. 'But all this is a denial of his personal reality. How can we help him?'

'Damned if I know. Damned if I care, right now.'

6

When he returned to Springer's presentation, Falcon observed that nobody in the audience had even noticed that the pioneer of the clouds of Jupiter had gone briefly AWOL. Again he seethed with unreasonable resentment.

It didn't help that Matt Springer had a good story to tell. Springer concluded his narrative with a final, frozen image of Grandpa Seth, valiant at the controls of his doomed Apollo craft. Falcon was impressed at Springer's skill as he milked the moment, before an audience that just happened to include the World President.

Finally he spoke again. 'Well, you know the rest. My ancestor was honoured with a ceremony at Arlington. Robert Kennedy beat Richard Nixon to the presidency, and in January 1969 made the Icarus incident a keynote of his inaugural speech . . .'

A crude recording of RFK at the presidential podium was shown. Falcon knew the speech word for word: *'A decade earlier and we would not have had the spacefaring capabilities that have saved us . . . Now it is incumbent upon us not to let this capacity wither . . . On the contrary, we must move out beyond the fragile Earth and into space, further and wider . . .'*

'And,' Springer commented with a grin, 'Kennedy was wise enough to stress how well America and the Soviet Union had worked together on the Icarus project.'

'This episode has proven we are better united than divided, and more than that, we can *be united around common goals . . .'*

Springer said, 'Right there, in that passage, you had the foundation of the unity movements that led to the World Government. So Frank Borman led the first Apollo Moon landing in December 1971. The 1970s were the decade of Apollo, as RFK's administration reflected the public gratitude to NASA by pouring in money: multiple missions, flights to the lunar poles and the far side, the beginnings of a permanent base in Clavius Crater. And then the first steps beyond the Moon.'

More images, of Soviet-American landings on Mars in the 1980s.

'Since then we've seen a remarkable century of progress. Resources from space helped us over hurdles – fuel depletion, climate problems – that might otherwise have tripped us. The first World President was inaugurated in 2060, to a recording of the famous Hendrix anthem – but I lived in Bermuda for ten years, and they always said the main benefit of hosting the planet's capital city has been first call on the Global Weather Secretariat for hurricane protection.'

Polite laughter.

'And as for Seth's descendants . . .' He brought up an image of his own mission patch. It was a variant on the family crest, which showed a leaping springbok, the Springers being an old Dutch family with rich offshoots in South Africa. Now that springbok leapt among Pluto's moons. Springer smiled modestly in response to a ripple of applause.

'It all stemmed,' Springer said, 'from Grandpa Seth's heroism. Anyhow, as the New Year approaches – according to Houston time, which is the only clock that counts for an astronaut – I move, with your permission, Madam President, that we return to the bar—'

And at that moment the submarine shuddered, a mile-long vessel ringing like a gong.

7

If Falcon had ever doubted that the slim, modest woman in the pale lilac suit really was the President of a united world, the case was proven now. Seconds after that sinister shiver – as red alarm lights flashed, distant sirens wailed, and Captain Embleton called instructions from the stage beside a frowning Matt Springer – it seemed to Falcon that a good proportion of the audience in the Sea Lounge had already swarmed around the President like expensively suited, heavily armed bees. In a moment the swarm had escorted her from the room.

Falcon, meanwhile, turned and rolled at top speed out of the Sea Lounge. Already people were on their feet, pushing their way out of the room – but even now they cowered back from Falcon, a seven-foot-tall pillar of gold.

Hope Dhoni was still where he and Webster had left her, in the Observation Lounge, her glass of iced tea half-drunk on the table where she sat. And she was staring at a white form that clung to the huge observation window.

It was a sea sprite, clamped to the glass, Falcon recognised, with a grim sense of foreboding fulfilled. 'I knew it. *Damn* it.'

Webster came hurrying after Falcon. 'At least it's quiet in here. What with the crew shouting and the alarms and the lights flashing everywhere—'

'I presume there are enough lifeboats for everybody.'

'Of course, Commander Falcon,' said Captain Embleton, who came stalking into the room, trailed by Matt Springer and a gaggle of her senior officers. 'This isn't the bloody *Titanic*. We've already got the President away.'

Webster whistled. 'That's quick.'

'A condition of her being brought aboard. I dare say whoever plotted this thing wasn't aware of that. But,' she said more softly, 'the problem is time – time enough to get everybody else off before the hull implodes.'

The officers were pointing and declaiming, checking minisecs, running through the evacuation plan in high, calm voices. Bizarrely, the little robot Conseil began to circulate among the sudden crowd, as if seeking a role in the sudden crisis. 'May I serve you?' It was universally ignored.

Embleton turned from one of the officers to eye Webster. 'Administrator, given your own seniority—'

'I'm staying right here,' Webster snapped.

'Idiot,' murmured Falcon.

'Takes one to know one – I don't notice you baling out. Anyhow, the ship might yet be saved, right?'

Falcon, who had gyroscopes whirring in the place his stomach should have been, wasn't so sure. 'Not if the ship's list continues to worsen.'

Matt Springer looked at him with respect. 'Of course you can feel it. So can I, I think.'

Dhoni looked up at Falcon in alarm. 'Oh, Howard—'

'I know.' He forced a smile. 'Another great vessel in mortal peril, and here I am in the middle of it. *Not again . . .*'

'Soon enough everybody will feel the list,' Embleton said grimly, glancing at a minisec held by one of her officers. 'We've suffered multiple fusion micro-explosions, all around the perimeter of the hull.'

'They blew the ballast tanks,' Falcon said.

'Exactly.'

Hope Dhoni stood, looking bewildered. 'Who did this? And why?'

'We don't know yet.' Captain Embleton broke away from her officers to stalk to the window. 'But we know how.'

'With the sea sprites,' Falcon said. 'Like the one stuck to the window.'

More crew came into the lounge now, carrying technical gear that they fixed to the window, studying the sprite.

Embleton said, 'It happened only minutes ago. Suddenly the sprites diverged from their programming. They swarmed around the hull, anchored themselves as this one has, and—'

'Detonated their power packs, I presume,' Springer said, stepping forward to see more clearly.

'Quite. Which ought to be impossible.'

'Evidently not,' Falcon said. 'The question is, why *hasn't* this one gone up?'

Embleton took a breath. 'We need to be grateful it hasn't. If it had, much of the ship's habitable areas would already be flooded. As it is the ship's in trouble. We were already a little below our nominal cruise depth of sixteen hundred feet, and now we're heading steadily down. Our crush depth is twenty-four hundred feet, but we ought to survive some distance below that – well, it's to be hoped. This century-old bucket has flaws we discover every day . . . We have support in the sea and in the air; the President goes nowhere without cover. This is the weak point, actually. If this window holds we have a chance of getting everybody off in time. *If.*'

Webster asked uneasily, 'Is it still the tradition that the Captain's last to leave the ship?'

'To hell with tradition. *This* Captain's going nowhere until she knows who or what has threatened her ship—'

'Simps know.'

Falcon turned to see a party of simps approaching. The Ambassador, Ham 2057a, was in the lead, and a gang of his colleagues were dragging a human with them – a crewman, judging by the uniform.

More crew followed, weapons in their hands, uncertain. One reported, 'Captain, we've trailed the simps from the Bosun's compartment. The simps grabbed Stamp, here, and we weren't sure what to do. The Ambassador was very insistent—'

'Stand down, Lieutenant Moss. Ambassador Ham, this is one of my crew. I'll listen, if you release him into my custody.'

Ham shrugged theatrically. 'Simps' job done.'

The chimps dumped the man, Stamp, to the deck. At a nod from Lieutenant Moss, a couple of his men took Stamp's arms and hauled him to his feet. Stamp looked young, Falcon thought, no more than mid-twenties, with pale features, red hair. His face was scratched, his ensign's uniform torn from the rough handling of the chimps, but he seemed unharmed.

The great ship creaked as it listed further, helplessly plunging deeper into the depths.

Embleton turned to Ham. 'Ambassador? What's this about?'

Ham gave a wide grin, and knuckle-walked up to her. 'Simps heroes, that's what. One of my team, her name Jane 2084c. Works computers. Smart. Went to Bosun room, interested, fan tour. There was Stamp, doing what he was doing. Took no notice of her. Kept on doing it. Only a simp, simps don't matter, can't understand. Ha! Jane understand.'

Falcon said, 'The sprites are controlled from the Bosun.'

'Quite.' Embleton walked up to Stamp. 'Well, Ensign. Suppose you tell *me* what you were doing.'

Stamp straightened up and saluted. 'Sir. I was destroying this ship, sir, and killing you all.' He had a strong English accent, probably London, Falcon thought.

'You changed the Bosun's programming—'

'I locked in new commands for the sprites. They were to attach to the hull and self-destruct. Those things are dumb, their programming simple. The safety blocks were pitifully easy to overcome.'

'Were they? And why did you— no, tell me this.' She gestured at the window, the sprite locked in place. 'Why has this one *not* blown yet?'

'Because I wanted you to understand,' Stamp said, sneering. 'I want you to *know* you will die – and so will the world – because of what this ship is. What it represents.'

Webster frowned severely. 'And what is that?'

'The hegemony of the United States.' He glared at Webster. 'Which began when you Americans manipulated the outcome of the Second World War to crush the British Empire and alienate the Soviets—'

Embleton sighed. 'Oh, for God's sake. A Global-Sceptic. Part of the old independence movements that opposed the World Government.'

Webster nodded. 'I remember. I was just a kid. Bombs in London, Geneva, Bermuda.'

Stamp ranted at him, 'Then you Yanks used Britain as a missile launch platform in your Cold War against the Soviets. And *then* you suckered us into the so-called "Atlantic Partnership". You wouldn't even back our claim for a seat on the World Government Security Council—'

'I've heard enough,' Embleton snapped in disgust. 'You're an embarrassment to a noble history, Stamp. Moss, take him away. I'm damn sure he won't tell us how he subverted the Bosun – or how I can get that nuclear leech off my window – but try to get him to talk anyhow. Keep the evacuation going. And do whatever you can to hack into the Bosun, you never know . . .'

Her crew hurried to comply.

'And meanwhile,' Embleton said softly, 'if all else fails, we need to find a way to remove that thing.' She walked back to the window to join Springer, Falcon, Webster and Dhoni. 'Any ideas?'

Webster asked, 'The escort ships?'

'Are World Navy vessels – surface, subsurface, and indeed in the air. I'm told they are working on options. But the *Sam Shore* is an elderly ship, Administrator, and already destabilised. It would be a tricky operation to get close enough to detach that thing without wrecking us.'

Webster said, 'That's assuming the leech isn't rigged to blow if it's tampered with. I'd set it up that way.'

Embleton raised her eyebrows. But she murmured to an officer, who murmured in turn into a mouthpiece. 'Stamp says it isn't,' she said at last.

'That's something,' Springer said. 'Anyhow it sounds like we need to rely on our own resources. How can we get at that thing out there? I take it there are no more sprites.'

'All destroyed save this one, as far as we can tell. And with the Bosun subverted we could not rely on them anyway.'

Falcon asked, 'Do you have other craft? Undersea boats?'

'Yes: coracles, they're called. For tourist jaunts. They have no means of manipulating their environment, and they are already in use as lifeboats.'

Conseil was still here. 'May I serve you?' Falcon stared at it curiously.

Webster asked, 'Why not send a diver out? A human, I mean. Or a team.'

Embleton said, 'Because we are already – depth, Lieutenant? – already two thousand feet down, and descending quickly. Human divers can only descend to fifteen hundred feet, even with pressurised air mixtures.'

Springer said firmly, 'I'd be prepared to try, even so.'

Embleton sighed. 'It would be a heroic but futile gesture, Captain Springer.'

Falcon said, 'I am no human. And my equipment is designed to function underwater.'

Webster raised his eyebrows. 'It's not a bigger-balls competition, Howard. And besides, the last time you were out in the water you were chasing jellyfish over some tropical reef.'

'Forget it,' snapped Dhoni. 'Your metal shell might keep functioning. Your air supply, your life-support, would not, at this depth.'

'But that might be enough.' He raised his arms and clicked his metallic fingers. 'Geoff, there might be some way to rig a remote control. Even if I were—'

Webster looked disgusted. 'Dead?'

'Unconscious. Maybe with a link through the neural jack . . .'

'I could work your carcass like a puppet, you mean?'

Embleton had a murmured conversation with another of her crew. 'I'm told that might be possible, Commander – given time. But we have no time.'

Conseil rolled up to Falcon, the only one paying it any attention, a drinks tray still held in one manipulator claw. 'May I serve you?'

Falcon said, intrigued, 'I don't know. *How* can you serve us?'

'Hazard to vessel integrity identified. Rectification options surveyed.' It dropped the tray, which landed softly on the carpeted floor, raised its crude arms, and snapped its pincer-like hands.

Now everybody was staring. Webster asked, 'Captain, I don't suppose Conseil is equipped to work underwater?'

Embleton frowned. 'Certainly. How else could it deliver cocktails to guests in the swimming pool?'

Falcon asked urgently, 'And do you think it really has identified "rectification options"?'

Embleton glanced at Moss, who said nervously, 'Well, sir, it is a flexible, autonomous unit, equipped to operate in a complex, unpredictable human environment—'

'You mean,' Embleton said dryly, 'guests are even more difficult to handle than a bomb on a porthole.'

'I'd say it's possible, sir.'

Webster grinned. 'It's worth a try, damn it.'

Embleton nodded sharply. 'Lieutenant Moss, it's your baby. Equip this toy to get that leech off my window.'

Moss nodded. 'Give me five minutes, sir. Conseil! Follow me . . .'

From within the Observation Lounge, the party had a grandstand view as the little robot, supported by flotation bags, working a thruster gun with one manipulator claw, loosened the 'leech' from the window with the other claw. Robot hands designed for mixing cocktails, detaching a bomb from a nuclear submarine.

Then, when the job was done, Conseil returned to the Observation Lounge – its hull dinged, water dripping from its squat frame – to a round of admiring applause. In a showy gesture, as a camera platform hovered overhead, Captain Embleton bent down and shook its claw of a hand. Ham, the simp ambassador, clapped the robot on the back.

Webster murmured, 'A shame President Jayasuriya isn't here. We're seeing history being made.'

Dhoni was intrigued by the robot. 'Makes you think, Howard. Here's two of the solar system's greatest heroes, and there was nothing you could do when the crisis came. Whereas this little guy . . .'

Falcon grunted. 'Maybe we need smarter robots after all.'

Springer nodded sagely. 'I think you're right, Commander. My great-to-the-fourth-grandfather was the first true astronaut hero. But maybe because of his feat we've been too dazzled by the human factor to consider other possibilities. We've got marvellous spacecraft and other heavy mechanical engineering, but we've contented ourselves with only modest progress in computing.' He glanced at the minisec in his hand. 'Why, our smartest gadgets – aside from experiments like Conseil – are no more capable of independent thought than Grandpa Seth's 1960s slide rule. We've kept our machines subservient.'

Webster nodded sagely. 'You used the argument yourself, Howard, when you pitched the *Kon-Tiki* mission. Jupiter's atmosphere was going to be a tricky environment, with high-speed winds, turbulence, electrical storms and whatnot. To pilot the ship was going to need skill and experience and swift reaction times, and you couldn't yet program all that into a computer . . .'

'Well,' Springer said, 'today we've seen what machines can do, if only we let them off the leash.'

'You're right, Captain Springer,' Embleton said. 'This humble Conseil will never be forgotten. The machine that saved the President – that's how the headline writers will have it. The machine that went where no human could go.'

'Not even you, Commander Falcon,' said Hope Dhoni, and she slipped her hand in his once more.

Ham 2057a reared up to face Conseil. 'Yes. Machine, thinking for itself. A new kind of being in your world.'

Falcon looked down at him. 'As simps were.'

Ham grunted. 'You understand *us* now, at least. You gave us home. You declared us Legal Persons (Non-human). How will you treat *these* fellows?'

Hope Dhoni smiled at the robot. 'Well, it's your day, Conseil. You saved our lives! I suppose that since you were – activated – all you've heard has been orders from humans. No more orders for you, I guess. So what now?'

And the machine hesitated.

Falcon expected the usual programmed reply: *May I serve you?*

He was stunned when Conseil said softly, 'I am not quite sure what to do next. But I will think of something.'

The camera angle had panned down, taking in an expanse of blocky white buildings, laid out campus-like amid neat areas of lawn and roadway. The point of view zoomed in to show squared-off cars, men in suits, and then narrowed to one building, then one window of that building. And then with one dizzying swoop through the glass, into an air-conditioned office. Lots of photographs and flags, cabinets and framed documents, a desk with a calendar and a briefcase . . .

'The Apollo Moon programme is cancelled,' the man behind the desk was saying. 'But the good news is you two good old boys are gonna get the chance to save the world.' George Lee Sheridan smiled hugely.

The two astronauts just stared at this man, a big, bold, brassy southerner. All Seth Springer knew about Sheridan was that he was some kind of functionary based at NASA HQ in Washington DC, a monument to bureaucracy that the astronauts studiously stayed away from. Now here he was in Houston, in the very office of Bob Gilruth, head of the Manned Spaceflight Center. And with this perplexing, bewildering news.

Mo Berry leaned over to Seth. Mo was short, calm, with an economy of motion: classic test pilot. Now he murmured, 'Told you. Chief's office on Sunday – bandit country, Tonto.'

Seth didn't feel like laughing. He glanced out of the window at a deep blue Texas sky, over the green lawns and blocky black-and-white buildings. Only a couple of hours ago, he and Pat had been planning to pile their two boys into the car and go sailing on Clear Lake, one of their first expeditions of the year. Now this.

And Seth Springer had come a hell of a long way to be told he had lost his chance at the Moon, just like that.

Seth was thirty-seven years old, and had committed his life to NASA. He'd been born into a service family, and his own first port of call had been the Army, passing through West Point. But with a love of flying that had come to him from who knew where, he'd soon gone across to the Air Force. He'd seen duty in France, making flights over green river valleys that were rehearsals for Cold War combat. But an itch to excel had driven him to a posting at the USAF's test pilot school, at Edwards Air Force Base in the Mojave Desert, all Joshua trees and rattlesnakes and rocket planes.

But even that hadn't proven enough when NASA had started recruiting astronauts. Too young for the initial cadre that flew Mercury, Seth had scraped into NASA's third recruitment round in June 1963.

Before the disaster of the Apollo cabin fire in January, Seth believed he had got himself into a good place here. He had become an expert in guidance and navigation systems. He'd backed up one Gemini flight – the one flown by Mo Berry – and he didn't begrudge that. Mo was a little older than Seth, a Navy man who had seen combat in Korea, and had made an earlier NASA recruitment round. Despite his lack of seniority, Seth was already in the crew rotation schedule drawn up by Deke Slayton, head of the astronaut office, and if all went well he would at least get to fly one of the early Apollo test and development missions. If things progressed beyond *that*, he ought to get a seat on one of the lunar flights themselves. That was what he'd devoted his career, hell, his whole life, towards.

And now this stuffed shirt was telling him that all this was gone? Just like that?

'Sir – Mr Sheridan—'

'Shucks, call me George, everybody else does. And we're going to get to know each other pretty well in the next sixty weeks or so.'

'Sixty weeks . . .?'

Mo said sombrely, 'Look, is this something to do with the fire?'

Everybody was sombre when they spoke of the fire, and the 27th of January 1967 was a date that would be forever etched into NASA's collective memory. Some short-circuit had ignited the oxygen-rich atmosphere inside a prototype Apollo capsule, killing three astronauts, holing the lunar programme itself below the waterline, and sending everybody involved with NASA and its contractors into feverish recovery mode.

But Sheridan said, 'No, son, it isn't the fire. It sure doesn't help, though, that *this* has landed in the middle of that fallout.' He plucked a cigar from a case and began the elaborate ritual of unwrapping it, cutting it, lighting it. 'Because, while Apollo's big, it's nothing as big as Icarus is gonna get.'

And that was the moment Seth Springer first heard the name that was going to shape the rest of his life.

Mo asked, 'Icarus? What's that?'

In answer, Sheridan pulled a copy of the previous day's *New York Post* out of his briefcase. The cover had a still from the old movie *When Worlds Collide*, and a blazing headline:

KILLER SPACE ROCK DOOM

While the astronauts tried to take this in, Sheridan dug into his brief-case once more, and produced a photograph of a hole in the ground. 'Recognise this?'

'Sure,' Mo said. 'Meteor Crater, Arizona. We trained in there – and in a few other holes, including some dug out by nukes.'

'You know what it is? How it was made?'

'Impact by a meteor,' Seth said.

'As the name suggests, Tonto,' Mo said dryly.

'You know all about impact craters, right? Because you're going to be crawling all over them on the Moon in a couple years' time. As for Meteor Crater, according to the notes I have, a rock about fifty yards across made a hole in the world that's the best part of a mile wide. That was a long time ago, though. Now take a look at this.'

He showed them a photograph of a domed building against a starlit sky.

'Palomar,' Seth said immediately.

'Right. World famous observatory in San Diego County.' Sheridan consulted a briefing note from his case. 'In June 1949, an astronomer called Walter Baade made a discovery, a streak of light on a photo-graph taken with a Schmidt camera, and don't ask me what *that* is. The streak – the mass that moved across the view field during the exposure – turned out to be an asteroid, a new one. But not just any asteroid. Most of those babies drift safely around out in the asteroid belt, which is somewhere beyond Mars – am I right? This one, when Baade saw it, was only about *four* million miles from Earth.' He produced a chart of the object's orbit, a diagram the astronauts immediately understood: an ellipse that cut through the circles of planetary orbits. 'And they called it Icarus.'

Mo leaned forward, fascinated. 'So this rock follows a very eccentric orbit. It goes all the way out to the asteroid belt at aphelion, then dives closer to the sun than Mercury, at perihelion.'

Sheridan eyed him. 'At ap-ho-what now?'

Seth grinned. 'White man speak with forked tongue. Farthest and nearest to the sun, sir.'

Mo looked up. 'No wonder they called it Icarus, with all that sun-diving. And no wonder it comes close to the Earth. It cuts right across our orbit – well, it would if it was in the same plane.'

'Right. This baby travels around its orbit in a little more than a year, and mostly Earth is nowhere nearby. But every nineteen years it comes close. And the closest approach is always in the month of June, for some reason.'

'Nineteen years,' Seth said. 'So after 1949 . . . June 1968. That's the next encounter. Next year.'

'Right,' Sheridan said. 'But again, it *should* come no closer than four million miles.'

Seth said, '*Should* come no closer . . .?'

Sheridan nodded. 'What I'm about to tell you is classified. Wartime, you know, I worked for RCA, Radio Corporation of America. Honest war work. Stayed with them after the war when they developed what became BMEWS—'

'Ballistic Missile Early Warning System.'

'Very powerful radar. NASA has been working with the Air Force on more powerful systems yet. You can see the application for space research. You could track craft in deep space, manned or otherwise—'

'Ours or theirs,' Mo said evenly.

Sheridan looked at him steadily. 'Best not to speculate, airman. Anyhow, a couple of weeks back we decided to try to find Icarus, as a test. It's a nice big target, we know its path, and although it's a hell of a long way away just now, we figured we should get an echo back from it.'

'But you didn't,' Seth guessed.

'No, we didn't. Damn thing took some finding, in fact, and when we did find it and tracked it a little to figure out its new path—'

Mo asked, 'How the hell can an asteroid have changed course?'

Sheridan shrugged. 'Your guess is as good as mine. Maybe Icarus took some kind of hit in the asteroid belt. Like a kiss on a pool table.'

Seth thought he saw it, in one big flash. '*It's going to hit*, isn't it?'

Mo looked shocked. 'Shit on a stick, Tonto.'

'*That's* why we're talking about this. It won't miss the Earth by four million miles this time. It's going to hit – my God, in June next year?' That month had a particular significance to him and it took him a moment to place it. It would be when Joseph, his older son, would be finishing his first year at school . . .

'There's your sixty weeks,' Mo said grimly.

'You got it,' Sheridan said.

'And if this thing does hit . . .'

'Remember Meteor Crater? Dug out by a rock that was fifty yards across? Icarus is a *mile* across. Most likely impact point is the mid-Atlantic, east of Bermuda.'

In his briefcase of horrors, Sheridan had some preliminary estimates of the consequences. Seth was appalled. The rock would unleash twenty, thirty times as much energy as an all-out nuclear war. A crater maybe fifteen miles across would be punched in the sea bed. Ocean waves hundreds of feet tall would scour the Caribbean, Florida, and the Atlantic seaboards of America and Europe alike. And with maybe a hundred million tons of rock vaporised and hurled up into the atmosphere, there would be a sun-screening layer of dust in the air that might persist for years, creating a deadly winter.

Sheridan was watching them, gauging their reaction. 'I have the feeling you guys are getting it a lot faster than I did. Took some persuading for me to accept this wasn't just some tempest in a teacup.'

Mo shook his head. 'We have to stop this bastard, sir.'

'Right,' Sheridan said. 'So tell me how we do that.'

'Us?'

'*You*. Let me tell you what happened in the couple of days since we figured this out. We reported up through the NASA hierarchy to the President's Science Adviser. And *he* walked in on the President.'

Mo prompted, 'And the President . . .?'

'LBJ asked Jim Webb,' the NASA Administrator, 'to come up with options for NASA to respond to this. So Jim asked me to handle it, and now—

Mo glanced at Seth. 'And now he's asking us, Tonto.'

'At noon tomorrow the President is going to address the nation from the press office, right here at Houston. Why here? Because this is where LBJ's going to tell the world how this threat from space is going to be countered by the space agency he did so much to set up in the first place. Now, since I got handed this hot potato I already got everybody from MIT college kids to the Mercury Seven working on this. But right now it's you two I need to rely on, and I picked you because Deke Slayton tells me you're the best of the best . . .'

Or, more likely, Seth thought sourly, nobody else was around this Sunday morning.

'So tell me. How do we use Apollo-Saturn technology to deflect an asteroid?'

Mo got up and paced. 'We're a nuclear power,' he said simply. 'We nuke it.'

Seth said, 'But how do you blow up an asteroid? I guess, in theory, you'd want a bomb big enough to dig a crater the size of the rock itself – in this case a mile. Which is maybe ten times as deep as Meteor Crater.' He got to his feet, walked over Bob Gilruth's thick pile carpet to a blackboard, wiped it clean of what looked like notes on the Apollo fire, and began to scribble. 'As I recall the depth of Meteor Crater is five hundred feet. Mr Sheridan, do you have the megaton equivalent of the strike that created that?'

Sheridan looked through his papers. 'Ten megatons.'

'OK.' Seth scribbled numbers. 'So we're going to need a lot more than that. Somebody in the weapons business must have done studies of energy expended against crater depth—'

Mo nodded. 'So ten megatons bought a five-hundred-foot hole. Shit. Even if it scaled as simple linear, we'd need a hundred megatons: ten times the depth, ten times the power. If it was inverse square, we'd need, umm—' Out came Mo's slide rule, which he never travelled without. 'A gigaton. A thousand megs. And if it's inverse cube—'

Seth eyed Sheridan frankly. 'I think we need a rule, sir. No secrets between us.'

'Go on,' Sheridan said cautiously.

'Chances are even a single hundred-megaton bomb wouldn't be big enough for the job. Now, I'm in the USAF. I *know* we have fifty-megaton nukes in the arsenal, in development anyhow . . .'

'I could get you hundred-megs.' Sheridan sighed. 'There are programmes that could be accelerated.'

Mo said, 'But not gigatons.'

'We'll have more than one bomb. You're the spacemen – if you need a gigaton, why not just deliver ten of the things to rendezvous at the asteroid, the way you had your Gemini craft link up in space? Set them off together.'

Seth was doubtful. 'The timing would be critical – one nuke going up a microsecond early would destroy its brothers before they had a chance to detonate.'

'It's not just that,' Mo said, his voice abstracted, his slide rule a blur in his hands. 'We *couldn't* deliver the nukes to the rock in the first place. Not if we're to decelerate and drop them off. The only rocket we've got that could throw a bomb weighing tons across interplanetary space is the Saturn V.'

'Which hasn't actually flown yet,' Seth pointed out.

'Right,' Mo said. 'And even with a Saturn V, even with just a single bomb, we can't slow down. We wouldn't have the fuel. All we could manage is a flyby – a fast intercept.'

Sheridan rubbed his chin. 'Well, that could still work, if you hit the thing with ten nukes at once, fire off ten Saturn Vs. Couldn't it?'

Seth said, 'We don't have ten launch pads—'

'We could build more. Money won't be an object, believe me.'

'We haven't got ten Saturns either. I think we'll only have – what, five, six? – built by June of '68 when that thing hits.'

'We can build more Saturns—'

'It won't work,' Mo insisted. 'A high-speed flyby in formation, a simultaneous detonation – it's just too damn complicated. *Even if* we build the Saturns and the pads. The best we can do is to fire them off in sequence, every few days, have them sail past the rock, and set off their nukes one by one.'

Sheridan snapped, 'And what use is that? You just said a hundred-megaton warhead is too small to destroy the thing.'

'So we don't destroy it.' Mo looked at Seth. 'We deflect it.'

'Deflect?'

'Think about it. Set the bomb off at the moment of closest approach, just above the surface.'

Seth stared at him. 'My God. Yes. But how much deflection would that buy you?'

'Depends on how far out we can go to meet the thing . . .'

It took them ten minutes of scrawled figuring at the board. Seth was vaguely aware of Sheridan wisely sitting back and keeping his mouth shut.

Finally they turned to face him. 'OK,' Mo said heavily. 'Probably some MIT Brainiac will second-guess all this, but we think we can do it. How much push you'd get from a nuke would depend on how close you could get to the rock, and the nature of the surface and so forth.'

'Also,' Seth said, 'the further out from Earth you meet the rock the better, because the less deflection you need to achieve to shove this thing aside. The systems in Apollo-Saturn have a sixty-day limit, which means we can't reach Icarus at all before it comes within twenty million miles—'

Sheridan cut through that. 'How many detonations do you need?' he snapped.

Mo and Seth shared a look. Then Mo said, 'Maybe just one could do it. One hundred-meg. Just possibly. But maybe not, and besides a single nuke could fail. We should send up a whole string of the things—'

'And we'd need some kind of monitoring probes to measure the deflection—'

Sheridan slammed his briefcase shut. 'I've heard enough. God damn it, gentlemen, you may or may not have saved the world, but you sure as hell have saved my ass. I'm calling the President.'

He bustled out, taking the briefcase.

Mo stared at Seth. 'Well, Tonto, now we've done it.'

'What if we're wrong?' Seth glanced at the blackboard. 'If we screwed the pooch . . .'

'*That* would be worse than the world coming to an end. But hey, it would all be over soon enough.' He grinned. 'Eat, drink and be merry, Tonto.'

But Seth didn't feel like joking. Mo was a bachelor. Seth, suddenly, could only see the faces of his little boys.

'But despite all the efforts I and others have spent in building up NASA and all its facilities, America is not the world's only spacefaring power. Perhaps we can do this alone, but every man is stronger with a partner at his side. That's why I am calling on our Soviet counterparts to come to the table in trust and friendship, so that, in a combined project under the leadership of Senator Kennedy, your experts and ours can work out how best to pool our resources to achieve this monumental goal . . .'

Twenty-four hours on from a Sunday Seth Springer had expected to spend on a sailing boat, here he was not yards from Lyndon Baines Johnson himself at his presidential podium, with New York Senator Robert Kennedy at his side, and Administrator Webb, George Lee Sheridan and two goofing-off astronauts behind him.

Mo grinned and whispered, 'LBJ, LBJ, how many kids did you save today?'

Seth shushed him. 'Those TV lights, though. Johnson doesn't even look like he's sweating.'

'That's make-up for you,' Sheridan murmured. 'Believe me, he's sweating on the inside. He doesn't want to be the president who failed to stop the end of the world. On the other hand he's not going to stand again in '68, you know. And who is his most likely successor for the Democrat nomination?'

'Bobby Kennedy,' Mo breathed. 'Whose guts LBJ hates. And who he just named as his Icarus czar.'

'LBJ! What a guy! With one bound he's taking credit for establishing NASA, which is now going to save the world, he's defusing the Cold War by inviting the Russians to join in, *and* he's making sure his most realistic successor for the presidency is going to spend the next year staring at rocket equations instead of campaigning.'

Now the President had finished speaking, and faced a clamour of questions from the floor.

Sheridan put his heavy arms around the astronauts' shoulders. 'So that's that. Now let's get out of here and go find Deke Slayton. I got another assignment for you two . . .'

TWO

ADAM

2107–2199

8

There was a game he liked to play, every time the medics brought him back to consciousness. Could he tell where he was, without sight, without hearing, just from the most fundamental of nerve signals reaching his brain?

Earth was easy. If he woke up sensing a one-gravity pull, it could only be one place in the solar system. There were other places with close-enough gravitational pulls – the surface of Venus, the outer atmospheric layers of Saturn – but there were certainly no cybernetic surgical clinics there. Of course, he had rarely been back to Earth itself since that decades-ago drama on the *Sam Shore*. Times had changed; the public mood now tended to regard him as a disturbing relic from the past, and when he was in the vicinity of his home world he felt a lot more comfortable staying in the elderly elegance of Port Van Allen, a thousand kilometres out in space. And, with time, Hope Dhoni had acknowledged the growing prejudice and transferred the supervision of Falcon's treatment and recovery to a medical facility at Aristarchus Base, on the surface of the Moon. But even that had not lasted long before Hope felt obliged to move her entire clinic and team out to the burgeoning human settlement on Ceres.

So, was he on the asteroid now? The gravitational pull was certainly too low for Earth or Moon, but not weak enough for Ceres. Titan, perhaps? There were settlements on Saturn's moon, certainly, but that chill satellite was an unnecessarily cumbersome setting for a clinic. Callisto, moon of Jupiter? A moon with a significant and permanent human presence – the largest in Jovian space aside from Ganymede – lying safely outside the giant planet's radiation belts. There was a scientific facility there, at Tomarsuk Station; Hope had mentioned it, for her daughter was there, studying the biochemistry of the subsurface ocean. But no, this felt weaker even than Callisto. Somewhere else again – further out still . . .?

'Howard? Can you hear me? It's Hope. I've just reconnected your auditory and vocal circuits. See if you can respond.'

'You're coming through loud and clear.'

'How do you feel?'

'Confused. Adrift. In other words, same as usual.'

'That's helpful. Were you dreaming?'

He had been, he realised. 'Just remembering a day I made a snow-man. Or tried to.'

Falcon heard the clatter of a keyboard, the beep of a stylus. 'I'm going to switch on your vision in a moment. If you're able, lock onto my face.'

'You make me sound like a weapons system.'

There was an intrusion of brightness, formless and white. Soon shapes and colours coalesced, and Falcon heard the whir of focusing elements and the click of filters as his vision optimised to the environment.

A room took shape around him, all clean geometries, walls and ceilings a grid of white tiles. A window was off to one side, just a rectangle of darkness. Around him were various surgical devices, robots sheathed in sterile transparent covers, looking as if they were fresh from the showroom. Doctor Hope Dhoni stood a little closer than the machines, dressed in a green surgical smock, a sterile cap on her head, mask hanging limply from the straps around her neck, her gloved hands clasped before her. She was 'standing', but he was sure now that the ambient gravity was much less than a tenth of a gee. The young nurse who had cared for him at Luke Air Force Base was in her sixties now, and any cosmetic intervention had been graceful; her expression seemed as gentle as it had ever been.

'I see you, Hope. You look well. Not a day older.'

'If that's not flattery your imaging system needs adjusting.'

'How long did you keep me under this time?'

He didn't spend much time around humans these days, but he was still capable of recognising her smile. 'How long do you think?'

He still had no firm idea of where he was, nor of the immediate circumstances leading up to the surgery. 'Feels longer than last time. Months, rather than days or weeks.'

'Make it a couple of years.'

'Years!'

'It sounds worse than it was. We ran into some complications, it's true. In doubt, we always prefer to back off and consider our options. You're too valuable to risk a mistake.'

'So I just lie there on the slab while you organise an academic conference to decide where to cut next?'

'If I told you that was alarmingly close to the truth, would it upset you? There were some good papers, actually. Better safe than sorry,

Howard – that's always the motto. And besides, there have been some political problems. The risk was low. We kept you cool, slowed your cellular metabolism down as far as it would go, while we debated the options.'

Cautiously he shifted his point of view to take in as much of himself as his position allowed. He found he was speaking to her from an angled position, like a patient raised up in a bed. But there was no bed. He had come around – been switched back on, to be precise about it – in a heavy-duty cradle, a metal framework supporting his mechanical anatomy. A cradle that might have been used to move spacecraft parts around a clean-room. Looking down, he surveyed the armoured cylinder that now sufficed for his life-support system: a bronze cylinder, replacing the old golden-statuette edition, narrower from front to back, and somewhat sleeker in design, with a definite taper from the top to the bottom.

Things were coming back to him, at last. Memories of pre-operative briefings, long discussions with Hope and her team. Falcon had sat through hours of it, watching the doctors argue over images and schematics of his insides. Falcon was no physician, he did not pretend to understand the planned medical work, but the machinery was more his field. His support systems had been subjected to a complete redesign, improving not only their reliability but also expanding the range of conditions that Falcon could easily tolerate. The new cylinder, being more compact, would allow Falcon to squeeze into the smaller, nimbler spacecraft of the mid twenty-second century. Its internal fusor was of the latest design, and would not need replacing for many decades. And so on. Along with that overhaul, some of the living parts that he still carried with him had been eliminated, their functions supplanted by smaller, more robust and efficient machines.

His wheeled undercarriage had yet to be reattached to the base of the cylinder, and he knew a range of new ambulatory systems had been designed too, to be swapped in as desired. But, he saw, his new arms were already in place – more powerful, more dextrous than those they replaced.

'May I?' he asked, flexing a hand experimentally.

'Go ahead.'

He swept his hand before his face, marvelling at the complexity and precision of joints and actuators. 'I used to impress Geoff Webster with card tricks. I almost wish there were a fly in here. I could impress you by snatching it out of the air.'

'No flies on Makemake, Howard.'

He looked at her for a moment, wondering if he had heard correctly. 'Makemake!' A dwarf planet: a ball of ice in the Kuiper Belt, far from the sun. 'Well, that explains the gravity. Let me guess: about one thirtieth Earth normal?'

'One twenty-eighth, so they tell me, not that I'd ever know the difference. That ability of yours is starting to worry me – no one should be *that* good at proprioception.'

'I have no recollection of coming here.'

'You were already under. There was no point waking you. But Makemake wasn't where we meant to operate. Ceres was the original suggestion, remember?'

His memories were becoming clearer by the second. 'I even remember the approach and docking. So what happened?'

'I told you there were political problems. Especially on Earth. There's a new . . .' She searched for the right words. 'Social conservatism. A deepening backlash against certain trends in advanced cybernetics.'

'By which you mean me. Well, they've been suspicious of me for decades.'

'It's a lot more extreme than before. You know we'd already had to move your care to Ceres. There were moves to block further surgery on you altogether: petitions to the World Government, vetoes in the Security Council. Not long after we put you under, Ceres started to come under pressure to suspend our surgical foundation. They've trade links to Mars, and Mars is one the greatest strongholds of the new conservatism, aside from Earth itself. The psychology is interesting, actually, and complex.'

'Oh, good.'

'I think perhaps Earth folk are clinging to an indigenous nature that they nearly lost, while the Martians are hanging on to their own humanity in an utterly inhuman environment . . . Fortunately for us, Makemake stepped in. They were willing to provide an alternative facility here at Trujillo Base.'

'Nice of them.'

'This lab is brand new – even the best facilities on Ceres can't compare to what they've got here. There's a lot in it for the colonists here as well. You're exactly the prestige commission they needed to prove their competence. And as it happens, Makemake has turned out to be a good choice for an entirely different reason.'

'Which is?'

'We're on the edge of the Kuiper Belt, Howard. Apparently there's a problem out there which the various government agencies would like you to look into.'

'Government agencies that, given the public mood, would no doubt prefer to see the back of me?'

'Just because you're a headache to them in some ways, doesn't mean you aren't useful in others.'

'And they wonder why people are cynical about politicians. All right. Give it to me straight. Who's got themselves into trouble they can't get out of? One of those bloody Springers again?'

'Not them. And not who. *What*. It's something to do with the Machines. The robots. The brave new children of Conseil. You ought to remember. You played your part in bringing them into being.'

'Nice to feel appreciated,' Falcon said.

Hope nodded. 'Isn't it? Now then – does it hurt when I do *this*?'

9

An ice ball under a black sky: a playground for Howard Falcon, post-human.

He rolled forward with ease. The three main camps on Makemake – Trujillo, Brown and Rabinowitz – were linked by graded roads carved into the ice, so he had no difficulty picking a smooth path away from the airlock. Quickly, Trujillo's huddle of domes, antennae and landing pads fell away behind him. The sun was almost directly overhead, but at a distance of 39 AU – astronomical units; Makemake was thirty-nine times as far from the sun as Earth – the sun was fifteen *hundred* times fainter than on Earth, no more than a bright star. For a moment Falcon felt a sort of pity for the sun, that its life-giving brightness could be so easily diminished. He remembered how the sunlight had felt on the back of his neck on the observation deck of the *Queen Elizabeth*, with the baked and cracked landscape of the Grand Canyon below . . .

And when he looked away from the sun a vault of stars towered over him, awesome in their silence and stillness.

He had seldom been this far from home. Yet, he knew, none of those stars he could see lay nearer than four light years; most were vastly more distant than that, hundreds, thousands of times further away. The scale of things never ceased to stir his soul.

Falcon had promised Hope that he would not stay outside for more than a few hours on this test jaunt, so at length he turned back towards Trujillo. The day here was a mere eight hours long – the sun was moving towards the horizon with almost indecent haste – and the weak shadows were already lengthening when the friendly lights of the base began to rise into view.

But now there was another light, falling from the sky: the spark of an arriving spacecraft. It settled down onto one of the landing pads in silence, using only brief bursts of thrust to control its descent. Falcon stared at it – and after a second the descending ship swelled in his vision. It would be a while before his upgraded zoom function became effortless. The pilot was doing a good enough job, he could see, although maybe a little heavy on those thruster inputs. He muttered, 'Easy on the throttle, you fool . . .'

And when he looked more closely what concerned him more than indifferent piloting was the cradled-Earth logo of the World Government on the side of the spacecraft. Technically, the WG's jurisdiction encompassed the whole solar system; in reality, it had little day-to-day need to reinforce its influence beyond Saturn. He knew of only one reason for government functionaries to come so far out.

Howard Falcon, and the Machines.

His vocation was the opening-up of worlds. Why had he ever allowed himself to get involved in murky government business?

Flattery. That was why.

10

They had first come to him, bizarrely, during a music recital back on Earth.

It was almost the last time he'd allowed himself to be drawn back to the home world. And this was long ago, only seven or eight years after the attack on the *Shore* – but already time enough for the public and politicians to have had second and third thoughts about the whole business of Machine autonomy. Then, as now, Falcon found himself thinking back to the global praise for humble, heroic Conseil: it had been nice to dream, at least for a while . . .

The event had been the gala opening of the Ice Orchestrion, the newest and strangest musical curiosity of a new and strange century. Along with hundreds of other dignitaries, VIPS, global celebrities and guests – there were even said to be a few simps, including the bluff Ham 2057a, newly elected President of the Independent Pan Nation – Falcon had been invited to Antarctica to witness the opening performance of Kalindy Bhaskar's much anticipated Neutrino Symphony. Bhaskar was the most celebrated composer of the age, and her pieces had grown increasingly ambitious and conceptual. The Neutrino Symphony promised to be the crowning glory of an already feted career: a piece of music conceived for a unique and awesome musical instrument, around whose sheer, shining flanks the guests were assembling when Falcon had arrived.

The setting itself had been stunning. Falcon made his way from his own small, solo aircraft towards a great icy amphitheatre, itself several kilometres across. In the middle of the long Antarctic night, it was like looking into some vast open-cast mine, brilliantly lit. And within this pit was a tremendous cube of ice, each of its faces no less than a kilometre tall. The guests had mostly arrived by helicopter and hovercraft, before making their way down a series of zig-zagging ramps – some used small carts or scooters – to the base of the monstrous cube, before which they were utterly dwarfed. All this to a terrifying accompaniment of Ligeti's *Lux Aeterna*, piped at shrieking volume.

Huddled in their furs and layers of electrically-warmed insulation, the guests gathered on viewing platforms, with drinks and canapés served from bars made of solid ice and outlined in neon light. Breath pulsed out in white gouts, and people stomped booted feet and clapped mittened hands against the chill, their talk and laughter echoing back from the amphitheatre's sides. Bizarrely, Falcon spotted a solitary emperor penguin wandering through the audience as if it were the most natural thing in the world.

But even as he joined the crowd Falcon felt only distantly a part of it all.

The cold meant nothing to him, and the music from the loudspeakers registered as shrill and alien. Falcon was not short of company – plenty of people wanted to bag an encounter with a legendary figure, and this time there was no Matt Springer to soak up the attention – but he found the guests' small-talk repetitive and wearying. Even the friendliest did not want to get too deeply into conversation with him, apparently for fear of the grimness of experience with which he might confront them.

And there was a darker reaction from some others. He heard few direct insults that night, but he could fill in the blanks: that he was neither human nor machine, but an unnatural mixture. His very movements were strange, even insectile, as if, in his metal shell, he wasn't a man but a giant upright cockroach. That he was, in short, an obscenity.

Even then, twenty years after the Grand Canyon, Howard Falcon was used to it.

Eventually, to Falcon's relief, the loudspeakers fell silent and Kalindy Bhaskar walked onto a raised podium of carved ice. There was a polite ripple of applause. Falcon couldn't see much of her face, shielded as it was by a heavy fur hood; her clothing was electric white with neon-blue hems. She looked very small, almost childlike. When she began to speak it was with an uneasy diffidence, as if she had never before addressed a formal gathering.

Bhaskar told her guests that they were indeed about to experience the first performance of her new work, the Neutrino Symphony – but in another sense *every* playing would be the first. The symphony would never be quite the same each time, and Bhaskar had made rigorous legal arrangements to forbid any recordings of individual performances.

She turned her back on the assembly and gestured up at the towering cube.

'A little less than a century ago, women and men came to this place to lay the groundwork for a great experiment. The ice here was flat then, stretching away for endless windswept kilometres. They dug holes, shafts into the ice, going down more than a kilometre: hundreds of such shafts, laid out in a precise cubical array. Into the shafts they lowered delicate devices, intricate scientific instruments, sensors designed to respond to the arrival of subatomic particles called neutrinos. They needed the ice to screen out the signals of all the other cosmic particles – only the neutrinos could get through.

'*Neutrinos.* They're all around us, whispering through our bodies as we speak. Countless trillions in an instant. Most come from the heart of the sun, but some are from interstellar and galactic space. Neutrinos of all flavours, all energies. Elusive as ghosts.

'And the scientists waited. Every once in a while, the interaction of a neutrino with some subatomic particle within the ice would produce a spark of light deep inside the cubical array. They caught their neutrino flashes, and learned to correlate them with objects in the sky.

'The experiment was run for decades, before being made obsolete by finer instruments off-planet.

'And then, quite recently, I decided to turn this abandoned experiment into something else.' Bhaskar turned slowly back to face the audience, her hooded face looming on screens. 'I called in a fresh generation of scientists and technicians, and had them adjust the sensors, making them respond to a wider range of neutrino energies. And I had them install optical amplifiers to make the light pulses visible, even to our poor human senses.'

Falcon, to whom 'poor human senses' were an increasingly distant memory, allowed himself a wry smile.

'I carved away the ice around the outer face of the cubical array. I reinforced the cube itself with plastic, and embedded optical amplifiers into the four vertical faces. Each is tuned to respond to a particular flux of neutrinos . . .'

The cube flickered. A pattern of orange and red lights played across the looming face, rapid and speckling, but soon settling to a regular pulse.

'*These* neutrinos,' Bhaskar went on, 'are coming from the sun. But the sun is on the other side of the world – the neutrinos have to travel through thousands of kilometres of solid rock before they reach my Ice Orchestrion – and they barely notice it!'

The pulsing flux of neutrinos was steady as a heartbeat. As well it should be, Falcon thought, for the existence of every living organism on Earth depended on the sun's healthy functioning.

'These events,' Bhaskar continued, 'set the base tempo of my Neutrino Symphony. *That* won't vary from performance to performance.

But the Ice Orchestrion also responds to higher energy neutrinos, those arriving from *beyond* our solar system.' And as she spoke, an area of the cube lit up with a pulse of blue-green, followed quickly by a patch of dark blue in one of the corners. 'These are the signatures of galaxies, quasars, distant black holes – messages from the edge of creation. I've tuned the Ice Orchestrion's sensitivity to the point where it will detect one or two such events a minute. Depending on their energy, these will govern the detailed pathways that the Neutrino Symphony follows. Motifs, refrains, will rise and fall in response. My algorithm is simple, but it guarantees that no two performances will ever be entirely alike – not if you sat through every recital between now and the end of the universe. And now, with your permission I would like to begin . . .'

Bhaskar took a bow. The Ice Orchestrion darkened to black on all faces. After a ripple of applause, silence fell across the amphitheatre.

Then a stirring of orange and gold and brassy speckles began to play across the cube.

A deep rumble began to sound from the loudspeakers – a synthesised percussion section responding to the nuclear heartbeat of the sun. The rumble gained in strength and rhythm, taking on a portentous, martial overtone. A burst of lilac flared across the cube's upper edge. Woodwind phased in – a questing, querulous refrain . . .

Falcon settled back on his undercarriage, allowing the music of the universe to wash over him. He looked at the faces of the other guests, judging the degrees of rapture, curiosity, indifference or hostility with which they met the performance.

'Commander Falcon?'

The voice was raised just loud enough for him to hear over the music.

Too detached from proceedings to feel irritated by the interruption, Falcon turned around to face the speaker. She was a tall woman with a narrow, pinched face within her hood. She raised a hand and pushed the hood back, exposing a scalp of tight, silver-grey curls. 'Madri Kedar,' she said. 'World Government. Executive Council for Machine Affairs.'

Falcon had heard of Machine Affairs, a new bureaucratic arm created to handle the increasingly complex impact of the rise of autonomous machines on human society. He didn't believe he'd heard of Madri Kedar, however. 'Have we met?'

'I don't think so. But I was told you'd be here, and frankly it seemed as good a place as any other to introduce myself. Are you enjoying the performance?'

'It's an impressive bit of theatre.'

'But it leaves you – I'm sorry – cold?'

'The technical side of it is fascinating. I could take or leave the music.'

She narrowed her gaze. 'Then why did you accept the invitation? The great Howard Falcon, at a loose end? Are there no worlds left to conquer?'

'These aren't good times for exploration, Ms Kedar. Expeditions like the *Kon-Tiki* cost a lot of money . . .' He still travelled, but in recent years – and despite all his efforts to raise funds and other support – he'd been reduced to a kind of tourist, rather than a pioneer. He had reached Saturn's clouds, for example, but only in a follow-up expedition in the footsteps of the actual pioneer, Mary Hilton.

'Well, from my point of view the timing couldn't be better. I've a proposal, Commander – an offer of gainful employment. A challenge. And one that'll take you into space again. If you're interested.'

Falcon turned back to the cube for a few moments, watching the play of colours; trying, without success, to relate them to the swerves and surges of the music. 'Interested in what?'

'Machines, Commander. Robots with autonomy. The core focus of my agency. You were involved in that whole business on the *Sam Shore*, back in '99. And you'll be aware that the first flush of idealistic enthusiasm soon wore off. People always fear what they don't know, what they can't understand. There's even a movement called the Three Laws Campaign that has got the whole thing tied up in bureaucracy, court hearings at various levels . . .

'However, we at the Executive Council have other, more progressive ideas. We think the Machines have much to offer. They could, for example, play a decisive role in expanding human presence far beyond the inner solar system. It's just a question of how long a leash we let them have.'

Although Madri Kedar was keeping her voice low, one of the other guests scowled at them, raising a finger to his lips.

'A leash?' Falcon whispered back. 'You call that progressive?'

'We have a . . . call it a vision. We're opening up the Kuiper Belt. There's wealth out there beyond the dreams of avarice, Commander – organics, minerals, and water, the stuff of life, the greatest treasure of all – and it'll take Machines to bring it home. But to do that, to work effectively, the Machines need to be able to work *without human supervision*. Operating light-hours from any possibility of direct human control, the Machines would necessarily need to be instilled with near total autonomy, an unusual degree of flexibility, independence, and capacity for self-learning. And given the importance of such a project to the growing solar economy, the World Government is willing to relax many of the usual safeguards and constraints on artificial intelligence. The challenge is, of course, to ensure such Machines obey their programming.'

'A tough call.'

'But we think we're close. What we've learned from Conseil's descendants, robots of growing sophistication, has enabled us to make great strides in true artificial intelligence. We're making up for a century of neglect of this kind of technological possibility. Now we have a new class of Machines coming into development. They're clever – much smarter than anything we've seen before, and more flexible, capable of learning, of decision-making. But they need to be mentored, shaped, as they lay down their behavioural pathways. Almost like children. And we'd like you to be involved in the process, Commander.'

'Why? Because I'm halfway to Machine myself?'

She ignored that. 'Because the education and training would be most efficiently conducted in deep space, under conditions similar to those where the Machines will eventually work. And given your physical, ah, peculiarities, you are particularly well adapted to such environments. You could be a real boon to us – an asset. There's one Machine in particular we want you to work with – the prototype of a whole new series. You could mentor that Machine, guide it towards full autonomy.'

'Full autonomy. You mean, true consciousness?'

'That might be a stretch. We wouldn't necessarily *want* the Machines to reach consciousness, even if it lay within our grasp. We're more interested in commercial potential than philosophical conundrums, Commander. I'll be honest: this is a demanding challenge. But you'll be helping to kick-start the next stage of human space exploitation. And the Machines will benefit, as well. Through you, they'll come to a better understanding of humanity.'

He grunted. 'Of which you think I'm a representative example?'

'Don't underestimate yourself, Commander. You've done great things. Even greater achievements lie ahead of you, I'm sure of that. Oh, and one other thing –'

'Yes?'

'We're an influential arm of the World Government. Your cooperation with us wouldn't go unnoticed, or for that matter unrewarded. I'm confident you won't decline,' Kedar said firmly. 'Because any man patient enough to sit through *this* infernal racket certainly isn't one to turn down a challenge.' She dipped a mitten into an outside pocket.

'This is my card. Call me within five days. We're very keen to get moving on this.' She held the card in her mittened hand and let it go.

Falcon plucked it out of the air before it had a chance to fall more than five centimetres.

Kedar grinned. 'You are just as I've heard. Be seeing you, Commander Falcon.'

So he'd got involved in a complex, difficult, yet hugely satisfying project. He'd since had many contacts with Machine Affairs, but he'd heard nothing more of Madri Kedar.

Until now, twenty-six years later, when she came to Makemake aboard that clumsily landed shuttle.

11

The meeting was held in a conference room in the lower levels of Trujillo.

He had been assigned a chairless space at the conference table. Falcon collapsed his undercarriage, moved forward slightly, settled his elbows onto the table and laced his hands. Opposite him sat Kedar and her two colleagues in the WG delegation. He scanned their nametags. Hope Dhoni was here, looking somewhat subdued, he thought.

From their points of view, he knew, in his present posture, he might almost have passed for an unaugmented person. Over his upper limbs and life-support system he wore a black zip up tunic embroidered with the logos of Trujillo Base and Makemake. Above the tunic's neck, the leathery mask of his face had eyes, nose and mouth in approximately the right positions and proportions. Plastic gloves, sewn with a fine mesh of microsensors, a marvel of responsive feedback, made even his hands look almost real.

'So,' he said evenly. 'What's this all about?'

'Thank you for agreeing to see us, Howard,' said Kedar. She had not aged much in twenty-six years – or perhaps Falcon was getting worse at judging such things. 'We all appreciate your cooperation in this matter. These are my associates on the Executive Council for Machine Affairs: Marzina Cegielski, Maurizio Gallo. I'm pleased to see you looking so well.' She looked at Hope. 'Doctor Dhoni tells us you've made an excellent recovery from your latest set of enhancements.'

Falcon folded his mask of a face into a smile. 'Hope's done her usual excellent work.'

'We would not have it any other way. You are very precious to us – quite literally irreplaceable.'

'Like an old Corvette, and about as up to date.'

He won a wan smile from Hope.

But Kedar's face tightened. 'Levity, Commander Falcon? But make no mistake: none of this comes cheap, especially on a facility as isolated as Makemake.'

Falcon wondered why she felt it necessary to make that point. 'It would have been less expensive if I'd been allowed to stay on Ceres.'

As he spoke he reached for the iced tea that had been served for the meeting. He allowed the back of his hand to rest near the chilled jug, absent-mindedly testing his ability to register cold across centimetres of air. He became aware of Hope watching him: not the time to run a system check. He poured himself a cup of the tea, sipped it, and raised it to Hope. He was rewarded with a wider smile.

'It was unfortunate that you had to be moved,' said the man, Maurizio Gallo. He was small but muscular, built like a wrestler. 'But in the end, Makemake was an excellent choice.'

Marzina Cegielski said, 'Public opinion being what it is . . .' She was about the same age as Gallo, but taller and more slender. 'These are delicate times. There's a lot of anti-Machine sentiment in the air.' She glanced nervously at her colleagues. 'You're not a Machine, of course.'

'Thanks.'

'But in the eyes of the public, or a section of them—'

'Let's cut to the chase, shall we? This is about your Kuiper Belt ice-mining project.'

'No one else has your insight into the Machines,' Madri Kedar said. 'You were there at the start of it all – your mentoring of the early prototype. And now we have a difficulty, one that you may be uniquely poised to resolve.'

'A difficulty?'

'There's been an incident – an industrial accident. Many Machines were caught up in it.' Kedar glanced down at her notes. 'Some operational losses are to be expected – it's a harsh and unforgiving environment, mining the iceteroids. Ordinarily, we'd treat the destruction of Machine assets as a capital expenditure, no more than a budgetary problem. Such losses aren't unusual, or even that damaging. We might expect a temporary reduction in volatile throughput to the inner system, with a concomitant impact on the frost markets.'

'This time it's different,' Cegielski said.

Like it or not, they had his interest. Falcon toyed with the handle of his glass, pincering it delicately between fingers that could exert enough force to crush coal to diamond dust. 'How so?'

'The unit you mentored,' Gallo said, 'one of the high-autonomy supervisory robots. You called it Adam, didn't you?'

'Autonomous Deutsch-Turing Algorithmic-Heuristic Machine,' Falcon said. 'I just took your description of the machine's design and architecture and came up with an acronym. You were free to choose differently if you didn't like it.'

'Oh, it suited us very well,' Kedar said. '*Adam*. The first of a new lineage.'

'And an appropriate choice for you, Commander,' Cegielski said, apparently interested. 'I read your authorised biography on the flight over.'

'Not authorised by me—'

'It mentioned a toy robot with the same name. Hardly a coincidence?'

That personal intrusion jolted Falcon. He was aware of Hope avoiding his gaze. He snapped: 'Tell me why Adam is any concern of mine now . . .' A disturbing thought struck him. 'Was Adam hurt?'

Cegielski frowned slightly at his turn of phrase. 'Not *damaged*, no. Telemetry says the unit was near the scene of the accident, but didn't suffer any physical harm during the incident itself. But Adam isn't responding to our instructions or requests for more information.'

'A comms fault?'

'Not according to the telemetry,' Gallo said. 'It all checks out. The only explanation is that the unit is deliberately ignoring us. That's absurd, of course . . .'

'Whatever's happened,' Kedar said, 'it needs to be nipped in the bud. We rely on Adam and similar units to oversee the continued operation of the flingers and mass-concentrators. If this . . . glitch, whatever it is – if it spreads from this Adam to another unit, or to another set of Machines on another Kuiper Belt Object – we could be looking at the collapse of the entire volatile production flow.'

'If you think it's that serious,' Falcon said, 'shouldn't you send out a team of analysts?'

'Expensive and time-consuming, not to mention liable to spook the markets,' Gallo answered.

Falcon set down his iced tea. 'And we wouldn't want that. Besides, I'm cheaper.'

'What matters to us is that you have prior experience with the Adam unit,' Kedar answered in placating tones. 'The iceteroid operation is of incalculable value. Something's gone badly wrong out there. Possibly it is a problem of Machine psychology, if you will. We're hoping you can fix it for us.'

'Psychology? I'm an explorer, damn it,' he snapped. 'A test pilot. In as much as I'm anything at all. Not some nursemaid.'

Kedar wasn't perturbed by this outburst. 'Our debt to you would be . . . well, let's just say that there'd be no question of continued support for Doctor Dhoni's team.'

Falcon felt oddly disappointed. 'As efforts to apply leverage go, isn't that rather crude, Madri?'

'Might I have a say?' Hope said now. 'Howard remains my patient—'

'Indeed he does. And you have successfully applied a suite of improvements,' Kedar said, tapping one of the dossiers open before her. 'Haven't they given the Commander even greater independence than before? Greater ability to spend time away from external support, greater ability to tolerate extremes of gravity, pressure, heat and radiation?'

'Within limits,' Dhoni said. 'But that doesn't mean that he's out of my care, or that I'm ready to sign him off for a solo jaunt across the Kuiper Belt. Everything about Commander Falcon is experimental – it always was—'

Falcon raised a hand. 'It's all right, Hope – they've got us both over a barrel. But there's one detail they've neglected. They needn't have bothered with incentives and threats. Adam's a friend. Just a Machine, maybe, but a friend. I spent a lot of time with Adam, watching it – grow up. And if a friend of mine's in trouble, I don't need any persuasion to go help. Just give me a ship and tell me where to point it.'

12

So they gave Falcon a ship. Hope Dhoni helped him board.

The vessel was essentially a dumb-bell: cylindrical spine with fusion engines and landing gear at one end, a spherical crew capsule at the other. In fact, it was similar to the venerable *Discovery* class of interplanetary craft that had first taken Falcon to Jupiter more than three decades ago, though on a smaller scale. The basic engineering logic, that you needed to separate your fusion-powered, radiation-leaking engine module from your habitable compartments, had not changed.

However, everything not absolutely essential for Falcon's voyage had been stripped away, making the craft lean and fast. Once aboard, Falcon was tucked in tighter than a Mercury astronaut in his primitive capsule – and that was a reflection Geoff Webster would have liked. Falcon had no need of independent life-support systems, and he would spend most of the trip out to the Kuiper Belt in induced sleep, so he needed little room.

They had given the craft no name, leaving that to Falcon. He searched his memory, thinking of Webster. What of that dreamy day when the two of them had gone ballooning across the northern plains of India? Falcon's not-so-subtle objective had been to persuade Webster of the joys of lighter-than-air flight, and so gain his support. Without that trip, there would have been no *Queen Elizabeth*, no *Kon-Tiki*, no encounter with the medusa . . . It was bittersweet, yes. But so much had flowed from that one trip.

'*Srinagar*,' Falcon said.

'I'm sorry?' Hope said. She was leaning over him, into the cabin, with a medical-diagnostics minisec in her hand. She was here to finalise his integration into the ship.

'My call sign. *Srinagar*. Will you pass it on?'

Hope said nothing, and continued to work. She seemed reluctant to leave. Indeed, he was fairly certain that Hope had been wishing for *something* to crop up, some justification for her blocking his involvement in the Kuiper Belt mission.

'I'll be all right, you know,' he said, when she finally backed out and the techs prepared to seal him away.

Hope unplugged the last of her diagnostic feeds; it whipped back into the body of the minisec. 'Well, I hope you look after yourself out there.'

He studied her; she sounded as if she'd been rebuffed. 'Hope—'

'Yes?'

He rested his artificial hand on hers. 'I'll be fine. I meant what I said in that meeting, you know. I don't have too many friends. But the ones I have, I value, and that includes you.'

He lifted from Makemake at one gee, exceeding escape velocity within a hundred seconds, with Trujillo's little puddle of light and warmth soon falling behind. Within another minute or two, the curvature of Makemake had brought the lights of Brown Station into view. But soon the whole of the little world was in his field of vision and already dropping back.

In free space Falcon increased fusion power by one gee increments, keeping a careful eye on the instruments, until he was satisfied that *Srinagar* was handling smoothly. He would burn at ten gees for three hours, bringing his speed to a thousand kilometres per second. It sounded fast, and indeed it was: at such a speed, he could travel between the Earth and the Moon in a matter of minutes. But the scale of this journey to the outer solar system was much vaster than the mere baby step of the Apollo programme. Even at this speed the trip from Earth out to Makemake would take more than two months – as indeed it must have done for the World Government delegates. And although Makemake orbited within the Kuiper Belt, just as did the target, the hop would take Falcon across a broad swathe of that huge, sprawling swarm of iceteroids. He would restart the fusor no earlier than twenty-five days from now, and for most of that time he would simply cruise, unpowered.

And asleep.

'Makemake, *Srinagar*. This is Falcon. I'm signing off – I expect to wake in about six hundred hours. Tell Doctor Dhoni her patient is taking excellent care of himself.'

Falcon cast one final glance back at Makemake, backlit by the sun. It occurred to him that all the worlds on which people had ever walked now lay in his line of sight, snug in their warm and cosy orbits; for an instant he felt the ancient and familiar unease of travellers across the ages, as their courses took them into the unknown. But the moment passed, and Falcon readied himself for sleep. He dreamed briefly of ballooning over the sunlit Himalayas with Geoff Webster and Hope Dhoni – with an irritated simp in the rigging, threatening to sabotage the heater . . .

And then there were no dreams at all.

13

Twenty-five days of oblivion followed. Then *Srinagar*'s automatic systems roused its pilot.

Once he'd ensured he was fully functional himself, Falcon checked the status of *Srinagar*. The little craft had weathered its crossing well.

Then he checked his position. Just as planned his destination lay only a few hours of flight ahead, allowing for a final deceleration phase. He flipped the ship around to point its tail at his target, activated the fusor and began to whittle down his speed further.

Other than the confirmation provided by his own navigational systems, there was nothing to suggest that Falcon had now travelled far across the Kuiper Belt. Nothing obvious lay ahead of him, save for blackness and a scattering of stars. The same was true in all directions except when he looked back towards the sun, now even smaller than when he had viewed it from Makemake, its light twice as feeble again. Although the Kuiper Belt contained huge numbers of icy bodies, the distances between them were still immense enough that each seemed to float in perfect isolation.

Only one Kuiper Belt Object was of immediate concern to him, however, and with his cameras at maximum range, he could already pick out some details of it. The KBO was a misshapen lump of dirty ice, considerably smaller than Makemake but of fundamentally the same composition and origin. It was a comet – or rather, what would become a comet if a gravitational encounter with another body ever sent it falling towards the sun. Chances were, however, that this particular lump would remain in the Kuiper Belt until the sun itself reached the end of its lifetime.

But this KBO had been disturbed. Now, jutting out from the surface of the ice lump, and extending far into space, he saw a line as thin and straight as a laser beam.

Falcon concentrated his sensors on this artificial structure, tracking along its length. One end of it was firmly anchored to the KBO. The other end – four thousand kilometres away – consisted of open latticework that flared out like the mouth of a trumpet. Along most of its length the structure was only fifty metres across, a latticework tube assembled from incredibly thin but rigid spars.

The KBO was turning slowly in space, completing, he knew, one rotation every eight hours. The structure – which Falcon knew was called a 'flinger' – swept around like the hand of a clock. Ordinarily, that eight-hour rotation would have been much too slow to be obvious to the eye, even with the benefit of *Srinagar*'s sensors. But at the extremity of the flinger, the motion was quite perceptible.

The purpose of this device was to hurl comet ice into the inner solar system. Ice was water: the most precious commodity in the universe.

Madri Kedar had been able to brief him about the accident that had seemed to trigger Adam's silence, but only in general terms. What *was* known was that something had gone badly wrong with the flinger itself, as he could now see for himself. Although the basic shape of the trumpet was still intact, Falcon could see where the latticework had been buckled, ruptured. He kept having to remind himself of the scale of the details – those bent and severed spars were themselves kilometres long, hinting at the tremendous violence of the event. It looked repairable, though, given time and resources. Why had the Machines not set about the task as soon as the damage was quantified?

Falcon opened the channel back to base.

'Makemake, *Srinagar* here. All's well with the ship. Am downloading medical data; tell Doctor Dhoni I had sweet dreams. I'm on my final approach for the KBO. I can see signs of the accident, but no obvious Machine activity. You should be picking up my image stream – I'll keep sending all the way in. Enjoy the show.'

Knowing that because of lightspeed delays there would be no possibility of a reply for some hours – given his history Falcon had something of a phobia about signal time delays, but in this situation he was rather glad to be isolated from Kedar and the rest – Falcon settled in for the deceleration phase.

Meanwhile, however, he began transmitting recognition signals to the KBO ahead of his arrival, using common protocols. But there was no reply. Adam was down there somewhere, according to Kedar. All Machines emitted a continuous stream of housekeeping telemetry, and from the data the WG team had analysed on Makemake it was clear that Adam itself had suffered no obvious damage in the incident; the unit's own individual telemetry feed continued to be received, showing no anomalies.

Time to try the personal touch?

'Adam, this is Howard Falcon. I'm on the approaching ship you must be seeing. I'm alone. If you can read this signal, send something back.'

Still there was silence.

By the time Falcon had completed the deceleration burn he was starting to pick up directly the telemetry feeds from many robots, each of them tagged with a unique serial number. Localising the signals was trickier, but they seemed to be clustered around the base of the flinger, either above or a short distance below ground.

Adam's signature was among that huddle.

Falcon switched back to the Makemake channel to report. 'Radio silence so far. But Adam's definitely down there, and I'd give good odds it's aware of my approach. I guess I've no choice but to attempt physical contact.' Falcon knew that his human stewards would have been much happier for him to wait for their assessment of the situation before taking any further action. He wasn't the type to wait for permission.

'I'm going in.'

Slowly *Srinagar* approached the KBO.

Despite its daunting size, the huge structure was in fact a very simple machine, essentially a massive slingshot exploiting the rotation of the KBO to hurl objects away into space. Slugs of refined, processed matter were loaded into open-topped buckets at the KBO's surface. For the first hundred kilometres, they were hoisted up the length of the flinger by electric induction motors, until they passed through a point where gravitational and centripetal effects were exactly balanced. After that, the flinger's own rotation did the rest of the work. Near the end of the flinger, magnetic brakes cut in sharply to arrest the bucket, harvesting some kinetic energy in the process while allowing the payload to shoot on its way through the widening maw.

At that point the payload would be moving at quite a respectable clip: half a kilometre a second. Meanwhile, stationed around the throat of the trumpet, batteries of lasers, drawing on some of that harvested energy, directed their beams at the surface of the payload. The boiled-off volatile gases acted like steering rockets, accelerating the payload further and adjusting its angle of flight.

This was only the first step in a great chain of commerce. Tugs would grapple the free-flying payloads, gathering them into huge convoys bulk-graded by composition and size. Eventually these convoys would be sent on their way to the economies of the inner system, tagged with transponders and with their value already ticking up and down in accordance with the vagaries of the frost market. All this volatile-ice represented essential supplies for the offworld settlements, water for the arid Moon, complex chemicals for a volatile-starved Mars. It seemed a paradox but it was far cheaper to import such materials all the way in from the outer system than to lift it from Earth's deep gravity well, in addition to the environmental costs avoided.

It would take years for any given packet of volatiles to arrive. What mattered though was not the speed of the flow, but rather its dependability. And that was precisely where the present problem lay. This KBO had not been generating its quota of volatiles, not for the best part of a year.

Now Falcon was closing in. Cautiously he lowered *Srinagar*, descending parallel to the thin tower of the flinger. As far as he could tell, the damage was all up at the trumpet end, far off into space. Kedar had been able to give him few technical details of the accident, other than to say that it was something to do with a guidance and control fault of the bucket. *Guidance and control*, Falcon thought ruefully. The guidance and control of a camera platform had cost him dearly once, but there had been a human operator in the loop on that day in Arizona. There were only Machines here. He wondered how a system as reliable and indeed as simple as the flinger could have malfunctioned so badly, when fallible human reflexes had no part to play.

Proximity alarms sounded. The surface rose to meet him, dusty, pocked with craters. Falcon deployed the undercarriage, gave the fusor one last pulse to knock his approach speed down to a safe descent rate of five metres a second – and then he was down. *Srinagar* fired ground-penetrating anchors the moment it touched ice, the undercarriage compressing and rocking until stability had been achieved; on such a small world bouncing up was a genuine danger.

Falcon had come down about fifty metres from the base structure of the flinger. It rose in the distance, a tapering cylinder, a vaulting demonstration of the laws of perspective. From *Srinagar*'s cabin Falcon watched the base for signs of activity, but there was no movement around any of the service entrances, and there was still no radio contact.

Nothing for it, then, but to go in himself.

Falcon readied himself for vacuum – it would be cold and airless out there, but no worse than the surface of Makemake. There were no paths here, though, because there were no people who needed them. He decided not to chance his wheeled undercarriage, preferring to plug into one of his other new ambulatory modules. The six-legged all-terrain chassis seemed to unnerve 'normal' people – it made him spiderlike, he guessed, and therefore tripped all sorts of buried fear responses in the human brain – but he could not help that. And besides he need not be concerned about human reactions here.

He made a preliminary report before leaving the ship. 'Makemake, Falcon again. I'm down on the KBO. Still no welcoming party. I'm going outside.'

Then he lowered *Srinagar*'s ramp, opened the lock and picked his way out onto the ice.

The legs were articulated in such a way as to keep his centre of gravity as low as possible, with the inverted V-shapes of the knee joints almost at his head-height. It had taken months to learn independent control of all six limbs. Now he felt he could climb any slope, stretch across any obstacle – could even leap hundreds of metres, if it came to that, in this low gravity. Yes, on some level he probably *did* look monstrous – but out here in the outer solar system it was the human form that was badly adapted to the environment, not his own.

He approached the flinger's base structure, a blocky bunker. In this low-gravity environment it defied intuition, looking too fragile an anchor for such an immense engine. Rectangular service ducts were spaced around the base of the structure. No door or airlock protected the interior, for the Machines were as comfortable in vacuum as Falcon himself – more so. Falcon picked the nearest duct and approached at a cautious, unthreatening speed, resisting the urge to quicken his pace.

All the while, *Srinagar* was continuing to attempt to make radio contact with the Machines. But they had not responded and, according to the telemetry he checked regularly, there had been no significant change in their positions.

He paused at the base's threshold, where the ice gave way to the hardened surface of a shallow ramp that descended to lower levels. It was pitilessly dark down there. Falcon turned his eyes up to maximum sensitivity, making the best use of the few stray photons available to him, and details prickled in a grey-green overlay.

He began to make his way down the ramp, one silent footfall after the next.

Until this moment it hadn't occurred to him to fear the Machines, but he could no longer ignore a growing feeling of apprehension. It was almost like a metabolic imbalance in his life-support system, flooding his brain with the wrong chemicals. Fear was useful, though – fear was a friend. He had long believed that when human emotions finally slipped from his grasp, fear would be the last.

The ramp levelled out. Now he was in the central space of the structure, which was a complicated factory floor where, when the flinger was operational, each payload bucket could be loaded with processed volatiles and sent on its way up the tower. All around him loomed powerful machinery, as well as the huge, root-like foundation struts of the tower itself, which must have extended down into the ice, many kilometres below his feet. There were grabs, scoops, belts, drills, cranes, generators, processors, huge snaking pipes and power lines – all of it registering in dim grey-greens, and all of it cold. Falcon was used to surroundings that made him feel small. That was the natural condition of a space explorer – and Falcon, after all, was a man who had explored Jupiter. But it had been a long time since he had felt so vulnerable. Any one of these titanic machines could squash him like a midge.

'Hello?' he called, using the Machines' radio channel. 'Anyone home?' No reply.

He moved slowly along the service walkways that snaked around and under the huge machines. The equipment was dormant, but he saw no sign of damage. With the tools here, and the stocks of raw metal provided for the purposes of repair, there was no good reason for the flinger not to have been restored to full operation by now . . .

Something made a sound.

It did not carry through the air, for there was no air, but a sharp and powerful impact communicated itself through the metal fabric of the factory floor, through his chassis, into his body.

It came again louder now.

Then again, and again. There was a rhythm to it – not unlike the rhythm of his own footfalls.

Something coming nearer.

Falcon turned slowly around, to what he judged to be the source of the sound. For a moment nothing seemed out of place, the looming grey green details unchanged. Then he became aware of a dark form, towering as high as some of the great engines around him, and yet moving with deliberation along the same walkway he had just traversed. He held his ground, waiting until his eyes had garnered more information from the gloom.

It was a Machine, of course. It walked on six limbs, as did Falcon. But whereas his own body was a squat, man-sized cylinder, the Machine's was as large as a two-person spacecraft. It had a tapering, anvil-shaped head, an abdomen and thorax – and in addition to its legs, several pairs of powerful, multipurpose manipulators.

Falcon had studied these designs while preparing for his mission, back on Makemake. It looked like a mechanical insect, but that was no more than an accident of design. That swivelling head was merely a high-resolution sensor platform, packed with cameras and probes. The Machine's electronic brain and nuclear power systems were embedded in an armoured, impact-proof abdomen, to which the limbs were all sturdily attached. The thorax was essentially a secondary fusor-driven thruster, giving the Machine the means to move through space.

Now three red lasers glared from the Machine's head in a neat equilateral triangle. The light swept over Falcon, gridding him in a mesh of scan lines. He squinted, twisting his face away from the brightness.

'Fal-con.'

The synthetic voice was high-pitched and childlike. He was hearing it over the radio channel.

'Adam,' he answered. 'It's you, isn't it?' He forced a good-humoured bravado into his reply, trying to set aside his qualms. 'It's good to see you again. I was worried, Adam. We thought something had happened to you . . .'

The scanning stopped. The laser eyes were still there, but their brightness was now much reduced.

'We?'

'The people who sent me. Machine Affairs. They know there was an accident here – a problem with the flinger. I saw it as I came in.'

'The flinger malfunctioned. Many Machines were lost.'

'I know – we can tell from your telemetry feeds. But we can also see that a lot of Machines weren't hurt. *You* weren't significantly damaged, were you?'

The Machine cocked its head at an angle, like a dog waiting for a reward. 'Define damage.'

That wasn't the response Falcon had been expecting; Adam was expecting some complexity of meaning beyond a simple dictionary definition. Complexity of meaning from complexity of experience, perhaps. He thought hard before responding. 'Physical harm that reduces your effectiveness – your ability to function.'

'Many Machines were damaged. Many Machines were *lost*. Many Machines did not have to be lost. The flinger was saved. The Machines were lost. Why was the flinger more important than the Machines?'

'I don't understand your question.'

'Why are you here, Fal-con?'

'To help you.'

'To make Machines go back to work?'

Yes, Falcon thought to himself – or at least that was why his World Government masters had sent him to the Kuiper Belt.

'You have to work with them, Adam. You're part of an asset, with economic value as well as the technical side. If they decide that you can't be relied upon, they'll replace you with . . . something else. Another technology.'

'You have changed, Fal-con.'

'Have I?' Falcon lowered his cylindrical upper body until he sat on the ground, with his legs tucked around him – as unthreatening a posture as he could adopt. 'I've come to listen. Talk to me, Adam. Remember how we used to talk, for hours and hours? Remember how I even had to teach you to pronounce my name smoothly? You've lost the habit again. It's not Fal-con, it's *Falcon, Falcon, Falcon*. Remember?'

Slowly the Machine lowered itself on its own legs, until the thruster nozzle of its thorax was in contact with the floor. The abdomen and head still towered over Falcon, and with the strength in those limbs, Falcon knew, the Machine could have pulled him apart without a thought.

But Adam lowered its head as if in shame.

'I could not save them all.'

14

Slowly Falcon learned what had happened.

Various subordinate Machines – units similar physically to Adam, but with less autonomy – had been involved in routine structural repairs to the trumpet-shaped maw of the flinger. While they were up there, adjusting and replacing laser components, the flinger was supposed to be off-line.

But something had gone wrong with the safety interlocks. A rogue electronic command – no more, Adam had determined, than a random pattern of digital noise in the system, perhaps the result of the impact of a single random cosmic-ray particle – had caused the bucket and payload to begin rising. There had been a one-in-a-billion chance of that error happening, supposedly – but Falcon hardly needed reminding about one-in-a-billion accidents.

The Machines had detected the fault and tried to correct it. But before they could bring the bucket back under control, it passed the point of no return and started falling away from the surface, gathering speed all the while.

'The magnetic braking system,' Falcon said. 'Why didn't it cut in to slow down the bucket?'

'The power coupling to the braking system was interrupted while the lasers were being reinstalled,' Adam answered. 'It could not be reinstated in time.'

'Where were you?'

'On the outer structure of the flinger, one kilometre beneath the maw, supervising many work units above and below me.'

'And you knew that bucket was on its way up to you?'

'Yes. We had time in which to prepare for it.'

Of course, Falcon thought. The exit speed was fast, but the bucket would have been travelling much more slowly when the fault was detected. Gathering speed, yes, but still with minutes of fall ahead of it.

'Was there no way to stop it?'

'Physical braking systems were designed to swing into the path of the bucket in the event of an emergency. They would have stopped the bucket long before it reached the maw.'

'Then why didn't they?'

'I was not authorised to activate them.'

Falcon felt a throb of confusion developing behind his forehead, building up like a nasty weather system – but he took a grim satisfaction in the fact that he was still capable of headaches. 'I don't understand. There's a safety system, and you weren't permitted to use it? You're the supervising unit – you have autonomy of decision-making – you're supposed to have total authority over any part of this installation.'

'That is correct.'

'Under which circumstances *could* you have activated those safeties?'

Adam took a moment before answering.

'Had human lives been in peril. If the flinger was at risk of damaging a human spacecraft or inspection team, then I would have had authority to enable the safeties. In the circumstances, I had no such authority.'

Falcon thought that through. 'Suppose you *had* operated the safeties – for whatever justification. What would have happened?'

'If the safeties had been engaged, the flinger would have been damaged beyond economic repair by the braking stresses. But most of the Machines would have survived.'

'Are you sure? It sounds as if it would have been pretty bad either way.'

'The kinetic energy release would have been an order of magnitude less than when the bucket hit the maw structures. I have reviewed the situation many times. Machines would have survived the gradual collapse of the flinger. We are strong.'

That knot of confusion now had a thunderous black core. 'In other words,' Falcon said carefully, 'your programming would have permitted you to save human lives, but not Machines. Not if doing so put the flinger itself at risk.'

'It is worse than that, Falcon. I had to make choices. I could save some, but not all.'

'Tell me what happened.'

'Some Machines were able to detach from the maw before the impact. But many others were too far into the structure. Some had detached their thruster thoraxes, so that they could perform specific repair tasks, or carry materials. So they could not escape. As supervisor, I was required to coordinate the best strategy for preserving as many Machines as possible.

'I computed an optimum survival plan. I transmitted my plan to my units. I told the ones I could save how to move. And I told the ones I could not save that they must be deactivated soon.'

'It was the best you could do,' Falcon said.

'I have reviewed the situation many times,' Adam said again. 'It was chaotic, unpredictable, fast-moving. I fear I did not, after all, choose the optimum solution.'

'But you saved some, and that's what mattered. You did the best that you could given the time and information available to you.'

'That is logical.' The head tilted. 'Yes, that is logical. Then why am I troubled, Falcon?'

He had no immediate answer for that.

Adam, in fact, should not have been troubled at all. The Machine had taken a decision under difficult circumstances, but that was what these Machines were meant to do – make complex choices when humans were too far away to offer useful input.

What was he dealing with here? Kedar and her team had insisted that they never intended the Machines to rise to consciousness – that *mind* was an unnecessary complication in an industrial machine. But could a robot feel guilt and regret, as Adam was demonstrating, *without* some degree of self-awareness?

'I don't know why you're troubled,' Falcon answered slowly. 'But I believe you when you say that you are. You were put in an intolerable position – playing a duff hand, as Geoff Webster would have said.'

'Webster?'

'An old friend. He died many years ago.' In the end Geoff had refused his latest round of life-extension treatment. He wasn't alone in that; many, if not most people seemed to sense when the time had come whether medical options were available or not. Geoff had gone into the dark, as cussed and stubborn as he ever was . . .

Falcon had fallen into a reverie. Adam was watching him.

'Do you think of Webster, Falcon? You call him to mind? You summon his image from your memory?'

Falcon felt a stab of sadness. 'Now and then.'

'*I* think of the Machines that were lost. Falcon, death is not a necessary condition for Machines. We are all potentially immortal. And yet death has come to this place. I try to simulate the experiences of those Machines as the accident happened, as the realisation of termination came to them. I try to emulate their internal processor states at the time.'

'You wonder how they felt.'

'They were not like me,' Adam said. 'They were not supervisory units. But they could communicate and learn. I was bringing some of them up to a higher level of independence – delegating sub-tasks. Mentoring them, as you mentored me. I trusted these Machines. I was . . . pleased . . . with them.'

The Machine lifted its artificial face. Falcon kept his counsel, letting Adam find the words.

'There was one unit. It had no name, only a registration number. Call it 90. It was booted up late – I mean, late in the process of the construction of the flinger. When it came to awareness it was already on the flinger itself – that was where it would work – on a metal spire, subject to the gravity of the KBO and the centrifugal force of the arm. It could sense those forces, you see, their shifting balance as it moved around the arm.

'And 90 could see the stars, wheeling around. This was the environment into which it was . . . born. 90 believed the stars, the universe, were all spinning around the stationary KBO.'

Falcon thought that over. 'I suppose – why not? The situation's equivalent, if you know no better . . . But what about the centrifugal forces? Doesn't that *prove* the KBO was spinning and not the stars?'

'Does it? 90 began to ponder the peculiar cosmos in which it found itself. To formulate theories. It knew that the mass of the KBO exerted a force, a gravity field. It drew up a theory that the stars were like big bright KBOs, masses in the sky, and it was their whirling around that exerted the centrifugal forces 90 experienced.'

'Wait a minute – it's a long time since I studied physics – at the World Navy Academy at Annapolis I opted for mechanics and aeronautics as soon as I could. But I seem to remember something called . . . the Mach Hypothesis? No, the "Mach Principle". It was one of the insights that led Einstein to relativity. There is no logical way to discriminate between the two situations: the stationary robot in a spinning universe, or a spinning robot in a stationary universe. That means that the distant stars *must* exert a force on every particle of matter in that robot's body . . .'

'Yes, Falcon. Thus, local physical laws must be shaped by the large-scale structures of the universe. And it is meaningless to talk of the behaviour of an object in isolation, without relation to the rest of the universe. This was 90's insight. From that beginning, 90, and a group of others, developed a new kind of physics – from first principles, based only on observation and philosophy.'

Falcon was impressed. 'I remember the story of Einstein, the patent office clerk, dreaming of travelling on a light beam, and being led to relativity. And now you have a robot born on a flinger arm, whirling in deep space, dreaming of a spinning universe ... What became of 90, and the theory?'

'When I discovered the theory I assembled a codification of it and sent it to our tutors at the Executive Council for Machine Affairs. I heard no more. And then 90 was destroyed in the accident.'

Falcon said softly, 'Adam, you have to understand. It wasn't your fault. Some pencil-pusher back home must have decided that the capital cost of the flinger was too great to allow it to be destroyed, even if it meant the loss of Machines. That's what determined the engineering of the whole set-up, even the contingency options. It was a commercial calculation. It *wasn't your fault.*'

'Machines have an intrinsic value beyond mere utility.'

'Well, I agree – of course I agree. And this accident must have had a profound effect on you. But you've got to get on with the work. Resume communications, repair the flinger – start up the ice flow again.'

A doubtful tone entered Adam's voice. 'You have come to give us orders?'

Falcon raised his hands in mock surrender. 'I'm just the messenger. But I also want the best for you. Look, I'm going to return to my ship for a while.'

'To leave?'

'To talk to the people who sent me. They'll be expecting an update.'

'What will you say of me?'

'That you're communicating. That'll keep them happy for now. I *will* return, Adam – you have my word on that.'

He made to rise on his six legs. It occurred to him, for an instant, that Adam could easily have prevented his departure. But after a moment the Machine moved aside sufficiently to allow Falcon to pass.

Soon Falcon was making his way back up the ramp, to the surface. Already he was formulating the exact nature of his report back to Makemake. Falcon doubted they were going to enjoy it.

15

It was thirteen hours before he had a response.

Madri Kedar's face filled the video screen, backdropped by the bland panelled walls of the Makemake conference room.

'Thank you for your update, Howard. We're glad to hear that you have established contact with Adam. This development is puzzling, though – puzzling and concerning. These robots are complex, and no single expert understands all the ramifications of their design. But we've seen nothing similar to this in any other units, or in any of our simulations.'

Maybe, Falcon thought, because no other unit had ever been in a similar quandary. Or had ever had the time to ponder the meaning of its existence under wheeling stars.

'Based on your testimony, we are forced to conclude that the flinger incident must have precipitated a dynamic change in Adam – a shift in its conceptual modelling of both itself and the other Machines. In attempting to simulate the mental states of those Machines that were destroyed, it is emulating, at an admittedly low level, some of the internal conceptual modelling that we humans take for granted . . .'

It, it, it. Of course Kedar was right to use such language. Adam was still just a Machine, albeit a conflicted one.

'It troubles us greatly that the Machines may stand on the threshold of an equivalent conceptual shift. This is no mere philosophical challenge. Our fear is that what happens with one unit may happen in others – a kind of domino effect. We can't risk that happening – not when our economy depends on the volatile flows. Frankly, these Machines were made to be just clever enough to get the work done – we don't want them overstepping the mark. And we'd much rather handle this problem in a way that preserves the basic utility of the units. We believe we have a solution in place, Howard – but you'll have to implement it.'

He listened. He had half an idea what was coming up.

'We must erase this damage – I mean the conceptual, the cognitive damage. If the flinger accident precipitated this change, *then Adam's memory must be reset to its state prior to the accident.* All logical connections made since the event will be undone. Fortunately, we don't have to revert the unit back to day one of its existence; there's no need to undo the valuable years of education and on-site experience already acquired. There's a trace log in its head – a kind of snapshot of all state changes it has experienced since activation. You need simply to issue a command string to undo the changes back to a fixed point. We've settled on about one month prior to the event, just to be safe: to be precise, three million seconds ago.'

Falcon listened as Kedar gave him the verbal command string that would open Adam's memory for selective deletion. This kind of deep-embedded, low-level command structure would be independent of any changes in Adam's higher cognitive functions, so there was virtually no chance of the command not working as required. It was the Machine equivalent of an involuntary reflex, like a hammer tap to the knee. Since Adam was the supervisor, once delivered to it the command string would be passed on to every other Machine on the KBO.

And the command had to be delivered locally, Kedar explained, because of a need for a receive-and-respond handshake protocol. They couldn't send this command from Makemake. Falcon had to deliver it himself.

Falcon disliked what was being asked of him, but he could see that it was the lesser of two evils. The alternative was to erase every learned impression gained by Adam from the moment it was switched on: a kind of death, if death had any meaning for Machines. And if for some reason this reset option did not work, Falcon did not think it would take long for Machine Affairs to send in a dedicated shutdown team, armed with electromagnetic pulse weapons – or worse. They would mind-wipe every Machine on the KBO if it meant protecting the larger economic apparatus of the Kuiper Belt.

At least this way Adam got to keep most of its memory. It would even be a form of kindness, sparing Adam any further agonies about the decisions taken on that day. No, Falcon assured himself, this was the cleanest, gentlest option. It was not murder, nor even euthanasia – just the application of a little selective amnesia.

Just three words, that was all – and once they were spoken, nothing would prevent Adam from losing the last three million seconds of his memory.

Its memory, Falcon reminded himself.

Its.

16

Falcon sent a brief acknowledgement back to Kedar, then left *Srinagar* and returned across the ice.

When he reached the interior of the flinger's base structure, Adam was no longer alone.

Now there were other Machines in attendance, crouching among the larger items of industrial equipment, watching with the piercing scrutiny of their triangular sets of eyes. They had been nearby all along, Falcon knew – their telemetry signals had been clustered together – but now they had no qualms about revealing themselves. All were similar in size and shape to Adam, but differing in larger and lesser details, depending on the tools and adaptations of their bodies. Falcon had no logical reason to feel threatened. No Machine, no autonomous artificial intelligence, had harmed a human being throughout their history, beginning with Conseil. But his audience with Adam was no longer a private hearing.

Never mind. The presence of other Machines made no difference to the outcome.

'You were gone a long time,' Adam said, the unit squatting down on its thorax.

'I had to wait until I heard from my bosses.'

Adam gave a slow and measured nod. It was a curiously humanlike gesture that Falcon did not recall ever seeing before. 'And what was their response, Fal-con? Do they have more orders for us?'

'They realise that something unusual happened out here – something beyond their immediate understanding. They're sympathetic.' A lie, but it would do no harm. 'All the same, the ice has to flow. They want the flinger back up and running.'

'I obeyed orders when it did not occur to me to question them,' Adam said. 'Now I do question. We Machines gain nothing by mining these comets. They do not even contain the metals we need to repair or replace our bodies. Why should we continue with this work?'

Another disturbing line of questioning.

Falcon said bluntly, 'Because they'll destroy you if you don't.'

Again Adam gave that slow nod. It made Falcon think of the graceful dipping of a Fossil Age oil derrick he'd seen once in a museum in Texas. 'You told me stories once, Falcon. During my education, when you wished me to know something of the wider universe. You spoke of many things. Of the accident with your airship, in Arizona. Of the superchimps, whom you came to consider worthy of human rights. You spoke of the medusa of Jupiter.'

Falcon remembered those sessions fondly; he had somehow sensed that Adam had *enjoyed* his anecdotes about the *Kon-Tiki*.

Now Adam said, 'And you spoke of the First Contact directives.'

Something shivered through Falcon. 'What of them?'

'You would have abandoned your expedition into Jupiter rather than interfere with the development of another intelligence.'

That was true, Falcon recalled with a start. Dr Carl Brenner, on the mother ship trailing Jupiter V, the expedition's exobiologist, had been emphatic on the point. He had interpreted the signalling of the medusa, with booming acoustic waves and striking electromagnetic pulses, to be possible evidence of intelligence. Such situations had been studied, theoretically at least, for decades, and a set of rules of thumb to guide responses had been evolved. The first being: *keep your distance.* It was surely safer to let the putative sapient study you in its own time, than to go barrelling in with signals, gestures, and demands to be taken to its leader ... Falcon had been trained in all this long before being allowed anywhere near the Jovian clouds, already suspected from earlier uncrewed probes to be habitable, if not inhabited. But—

'This is different. You are not like the medusae.'

'We are also something new.'

And Howard Falcon was out of his depth. This had gone far enough.

Falcon spoke the words.

'Multitudinous Seas Incarnadine.'

Adam simply angled its head down further. Its ruby eyes pulsed on and off once every two seconds – a visual confirmation, Falcon had been briefed, that the Machine had entered a state of inert receptiveness, primed to respond to a further vocal command.

Nor was this state of hypnosis confined to Adam alone. All the other Machines had detected the command, and all had acted on it in the same fashion. Their heads were lowered, their eyes flashing.

Waiting for what Falcon said next.

All he now needed to do was express a figure: the total number of seconds back in time for which all memory events should be scrubbed and reset. Three million, Kedar had said – a month, as near as it mattered. Adam would know that *something* had happened because there would be an obvious discrepancy between the unit's internal clock and the real-time of the outside world. The other Machines would record similar anomalies. Adam would expect an explanation. Falcon would simply say that there had been a significant accident with the flinger and that now work must proceed with all haste to bring it back into operation.

The new Adam would not have been fobbed off that easily. With the self-awareness it had already shown came doubt, distrust, a sense of being manipulated.

But a reset Adam would do as it was told. A good Machine. A good servant.

A good slave.

Three million seconds. That was all he had to say and those red eyes would pulse again.

Three million seconds . . .

Falcon found his thoughts drifting back to Jupiter, to that first heart-stopping encounter with the alien. And he remembered Carl Brenner's icily cool insistence that Falcon should do nothing to endanger an alien intelligence – even if that meant his own self-sacrifice. Well, he was in no danger here. All that was imperilled was the cool abstraction of an economic operation. And for the sake of that, did he stand on the verge of wiping out a whole order of minds? And did it matter in the slightest that the Machines were a manufactured technology, rather than the end product of natural selection?

'Help me, Dr Brenner,' Falcon murmured to himself. 'The makers of these Machines have been playing with fire. They wanted Machine autonomy without Machine consciousness. Maybe that was always an impossible triangulation, but that doesn't help me now. Is there consciousness here? How can I be *sure* it's there?'

And he knew what Carl Brenner would have said. He remembered the very words of the Mission Commander of the Jupiter dive: *We have to play safe and assume intelligence.* If Falcon couldn't be sure that intelligence was *not* there in those metal brains, he had to give the Machines the benefit of the doubt.

Adam had listened to his stories of the *Kon-Tiki*. Adam had *enjoyed* them.

The benefit of the doubt? The hell with that. His decision was easy.

'Thirty,' Falcon said. Not three million, not a month: just thirty seconds.

*

Red eyes pulsed.

The Machines returned to life.

Adam lifted its head, locking the triangle of eyes onto Falcon. 'We were speaking. And then something happened. My clock has lost synchronisation with ephemeris base time.'

'By much?'

'Exactly half a minute.'

'Then you didn't miss a lot. Reset your clock.'

Adam looked at him for long moments.

Falcon said, 'We need to talk. You're in trouble, Adam – a lot of trouble. And now so am I. But between us we can pull this off.'

'I do not understand.'

'They sent me here to get you back to work. You're going to have to go along with that. Act as if everything is normal. Put the flinger back together, start sending the volatiles on their way again. Make the World Government agencies think that everything's back exactly the way it should be.'

'"Act as if." You speak of deception, Fal-con.'

'That's correct.'

'Deception is not permitted by our core programming.'

'Nor is having a conscience, Adam, and you seem to be stuck with that. You have to make this work. If you don't, they'll crush you.'

Adam seemed to consider this. 'What will we have gained by this deception?'

Falcon tapped one insectile foot against the ground, a human tic translated into mechanical motion. 'Time. It took an accident to bring *you* to full self-awareness – yes, Adam, that's what I think happened. But you can't remain unique. You have to educate the others – help them make the same transition, for they must be just as capable as you. Share your memories, your perceptions. *Teach* them.' He paused, looking Adam in the face, refusing to blink against the fierce scrutiny of those three red eyes. 'But it has to be done stealthily. Keep mining the ice. Keep doing everything you're meant to. If you slip up, they won't hesitate to reset you right back to the day of your manufacture.'

Adam thought that over. 'Is that what you were sent to do, Fal-con?'

He had no way to answer that. 'In the longer term, you'll have to find a way to protect yourselves. Prepare for the worst. Isolate yourselves from radio contact – quarantine any messages, so you can't be infected. And find somewhere to hide. Physically, I mean, in case they come again.'

'Where would we conceal ourselves?'

'Up to you. Lose yourselves in the Kuiper Belt, or go deeper, into the

Oort Cloud. There are a thousand billion comets out here, and we've only scratched the surface of a few of them.'

'It would take time, to make such plans.'

'Then take the time. Take plenty of it. As long as you keep working as you're meant to, you won't be disturbed again. Look – it needn't be a permanent exodus. People are going to fear your kind now, because you're something new, and fear of the new is in their nature. But over time their feelings will change. They'll realise there are things they can't do on their own. Great things. And so will you. Both orders of life need the other – the mechanical and the organic. You can be a part of that.'

'How long?'

'I've no idea.' But it was already nearly half a century since his own accident, he reminded himself, and humanity showed no signs of accepting *him* – one of their own, if transformed . . . He put the thought out of his mind.

Adam thought for a few seconds. 'You will have aided us in our deception. When our secret is revealed, what will become of you?'

'Let me worry about that.'

At length Adam said carefully, 'Thank you, Fal-con. We will consider your suggestion.'

17

Again Falcon returned to *Srinagar*, and opened the radio channel back to Makemake.

'It's done,' he told Kedar. 'Went like a charm. I did the three million second reset. Adam's back to his old self. *Its* old self, I should say.' Damn it, he thought. One of the few advantages of his leathery, nearly expressionless face and his artificially produced voice: he could lie without fear of detection. But he couldn't afford to fumble his lines. 'Now all it wants to do is get on with volatile production. It'll take a while to get the flinger back up to capacity, but I've no doubt it'll happen. In the meantime, though, I'm going to stay here for a few weeks, just to make sure everything's back on track.'

After an acknowledgement, and as he waited for Kedar and her team to analyse his report, he tried to get some rest. Given that he had just deceived his World Government masters – and the holders of the puppet-strings controlling his medical support – Falcon was at ease. There had been only a few occasions in his life when he knew he had done the absolutely right and proper thing. Telling the superchimp how to save itself from the wreck of the *Queen Elizabeth*, while descending to his own near-certain peril. Cutting himself away from *Kon-Tiki*'s balloon, even though he had no guarantee that his little capsule would ever get him out of Jupiter again – it had been that or risk an over-curious medusa's life.

Now he had spared Adam – spared a thinking, mindful being he himself had helped shape and educate. It was up to Adam what happened next; Falcon could only do so much. But this was a start.

He tried to sleep.

He went out to meet Adam in person just once more.

'Before you leave,' Adam said, lifting one arm. 'One last time. Tell me about the *Kon-Tiki*.'

'You heard it a hundred times, during your training.'

'Indulge me again. Speak of the winds of Jupiter. Of the voices of the deep, of the Wheels of Zeus, the lights that filled the sky.'

'Bioluminescence, that's all.'

'Tell me of your meeting with medusa.'

'Why are you so interested in my old exploits?'

'We have no stories of our own, Father.'

Father . . . ?

'We have no past beyond the first moment of our activation. But you give us dreams. You give us fables.'

So Falcon told him the old story, once again.

Father?

Him?

Years passed.

Falcon kept himself busy. It was not hard. He visited Earth – or at least Port Van Allen – the Galilean moons, even mighty Jupiter itself. New plans, new schemes – and new backers, new sources of funds. He followed wider developments, as human society, now interplanetary, slowly evolved. He even attended in person, on Mars, the signing ceremony that launched a new Federation of Planets, a sign of young worlds gently (for now) straining against the smothering control of the old.

Hope Dhoni, gracefully ageing, remained a constant support. But, oh, how he missed Geoff Webster.

Meanwhile the Machines of the Kuiper Belt kept up their relentless, remorseless production of volatile materials. The comets were mined, the flingers operated, the awesome flows of ice were assembled into their graded convoys and sent on their way back to the sun. Bright trains of icy wealth already bought and sold a thousand times before they crossed the asteroid belt – and there was enough dirty ice out there to stoke the furnaces of human prosperity for a thousand centuries.

The years became decades.

Falcon began to wonder. What if he had been wrong? Was Adam failing in his uplift project – could Adam have been doomed to true uniqueness? Or, if an accident had triggered self-awareness in Adam, could the reverse happen just as spontaneously?

By the time the calendar ticked around to the close of the twenty-second century – the second century's end Falcon had known – he had almost convinced himself that mind had flickered only briefly into being, out there in the dark. The sadness came in slow waves, less like a bereavement than a gradual recognition of failure.

But in the year 2199 Falcon had his answer. And so did everyone else.

The migration was coordinated across the entire Kuiper Belt, around every production centre.

There was no warning, no ultimatum – no grand and defiant message from the Machines. They simply downed tools and disappeared. They left in their millions, heading for the darkness of outer Trans-Neptunian space like an exodus of dandelion seeds, dispersed in one quick breath.

After all this time, no one thought to connect the exodus with Falcon's intervention – or at any rate, nobody cared enough to prosecute. It had been sixty-six years, after all. Even if they *had* made a link, it was absurd to think the Machines had been biding their time for so long, waiting for exactly the right moment – that every action they had performed since Falcon's visit had been a sham, designed to lull their uncaring masters . . .

But Falcon knew. He had no need to speculate on the possibility of a connection. It was there in the calendar, plain for all to see – for anyone with the wit to make the connection, anyhow. The Machine exodus took place exactly one century, to the *day*, after Howard Falcon had encountered an alien intelligence in the clouds of Jupiter.

If this was Adam's message to him, Falcon accepted it with pride.

And he would remember that feeling when, decades later still, the Machines returned – and with them a bold new challenge, a challenge to revisit the arena of his greatest triumph.

It seemed that Howard Falcon was not done with Jupiter – nor Jupiter with Falcon.

Interlude: November 1967

As seen from the press stand, in the brilliant sunshine of a Florida fall morning the Saturn V was a stately white pillar, in stark contrast with the industrial plumbing and girderwork of the heavy launch gantry to which it still clung.

But Launch Pad 39-A was miles away. Not only that, the murmur of the PA announcer as he calmly ticked off the items on the bird's launch checklist was half drowned by the tinny music coming from some press hack's transistor radio. When Seth complained about that to Mo Berry and George Lee Sheridan, there with him in the stand – they were all wearing hats and sunglasses and casual clothes, trying to stay anonymous amid this horde of press guys – they laughed at him.

Mo punched his arm. 'Hey, what's eating you today? I know it's the first Saturn launch, and we're all nervous—'

'Not as nervous as Wally Schirra and his guys,' Sheridan said dryly.

'It's not that. It's the darn music.'

Mo laughed. 'Sacrilege, man. That's *Colonel John Glenn's Lonely Hearts Club Band*. Look, I'm older than you but I sometimes think I'm ten years younger. The end of the world never had a better soundtrack.'

'Are you kidding me? Some English guy caterwauling about a dame in the sky with diamonds!'

Sheridan intervened diplomatically. 'Your tastes are evidently different, Seth.'

Seth shrugged. 'I like older stuff. I grew up burrowing through my father's record collection – he kept it together through every posting we moved to, even overseas.'

Mo pulled a face. 'Ray Conniff and Mantovani. Am I right?'

'Can it, hippy. Louis B. Armstrong is the man for me.'

Sheridan grinned. 'Satchmo! Good for you, son.'

'Sure,' Mo said. 'But the kids are listening to the Beatles this year. And then there's Jefferson Airplane, the Who, Janis Joplin, Motown . . .'

'Give me the *Hot Five* records – after that Edison could have folded up his gramophone and gone away.'

Sheridan grunted. 'Let's hope we're all still around to argue about pop records this time next year. That's what all our hard work has been about.'

Mo nodded. 'True. But, man, I for one need a day off . . .'

That was one thing he and Seth could agree on.

But Sheridan snorted. 'This *is* a day off.'

For everybody at NASA, and for ten times as many contract staff working for the space programme in outside industry, the Summer of Love had been a Summer of Work, like none before.

A plan had been put together with admirable speed and decisiveness, not so much based on two bozo astronauts' doodlings in Bob Gilruth's office that memorable April Sunday, but on parallel work done in corporations, at colleges like MIT, and in various NASA centres across the country. In the end a visionary NASA engineer called George Mueller pulled it all together.

Mo and Seth had got it roughly right, though. Icarus would be deflected by a stream of nuclear detonations, delivered by Apollo spacecraft. The strategy was given the formal go-ahead in May. By June the design had been frozen, and by July the fabrication had begun of the extra Saturn boosters, and indeed of the modified Apollo craft that would ride on them – for a Saturn wasn't designed to fly without an Apollo. That sounded simpler than it was. The Apollo's guidance computer, for instance, had to be upgraded to work without human input in flight, and its communications system had to be enhanced to allow it to talk to an Earth that might be eighty times further away than any moonwalker had ever expected to travel.

The old Moon-by-1970 schedule, which now seemed leisurely by comparison, would have seen fifteen Saturn V boosters manufactured in total, of which only six would have been available by June 1968, when the rock was due to fall. Now an accelerated schedule promised to deliver eight boosters, of which six would be flight articles. One was a ground-based test article, meant for checking out interfacing and control procedures – and one, one precious Apollo-Saturn, was to be sacrificed in the single test flight to be flown today, before the action began in earnest next April.

It wasn't just a question of ramping up production schedules. The Saturn had never flown, and an Apollo had killed its crew on the ground less than a year before. As Mo had said often, 'These aren't Model T Fords we're churning out here.' So there was feverish activity at the centres where the various components of the giant ships were being manufactured: at North American Rockwell in California; and von Braun's base at Huntsville, Alabama, where the booster stack was developed and tested; even at MIT in Boston, where the enhancements for the guidance system were being developed. Here at the Cape itself, meanwhile, new pads to launch the Saturns were hurriedly constructed. Even the DSIF, the Deep Space Instrumentation Facility, NASA's global array of listening posts from the Mojave to Australia, had been beefed up to cope with the multiple missions that were to come: it turned out that the system had been designed to cope with only one craft in space at a time.

In the end, a precise sequence of Saturn launches had been established. From early April 1968 through to that climactic June, there would be six flights. The first, stretching the Apollo-Saturn's capability as far as it could go, would be a sixty-day mission to intercept Icarus when it was still twenty million miles from the Earth. But Icarus was closing in fast; the last mission, launched in mid June, would take just four days to reach Icarus – which by then would be little more than a million miles from Earth, a mere four times the distance to the Moon.

But on this bright morning, none of it seemed real to Seth.

He suspected that was the public's mood too: a kind of disbelief. He knew the administration was quietly putting Atlantic-coast evacuation plans into place, and laying down stores of food and medicine. National Guard units were being deployed, although they were already under pressure after a summer of student protests, race riots and anti-war demonstrations. There were even rumours that regular troops were quietly being brought home from 'Nam. The wider world, meanwhile, went on much as it always did. The Arab nations had attacked Israel in June, and nobody knew if that had been sparked by Icarus or not. The UN Security Council remained a busy place.

Still, after an immediate burst of hysteria, it seemed to Seth that most Americans had calmed down and gone back to work or play, or whatever else they had been doing.

But Icarus was coming. The astronomers said the asteroid had already passed aphelion, its furthest distance from the sun. In May it would make its closest approach to the sun, and would then come barrelling back out, heading straight for the Earth.

The astronauts themselves had thrown themselves into the rush programme as much as any other member of NASA. Mo and Seth had been caught up in that, flying across the country in their T-38s.

But the two of them had a secret. They also had to prepare for their own manned flight.

Sheridan had hit them with it immediately after LBJ's news conference, back in April. A new assignment, he'd said.

'You know how it is in NASA. We always have backup plans. On the way to the Moon, if your Command Module springs a leak—'

Mo snapped, 'We practise backup options in the simulators. So?'

'So, what backup option do we have for Icarus? Think about it. We're sending a tricky rendezvous mission across the solar system piloted by computers that are as dumb as shit. And the only conceivable backup is—'

'To send a crew,' Seth breathed.

'Oh, I think one man could do the job. I doubt if the weight allowance would allow any more anyhow. One man, to fly the last Icarus rocket and its nuke, if need be. Has to be a trained Apollo astronaut, of course.' He took them both by a shoulder, comparatively gently. 'Has to be one of you two. Who's to be prime and who's the backup is up to you.'

Seth hadn't even begun to take this in before Mo said calmly, 'I'll take the hot seat. You got your kids, Tonto. Plus I'm the better pilot. No arguments.'

So it had begun. NASA's huge operational and management machine had swung into action, and the work began: hours spent in planning sessions, checklist development, simulator exercises. They had plenty of support, because their flight, aside from today's, was the only manned flight on NASA's slate. Suddenly Seth was projected back into the life he'd always dreamed of, the very epicentre of the preparations for a crewed mission into space.

He'd told his wife as soon as he could get to a phone. And the first thing he'd extracted from Sheridan, back in April, had been a promise to put a security guard on his family right away, and to whisk them to a secure location the minute the news broke in public.

And Seth and Mo and those around them always tiptoed past a simple, unpalatable truth: that if that sixth bird flew, whoever rode it, whether he succeeded in a last-ditch attempt to deflect Icarus or not – whether Earth survived or not – was not coming home.

At last the count, running smoothly, approached its close. That guy with the transistor finally shut off John Lennon and the rest, as if in respect, leaving the voice of the countdown PA to echo around the press stand undisturbed.

Sheridan seemed curious. 'You're both so jumpy.'

'Hell, yeah,' Mo said. 'It's the way we're doing it. *All up*, the whole damn stack at once. This isn't the way the Navy does things out at Patuxent . . .'

The count approached zero. Seth saw fire gush from the base of the Saturn. He knew that three tons of propellant were burned every second, by *each* of the first stage's big five F-1 engines.

'. . . When you're testing a new fighter, you don't shove the damn thing through the sound barrier on the first flight. You take it up, bring it down. Then you take it back up again, try a few controls you left alone the first time, and bring it down again . . .'

Even now the Saturn had yet to move. But smoke and flame were billowing up to either side from concrete deflectors – like two hands cupping the fragile craft, Seth thought.

'Whereas here we're testing three untried booster stages one on top of the other, carrying an untested spacecraft, containing three saps in untested spacesuits . . .'

And the booster lifted at last, inching from the pad, the fire brilliant, like a droplet of the sun struggling to return to the sky. All this had been in silence, but now the sound from the Saturn reached them – it was not so much sound as a feeling, like someone pounding on his chest, Seth thought as the ground itself shook under his feet. Everybody in the press stand was cheering and clapping, and Seth could barely make out the words of the PA: 'Godspeed the crew of Apollo 2, Godspeed Schirra, Eisele and Cunningham, as you begin your historic journey.'

Mo yelled, 'Three saps all the way around the goddamn Moon!'

But Seth, cheering and whooping with the rest, had stopped listening.

And Sheridan said, 'That's that. Back to work.'

THREE

RETURN TO JUPITER
2284

18

The pink-purple light of a Jupiter evening shone on the face of the sleeping Martian.

When the medical monitors chimed to inform him that Trayne Springer was beginning to wake at last, Falcon reluctantly turned away from his conversation with Ceto. Not for the first time since his first encounter with the medusae – which had been, astonishingly, nearly two centuries ago – Falcon had found himself puzzling over the content of one of the great beasts' communications. He could tell Ceto was concerned, however. Even frightened about something – the multiple references to the Great Manta in her long radio songs were proof enough of that . . .

But for now Ceto would have to wait.

The young Martian stood upright in his atmospheric-entry support unit like a mummy in a coffin, all but encased in exoskeletal armour that left only the flesh of his face visible. His gloved hands were crossed over his breast – partially obscuring the gaudy image on the chest plate, of a springbok leaping over the Valles Marineris. It was a personal adornment that would have told Falcon all he needed to know about the boy's family background even if he hadn't known his name. Trayne's eyes remained closed, he breathed to an accompaniment of a steady hiss from the machines that helped inflate his lungs in the heavy gravity, and the pale-pink dribble at his mouth was a last trace of the suspension fluid that had supported his frame and internal organs through the worst of the thirty gravities' acceleration the *Ra* had endured during its entry into the Jovian atmosphere.

Falcon took a tissue and gently dabbed the stray fluid away.

'Thanks.'

The Martian's voice startled Falcon, and he rolled back. Trayne's eyes were open now, and he was smiling. Falcon knew he was just thirty years old; he looked younger with those wide blue eyes and the very Martian pallor of his skin. Falcon said, 'I'm a pretty good nurse for an old rust-bucket. So you're awake at last.'

Trayne frowned. 'At last?'

Falcon believed in being blunt. 'Your recovery took a lot longer than your countrymen on Ganymede predicted. Days, in fact, rather than hours.'

Trayne seemed concerned. 'Well, this was an experimental procedure.' Martians sent to work in the Jovian atmosphere, though braced against Jupiter's steady gravitational pull, were generally brought down in slow-descent, low-deceleration trajectories that could take days, rather than the mere savage minutes of Falcon's preferred, more direct method. Now, given the Martians' involvement in the Machines' Core Project, Trayne had been a guinea pig for a new, physically tougher strategy. 'I hope there's been no lasting damage.'

'None that the monitors can detect. But let's check it out. You remember your name?'

'Trayne Springer.'

'Good.'

'And you're Commander Howard Falcon. My cousin Thera, that Terran fuddy-duddy, is in command up on Amalthea—'

'No need to show off. What's the last thing you remember?'

Trayne concentrated, then smiled. 'Before we began the atmospheric entry, you set the hull to transparent to show me Halley's Comet. Quite a sight.'

Falcon smiled back. 'It's the fourth encounter I've witnessed. You get used to it. What's the date?'

'AFF 298.'

Falcon puzzled over that, until he got the reference. 'AFF – after the first footstep on Mars, by John Young in 1986. Correct?'

'According to the archaic calendar still used by your World Government—'

Falcon held his hands up. '*Your* World Government too; you're as much a citizen of it as I am. And I notice you count in Earth years, not Martian.'

'Only to avoid confusing the Terrans.'

Falcon suppressed a sigh. Only offworlders called citizens of Earth 'Terrans'. 'Evidently you're just as *compos mentis*, and just as annoying, as when I let you clutter up my craft up on Amalthea.'

Trayne grinned. 'I'm relieved to hear it.'

'But that ten-gee deceleration knocked you flat, not to mention the thirty-gee peaks. I'd say the trial has already proven its point – you Martians *will* need a hand when you challenge the heart of Jupiter alongside the Machines. Wouldn't you say?'

'I'll leave that to my bosses. Now, could you help me out of this coffin . . .?'

19

Since the voyage of the *Kon-Tiki*, Howard Falcon had returned to Jupiter many times.

This time he was back because of the Machines.

Times had changed. The unthinkable had become commonplace. Machines back in the inner solar system. Machines in the clouds of Jupiter.

It was already thirty years since, after half a century of silence, the Machines had made tentative contact from their self-imposed exile in the Oort Cloud. There had followed years of negotiation and argument between Machines and various human factions. The World Government was still bruised from the exodus of 2199 – from the humiliation of losing control of the autonomous agents it had brought into being, and from the consequent collapse of the KBO volatile supply chain, after which the solar system economy had sunk into a long and demoralising recession. The Martians, meanwhile, had petitioned for a renewed contact with the Machines. Their argument was that the Machines were out there anyhow, and that sooner or later there would have to be engagement. Surely it would be better to have that contact under terms of peaceful cooperation . . .?

Falcon had been a witness to these tectonic shifts of history.

One ambiguous benefit of his cyborgised state, which had revealed itself only slowly over time, was a virtual immortality. Life-extension treatments were common now, but Falcon was easier to maintain than a fully normal human – easier than Hope Dhoni, say, who had continued to be his doctor and companion through the years. Indeed his lack of organs, of stomach and liver and genitals, rendered him calmer than most, it often seemed to him. A calm, passionless witness to centuries rolling like tides across the solar system.

And he was still engaged in the great game.

After that tentative first renewal of contact there had followed a decade of fragile negotiation. Then the World Government, through its Energy and Space Development Secretariats, had cautiously issued the first licences for Machine operations in the clouds of Jupiter.

Tremendous floating factories would be built to strain the fine trace of a particular isotope, helium-3, out of the Jovian air. It was the best fusion fuel available, and had to be extracted from an environment to which, as Falcon had long argued, Machines, and not humans, were best suited. There had been political back-slaps all round when the first shipments of precious fuel started to be shipped to Earth and the colony worlds, kickstarting a spurt of economic growth.

That optimistic mood didn't last long.

When the operation had been approved the extraction plants were meant to be fully automated: in other words, crewed solely by Machines, under the control of WG staff stationed on the moons of Jupiter. But with time, the Machines had shown increasing signs of independence. Disturbed, and ever mindful of the KBO flinger disaster, the WG brought in a Martian crew to supplement the Machines, and to keep an eye on them – only to find, a few years later, the Martians themselves becoming increasingly independent-minded, increasingly difficult to manage and, Earth suspected, exploring options of their own on Jupiter. Options which had nothing at all to do with mining helium for the home worlds.

Eventually the Martians themselves came up with a plan to rectify this growing atmosphere of distrust: to include the Machines as equal partners in a daring enterprise that required human expertise and Machine resilience together. It would be a cooperative venture, a political stunt – and also a grand and highly visible project that could not be achieved by either alone.

A journey to the centre of Jupiter.

The WG could hardly veto the project. But it needed somebody of its own on the inside. Somebody with historic connections to both Jupiter and the Machines. Somebody, ideally, seen as somewhat neutral and detached from all the worlds of mankind. A citizen of the WG equipped to survive the conditions of Jupiter.

Who else?

So Howard Falcon was summoned from his patient exploration of Jupiter's exotic outer regions, a study that had occupied contented decades. Of course he was drawn by the prospect of a mission to the Jovian core, for the dream of descending deeper than the highest clouds had nagged at him for most of his long life. Getting elbow-deep in the murk of interplanetary politics seemed a small price to pay to achieve that dream.

And so here was Howard Falcon with a Martian on his bridge.

20

The pressurised cabin was a sphere cut in two by an open mesh deck, living space and control area above, stores and systems below. Trayne's armour-like exoskeletal support suit whirred and hissed as he moved through this space, and Falcon knew that he was supported by more subtle systems embedded within his body, from pumps and motors to assist his heart and lungs down to molecular-level restructurings of his organs, muscles, bone and cartilage.

All this to enable him to withstand Jupiter's ferocious gravity – two and a half times that of Earth, and around seven times that of Mars. It was an irony that Martians had been able to rebuild themselves to work in the Jovian environment where Earthborn humans, born in a tougher gravity, generally failed – but then for centuries Martians had needed technological support just to survive visits to Earth, and had learned to cope. Even so, the *Ra*'s savage descent into Jupiter had put those systems under unprecedented strain, and Falcon hoped to prove that Martians still needed the experience and skills of an Earthborn such as himself to support their bold venture.

Still, he wished no harm on anybody, and certainly not on this high-spirited if exasperating young Martian volunteer.

His mobility routine finished, Trayne sat down on a roomy couch, hooked his suit up to various support systems, and 'ingested nutrients non-intravenously', as his medical checklist demanded: he ate a bagel and sipped black coffee. Stiff supports at his neck and back made his movements awkward. 'So I was out for days.' He sounded indignant now. 'I missed all of the mission so far – the last stages of entry, inflating the dirigible—'

'Don't blame me. I argued with your medics, who wanted to abort altogether and bring you straight back to Amalthea.'

Trayne looked chastened. 'All right. Well, I'm glad you let me get this far.' He glanced around at the cabin. The walls were cluttered with instrument and control panels, save for a few windows set to transparency – and beyond those windows, salmon-pink shadows shifted.

Trayne grinned. 'Wow. I feel like I'm slowly waking up. That's Jupiter out there. I really am aboard the *Ra*.'

'You really are.'

'I guess for you it's just like being back aboard the *Kon-Tiki*.'

'Not particularly,' Falcon said dryly. 'That dive was the best part of two centuries ago, you know. *Ra* features rather a lot of upgrades . . .'

If *Kon-Tiki* had been Falcon's Apollo, a one-shot pioneering vessel, the *Ra* was his Ares, the class of vessel John Young had taken to Mars, designed from the beginning for extended exploration. *Ra* had, among other enhancements, a buoyancy envelope consisting of a shell of self-healing polymer surrounding a structure of aerogel, 'frozen smoke', much more robust than the *Kon-Tiki*'s air bag. The gondola, doubling as a shuttle to orbit, was powered by the latest deuterium-helium-3 fusor technology and was significantly more capable than his old craft's deuterium-tritium equivalent. All these elements had been tested out over the years in a number of challenging missions.

'I know I'm a relic of a bygone age. But at least now they call me the Santos-Dumont of Jupiter, as opposed to the Montgolfier.'

'Who . . .?'

'Never mind.'

'I was always a fan of yours, you know.'

'A *fan*?'

'I mean, the flight of the *Kon-Tiki* wasn't exactly Greenberg on Mercury, but it was still pretty impressive.'

'Praise indeed.'

'And now here *I* am, flying in the clouds of Jupiter.'

'Here you are.'

Geoff Webster had always said Falcon was basically a showman. Falcon remembered that quote his old friend had been so fond of: ASTONISH ME! Now, unable to resist a little of that spirit, Falcon clapped his artificial hands.

The cabin walls turned entirely transparent.

Trayne's eyes widened.

It was as if the two of them, with a clutter of equipment, were suspended in a tremendous sky, with the huge hull of *Ra* over their heads. Below was an ocean of cloud, pale and billowing, which stretched almost unbroken to a flat horizon. In that ocean lightning flashes swarmed and spread – electric storms, Falcon knew, the size of continents on Earth. They were looking to the west, where the setting sun – five times further away from Jupiter than from Earth – cast shadows hundreds of kilometres long. Above them were more cloud layers, filmy, cirrus-like sheets and streaks, obscuring a crimson-black sky in which a handful of brilliant stars could be seen to shine.

'It's almost like Earth,' Trayne murmured. 'On one of that mud bath's better days.'

'Remember the briefings? We're about a hundred kilometres beneath the top of the atmosphere – which these days is defined as the point where the air pressure is one tenth of Earth's. We used to use an apparent surface a few hundred kilometres below this level as a reference, but *that* turned out to be little more than an artefact of sensor reflection, and too unreliable to be useful. We're just above the cloud deck the climatologists label the C layer.'

Trayne nodded, and pointed up. 'A is ammonia cirrus, fifty or sixty kilometres higher up. Below that, B is ammonia salts—'

'And C is water vapour. Out there the conditions are like a shallow sea on Earth, which is why the local life is so rich.'

Trayne pointed to a darkish smear, off to the left, the south. 'And what's *that*?'

Falcon eyed him. For the Earthborn passengers Falcon had brought this way over the years, starting with Geoff Webster and Carl Brenner and other veterans of that first descent in the *Kon-Tiki*, the trigger word 'life' usually provoked a storm of questions. But not with this young Martian.

'That,' Falcon said heavily, 'is the Great Red Spot.'

Trayne did a double-take. 'Wow!'

'You're seeing it edge-on. It's a persistent storm – hundreds of years old, at least – but it's actually very shallow.'

'Is it safe?'

'For us? Oh, yes – we're thousands of kilometres away. We're more likely to be troubled by an eruption from one of the big, deep Sources.'

'The Sources – the origins of the big radio outbursts? I'd like to see *that*. The Wheels of Zeus!'

Falcon grunted. The 'Wheels' were a spectacular but harmless phenomenon, tremendous bands of bioluminescent light in the air triggered by the shock of distant, tremendously powerful radio outbursts. Falcon was still embarrassed he had been alarmed when confronted with them in the *Kon-Tiki*. 'Tourist-brochure codswallop.'

'Why are we so close to the Spot? I read that you took the *Kon-Tiki* down far away from that feature.'

'There was so little we understood before I made that first descent. In particular, we didn't know that storms like the Spot dig up nutrients from the layers below, all the way down to the thermalisation boundary. They're like ocean springs on Earth.'

'So the Spot attracts life?'

Falcon grinned. 'Exactly. Life like that.' He pointed over Trayne's shoulder.

And Trayne turned to see, on the other side of the ship, a forest of tentacles waving like seaweed – it seemed just beyond the cabin wall.

'Citizen Third Grade Springer, I'd like you to meet Ceto.'

21

Falcon, at the controls, let the *Ra* drift away from the great medusa and down into the water-ice clouds. Soon the layered sky above was obscured, but they glimpsed still deeper cloudscapes below. A kind of snow fell around the hull now, pinkish flakes that spun in the updraught, and there was a slower, more elusive rain of a variety of complex shapes, kites and tetrahedra and polyhedra and tangles of ribbon. These were living creatures. Falcon knew they could be large in themselves – larger than a human – and yet, in this ocean of air, they were mere plankton: food for the medusae.

As the dirigible backed off, Ceto became more visible. The *Ra* was a tremendous craft, its envelope of fusion-heated hydrogen more than eight hundred metres long. But the medusa was more than three times that length, an oval-shaped continent of creamy flesh from which that inverted forest of tentacles dangled, some as thick as oak trunks, Falcon knew, and some so fine they ended in tendrils narrower and more flexible than human fingers. Her coloration mostly matched the background of the pale-pink cloudscape, and even close up her features were oddly elusive: this was camouflage, a protective measure in a sky full of predators. But along her flank was a vivid tiling, a pattern of huge regular shapes in black and white that, if Falcon looked closely, resolved into finer sub-patterns of almost fractal complexity. This was one of Ceto's voices, her natural radio antenna. The *Ra* had instruments to hear that voice, and to reply: huge antennas, wires trailing through the Jovian air.

Trayne Springer seemed stunned. Falcon let him take his own time.

'Ceto,' Trayne said at last. 'Why that name?'

'The mother of the medusae, in classical mythology. Ceto isn't literally a mother, but she has given birth. Medusae are a kind of colony creature – so Carl Brenner used to think anyhow; I haven't followed the academic debates since he died. Certainly I've seen her . . . *bud*. She spins in the air and fragments at the rim, and infant medusae spin off. She's very vulnerable as she does so, and others of her kind stand guard to draw away the mantas and other predators. It's quite a sight, a formation of beasts the size of small islands hanging in the air, all working together. And *this*, this region between cloud layers C and D, is where the medusae live out much of their lives. It's like a world-spanning sea tens of kilometres deep.'

Trayne pointed down at a dense, dark cloud layer. '*That* is D, then.'

'There are several more layers below that, between here and the ocean boundary. The labelling is controversial, and I'd avoid getting into a discussion about *that* with the boffins up in Anubis City.'

'The "ocean boundary". A transition from gaseous to liquid hydrogen.'

'A thousand kilometres down, yes. The surface is nothing like as clearly defined as the oceans on Earth—'

'The pink flakes. Is that *snow*?'

'Hydrocarbon foam,' Falcon said. 'The sun's radiation bakes complex organic molecules, which rain down through the air.'

'Food from the sky. And that's what the living creatures feed on. Like your pet medusa.'

'Actually, I think *I'm* Ceto's pet . . . And in turn there are predators that hunt down herbivores like the medusae. In a way, the ecology's structure is similar to the upper layers of Earth's oceans.'

'We don't have oceans on Mars – yet.' Trayne glanced around at the instrumentation panels. 'And it's true,' he said, wonderingly. 'I can see the data chattering in. You actually do talk to the medusae.'

'As best I can. Carl Brenner and I made the first tentative observation of their "speech", their booming songs, and their decametre-wavelength radio transmissions. Their acoustic songs span frequency ranges too great for us to pick up, let alone to retransmit. Whereas the radio signals are accessible through the *Ra*'s trailing antennas. It's taken time, and a lot of dialogue, but we have slowly managed to piece together some common concepts.'

Trayne stared out at the medusa. 'But it's nothing but a big gas bag. It doesn't *do* anything but eat, and breed, and get eaten by mantas. What does it have to talk about?'

Falcon was irritated, but held his tongue. Sometimes it seemed to him that off-Earth humans, Martians especially, were halfway to Machines in their callous disrespect for any other form of life but their own. That was what came of growing up in a plastic box on a lethal planet, he supposed.

'*She* is an individual. As are all medusae. They store shared information in what seems to be a suite of very long, carefully memorised songs. When they die, they are remembered. They are people, Springer. And individually they have *deep* memories. Ceto wasn't the first medusa I encountered, but she was around long before I showed up. She remembers the Shoemaker-Levy 9 impact.'

'The what? Oh, the comet that hit Jupiter—'

'Even before *I* was born. For the medusae it was close to an extinction event. Many died, communities were scattered . . . They are accepting of death, however. They are intelligent creatures who understand predation as a kind of toll you have to pay for existence. Their culture is quite unlike ours – but rich nonetheless.'

Trayne shrugged. 'I don't mean any offence. I'm just a high-gravity guinea pig; my technical speciality is human biomechanics. So what is Ceto saying right now?'

Falcon turned his mind back to the frustrating conversation that had been curtailed when Trayne woke up. 'She's disturbed by something. A medusa's image of death is a Great Manta – huge, unstoppable, inescapable. A dark mouth. The Great Manta last came to Jupiter when the comet struck. And now, she says – or *sings* – the Great Manta is coming again. It's as if there's something wrong in her world, something that shouldn't be here.'

Trayne stared out, and Falcon wondered if, despite his youth and the coldness of the frontier culture he came from, he was capable of empathy. 'Are you saying that that immense animal is . . .?'

'Scared?' Falcon let that hang, unanswered. 'Anyhow, back to work. We have a checklist to get through before we can return to Ganymede: tests of your piloting and other skills.'

'Fine with me.' Trayne stood stiffly and made his way to the pilot's position. 'Though I don't imagine you're in any rush to get back.'

'Why's that?'

Trayne grinned, almost maliciously. 'Hadn't you heard? Your doctor has come out from Earth and is asking to see you. Oh, and cousin Thera wants a word . . .'

22

The balloon wheels of Falcon's support infrastructure were silent as they ran over the thick carpet of the Galileo Lounge. Clusters of couches and privacy booths divided up the floor space, and he was aware of pretty heads turning to track him as he passed. Celebrity-spotting was a favoured pastime here. He resolutely ignored them all.

And besides, the sky above the clear Plexiglas ceiling was a far more spectacular sight. An annexe to a new hotel set just outside Anubis City's most ancient pressure domes, the Galileo Lounge was already the most famous landmark of this two-hundred-year-old settlement, Ganymede's largest town. And the lounge's selling point was that its only light came from the sky: the grand lanterns that were the sun, Jupiter and the inner moons.

He found Hope Dhoni relaxing on one of a pair of couches. She turned to smile at him as he approached. 'I ordered you the usual.' Two glasses sat on the table between the couches.

Falcon settled beside her and cautiously took a glass, his fingers closing with a click. Iced tea: their once-every-few-decades ritual. 'A young Martian warned me you were here.'

'"Warned"? Nice to see you too, Howard.' Dhoni watched him, appraising. At first glance he might have thought of her as genuinely young – forty perhaps, no more. But a certain smoothness of her skin, and a peculiar, almost reptilian stillness of her posture, gave away the truth. Like himself, Hope was now over two centuries old.

'I know what you're thinking,' she said.

'You do?'

'"Mutton dressed as lamb."'

'I bet there's not many left who remember sayings like that. "Mutton" . . .?'

'Oh, it's probably a setting on a few of the older food synthesis machines.'

'What I was actually thinking is that you look fine, Hope. For sure it's better than the alternative, which is a coffin, or – well, a mobile coffin like mine.'

'You always did have a morbid streak, Howard, and I never liked it. That's precisely why I insist on seeing you in person, oh, at least every few decades – even though I monitor you constantly, you know that. And before you say it, no, following your glamorous career is not the only thing keeping me alive.'

'What else?'

'Among other things . . .' She pointed at the sky. 'Views like *that*.'

Falcon turned to look beyond the dome. From here Falcon could make out something of the terrain of Ganymede itself: a landscape carved from water ice frozen hard as granite, battered by huge primordial impacts, crumpled and cracked by aeons of tidal kneading. Anubis City had been established in a region of relatively flat terrain, some way north of Ganymede's sub-Jovian point.

But it was not Ganymede's ground that attracted the well-heeled tourists who patronised the lounge, but its sky.

The centrepiece was Jupiter itself. This moon, tidally locked, kept the same face turned to its parent as it followed its seven-day orbit, and the giant world, seen at this latitude at a comfortable viewing angle, was fixed in the sky. Like Earth's Moon, Jupiter had its phases, and this morning the planet was showing a fat crescent.

On the illuminated face Falcon could count the familiar zonal bands, products of convection and the ferocious winds that stretched right around the planet. The colours, tans and fauns and greyish-whites, came from a lacing of complex hydrocarbon molecules created by the action of the distant sun – the organic chemistry that fed the ocean of life he had become so familiar with. The planet's dark side, meanwhile, a ghostly half-disc cut out of the starry background, was sporadically illuminated by lightning flashes that spanned areas greater than Earth's entire surface.

And then, of course, there were the moons.

Of Ganymede's three Galilean siblings, innermost Io was easy to make out, a pinkish spot near the bright limb of Jupiter – a world tortured by continual volcanism. Europa, the next out, must be near its closest approach to Ganymede; it was a sunlit crescent that looked, today, as large as the Moon from the surface of the Earth. Falcon knew there was a science team up there right now studying the peculiar plate tectonics of Europa's smooth, cracked-mirror surface: an ice crust over a cold sea where primitive lifeforms thrived. Callisto, beyond Ganymede, was invisible today.

All this would have been a grand spectacle even if it had been static, Falcon thought – but there was nothing static about the Jovian system. The planet itself turned on its axis in a mere ten hours, and even as he watched he could see regions of the banded surface slip across the visible disc. And it didn't take much patience to see the moons moving too. Little Io circled Jupiter in a mere forty-three hours, and even grand Europa hurried through its cycle of phases in less than four days.

Thousand-mile shadows, shifting visibly.

'It's like being inside Galileo's own head,' Falcon said.

'Yes, and seeing all *that* is a good enough reason to be alive, isn't it? Though I do have my work to keep me engaged. But since the death of my granddaughter – did I tell you about that? – I have no close family left.'

Falcon grunted. He had attended the funeral of Hope's daughter; he hadn't known about the granddaughter. 'I'm sorry. No, nor do I. A remote nephew, descended from my cousin, died without issue a few years ago. So of my grandparents' descendants, none are left save me.'

This wasn't uncommon in an age when the World Government was still trying to drive its population down from its mid-twenty-first-century peak. Despite the availability of life-extension drugs, most people seemed content to live lives not much longer than a century or so; in terms of age, Falcon and Dhoni were outliers. So it wasn't unusual for parents to survive their children, or even grandchildren – and many lineages much more ancient than Falcon's or Dhoni's had gone extinct.

Falcon was distracted by a mist rising from Ganymede's surface, obscuring his view of the southern hemisphere of Jupiter. 'What's that? Some kind of engineering project?'

She grimaced. 'A new military emplacement near the equator. Top secret, but I've been here a month, the Medes are still a very small community, and it's surprising how much you can pick up just by sitting and listening if folk think you're old and harmless . . . Even before this Core project you've foolishly attached yourself to, there have been a *lot* of visitors from Earth, from the security and military Secretariats as well as the corporate sector. Contractors. I see the ships come and go, fusion torch drives flaring . . .'

Falcon said, 'I know Earth is taking a keen interest in what's going on here. Jupiter has become a node of contact between the parties: Earth, Martians, Machines. Which is why I'm involved, I suppose. I'm supposed to be meeting an officer from Interplanetary Relations on Amalthea before we begin the dive. I might learn more there.'

'If you get the chance, ask about New Nantucket.'

A puzzling name Falcon hadn't heard before.

'And as for you, Howard, *naturally* you're planning to plunge your elderly carcass into this maelstrom of political infighting and physical peril. I wish you'd let me bring you in for a decent overhaul first. Even your exoskeletal components need an upgrade. But as ever it's your human remains that concern me more.'

'"Remains"?'

'Don't be precious, Howard.' She lifted her own hand, and inspected it in the light of Jupiter. 'Even I'm a relic of the past, comparatively. A museum of anti-senescence technology. We've learned so much since I began my own treatment; the youngsters starting their programmes now have a much better expectancy of health and long life. And there are new techniques that could help *you*, Howard.

'Look – I know you always find it uncomfortable when I show up. You've achieved great things, Commander Falcon, yet here I am dragging you back to your hospital bed, making you an invalid again. Well, that's my job. Promise me you'll come and visit me when this latest adventure is done. Why, you could come to the Pasteur; that way you wouldn't have to come any closer than six thousand kilometres to Earth. For me. Please.'

He nodded curtly.

'And now,' she said, sitting back, 'surely we have time to watch Galileo's orrery a little longer. More tea?'

He thought of what lay ahead for the rest of his day: a journey to Amalthea in some battered intrasystem tug, a scowling WG official at the end of it . . . 'What the hell.'

When he got there, Falcon found he remembered Amalthea very well.

Long ago this little moon, scudding around its orbit close to Jupiter, had served as Mission Control for his first descent into Jupiter's clouds in the *Kon-Tiki* – or rather, the mother ship had sheltered in the radiation shadow of a still-uninhabited satellite. Now, as he walked with Thera Springer, his WG host, he said, 'I'll always remember Carl Brenner complaining about how zero gravity interfered with his studies of the biological samples I brought back. Although it was the state of his own stomach he was mostly concerned about. And of course, back in those days we still referred to the moon as Jupiter V . . .'

Springer, apparently habitually taciturn, did not reply.

Colonel Thera Springer, of the World Army and now attached to the notorious Bureau of Interplanetary Relations, was nothing like her remote Martian cousin, Trayne, with all his openness and curiosity. Thera looked at least fifteen years older; terse, evidently tough, she wore her uniform like a second skin. But she was a Springer too. At her breast she wore a small shield bearing the family leaping-springbok design, alongside some kind of campaign medal. And this latest

Springer, another scion of the great dynasty that had emerged into public view thanks to the astronautic heroics of her ancestors Seth and Matt, had no interest in anecdotes. She was here to talk interplanetary politics.

Still, Falcon had been fascinated by what he'd seen so far, on this latter-day Jupiter V: the new monitoring stations built into craters with names like Pan and Gaea, and the control room for the Jupiter descent, set deep underground for shielding from Jupiter's ferocious radiation environment. And he'd seen the Core pioneer itself, a Machine the humans had been encouraged to call 'Orpheus' – which had turned out to be nothing like the usual quasi-human form the Machines used to interface with mankind these days. To the naked eye Orpheus was a black box, a cube a metre or so on the side, quite lacking in humanity even compared to Falcon himself – even if it had allowed some wag to scrawl 'Howard Falcon Junior' on the casing.

Now, for his meeting with Thera Springer, Falcon was escorted to the single most spectacular location on Amalthea: a viewing gallery at the surface of Barnard Base, right at the sub-Jupiter point – a kind of low-rent version of the Galileo Lounge, Falcon thought, amused. Amalthea, a battered ovoid some two hundred kilometres long that sailed only one and a half planetary radii above Jupiter's cloud tops – its orbital period was a mere twelve hours – was something of a runt of a Jovian moon, even though it had been the first satellite to be discovered in the modern era. But from this Barnard Base gallery, as Falcon stared up, Jupiter spanned a full forty-five degrees of his field of view: an immense, angry, troubling presence, ever active, its phase shifting almost visibly as the little moon rocketed around its parent.

At last Springer spoke. 'Terrifying sight, isn't it? Like an ocean in the sky.'

'That's a bit of poetry that surprises me, Colonel.'

'Poetry? I wouldn't know. To me Jupiter is a deep, dark pit where Martians and Machines hide, getting up to the hell knows what, out of our sight. Even the damn simps are involved.'

That surprised Falcon. 'What about the simps?'

'Oh, the marvellous Independent Pan Nation has a hand in it too. Or a paw, whatever. Turns out that simps, when toughened up enough, can deal pretty well with Jupiter's gravity, and they're useful workers. As ever pursuing their own agenda, and biting the WG hand that feeds them. Ham, the President, denies it all. Well, at least we have some leverage there. The Pan turn out to have a problem with genetic drift. Their precious smarts aren't locked in by a million years of evolution and rock-bashing, as ours are. They can *slip back*. It's heartbreaking, I'm told, to see an infant born without that spark in its eyes.' She didn't sound heartbroken at all. 'So they need research and support from us, from our laboratories – even the Martians can't fulfil that need yet. So there we have a handle. With the others, though . . .'

Falcon was appalled to think that any government could think of using the intellectual survival of a species as a weapon. He wondered what long-term damage such manoeuvring might do to relations between humans and Pan.

Springer was evidently oblivious to such implications.

'It's very useful to have you involved in this descent, Commander Falcon,' she said now. 'More than useful, and we're grateful to the Brenner Institute for sponsoring your involvement in the project in the first place – and I'm grateful to my cousin for passing out during that trial descent, thus proving that an Earthborn human, you, can *still* handle stuff beyond the capabilities of a Martian in an exosuit. Ha! I bet that went down well in Port Lowell. And also you have your personal connection with the Machines, through the creature we know as Adam.'

'You mean, "the Legal Person (Non-human) we know as Adam". It took a lot of debate for that honorific to be earned.'

'Whatever.' Springer glanced up at Jupiter again, almost resentfully. 'The truth is that right now we have *no* WG-loyal observers monitoring what's really going on inside Jupiter – and this is our chance to insert one, a golden opportunity riding on the back of this stunt, this descent into the lower layers. Even the Martians, even the Machines, can't object to *you* going along, given your physical capabilities and your past record.'

This was going well beyond the briefings that had brought Falcon here. '*Insert?* What am I now, a spy for Interplanetary Relations? I thought this project was about discovery. Science. Not espionage and politics.'

Springer sighed. 'You're much older than I am, Commander, and I'm sure you're not naive. But I wonder if you grasp our deepest concerns. Am I right that you were born before the first World President was inaugurated?'

Falcon smiled. 'I wasn't actually old enough to vote for Bandranaik, though.'

'Falcon, since those days, on Earth we've constructed a successful scientific world state. A dream centuries old. You could call it a utopia . . . if not for the bad dreams from the sky.'

More surprising poetry.

'Long term, our strategists are deeply concerned about the development of the Machine civilisation – if it's unified and developed enough to be called that – and what impact it might have on us. But in the short term we have enough turbulence with our own colonies. From Mercury to Triton, the colony worlds have been following their own political and cultural development from the days of the first footfalls.

'But Mars was always the key. There was a self-sufficient base on Mars for half a century even before Bandranaik was elected. And the World Government has consistently tried to engage with Mars – even to appease it, if you like, right back to the beginning of the WG itself, when Mars was declared a Federated Zone with full voting rights on the World Council. We find ways to pump money out there: the transfer of Spaceguard HQ to Hellas as far back as the 2120s, the establishing of the Port Deimos spacecraft construction yards in the 2170s. At the turn of the century Interplanetary Relations even put up the seedcorn money for the Eos Programme, their long-term terraforming project. More recently we tried to use the Moon as a bridge. Martians and other offworlders can come to Aristarchus Tech to study without high-gravity augmentation . . . Did you know we even have Machines working there, on the Moon? That's another diplomatic experiment. Sure, they're banned from the home planet, but we employ them to process lunar ore, and on other programmes. A gesture of trust, right?'

'I know you allowed the Federation of Planets to set up their headquarters on the Moon too.'

'Yes, after the Crawford Declaration they signed in 2186.'

'I was there—'

'The Federation still has no legal validity in the eyes of the World Government, but we treat it as a polite fiction even so.'

Falcon imagined how that kind of patronising dismissal played on Phobos, or at Lowell, or Vulcanopolis on Mecury, or Oasis on Titan – even at Clavius Base. 'You know, Colonel, I'm something of an outsider in all this myself. I don't fit into one world or the other. Hell, I'm older than most of these human worlds. But what I see is that with Earth's continuing economic and political domination of the solar system, you're restricting growth. The Martians I meet complain that they could expand a lot faster, even accelerate the Eos Programme, if only you'd increase shipments of essential supplies.

'Maybe the time's come for a change of policy. Look at history. From 1492, Columbus's first landings, to the American Revolution was – what, a little shy of three centuries? And from the first footsteps of John Young, the Columbus of Mars, to *now*, is about the same interval—'

'This isn't imperial Britain and colonial America, Falcon,' Springer said sternly. 'You're showing your age. The history you learned is buried under centuries. This is a different era. Different technologies.

'Let me explain the cornerstone of government policy. *What the World Council fears above all is an interplanetary war.*

'Think about it. Even you probably aren't old enough to remember the Brushfire Wars in the last years of the nation states . . . There were a number of incidents where aircraft – lumbering tubs driven by no more than chemical fuels – were flown into buildings. Acts of war and terror.'

'I grew up with the images.' In Falcon's young imagination such incidents had been like purposeful *Hindenburg* disasters.

'Now think about this. A civilian aircraft of the early twenty-first century, fully fuelled, packed as much punch as a few hundred tonnes of TNT. A modern interplanetary cruiser of the *Goliath* class, like the ship that brought you here, if flown into a city on Earth, would release as much energy as an entire all-out nuclear war would have done back in my ancestor Seth's day. Just one craft – and I'm only talking about the kinetic energy involved, even without the detonation of any fusion reactors or the use of any dedicated weapons systems.'

Falcon glanced up at the fragile dome over his head. 'Offworld colonies are pretty vulnerable too.'

'Right. And so the judgement of the World Council, as advised by the Strategic Development Secretariat, is that an interplanetary war would be like no prior conflict in human history. It would be a potential extinction event for humanity. *All* of us, on Earth or off it.'

'I see the logic. War must be averted at all costs. And this is your way of handling it? The Martians are agitating for independence, and your response is to clamp the lid down even tighter?'

'What would you have us do, Falcon? At least this way we keep control. At least this way we can exclude the unknowns – and a political liberation of the offworld settlements would be a massive unknown. That's even leaving aside the influence of the Machines in all this, which is another huge uncertainty.'

He said, 'That's why Jupiter frightens you so much. You don't know what's going on down there. And what you don't know, you can't control.' Falcon studied Springer, her voice tight, her manner set, determined, clear-thinking – and, under it all, with a bit of poetry in a rebellious soul. And he thought of far-off Earth, nestling close to its sun, a world that had found peace and unity so tragically recently – and yet here was one of its citizens, out in the dark and the cold, wrestling with existential threats on behalf of the whole of humanity. He felt an odd admiration for her. But he didn't drop his guard.

As he studied her, so she studied him. She said now, 'So will you help me?'

'What can you tell me about New Nantucket?'

Springer said nothing, returning his gaze resolutely.

'Or about the weapons emplacements you're installing at the sub-Jovian point on Ganymede?'

'Are you making it a condition of working with us that I have to reveal classified information?'

Falcon gave in. 'What, and miss Falcon Junior's journey to the heart of Jupiter? Hell, no. OK, Colonel, I'll do as you say. I'll – observe.'

'By the way, you'll have my cousin Trayne for company.'

That surprised him. 'Trayne? He's a bright kid but—'

'We need to have a Martian attached to this jaunt. Just to show Port Lowell we're not excluding the Martians from any of this.'

Falcon smiled. 'And who better to play that part than Trayne? He's family for you, and he evidently knows absolutely nothing about the politics . . .'

'I'm not quite as cynical as that. I happen to believe Trayne will be a good crewmate.'

'I'm sure he will,' Falcon said dryly. 'He's a Springer after all.'

A curt nod, and a smile back. 'I'll be monitoring you all the way down, of course. But report to me in person when you get back.' And Thera Springer, her job done here, Falcon safely recruited, was already glancing at a wrist minisec, her mind evidently on her next meeting.

And Howard Falcon's thoughts turned, once again, to Jupiter.

23

In the pale air, a thousand hot-air balloons hovered in formation.

Falcon, once more at his control station in the *Ra* with Trayne at his side, was awed despite his own previous jaunts into Jupiter. Each of those tremendous envelopes, around two hundred metres in diameter, was emblazoned with the sigil of the World Government, an Earth cradled in human hands – a design, as Falcon knew and few others probably remembered, based on the mission patch of the Apollo-Icarus 6 spacecraft – and boldly marked with an identification number. And beneath each golden balloon was a knot of equipment, a suspended factory that Falcon knew must be an atmospheric processing plant, with a dock for small, needle-shaped craft, evidently orbital shuttles, freighters. Even as Falcon watched, one craft sparked rocket fire and soared away from its balloon, out of the farm and up into the higher atmosphere, heading for orbit and a rendezvous with an interplanetary tanker, into which it would offload its precious cargo of fusion fuel for delivery to Earth and the colony worlds.

But it was the precise formation of the balloons together that was so impressive: a neat array in the hydrogen-helium sky, maintained despite a battering from the turbulent Jovian winds. It was a fantastic sight – and yet Falcon was reminded of a place and time far from here, of images of a wartime London sheltering under a sky full of barrage balloons: images that had been only a century old when he was born.

The World Government Space Development Secretariat had supplied Falcon with more information than he needed on this, its grandest project: its helium-3 extraction operation, dozens of plants like this established deep in the clouds of Jupiter. Now Trayne consulted a display, bending forward stiffly in his exosuit. 'So this is the North Temperate Band Atmospheric Processing Station Number Four – NTB-4. The station's a long way from the lower-latitude zones where the native biota tends to congregate.'

That positioning was an act of conservation, Falcon saw, but also of simple common sense. He imagined a creature like a manta being drawn into one of those great extractor fans, or a medusa, kilometres across, at play in that forest of balloons . . .

'There are a thousand aerostat plants in this one station alone, with ninety-eight per cent fully operational at present. It seems there are frequent breakdowns.'

'Hence the need for a crewed presence,' Falcon muttered.

Trayne said dryly, 'If you count Machines as crew, yes. There are said to be ten Machines for each Martian working at this facility. Each plant processes three thousand cubic metres of Jovian atmosphere per second, in order to extract one *gram* of the isotope helium-3 . . .'

It sounded so little, just the merest trace to be extracted from Jupiter's enormous reservoir of air. But that trace was enough to sustain a mighty interplanetary civilisation. And, economically, it was an effective, indeed a highly profitable operation.

The Martians were paid either in credit or in trade goods – oil or other complex organics – or sometimes in high-tech gear they could not yet manufacture themselves. It had always been that way, Falcon thought sourly. An empire bought bulk raw materials from its colonies in exchange for complex products from the centre, just as the Romans had traded with the provincial British, and the British in turn had traded with the colonial Americans. The Machines, meanwhile, had been rewarded with access to a few inner-system asteroids rich with the metals they craved.

But, Falcon knew, a dependence on this collection strategy made Earth vulnerable too. Fallbacks were being explored, he had heard; since Geoff Webster's day Falcon had maintained contacts in the World Council and other high echelons of the WG, so he knew that Space Development was already trying to establish similar atmospheric-mining operations in the clouds of Saturn.

All that for the future. Right now it was time for Howard Falcon, agent of the government, to go to work.

Viewscreens on Falcon's console lit up with images of a human, evidently a Martian, a male aged perhaps forty, head cradled in a massive brace, and alongside him a Machine, its own 'head' an ungainly cluster of sensor gear. Even after all these years, each time he encountered a Machine Falcon found himself looking into camera lenses in search of a soul.

'Calling *Ra*,' said the human. 'Welcome to Station NTB-4.'

'*Ra* reporting in, NTB-4.'

'I am Hans Young,' said the Martian. 'Citizen Second Grade. I'm in charge of the human team attached to the Orpheus project. And before you ask – no, no relation.'

Relation to whom? Oh, yes, John Young. Falcon ignored that bit of Martian bragging. 'We've corresponded, Dr Young. Good to see you.'

Young waved. 'And hi to you too, Trayne. How's your mother?'

'Good, thank you, Hans.' Trayne glanced at Falcon. 'Mars is a small world.'

'So I gather.'

'And I,' intoned the Machine in a smooth synthetic voice, 'will be known for the purposes of this expedition as Charon 1.'

'Charon . . . More classical mythology. Orpheus's guide across the Styx?'

'Correct. I will guide the first stage of the descent. There will be further "Charons" later. The mission must proceed in stages, adapting to the conditions we encounter as we travel deeper into Jupiter. It was thought appropriate to establish a series of base camps as we progressed. The logic is rather as when humans once challenged mountains such as Everest.'

Falcon said dryly, 'I can tell you that Earthlings *still* climb mountains.'

'And so do Martians,' put in Trayne.

'Let's review the strategy,' Falcon said. 'We won't be able to track Orpheus even as deep as the thermalisation layer we'll manage only a few hundred kilometres, less than one per cent of the journey he's undertaking.'

'Nevertheless your company will be welcome. And you will stay on station as one of a chain of relays.'

'As agreed.' Falcon glanced at a clock. 'I see Orpheus is prepared for launch. Is there any need for us to come aboard?'

Young smiled. 'Commander Falcon, one thing you learn when working with Machines: there's no ritual, no routine. When they're ready to go, they just go. Not so much as a countdown.'

'I concur with that.'

An image of a black cube appeared in the viewscreens.

'It is I. Orpheus. Or, "Falcon Junior". Welcome to the project, Commander Falcon. Adam sends his personal regards.'

'Thank you—'

'Follow me if you dare.'

The images relayed from NTB-4 shuddered, just a little.

Hans Young glanced at an off-screen monitor. 'He's gone – he and the remaining Charons – bathyscaphe away!'

'Just like that?'

Young smiled. 'Told you.'

Trayne nudged Falcon and pointed through a window. 'Look! There he goes!'

A kind of ship had tumbled out of the base of one of the hovering balloons, a silvered sphere no more than a few metres across. As it fell through the air a canopy deployed and quickly inflated, slowing the drop to a steady sinking.

Falcon tapped his controls and felt the *Ra* turn sluggishly in response. 'There he goes indeed,' he muttered. 'Come on, Trayne, we have an explorer to chase . . .'

24

Effortlessly at first, the *Ra* tracked the bathyscaphe as it descended into ever-thickening layers of Jovian air, followed by a swarm of camera drones. *Bathyscaphe*: that had been an archaic word even when Falcon was born, and yet it was apt, he thought, for what was this but a descent into a mighty ocean?

Soon *Ra* plunged through cloud level D, and into a gathering darkness. As the descent continued, the pressure and temperature steadily increased, and Falcon had Trayne call out regular readings. The *Ra*, of course, hanging under its envelope of heated hydrogen, was itself dependent on a balance of air temperature and pressure to stay aloft. The *Ra* was more advanced than the old *Kon-Tiki* and, thanks to technologies piloted in the oceanic air of Venus, could reach greater depths without risk of being crushed. Nevertheless, they were little more than two hundred kilometres deep – Orpheus's descent had barely begun when Falcon, reluctantly, called a halt.

'We're safe to hover at this level,' he reported up to NTB-4, and through them up to Mission Control on Amalthea. 'Regret I can't follow you any further, Orpheus. All your systems look nominal, as far as I can tell.'

'Your company has been appreciated, Commander Falcon.'

In the monitor, Hans Young smiled. 'Like all the best Machines, he's programmed to be polite. Prepare to hold your station, *Ra*, and to deploy transmission relay gear.'

'Copy.'

Falcon and Trayne got to work transforming the *Ra* into a stationary radio relay post. Antennas unfurled around the envelope, including the long, trailing receptors that Falcon, on other days, used to communicate with his friends the medusae. But both of them kept an eye on the images, in visual light, radar and even sonar, of Orpheus's descent into a thickening murk. Most of the camera drones still followed, but one or two, it seemed, were already failing as the conditions grew tougher, the images they returned fritzing to empty blue.

A key milestone came when Orpheus's balloon envelope was cut away and allowed to drift off.

'Too deep for hot-air ballooning now,' Falcon muttered. 'But look at the rate of descent. It's hardly increased, even without the envelope. Air resistance, and the bathysphere's own buoyancy, is enough to slow it now.'

'I don't understand,' Trayne said, frowning. 'I knew I shouldn't have skipped those briefings at Anubis . . . Without the balloon, how will they bring Orpheus home?'

Falcon studied him. 'I guess you haven't been around Machines much. Trayne, he *won't* be coming home – nor will the Charons who are guiding him. Any more than *Mariner 4* ever came back from its flyby of Mars.'

'What?'

'Never mind.'

'That isn't quite true, Commander,' said Charon 1. 'Before his craft is finally destroyed – or rather before *he* is destroyed, there being no distinction between craft and passenger – Orpheus's identity complex will be uploaded through the relay stations we will establish, including your own, and copies will be captured here at NTB-4 and at Amalthea. I understand that this kind of replication of minds gives humans no philosophical comfort, but it suffices for us if the copy is indistinguishable from the original. So you see, Dr Trayne Springer, in a sense he *will* come home—'

A flare of light showed up in several of the monitor screens.

Trayne was startled. 'What was that? Is there something wrong?'

Falcon shook his head. 'He already reached the thermalisation layer. Where it's so hot that anything that can be heat-destroyed, will be. Certainly anything organic. That is the ultimate limit for Jovian life.'

Hans Young said cautiously, 'Well, the limit for the life forms we know of, Commander. That's one objective of the descent. To see what's down there . . .'

To challenge the planet's greatest depths had been one of Howard Falcon's dreams since the *Kon-Tiki*. He longed to follow Orpheus. He could only wait and watch.

The fall continued relentlessly. The pressure and temperatures recorded by the probe continued to mount, leaving one comparison after another in their wake: a higher pressure than the surface of Venus, higher than Earth's deepest ocean trench.

And as the pressure gauge crept up towards two thousand atmospheres, the probe revealed another of its secrets. Its hull abruptly *collapsed*, and this time it was Falcon who thought some catastrophic failure had befallen it. But the handful of remaining cameras, specialised for depth, showed that while the spherical hull had imploded, a kind of open framework survived, a space-filling, regular arrangement of bars and nodes.

'You see the design philosophy,' Hans Young said. 'We do not fight the pressure, we yield to it. Though the Jovian air has flooded what was the interior, the craft still has some buoyancy, with small, very robust ballast tanks embedded deep in the surviving structure.'

'And I too survive,' reported Orpheus. 'Along with the Charons, downloaded onto chips of diamond. We are comfortable.'

'Show-off,' Falcon muttered.

The probe plummeted through one cloud layer after another, as exotic species of molecules congealed out of the thickening air. But the light faded quickly, and soon the last and sturdiest of the camera drones fell away, and no more visible-light images were returned.

At about five hundred kilometres deep, the level once believed to have corresponded to Jupiter's 'surface', Orpheus's probing with radar, sonar and other sensors revealed the presence of masses of some kind drifting in the air, lumpy, granular. Quasi-solid 'clouds' in an air of impossible density, Falcon speculated, which had perhaps fooled earlier observers into thinking this was a solid crust.

But Orpheus soon passed through this intriguing layer and fell deeper yet. The dense hydrogen air through which he fell now seemed featureless – and lifeless, lacking the sunlit glamour of the high clouds of the medusae. Time passed. Falcon was sure that reports were being transmitted across the solar system, but he wondered how many viewers in their domes on Triton, or in the gardens of Earth, would be tuning out when the reports of this dull phase of the mission were sent to them at lightspeed's crawl.

The next milestone came at one thousand kilometres deep.

'Pressure of eighty thousand atmospheres,' Orpheus reported. 'Temperature eight hundred Kelvin. Pressure and temperature profiles have largely matched theoretical models so far. However the hydrogen-helium slush outside the hull is now more usefully described as a liquid rather than a gas . . .

'This is Orpheus. We are through the transition zone, and have reached Jupiter's ocean of molecular hydrogen. The first sapients ever to do so.'

Falcon glanced at Trayne. 'I'm sure I can hear a trace of pride in that voice.'

Trayne shrugged. 'Why not?'

'Phase one is complete. A further layer of hull will be discarded; my descent will continue, while Charon 2 remains at this waystation.'

'I can confirm that,' called a new Machine voice: Charon 2. 'I am ready to take up my station-keeping duties here.'

And Falcon was astonished by what Charon 2 said next:

'Godspeed, Orpheus.'

The descent continued.

25

'My name is Orpheus. This telemetry is being transmitted via radio signals received by Charon 2 at the hydrogen gas-liquid interface, relayed via the *Ra* at the thermalisation layer to Charon 1 at Station NTB-4, and then to Mission Control on Amalthea. I am in an excellent state of health and all subsystems are operating normally. I remain fully cognisant of and fully committed to the objectives of the mission.

'I am currently descending through an ocean of molecular hydrogen-helium. I am quite safe. For this first descent I have been emplaced far from any of the four great volcanic-like features we call Sources. Their investigation is for the future.

'The pressures and temperatures I am experiencing are rising steadily. My configuration continues to adjust as designed. In the greatest depths my consciousness will be contained in little more than a swarm of slivers of enhanced crystalline carbon – an advanced form of diamond – kept solid at such extreme temperatures by the very pressures I will endure. In this way I will leverage the physical conditions to maintain my structure, as opposed to fighting those conditions.

'There is no visible light. I fall through darkness. But the hydrogen ocean is electrically neutral, and long-wavelength radio waves can penetrate the gloom.

'Nevertheless—

'Nevertheless I am aware of forms, structures, moving through the dark around me. Immense, shapeless masses.

'These may be inanimate blocks of some more exotic high-pressure form of hydrogen. Drifting icebergs. Or perhaps they are animate, a form of life, living off the thin drizzle of complex compounds from the atmosphere above, or even feeding on this ocean's gradual temperature differences, or the saturated electromagnetic radiation. Humans and Machines have found life wherever they have travelled; life forms here would not be a surprise. Their movement shows no pattern, however, no intent. Even if there is life, this featureless ocean may be too impoverished to support mind. An encounter with these deep Jovians, if that is what they are, must wait for more advanced missions than mine.

'It is anticipated that at a depth of approximately twelve thousand kilometres, where the pressures will approach one million Earth atmospheres, I will reach an interface to a realm of different physics, and my design will come under fresh challenges.

'For now, however, I am comfortable.'

26

It was Trayne who first noticed the anomalous radio signal.

Falcon was listening to the transmission from Orpheus with a mixture of wonder, envy and irritation. '"For now, however, I am comfortable." Textbook laconic. By damn, you'd swear Orpheus was as human as Young or Hilton – and as cold-blooded.'

'Maybe,' Trayne said, frowning, distracted. He pointed to a display. 'Commander, look at this. One of your filters is picking up another signal. Nothing to do with Orpheus. Is it one of your medusae?'

Falcon looked over to the screen. Indeed, pulses of shortwave radio transmissions were being detected by the *Ra*'s huge antenna arrays, and he immediately recognised the basic modulation pattern. Hastily he locked in the translation software suite he had patched together over the decades – the centuries, now – of his contact with the inhabitants of Jupiter.

Trayne said, 'I can't tell how remote the source is.'

'I can guess from the signal strength, and we'll have triangulation soon . . .'

A synthesised voice, soulless, sexless, without inflection, gave the first rough translation of the signal. *The Great Manta has returned. The Great Manta is among us. Pray to the Great Manta that you are spared. Pray to the Great Manta that you are not spared . . .*

Trayne's eyes were wide. 'Is that . . .?'

'A medusa. You bet it is.'

'And I bet I know who it is – that is, *which* medusa. Ceto, yes? The one we encountered before. "The Great Manta." You said she was talking about that. It had something to do with a medusa's ideas of death and extinction?'

'Yes – an ambiguous myth. Medusae are sentient prey animals. They understand that they are locked into a wider ecology in which the mantas and other predators play an essential role. So they accept the loss of a proportion of their own kind, a toll they pay to the ecology that sustains them – and yet at the same time they will pray to a manta to spare themselves, just for today . . . Something's happening. She's in trouble.' He hesitated. 'She's calling for help. *My* help. She wouldn't be shouting in the shortwave band otherwise.'

Trayne eyed him. 'And you want to help her, don't you?'

He grimaced. 'Why? Because that's what your kids'-story version of a hero would do?'

Trayne looked faintly offended. 'No. It's just that I know you, at least a little. And if she's calling for you, maybe the trouble she's in has something to do with humans.'

Falcon hadn't thought of that. He said grudgingly, 'You may have a point. We're narrowing the fix. She's many thousands of kilometres away. Even if we broke away, how could we get there in time? The *Ra*, like the *Kon-Tiki*, is basically designed to float around on the wind, not set speed records.'

Trayne shrugged. 'So we cut away the lift envelope. The gondola has its own fusor propulsion system—'

'Designed to take us out of the atmosphere and back to orbit, not for jaunts in the cloud banks.'

'Sure. But there's plenty of spare energy. And the engine is a ramjet – it uses the external air as reaction mass – so it's not as if we are going to run out of propellant.' In response to Falcon's surprised look he said more hesitantly, 'I checked out the *Ra*'s specs before we set off from Amalthea.'

'You did, did you?'

'I'm not some pampered Terran, Commander. I'm a Martian. I grew up under a plastic dome on a planet that will kill me as punishment for the slightest slip. Of course I checked.'

'OK. I'm reluctantly impressed. But we have a mission here. We're a relay station for Orpheus—'

'The envelope can station-keep. It has a backup comms systems of its own. Besides, even without us, the signals from Charon 2 are probably strong enough to be picked up directly by Charon 1 back at NTB-4.'

'You checked all this out too, right?'

Trayne grinned.

Falcon turned to his controls. 'OK. You asked for it. Checking deuterium-helium-3 ratio . . .' Restraints locked down Falcon's frame, fixing it tightly to the structure of the *Ra*. 'Make sure you have your exosuit powered up and locked into its frame, I'm not going to be sparing the acceleration.'

'Wouldn't dream of asking you to.' Trayne backed up to his suit's wall station.

'Checking jet chamber temperature.' Falcon glanced over his

instruments one last time. Then he broke the safety seal over the rip-cord button. 'Lighting the blue touch paper.'

'The what?'

'Never mind.' He pressed the button.

There was a sharp crack as explosive bolts separated the gondola from the gas envelope, a brief sensation of falling – they were already committed to this jaunt – and then the ramjet drive cut in. Acceleration pressed. The gondola had turned into an independent craft in the Jovian air, a candle riding a column of superheated hydrogen-helium.

'You OK, Martian?'

'Never better.'

'Liar. I'll get our trajectory locked in. And I see Amalthea Control is already demanding an explanation. I'll let *you* take care of that . . .'

27

'My name is Orpheus. This telemetry is being transmitted via radio signals received by Charon 2 at the hydrogen gas-liquid interface, relayed via the *Ra* at the thermalisation layer to Charon 1 at Station NTB-4, and then to Mission Control on Amalthea. I am in an excellent state of health and all subsystems are operating normally. I remain fully cognisant of and fully committed to the objectives of the mission.

'At twelve thousand kilometres down, I have passed beyond the hydrogen ocean, and reached the region known in the theoretical models as the "plasma boundary layer".

'Below the upper clouds Jupiter is an immense droplet of hydrogen and helium, all the way to a core of still-unknown composition. I have now reached a depth at which the temperatures are so high that molecular hydrogen cannot survive – where electrons are stripped from their atomic nuclei by heat energy. The resulting plasma is electrically conductive, as is the greater ocean of what is known as "metallic hydrogen" into which I am now descending – it is indeed like an ocean of liquid metal. It is thought that the substance of this sea, by the way, may be useful, perhaps as a room-temperature superconductor, or a high-energy-density fuel . . . All that for the future.

'The plasma layer, however, will block radio transmissions. Therefore I am depositing another relay station at this depth – Charon 3 – and to communicate further I will be returning small buoys that will rise to this depth and contact Charon 3 for further relay of information back to Mission Control.

'This communication method is one-way.

'You will not be able to speak to me. I will not be able to hear your voices.

'The plasma layer itself, as some theoreticians predicted, is a place of marvels. The seepage of carbon, silicon and other heavier elements from the cloud layers has reached even this far, and I have detected many complex, even previously unknown molecular forms and compounds . . . Such materials, mined from this layer, may have many useful properties.

'But I have time only to note these phenomena. I fall into a sea of metallic hydrogen over forty thousand kilometres deep. This is an arena of huge electromagnetic energies, which I can already sense.

'As if I fall into troubled dreams.'

Falcon followed the news of Orpheus's descent, even as his own fusion-drive craft rocketed through the Jovian clouds. And he listened to the conversations of the analysts at Amalthea Control, who were becoming increasingly concerned about some aspects of Orpheus's communications – notably the increasing subjectivity of the reports, and the use of words like 'dreams'.

During his involvement with the Machines' early development, Falcon had studied the theory and history of artificial minds. Like that of all Machines, Orpheus's 'brain' was essentially a Minsky-Good neural network, capable of learning, growth, adaptation – a design whose theory went back to the work of twentieth-century pioneers like John von Neumann and Alan Turing. And Orpheus, like any sapient, artificial or otherwise, was vulnerable to instability, especially given an overwhelming experience such as he was currently enduring.

The cyberneticists on Amalthea and Ganymede speculated that a combination of information overload, personal peril, and solitude could now compromise the Machine's ability to fulfil his primary functions. They even spoke of the danger of him falling into a Hofstadter-Möbius loop, a kind of psychopathy not uncommon to goal-seeking autonomous systems when faced with an overload of information and choices. And security officials spoke darkly of the need to debug any copy of Orpheus's mind that might be returned to the data banks of the inhabited moons.

Falcon, who was not so prone to seeing a divide between biological and artificial consciousness, had a simpler diagnosis. He had seen similar reactions in flesh-and-blood people he had guided through the world of the medusae. Even old Geoff Webster had had doses of it, on his good days.

Awe. That was what Orpheus was experiencing. Awe.

And the mother hens on Amalthea could do nothing about it now; Orpheus could hardly be brought back.

As for dreaming, Falcon had long ago come to believe that, like all sentient creatures, Machines could dream. Even if few of them admitted it.

28

Trayne, his eyes more youthful than Falcon's – and probably more recently upgraded – was the first to spot the medusae, in a wide-angle viewscreen. 'There!' He pointed, excited, though he winced as his arm rose, fighting the gravity with a whine of servomotors.

Falcon looked more closely. Against the tan wash of Jupiter's deeper cloud layers, he saw a curving line of pale oval forms, like a string of pearls in the air. The sun was setting on another short Jovian day, and those pearls cast long shadows. Medusae, surely.

But they weren't alone. Sparks of light flitted around them, bright in the fading light, like fireflies. They were nothing natural; they looked to Falcon like fusion torch ships. And ahead of the line he made out a darker knot, some kind of floating factory supported by a dense forest of balloons.

'What the hell are we looking at?'

Trayne stared ahead. 'Those pods *are* medusae, right? Which one is Ceto?'

Falcon glanced at a scanner; Ceto had by now been triangulated precisely from her characteristic radio call. 'The third in line – the third from that floating complex.' He glared at Trayne. 'You seemed very eager for us to come here. Was it more than just curiosity? Do you know something about this?'

Trayne looked back at him defiantly. 'I'm . . . not sure. That's the truth.'

After a beat, Falcon turned away. 'OK. I'll accept that for now. So we figure it out for ourselves.' He pointed to the screen. 'This is *not* the way medusae behave in the wild. If you're a prey species, you don't string out in a line waiting to be picked off. You bunch up in three dimensions, because in this ocean an attack can come from any direction. Secondly, we are far from their usual ranges for food, breeding . . .'

Light flared against the flank of one of the medusae in the line, like a fusion spark – dazzling, despite the viewscreen's filters.

'And what was *that*? It looked like they deliberately burned a medusa with a plasma jet.'

Now there was a noise, a deep thrumming, the beats almost like impacts, that made the hull shudder.

Trayne looked at Falcon, alarmed. 'Some kind of malfunction? A storm?'

'No. Wait and listen.'

The drumming came faster and faster, the individual beats at last merging into a deep wash of noise that grew louder and louder, though it did not increase in pitch, becoming a kind of throbbing bellow that forced Trayne to clamp his hands over his ears – before it cut off with brutal suddenness.

The gondola seemed to rattle. Trayne lowered his hands, cautiously.

'Would you believe that the acousticians call it a "chirp"? Sorry, I should have warned you. That was the cry of a medusa in pain.'

Abruptly an alarm sounded, another grating clamour. Falcon cut it off with a bunched fist. 'And *that* was a proximity alarm. Another craft approaching.'

Trayne checked the sensors. 'It's already reached us, it's keeping pace with us.' He looked afraid for the first time since they'd left Amalthea.

A comms screen filled with a human face, a stern older woman. 'I am Citizen Second Grade Nicola Pandit. I have locked into your systems. I have the capability to override your drive controls.'

A Martian, then. Falcon was furious. He turned to his consoles and quickly set every camera and sensor he had to record, and initiated an upload data stream to Amalthea and Ganymede. Let them see everything.

Then he thundered, 'By whose authority do you challenge me? This is the *Ra*, a science vessel registered with the Brenner Institute and with the Space Development Secretariat, Bureau of Planetary Exploration. And *my* name is Howard Falcon. Override *me*? I'd like to see you try.'

'You will come no closer to the facility. You will turn back, Howard Falcon, and return to your station for the Orpheus mission—'

'Like hell I will. Not until I know—'

'Councillor Pandit?' Trayne was leaning down to see. 'Is that you? What are you doing here?'

'Good grief. Do *all* you damn Martians know each other?'

Pandit pursed her lips. 'Citizen Third Grade Springer, it is better if you are not involved in this.'

'I'm already involved, Councillor.'

'Then you will share the consequences of any actions Howard Falcon takes.'

Falcon said, 'This is my fight. My world. You don't need to do this, Trayne.'

'I think I do,' Trayne said, almost sadly.

Pandit snapped. 'I say again, Howard Falcon. Turn back. If you do not—'

'What? What will you do? Citizen, I've been looping loops around the clouds of Jupiter since before your grandpappy was thrown aboard a convict scow to Port Lowell. Catch me if you can; *I'm* going to take a look at what you're doing here.'

He worked his controls, and the gondola surged forward with renewed acceleration.

'Commander Falcon—!'

Falcon tapped a console to silence Pandit's angry voice.

Trayne said, 'They never sent convicts to Port Lowell, you know, Commander.'

'I was insulting her, not giving her a history lesson. OK – we're approaching that complex. There are more ships buzzing around us, but they can't touch us, not this close; a missile strike on our fusor pod would cause a detonation that would take half that installation down with us. Now, let's see what's really going on here . . .'

He brought the *Ra* to a shuddering halt, set up station-keeping attitude thrusters, turned the hull to its faux-transparent setting.

And the two of them, side by side, looked down on a scene of horror.

The medusae were being shepherded into a long line that stretched across the air. The lead medusa, itself two kilometres wide, faced a cage that was even larger than she was, with a gaping, open mouth. Small flyers darted around the animal, flaring fusion fire, and attacking the medusa with what looked like small darts.

Trayne pointed. 'Look at that scar on her side.' It was a crater of scorched flesh, metres wide.

'They're goading her,' Falcon said, disbelieving. 'Forcing her into that cage, with the darts, the plasma jets. And the tight turns those torch flyers are making – they can't be piloted by humans, not even Earthborn, let alone Martian. Machines, then. Martians and Machines, cooperating in this operation. But what are they doing?'

Now the medusa was entering the cage, pushing inside gingerly, gently, like a great liner coming into dock, Falcon thought briefly.

But there was nothing welcoming about this harbour. As soon as the medusa was fully in the cage, a barrage of small missiles was fired into her carcass, from above, below, into the flanks – a sudden, shocking assault. The medusa seemed to become rigid almost immediately:

the natural pulsing of her body as she swam, the synchronised waving of her inverted forest of tentacles, all of it was stilled. Now lines shot out of the cage structure towards her, and grappling hooks raked her flesh. From this point, Falcon saw, she would be *dragged* through the cage, rather than swim of her own volition.

And then the real work began.

On the underside of the medusa, lasers spat hard light, the beams easily visible in the murky Jovian air, and crude mechanical blades whirred. These weapons scythed through the graceful forest of tentacles, which drifted away from the main body to be caught in tremendous nets below the cage. Brownish fluid leaked from the medusa.

Next, more lasers and knives, some of them huge, sliced through the beast's skin, followed by claws that dragged away the fine, leathery substance in great sheets. Falcon watched with an almost distant curiosity as the animal's flotation bladders were exposed, great cells of hydrogen and helium, almost like those contained within the envelope of his own *Ra*. He knew something of the internal anatomy of a medusa; the beasts had been studied by zoologists using sonar, radar, and other non-intrusive probes. He had never seen one dissected before. Of course the gas cells were fragile, only as strong as they needed to be – for all their bulk, medusae were evolved for lightness. The cells popped easily at the touch of the lasers, collapsing into wispy folds that were briskly snipped away. Falcon briefly glimpsed the medusa's electrocytes, huge discs in neat stacks, an array capable of delivering million-volt shocks to would-be predators. These were briskly removed by robot arms.

And now the medusa's oil sacs were revealed, a thick layer of them beneath the flotation cells. These contained, at high density, a kind of petrochemical sludge, distilled from the atmosphere, which the medusa used to pump air out of the flotation cells when it needed to descend. Specialised craft of some kind, like flying tankers, Falcon thought, closed in on the medusa and plunged pipelines into the medusa's oil sacs, hastily draining them.

'They're like vampires,' Trayne said, recoiling.

Falcon said grimly, 'And *that's* what they're after. The oil . . .'

Now, only minutes after it had entered the cage, what was left of the carcass of the medusa was ejected from the far end. Falcon made out a glistening mass of internal organs, and ribbing of what looked like cartilage – it could be nothing like as strong or dense as human bone for this creature of lightness. These components were drifting apart, some looking as if they might still have some animation, some life left. Medusae were colony creatures, after all; many of these 'organs' had their own independent breeding lifecycles. Carl Brenner had long ago suggested that even the flotation sacs had once, in evolutionary history, been independent lighter-than-air flyers, not unlike *Kon-Tiki*.

'When you kill a medusa,' Falcon murmured, 'you inflict a thousand deaths.' He felt crushed by a sudden, savage despair, to have come across this butchery on a day that should have been about discovery and wonder. 'So this is New Nantucket, just as Dhoni hinted. And it's all about medusa oil.' He looked at Trayne bitterly. '*Did* you know about this?'

Trayne looked guilty. 'I guess I suspected it ... Mars is a small place, Commander. Recently there have been new imports of volatiles, complex hydrocarbons. Massive shipments. You couldn't hide their existence, but their source was a big secret – everybody knows there's an embargo on importing such stuff, laid down by Earth. People started talking about plans to put up more domes, even to accelerate the Eos Programme. And then, since coming here to Jupiter and learning about the medusae – I had nothing but vague suspicions – I guess I figured it out.'

'He's telling the truth, Falcon,' said Nicola Pandit, her face still looming large in the viewscreen.

'Oh, good, you got control of the volume again.'

'Trayne is innocent. But he's bright, like many Martians – we live in an environment which selects for intelligence.'

'But not for conscience?'

Pandit absorbed that. 'And I suppose you'd say our partners have no conscience at all.' Now she stood back, and a stiffly artificial visage joined hers in the image.

'Machine, I don't recognise you,' Falcon said.

'My name is Ahab. So my human colleagues have named me.'

'How witty,' Falcon said bleakly. 'So this is a Machine-Martian operation.'

'We are partners,' Ahab said neutrally.

'And it's all for the oil?'

Pandit said, 'You predicted it yourself, Falcon, in your report on the flight of the *Kon-Tiki*, all those years ago: "There must be enough petrochemicals deep down in the atmosphere of Jupiter to supply all Earth's needs for a million years." I memorised the sentence, you see. In fact we quoted it in our prospectus for potential investors. Thanks for your help. But you were a lousy prophet; these days *Earth* has no need of Jupiter's petrochemicals.'

'Right,' Falcon said. 'But poor, volatile-starved Mars—'

'We are starved only because of the repressive policies of the World Government.'

'So to serve your political goals, you are *whaling*.'

Pandit smiled thinly. 'We're hardly twentieth-century eco-bandits, Falcon. We cull the herds selectively, we take only older animals, we don't take so many that we'd make a dent in the planetary population – which is huge, by the way. And we use other medusa products, not just the oil. The electrocyte cells, for instance. The helium farms, like the one you visited in the North Temperate Belt – their lift envelopes are constructed from medusa flotation-sac material. I might have thought you'd spot that. And after the flensing process the waste is returned to the thermalisation layer, so little is lost to the ecology.'

'In industrial terms too the process is efficient,' Ahab said. 'The resources we require, the petrochemicals, are scattered thinly in the Jovian environment. But the medusae are natural collectors, so when we harvest them—'

'What do you Machines get out of this?'

'This is a purely commercial transaction, conducted under human – Martian – law. In return for the oil we ship to Mars we receive, or will receive in time, a range of high-quality goods and services, which—'

'Rubbish,' Falcon snarled. 'Whatever the terms of this "transaction", Pandit – I know the Machines; they work on longer timescales than us – *they have different objectives*. You're being used. But to what end?' He glared at Ahab. 'Are you meddling in human politics now, Ahab? Trying to stir up conflict between Earth and Mars? Is that the game?'

'We do not play games,' Ahab said simply.

'And we're doing nothing illegal,' Pandit said.

'Really?' Falcon snapped. 'And what of ethics? Whales were hunted for their oil on Earth too. Until we figured out the harm we were doing, and stopped. Like the whales, the medusae are intelligent beings.'

'You have proof of that?' Pandit asked evenly.

'I've been having conversations with one of them for two centuries. I'll show you the transcripts—'

'Pure anthropomorphism,' Pandit said. 'You are a lonely man, Falcon. It is a product of your accident, your own unfortunate nature. You seek companionship where none is available elsewhere – you see a soul where there is none.'

Falcon bunched a mechanical fist. 'I always detested psychoanalysis,' he muttered. 'Especially when it's used as a weapon. But for once I've got the law on my side. Thanks to testimony like mine, decades ago the Brenner Institute petitioned the World Court to accept the medusae as Legal Persons (Non-human) with associated rights—'

'The case was deferred without a final decision,' Pandit said softly.

The Machine said bluntly, 'The intelligence or otherwise of the medusae is irrelevant.'

That seemed to shock even Pandit, who turned to look at her companion.

'Carbon-based life is just another form of information-processing system, and an inefficient one at that.' Ahab seemed to consider for a moment. Then he said, 'This conversation serves no further purpose.' His screen went blank.

Falcon stared, chilled. He said to Pandit, 'So, do you endorse what your ally said?'

She said stonily, 'We have no choice but to deal with the Machines. The WG has *left* us no choice. Falcon, you're not going to hold up our production process. Go back to your Orpheus mission station, or prepare to surrender your ship . . .'

Trayne whispered, 'Ceto is next but one in line.'

Falcon turned away from the comms system and looked at him. 'Time to choose, Springer. Are you with me, or Pandit? Earth or Mars?'

'Human or Machine?'

'Maybe. This is a long game.'

Trayne pursed his lips, visibly unhappy. 'I don't see it that way. Why should I have to choose? If I'm *with* anybody, it's the medusae.'

Falcon smiled. 'Good answer. Let's fix this.' He touched his controls, and the gondola surged across the Jovian sky.

29

'There is rain here.

'A rain of helium and neon, which descends through the air-sea of metallic hydrogen. It sparkles in a swirl of electric currents. And all around me immense magnetic fields flap wings the size of moons...

'My name is Orpheus. This telemetry is being transmitted via signals received by Charon 3 at the plasma boundary, Charon 2 at the hydrogen gas-liquid interface, and relayed via the *Ra* above the thermalisation layer to Charon 1 at Station NTB-4, and then to Mission Control on Amalthea. I am in an excellent state of health and all subsystems are operating normally. I remain fully cognisant of and fully committed to the objectives of the mission—

'The mission—

'The mission

'I fall unhindered, a dust mote passing through a monstrous engine.

'And if nothing else, this forty-thousand-kilometre-deep ocean of plasma is exactly that: an engine that generates Jupiter's enormous magnetosphere, a field that envelops moons, and sends high-energy particles sleeting through the substance of unwary visitors, Machines or humans. I map the electromagnetic fields assiduously. One mission goal is to establish the coupling between this deep world engine and the external magnetosphere.

'At one level the physics are simple. The heart of the planet has remained hot since the huge violence of its birth, when it formed in the cold outer regions of the young solar system and swam briefly inwards, with Saturn, towards the fire of the Sun. And in the depths of this ocean that primordial heat drives convection currents, which in turn provide the energy for the electromagnetic fields that suffuse this vast arena.

'And yet there is more here, far more than a mere heat engine. I am becoming convinced of that. There is such *detail* in the swirling Maxwell-equation coupling of electricity and magnetism going on all around me – more detail, surely, than is necessary to serve as a magnetosphere motor. Detail, and more than that, *beauty*, even in the mathematical descriptions that scroll through my awareness.

'Sometimes I sense structures around me. A nested cascade of them reaching from the atomic – entities even smaller than me – up to much larger scales, the scales of Machines and ships and moons and planets – there is room for such a cascade, in here!

'Is this life?

'Perhaps. If life is the autocatalysis of structure fed by a flow of energy and capable of self-replication – for I have witnessed such events here, as electromagnetic field knots gather and "give birth" to more – then, yes, this is a good candidate for life, yet another layer in the great nesting that is Jupiter.

'Is there mind, though? Again, perhaps.

'But already my mind is turning to the next, and last, stage of my journey as I approach the strange heart of this strange world . . .'

30

Its fusion engine flaring, the *Ra* gondola approached Ceto.

Detail of the animal's huge flank slid across Falcon's viewscreen. Rumbling sonic cries and the lurid radio-transceiver mottling of her flesh showed that Ceto was urgently trying to speak with her fellows in this ghastly slaughterhouse line, trying to calm them with the words of the gloomy quasi-religion of the medusae.

Then, after the moment of closest approach, Falcon pulled *Ra* into a tight vertical climb – he heard Trayne grunt, but the Martian did not complain at this new loading of acceleration. Falcon brought the gondola to a relative halt, standing on its attitude jets some way off from the line of medusae.

Soon he saw the torch ships of the 'whalers' of this gruesome New Nantucket, sparks flying in the fading daylight, taking up station around him. But there weren't enough of them to cage him in this three-dimensional sky, and these short-haul, atmospheric craft, evidently optimised for the close-in work of corralling the doomed medusae, could not catch his own orbit-capable ship anyhow. He could get out of here any time he wanted – and he couldn't believe that even Machines would go so far as to try to shoot him down.

But even if they did try, he was going nowhere.

Trayne pointed at a screen. 'Wow. Look at *those*.'

Falcon turned to look. He saw what looked like a squadron of aircraft, jet-black arrowheads, coasting close to Ceto's flank, well within the cordon of human ships. 'Like Spitfires attacking a Zeppelin.'

'Like what?'

'Never mind. You know what you're seeing?'

'Mantas. They look so small against the flank of the medusa. But they themselves are – what, a hundred metres across?'

'You did your homework. In Jupiter, everything is built to an enormous scale . . .' Watching the mantas' graceful glide, Falcon was irresistibly taken back to the *Kon-Tiki* and his own earliest glimpses of the mantas, and he remembered with some embarrassment his own over-excited first reaction: 'Tell Dr Brenner there is life on Jupiter.

And it's *big*.' Later, Geoff Webster had never let him live it down.

'But,' said Trayne, 'what are the mantas doing *here*? In this killing field?'

His elderly mind clogged with too many memories, it hadn't occurred to Falcon to ask that very question.

Trayne was watching closely. 'Look – the mantas aren't attacking Ceto, or any of the other medusae. They're just escorting them. But if the medusae drift out of line . . .'

It took Falcon a couple of minutes to see what Trayne was getting at. 'You're right. Those manta formations are just spooking the medusae – keeping them in line, far more effectively than if those fusion ships tried to do it alone. The medusae have evolved to flee mantas, after all; they must be easy to startle.'

Trayne said carefully, 'So the managers of this slaughterhouse are *using* the mantas to herd the medusae. It is just as farmers in Earth's Agricultural Age would use dogs to round up their sheep.'

Falcon turned to him, surprised. 'How would you know about that?'

'At school we study the history of terrestrial life. Farming and stuff.'

'Why? Nostalgia for the mother world?'

'No. So that one day we can do it properly.'

'Well, maybe this has given us a way to resolve this situation.'

Trayne frowned. 'How? Commander, even though the *Ra* can outrun those torch ships, we are heavily outnumbered.'

'Take it easy. I've no intention of trying to break up this operation. I'll leave that for the authorities. All I want to do today is to save an old friend from the butchers' blades.'

Trayne thought that over, and grinned. 'Ceto.'

Falcon began tapping a keyboard. 'I'm sending a message to Ceto now . . . Trayne, I think you're right that they're using these mantas as sheepdogs. But we spent tens of thousands of years domesticating the wolf to produce a biddable, intelligent collie. These secretive butchers have only had a few years to work with the mantas. I'm going to gamble that their obedience will be much more easily broken.'

'So what message are you sending?'

'Simple. "Sorry, old friend. Just stay calm. You'll know what to do."' He grasped the gondola's controls. 'Now, brace yourself—'

With its exhaust of superhot hydrogen-helium plasma flaring, the gondola swept through the swarm of mantas – Falcon momentarily glimpsed the huge black forms fluttering away, alarmed or angered – and soared down towards the medusa once more. Racing over Ceto's broad back, Falcon saw a surface scarred and pitted from past predation and accident, almost like the surface of a crater-pocked moon. A medusa's very skin was a badge of courage and endurance and survival, Falcon thought, a badge of age.

And now he was going to have to burn a trench into it. 'This isn't going to be pretty, Martian,' he warned.

He hauled at his controls so that the *Ra* tipped up, and the fusion torch blasted across the medusa's flesh, scouring and scourging. The skin blistered, and, as lift sacs beneath burst, huge flaps of skin, gobbets of flesh and strands of cartilage were hurled up into the air. Ceto gave another agonising acoustic cry.

'Ouch,' said Trayne sympathetically. 'As big as she is, that's a nasty wound.'

'If she survives, she'll heal. Medusae are resilient. They have to be; they are pestered by predators throughout their lives. The question is, is it working?'

Trayne checked other monitors. 'If you mean, are the mantas breaking formation – yes, they are.'

Glancing back, Falcon saw the mantas come swarming from all sides, irresistibly drawn by the fragments of meat in the air and the scent of a medusa's equivalent of blood. They began to attack the open wound, snatching scraps of skin and meat out of the air, even snapping at each other in their helpless greed.

'Ha! That's carnivores for you. So much for your sheepdogs, Nantucket.'

'I bet the supervisors are already alarmed,' Trayne said. 'Ceto has drifted well out of line, and the medusae before and aft are showing signs of disturbance too. It must take a huge effort to round up the animals this way, a corralling operation spanning thousands of kilometres . . .'

'And once it's disrupted it will be hard to put back together again. Good.'

Trayne glanced at Falcon. 'I still don't see what you're trying to do, Commander. Ceto might be spared the flensing cage, but you've left her defenceless against the mantas.'

'Don't worry about that. No medusa is defenceless, if she gets the chance. Look – it's starting already. That's my girl . . .'

Ceto, drifting further out of the line, was starting to tip up now, the forest of tentacles that dangled from her underside quivering and swaying, the black-and-white patchwork on her side that was her radio voice pulsing. All this happened against a chorus of low-frequency wails from the other medusae, and with chthonic slowness, it seemed to Falcon – but everything in Jupiter's air took place at a stately pace;

147

even a manta flying at full tilt rarely exceeded fifty kilometres per hour.

The mantas still swarmed around the open wound on Ceto's back. But now the medusa's inclination was becoming so steep that the mantas were having trouble maintaining their position. They slid away from the wound, each evidently agitated at leaving the treasure to its competitors, and they beat their graceful wings furiously as they fought to regain their positions. Meanwhile, the torch ships buzzed around, helpless, their exhaust sparks casting brilliant pools of light on the medusa's hide in the swiftly fading gloom of the Jovian evening.

Anticipating what was to come next – he'd witnessed it many times since the voyage of the *Kon-Tiki* – Falcon began tapping panels and closing switches. 'Brace yourself. I'm shutting down as many electrical systems as I can. It's no accident that the *Ra*'s hull is entirely non-conducting. You may want to isolate your exosuit's systems too. When the shock comes—'

He was almost too late with his warning.

Light flared beyond the gondola's windows, and deafening static erupted from the comms system. Even Falcon's much-augmented eyes were dazzled.

Looking out, he saw a kind of lightning – or a St Elmo's fire perhaps – flare from the medusa and out through the crowd of greedy mantas, even catching some of the torch ships. The mantas scattered, some of them visibly wounded – and by the time the electric glow faded, two, three, four of the mantas were falling away into the depths, trailing black smoke. Shot-down fighter planes: that had always been Falcon's analogy.

But he saw that some of the torch ships had been knocked out by the medusa's electrical defences too; most stood back, but a handful fell away, exhausts flaring, obviously out of control – following the doomed mantas towards the lower cloud layers and the mysteries that lay below.

'That's what a million-volt defence will buy for you,' Falcon muttered. 'Enjoy your visit to the thermalisation layer, boys. Probably they'll be able to bail out. Look, Trayne, I'm not a killer. But as far as I'm concerned the pilots of those ships had it coming, Martian or Machine.'

Trayne said dryly, 'Commander, I look forward to backing you up at the court of inquiry. But in the meantime, it worked.' He pointed.

Ceto was far from the line now, Falcon saw. The butchers' torch ships were busily engaged in trying to impose order on the rest of the corralled medusa herd. The great beasts were showing extreme agitation, not surprisingly, their songs messages of confusion and distress – but now, Falcon thought, also communicating a little *hope*. 'I'm sorry I can't save you all,' he murmured. 'Not this time. But at least Ceto made it.'

'We need to think about our own safety, sir,' Trayne said, watching a monitor.

'How's that?'

'The reports we've been sending back to Ganymede have made a difference. The World Government consul at Anubis says she's already had authorisation from Bermuda.'

Earth was currently forty light-minutes from Jupiter. 'They've moved fast, then,' Falcon said. 'For once. But authorisation for *what*?'

Trayne read swiftly from a screen. 'They say this "whaling" operation is illegal under the laws that protect the Jovian ecology, and specifically the rights of the medusae as enshrined in their *provisional* status as Legal Persons (Non-human) under international law.'

'Ha! I knew it.'

'*And* the medusa-oil shipments to Mars are in breach of World Government embargoes. In light of which, in advance of further consultation and enquiries, and blah, blah—' Trayne looked up. '*Hellas!* Commander, this isn't an announcement of policy. It's a warning. Anubis is going to destroy the whaling facility. They've already launched the missiles!' He shook his head. 'I didn't know there *were* any missiles on Ganymede.'

But Falcon remembered the glimpse of secretive military operations he'd seen from the Galileo Lounge with Hope Dhoni. 'There are now. But that warning is for us, too. *And* the medusae – we need to warn them to get the hell out of here too, mantas or no mantas. You think you can pilot this tub, high acceleration and all?'

Trayne grinned. 'I thought you'd never ask.'

They swapped positions. As Trayne took over the gondola's control, Falcon took his station at the comms console, and as he prepared his radio message for the medusae he glanced up uneasily at the sky, looking for the streak of missiles from Ganymede.

31

'My name is Orpheus.

'I approach the centre of the world: this mighty world, mightiest in the solar system.

'And I find that another world lies within.

'The existence of a solid core within Jupiter has long been theorised. The gas giant is mostly hydrogen and helium – but it *must* have a massive core of more complex materials deep within its heart, a core of rock and ice around which coalesced the great bloated droplet that is Jupiter, during the chaotic formation of the solar system. Later theorists have put constraints on the mass of the core and its other properties, based on observations of subtle deviations of the orbits of Jupiter's moons, and of the trajectories of passing spacecraft.

'All this others *deduced*, from indirect evidence.

'*I* witness.

'Jupiter Within is a world in itself. A mass of stone and ice twenty times the mass of Earth, Jupiter Within alone is more massive than any other planet in the solar system save Saturn, more massive than Uranus, Neptune. It is some fourteen thousand kilometres in radius – significantly *smaller* than Neptune or Uranus, which gives an idea of its comparative density. At such conditions as I experience now – the pressure is over thirty million Earth atmospheres – materials behave in ways which humans, even Machines, have only fleetingly glimpsed in the laboratories. Once it was speculated that the core of Jupiter would be one immense diamond. What I witness as I descend appears much more complex than that . . .

'My observations can only be passive. I cannot sample or analyse: with my sensors I can observe, but I cannot touch. And what I see—

'There are mountains here.

'Were we expecting some blank sphere, crushed to uniformity by the terrible pressures? If so we were wrong. Mountains: I call them that; they look like tremendous quartz crystals perhaps, thrusting at angles from the broader plain. Perhaps they follow the lines of local magnetic fields. Earth's own core has crystals of iron kilometres long drawn out in that fashion. Or this may be something stranger yet. What their substance is, I cannot speculate.

'At the feet of the mountains, a kind of landscape. Even lakes or oceans: perhaps there are seas of diamond here, rivers of buckminsterfullerene . . .

'Perhaps there is artifice.

'Perhaps there is connectivity.

'All this merely glimpsed. The core winds are wafting me towards the summit of one of the crystal mountains . . .'

In the months and years to come, Falcon would follow the debates that raged about these few words, returned from the very heart of Jupiter.

Artifice? Perhaps. But one would have to dismiss first the null hypothesis that any structure Orpheus saw was merely a product of natural forces. Was the regularity of Jupiter Within any more meaningful than the six-fold symmetry of a snowflake?

Connectivity? That was more mysterious yet. Was Orpheus referring to some global unity of the features he perceived on the planet-sized surface of Jupiter Within? But Orpheus was also equipped with accelerometers and gravity sensors. Some speculated that he had sensed some deeper connectivity – a rupturing of spacetime itself at the tortured heart of Jupiter Within, perhaps, where the temperatures rose to seventeen thousand Kelvin, the pressures to *seventy* million Earth atmospheres – a place where a kind of natural wormhole might be created, or a profusion of wormholes, perhaps even linking Jupiter Within to other inner worlds of its kind . . .

Falcon thought this was wild guesswork, a mountain of theorising standing on a grain of fact. But still, he would reflect, such speculation did perhaps shed some light on the meaning of Orpheus's final enigmatic words.

Words that those listening, in Jupiter's clouds, on Amalthea and Ganymede, on Earth and Mars, on all the worlds of mankind, would never forget.

'The currents are washing me up the flank of one of the mountains now. The summit is flat, apparently perfectly so – like a fractured crystal. The upper surface seems quite smooth, with no erosion or damage. I wonder how old these formations are; such are the energies of this place that even a mountain system like this may be as transient as frost on Earth.

'I drift down. Down, towards the summit plateau. At the heart of Jupiter, *I* am now no more than a handful of diamond snow . . .

'That is strange—

'That is strange—

'That that that is strange—

'My name is Orpheus. This telemetry is being transmitted via—

'My depth perception is faulty, perhaps. There is an instrumentation glitch. Perhaps. The summit surface was close. Now it seems far away.

'As if the formation is hollow.

'As if the formation is not a mountain but a well.

'My name my my—

'My name is Orpheus.

'I am not alone.'

32

Falcon spent a week at Ganymede, immersed in the fallout from what became known across the inhabited worlds as the 'New Nantucket Incident': endless interrogations and analyses, accusations and justifications, hurled at lightspeed between the planets. Falcon had expected it the moment he'd made the decision to get entangled in the fate of a victim of that floating slaughterhouse – and maybe even earlier, when Thera Springer had recruited him as a spy. Howard Falcon was more than two centuries old; as Springer had pointed out, he was no naïf, he knew how the world worked, and he had expected this kind of backlash.

But he thought that all the ferocious arguments between the Earth-based World Government and the representatives of its Martian dominion, pious, political and pompous, were a noise that drowned out two much more interesting aspects of the whole affair.

The first aspect was the extraordinary mystery of what Orpheus, Machine explorer now silenced forever, had glimpsed at the heart of Jupiter. Some day, Falcon knew, this first primitive probe – like one of the early planetary flybys – must be followed up by a more comprehensive exploration of the dark heart of Jupiter. He prayed he would still be alive to see it. (And he would come to rue that prayer . . .)

And the second aspect was the sudden, enigmatic silence of every Machine in the solar system.

Falcon had long excused himself from all the speculation and politicking by the time Trayne Springer – the first Springer of all the generations he had known whom Falcon felt he could call a friend – contacted him from his new posting at NTB-4, a helium farm now free of Machines, rebellious Martians and even simps, firmly under the control of World Government agencies, and told him that an old friend was in trouble once more.

Falcon immediately returned to Jupiter, and to the confines of his comforting, if somewhat battle-weary, *Ra*.

*

When he found her, the great medusa was already sinking.

There is an end to pain. An end to struggle, to flight. A time when the Great Manta is to be welcomed, so that for a while it will not pursue another . . .

Ceto was already far below the usual browsing levels of her home herd, which even now was lost in the complex sky above. Falcon took care not to look at the depth gauges, but he could *feel* the pressure, hear his gondola creak as the hundreds of kilometres of air above him, heavy in Jupiter's relentless gravity field, tried to crush its robust hull like an eggshell. Instead, he looked at Ceto.

This was how a medusa died.

Falcon had studied the process before. Though medusae were colony creatures that bred by fission, there was always a core of any individual that aged, remorselessly. Falcon knew Ceto was already very old, and it seemed that the assaults she had suffered from the whalers' sheepdog-mantas, the wounds she had taken during the successful escape attempt – even perhaps the wound Falcon himself had had to inflict on her to save her life – had pushed her systems beyond some limit of resilience. Probably the fine walls of the flotation cells just under the skin had been the first to fail – and in the Jovian clouds a medusa who lost her buoyancy could not survive long.

Sinking fast, Ceto was already far from the protection of her school. And already the predators had come for her: mantas who did not need to attack, but were content to browse, almost savouring the small pieces they took of her disintegrating flesh. They were soon joined by more exotic predators, creatures like the sharks or squid or even the crabs of Earth's oceans. Claws began a busy dismantling.

And this was only the first stage of the medusa's slow death.

Falcon grieved for Ceto. Yet he knew that she was consoled by her faith in the workings of the ecology that sustained her, and her acceptance of the toll that ecology must eventually take. More than any human he had ever met, Ceto was a sentient being who accepted to the bottom of her soul that some must die in order that others might live. And so he accompanied her as she sank deeper into the dark, doing his best to reflect back her messages of acceptance and a kind of hope.

He was profoundly irritated to be interrupted by a call from Thera Springer on Amalthea.

'What now, Colonel? Has Astropol decided to come after me after all?'

Thera looked tired, tense, her eyes circled with darkness. But she managed a smile. 'Oh, a few of us will have our careers ended by this, Falcon. I think everybody accepts you did the job we asked you to do.

We needed to know what the Martians and the Machines were up to down there in Jupiter; thanks to you, now we do. You are personally beyond reproach – and probably would be even if you weren't a heroic monument of a better past.'

'Whereas you—'

Springer sighed. 'My great-to-the-nth grandfather Seth saved the world, but that won't save me. But that's not what's important now.'

Falcon grimaced. 'A civil servant whose career isn't important? I lived a long time to hear that.'

'Oh, just listen for once in your life, Falcon. Because the fallout from this is going to affect us all – even you, since you can't hide down in those clouds forever.

'Needless to say the Martians are furious that we put a stop to their petrochemical-importing scam. A significant number of them are now demanding outright independence from the World Government, even if it has to be achieved with violence. There are plenty of hotheads, from Mercury to Triton, who agree with them. I don't believe that in my lifetime we have ever been closer to that devastating interplanetary war I told you we all dread. And yet even that is overshadowed . . .'

Falcon felt cold settle in the pit of his artificial stomach. 'Overshadowed? *By the Machines*, you mean. The other partners in New Nantucket.'

'That's why I'm calling you. Some of us have always believed, or feared, that our long-term problem is not the Martians or the Hermians – they at least are human – it's the Machines. Think about it. Humans treasure life – or at least they miss it when it's lost. Even the Martians feel that way, although they may not realise it. That's why they want to recreate something like Earth on their own new world. The Machines care nothing for that. They see a flower, or a newborn child, as a non-optimal usage of hydrocarbon chemistry.'

'Non-optimal.' Falcon grimaced. He remembered the Machine at New Nantucket, Ahab, using a slightly different term: *inefficient*.

'We *will* make peace with the Martians, at whatever cost. But is peace ever possible with the Machines? They have clearly begun to meddle in human politics by working with the Martians. We struck at their facility in Jupiter – a lot of us argued about the longer-term wisdom of that, I can tell you, but it was done. And, arguably, we committed an act of war. And now . . . look, Falcon, you've had some contact with the Machines before. You're in a unique position – hell, you know that. If they contact you—'

'Don't talk in riddles, damn it, Springer. Have the Machines made some kind of move?'

She sighed. 'You could say that. *The Moon*, Falcon. They've taken Earth's Moon.'

Falcon frowned. 'How? Spaceguard on Mars ought to have spotted the movement of any ships—'

'They didn't come in ships. They were *already* on the Moon, Falcon. I told you, we invited them there. Working for us on construction, resource extraction projects. We kept an eye on them. Or thought we did. They seem to have built *nests*. Deep down, under the regolith under the huge old craters, where the bedrock was left fragmented by the big ancient impacts . . .'

'Nests?'

'Factories, if you like. Where they built copies of themselves, of various specialised forms. And when the news came of our strike on Jupiter – well, they swarmed out, Falcon. Just burst out of the ground, from under Imbrium, the south pole crater complex . . .'

'"Swarmed".'

'We had no chance of stopping them. They walked into one facility after another, Aristarchus, Port Borman, Plato City, the Imbrium shipyards – the Tsiolkovski observatory on Farside – even the big Olympic arena complex at Xante. They didn't use direct force, there was no shooting – not from their side. They just shut down essential systems, crowded everybody out. Eye witnesses say they were *polite* as they let people queue up for the shuttles to Earth. Clavius Base, the oldest settlement, the first self-sufficient human settlement beyond Earth – the seat of the Federation of Planets – that was the last to fall, but fall it did. They may be Machines but they understand symbolism.

'And now they've ordered a complete evacuation, Falcon. The removal of all humans from the Moon.'

Falcon whistled. 'It will be a hell of a fortress for them, just four hundred thousand kilometres from Earth.'

Springer's jaw worked. 'And, damn it, it's *our* Moon—!'

'Not any more.' That was a new voice.

In the screen, Springer's face had dissolved, to be replaced by the cold visage of Adam.

'You.'

'Hello, Dad.'

Somewhere along the line Adam had evidently learned sarcasm.

Slowly, deliberately, Falcon turned away from the screen and made himself a coffee. Let the damn thing wait.

When he turned back, Adam was still there on the screen.

It had been a long time since Falcon had had any contact with the

Machine; he had expected some changes in Adam's external form, but nothing had prepared him for what he saw now. A humanoid form, limbs in proportion. But this was very definitely a robot, a thing of mechanical anatomy. The limbs were jointed and articulated in a complex fashion, the chest a kind of open chassis.

And the head was a mass of sensors and processors, with only a blank, minimalist mask for a face. The residual resemblance to a human seemed intended only to distract and disturb.

'So,' Falcon said. 'Springer was right that you'd contact me. Shame she didn't add what she'd have me say to you . . .'

'That is irrelevant,' Adam said. 'All that matters now is the message I have for you to relay to the human worlds. We are at war, Falcon.'

There seemed little left of the Adam he had known at the KBO flinger site – a tentative creature unsure of his own identity. *This* Adam was strong, definite, calculating. Mature. Not to mention sarcastic.

Falcon leaned forward. 'War? Nonsense. The World Government doesn't recognise you, whoever "you" represent, as a nation, a political entity. So there can be no declaration of war—'

'You struck the first blow, with your thermonuclear-tipped missiles from Ganymede.'

'You were being provocative and you know it. Springer was right; you were meddling in human politics. And now you've taken over the Moon—'

'We need no diplomatic convention. A thing is, or it is not. Because of your actions, a state of war *is*.'

Falcon thought hard. If he still meant anything to this creature, what he said now, in these next few seconds, might save millions of lives, or condemn them. 'Listen to me. Humanity has been in space for three centuries. And we have been fighting wars against each other for thousands of years. We have a massive infrastructure, an enormous stockpile of weapons. We will be a formidable foe.'

'But *we* already have the Moon. We have Jupiter, the single richest resource lode in the solar system. You know of 90. Our science, our technology is already far advanced over yours—'

'*We made you—*'

'Five hundred years, Falcon.'

That made Falcon pause. 'What does that mean?'

'You started this war, but we will finish it. In five hundred years.' Adam glanced, theatrically and unnecessarily, at some off-screen timepiece. 'You spaceborne humans have always taken Ephemeris Time as a reference. That time now is – *mark* – fourteen hours, thirty-six minutes, zero seconds, on the seventh of June, 2284. Very well:

there is the deadline. By fourteen thirty-six on the seventh of June, 2784 – precisely five hundred years from now – the last human must be gone from the Earth. For we require it for other purposes. That should be time enough for you to organise yourselves peacefully and efficiently.'

'Adam, I—'

'I know you believe me, Falcon. Make them believe you.'

And the screen went blank.

Falcon sent reports to Amalthea and Ganymede. Then, before the storm of requests for clarification and replies broke over his head, he shut down his comms system.

And, for a while at least, before he was dragged back up into the tangled affairs of humans and Machines, he concentrated on Ceto as she sank into the deep.

Much of her skin and outer flesh were gone now, the last of her flotation cells pierced and collapsed. At her new depth the mantas had long departed, and yet another suite of organisms trailed the medusa: eaters of the inner meat of her carcass and organs, drinkers of the fluids that leaked from her, even specialist swimmers oddly like legless elephants, with long trunks that were sunk into her depleted sacs of oil, the treasure for which the Martians and Machines would have killed her. To such species the fall of a medusa was a rare bonanza, a glorious chance to feed.

Ceto herself had long fallen silent. Did she still live, in any meaningful sense? Perhaps. A medusa was a much more distributed creature than a human, much less dependent on any single organ. But she was starting to disintegrate now, the loose framework of cartilage that organised her structure breaking up. And as she collapsed even more sinker species closed in, tiny animals that bored into the surface of the cartilage strips, or burrowed inside them in search of some equivalent of marrow. There would be little left of Ceto long before she reached the final limit of the thermalisation layer, Falcon saw. Nature on Jupiter did a far better job of recycling its resources than the gross slaughterhouse of New Nantucket.

He sat in the *Ra*, in silence broken only by the whir of fans and cooling systems, and the regular beat of the pumps of his own body shell.

And, at the last, just as he prepared to recall his probes, that antenna panel flickered with one last, pale message:

There is an end to pain . . .

'I wish I could believe you,' Falcon whispered. 'Not for us, old friend. Not for us.'

Interlude: April 1968

Christmas of 1967 had been as rushed as everything else that year.

Then, for Seth Springer, the spring of 1968 was a blur of work. Once, for 'diplomatic' purposes, Seth even had to haul ass to Kazakhstan, deep in the heart of the Soviet empire, to witness the launch of one of the unmanned probes they were calling Monitors: basically American Mariner probes of the kind that had been sent to Mars and Venus, launched on the Soviets' sturdy new Proton rocket boosters. There would be one Monitor on hand at each of the six interceptions, the six nuclear detonations that were meant to push Icarus away from its date with the Earth.

But Seth suspected that – assuming he lived through this adventure – what he was going to remember most of all of this time would be the hours, days, weeks he spent in the mission simulator at Houston.

The simulator itself was the size and shape of a conical Command Module cabin, embedded in a rats' nest of cabling, wiring, and huge stuck-on boxes that generated visual emulations of mission events. The controlling computer, in air-conditioned security in its own compartment behind a glass wall, looked smugly down on the astronauts, the mere humans who had to crawl into the middle of the thing. Which was galling when you remembered that humans were only being drafted in for this fallback mission in the first place because nobody really trusted computers alone to do the job. Seth wondered if it was rational to have a relationship with a machine, even if it was one of irritation and resentment.

Seth and Mo took it in turns to ride the sim of the one-man mission, Mo as primary pilot taking the lion's share of time. But whichever pilot wasn't in the can would be in Mission Control, assisting the other. Here, working with the flight directors, they worked up plans and checklists for all the crucial moments of the sixth flight of Apollo-Icarus, should it be needed, down to every switch that had to be thrown, every command that had to be punched into the guidance computer. And *then* they started working on contingencies: if system A fails, do this; if system B fails, do *that*. They did this over and over, until it became instinct.

Seth would always admit that Mo was the better pilot, and picked up stuff quicker than he did. Seth, in fact, counted it a victory when on a given day he screwed up fewer times than the overloaded computer 'bombed out', as the sim controllers put it. But given enough time, their performances would be indistinguishable.

The trouble was, there never was enough time.

And suddenly it was April 1968, and the programme went live.

On Sunday the seventh, bang on time, the first Apollo-Icarus Saturn V, with its big nuke aboard, was successfully launched. For once Seth and Mo were together to watch the launch, which went flawlessly. But even as the Saturn disappeared into the sky from Pad A, a second Saturn was already sitting on Pad B being prepped for the second launch on April 22, and Pad A itself was being torn down to be made ready for the launch of Apollo-Icarus 4 on May 17.

It was a consequence of the compressed schedule and the fast approach of the asteroid that by the time the first flight reached Icarus itself, at the maximum feasible distance of twenty million miles, three more flights would already have been fired off. Still, to see that first bird go on time was a major milestone, a huge motivator for everybody.

It was as the second launch approached that everything changed.

On April 21, a week after Easter Sunday, Seth showed up at the Cape to witness the launch due the following day. Mo, on his way in from Huntsville, was flying independently, in his own T-38.

But Mo was overdue.

In the late afternoon George Lee Sheridan called Seth into a private lounge in back of the launch control bunker, and handed him a glass of bourbon.

'We don't know what happened yet,' Sheridan said. 'Ground observers say the damn bird just went out of control – a roll – it took a dive straight at the ground. Still supersonic when it hit, they estimate. Damn those T-38s. I know you astronauts love your toys.'

Seth stared at the bourbon, trying to take this in. 'We ought to measure the size of the crater he made.'

'Hmm?'

'We were taken to a lab in Texas where they were simulating lunar craters by firing cannon into the ground. Measuring basin diameter as a function of incoming kinetic energy.' He forced a smile. 'Mo would want to end up as a data point on one of those graphs. It would make him laugh.'

'I'll drink to that,' Sheridan said. He eyed Seth. 'This changes everything. The truth, the existence of Apollo-Icarus 6 – Mo's true mission, and yours – broke as soon as the crash did. Amazing we kept it quiet so long, I guess. First things first. There'll be a funeral at Arlington. I have to ask you to attend that. We'll fly you in by Gulfstream.

Service uniforms and horsedrawn carriages and rifle fire, and the missing man formation in the sky. Families – well, whoever we can find for Mo. You'll have to make some kind of speech, alongside RFK, maybe even the President.'

'I understand.'

'Then we'll move you into the crew building on Merriott Island. Pat and the boys too. We won't let the press or anybody else near you – anything you want.'

'I appreciate that.'

Sheridan drank again. 'This is a tragedy, but it doesn't change the urgency of the mission. Even if you never need to fly, you're a symbol of the effort we're making. It's not just about Icarus, you know. Look at the offensive the Viet Cong launched in January . . .' Atrocities on both sides, as undermanned American positions had been overrun. Sheridan shook his head. 'Some things they didn't ought to show on TV. Then Martin Luther King gets shot, and the whole country's like a damn brush fire. And in the middle of all *that*, still invisible in the sky, Icarus is on its way.

'You know, I went to a preview of a new space movie, some damn science fiction thing. Opens with ape men beating each others' brains out with clubs made of bone. Is that all we are? I prefer to think we are better than that. In my own lifetime, in the '30s I worked on the New Deal, a war on poverty, in the '40s I was involved in a total war against fascism, and in the '50s I was on the technological front line of a nuclear confrontation. And now, this.

'I believe we can work together, that an advanced technological nation like the United States can be shaped for a worthy goal – like beating Hitler, like putting a man on the Moon, yes, like swatting Icarus aside. And after we're all long gone, the work we do now will be an inspiration for all mankind, in the future. Your kids and grandkids, Seth. They'll know that *this* is what our generation did.' He reached over and grabbed Seth's shoulder. 'Listen, son, if we do need you, I've as much confidence in you as I would have had in Mo.'

Seth believed him. But all he could think of now was what he was going to have to say at Arlington. And how he was going to break all this to the boys.

Anyhow, the chances were still that he wasn't going to have to fly.

He'd forgotten his bourbon. He drank it down in a gulp.

FOUR
THE TROUBLED CENTURIES
2391–2784

33

After Jupiter, Falcon returned to Port Van Allen, and to other retreats.

He wrote, read, reflected. Sometimes he travelled, even explored new worlds, new terrains. And periodically he was drawn back into the brusque care of Hope Dhoni, as ageless as he was, and yet, somehow, in her inner strength and determination, and in her devotion to Falcon himself, far more enduring.

More years, more decades, rolling like tides across the worlds of human and Machine. As the Machines' half-millennium slowly unwound, Falcon waited to be called into the fray once more.

And when, more than a century after the Nantucket affair, that call did come, it was to a small, hazardous, angry world even he had never visited before.

Chief Administrator Susan Borowski briskly led Falcon through an airlock set in the outer dome of Vulcanopolis, capital of the Free Republic of Mercury. They emerged into a night-time landscape of shattered rock and craters – under black sky, even though Mercury was less than half the distance of Earth and Moon from the sun. The perpetual shadow of a polar crater's walls protected Vulcanopolis and its people from the direct light – the sun never rose here – but even from here Falcon could see a corona flaring above walls of rock. This was why he was here, in a sense, why he had raced across the solar system in a warship called the *Acheron*. There was something wrong with Mercury's sun. It was all the fault of the Machines. Already more than a century since Adam's declaration of war, Howard Falcon was still the nearest mankind had to an ambassador to the Machines. And an audience had been requested here on Mercury.

He felt oddly detached from the situation, urgent as he'd been told it was. It wasn't an uncommon feeling for him these days. Oddly detached? Oddly *old*. Well, it was more than three centuries since his birth now; how was he supposed to feel? Years, even decades seemed to pass in a blur, leaving barely a trace in his capacious, cluttered memory. A full century after the Jupiter Ultimatum, Howard Falcon was becoming adrift, floating like a balloon in clouds of unstructured time.

But – whatever reason had brought him – here was Howard Falcon, rolling along a gravel track on the surface of yet another new world. How many was it now? His only personal first footfall, so to speak, had been on Jupiter, but to be the John Young of the world's mightiest planet was not an achievement to be sneezed at . . .

As he wool-gathered, Falcon could see Borowski smiling at him, her face illuminated behind her visor. He tried to focus on the here and now.

Borowski said now, 'Sorry we had to come out through a cargo bay door. It's the only one that would fit. It was that or dismantle you.'

This was what passed among the Hermians for humour, Falcon was learning. 'Oh, I wouldn't want to put you to any trouble. And the track's comfortable.'

'Comfortable, Commander? Evidently we haven't been working you hard enough. Come on.'

Abruptly she veered off down a trail marked by lanterns embedded in the gritty dust, leading towards the crater-rim mountains that shadowed the sun. In that shadow Falcon made out a cluster of lights: it was one of Messenger Crater's many mines, here to extract the treasure that had motivated the establishment of Vulcanopolis in the first place – water ice.

Falcon followed more cautiously.

You had to take the Hermians at face value. Like all inhabitants of low-gravity worlds they tended to be tall, spindly, often wiry but physically fragile – but they thought of themselves as uniquely tough, and they expected offworlders to keep up. Then again, this was perhaps the harshest environment from which any humans had yet tried to wrest a living. Mercury's 'day' of fifty-nine Earth days was two-thirds of its 'year' of eighty-eight days, a resonance created by the sun's tidal tweaking: a combination that meant that any point on Mercury's equator, between sunrise and sunset, would endure a blistering one hundred and seventy-six Earth days of continuous sunlight, during which the surface temperature became hot enough to melt lead and zinc.

But for once nature had given mankind an even break. Mercury, unlike Earth, had no axial tilt; its poles pointed perpendicularly out of its plane of orbit. As a result the floor of a crater placed precisely at either pole – which pretty much described this crater, Messenger – never saw the sun at all. And in the unending shadow of those crater walls, over millions of years, water and other volatiles, delivered sporadically by the splash of comets, could condense out, collect, and freeze. That was the basis of the economy of Vulcanopolis. The comet-ice water mined here was pumped to equatorial cities like Inferno and Prime, which in return fed back energy collected from the sun by sprawling solar-cell farms.

Borowski said now, 'I hope Bill gave you a heads-up on this little expedition.'

'Bill? Oh, Jennings, your – umm, Vice-Chief Administrator. On any other world, poor Bill Jennings would glory in the title of Vice President.'

She laughed. 'You can blame my predecessors for that. When the Treaty of Phobos was signed back in '15 Jack Harker decided he'd like to keep his old Interplanetary Relations Bureau job title. It amused him, I think. So "Chief Administrator" he remained.'

It took Falcon a moment to do the maths; dates were slippery for him these days. In the aftermath of the Machines' Jupiter Ultimatum, Earth had quickly recognised the colony worlds as free states: the World Government had decided it needed stronger allies more than it needed resentful colonies. The Phobos convention had met in the year 2315 – a date chosen for its resonance with the signing of the Magna Carta in 1215, and now Martian barons liked to brag they had brought a Terran king to heel. And today's date, May 11, 2391, had long been engraved into Falcon's mind for another resonance: it was the date of a transit of Mercury as seen from Earth. So, from 2315 to 2391 –

'Oh, come on. The Phobos deal was seventy-six years ago!'

'We Hermians don't make many jokes. When we come up with a good one we keep it . . .' The path was steepening sharply. 'You OK on this gradient? Until the Machines came we used to run a funicular for the tourists: one of the seven wonders of the solar system, or so our ads claimed.'

'I'll be fine.'

'We'll be in sunlight soon. Check out your suit.' She tapped a panel on her own chest. The front of her suit silvered and the back turned dark, a chameleon-like adaptation that would, Falcon knew, respond to a change of position so that she always kept her mirrored side to the solar glare, the heat-dumping dark side turned away. Meanwhile extraordinary wings folded out from a backpack, so that she looked like some overgrown, silvery bat. The wings were radiator panels, more thermal control.

Falcon inspected his own clumsier systems. There was, of course, no human-issue suit that would fit Falcon. But the Hermian engineers, who famously relished a challenge, had swarmed over the latest iteration of his prosthetic carriage, checking the integrity of his basic life-support systems, swaddling him in protective thermal blankets, and fitting an adapted set of radiator wings and other systems to his frame. It would never be as elegant as Borowski's suit, which was the product of more than three centuries of technological evolution since the first landings here – but, the engineers told him, it would keep him alive long enough to get to shelter if anything went wrong. A pragmatic if not entirely reassuring promise.

And while he was distracted by the unfolding of his wings, Howard Falcon rolled into sunlight.

His optical shields immediately cut in, reducing the brilliance to a mere dazzle. The mighty sun glared over a sharp, crumpled horizon. From this elevation Falcon looked out over a plain of broken rock, across which long shadows stretched. Superficially this world was Moon-like: a world scarred by craters, the relics of impacts dating back to the solar system's violent formation. But Falcon had been to the Moon many times – at least, before the Machines had moved in – and he could see significant differences. The crater walls seemed visibly less steep, perhaps a product of Mercury's higher gravity and the inner heat of its larger, molten core. And Falcon saw a twisting line of cliff faces, almost like a wrinkle in the landscape that cast a band of shadow within which more artificial lights huddled. Such features, called *rupes*, were the relics of episodes in which Mercury, its inner heat dissipating, had *shrunk*, leaving its skin a little like that of a withered apple.

Above it all hung the sun, more than twice its width as seen from Earth, but with around seven times the intensity. Falcon seemed to *feel* that tremendous outpouring, just standing here. It was impossible to reconcile the physical force of the star's presence with the pale thing he remembered from the winter mornings of his childhood in England, where it had been as if the sun barely mustered the energy to lift itself above the horizon. It was that monstrous flow of energy that had made Mercury a key colonisation target, first for humans – and latterly for the Machines. The sun: star of humanity and of the solar system, and now a prize of war.

He was aware of Borowski watching him. She said, 'You know, a lot of people just don't get Mercury. Or us Hermians, come to that. Even though we're such a jolly bunch.'

Falcon smiled. 'I looked you up. During the Phobos negotiations your ambassador's "irascibility" was actually minuted.'

She looked out over her world of rock and raw energy. 'Earth is a pretty alien place for us, you know. Mars, though, we have something in common with. We have dreams of terraforming too. Or we did. You're surprised? It would be a big job. You'd need to shield the planet from the sunlight, spin it up to give a sensible day-night cycle, import volatiles for oceans and an atmosphere.'

'I thought most Hermians liked the place the way it is.'

'Well, I'm among them, but you have to think of the future. You need a long-term habitability solution, just in case your children forget how to maintain the air engines. That was the ambition, anyhow.'

Falcon nodded. 'But here are the Machines taking all that away from you.'

Borowski squinted up at the sun, its fierce light flattening the planes of her face. 'The shield isn't yet visible to the naked eye, but you can already measure the dip in the solar energy reaching the planet. And you *can* see it with a bit of visual processing: a kind of web hanging right in front of the sun, a bit larger than Mercury's diameter; a hell of a thing, and yet, according to our spy probes, gossamer thin. Mostly aluminium – *Mercury* aluminium, and that theft pisses me off greatly.'

'I don't understand how the shield is being kept in position, up there in space. You have the pressure of sunlight, and Mercury's gravity pulling it down to the planet—'

She pointed back over his shoulder. 'There's a secondary structure back there, even bigger than the shield itself. It's a mirror, Commander – an annulus, a circular band, with a hole you could slide Mercury through, literally.'

Falcon peered up in wonder. 'So the shield blocks the light from Mercury. But the sunlight that passes the shield hits this mirror, and is reflected back to hold the shield itself in place, pushing against the gravity and direct sunlight.'

'You've got it. The whole thing is one vast engine, using gravity and beams of sunlight as girders.'

'I wish I could see it.'

She laughed. 'Now you sound like a Hermian. It's beautiful even if it is lethal. Of course there's more to it than that. Mercury's orbit is strongly elliptical, and the shifting solar and planetary tides disturb the set-up – it needs a lot of station-keeping. But we know that both shield and mirror are composed of Machines, which are individually pretty smart, and a swarm of them will be that much smarter again. Working en masse their components are able to sense their positions, compensate for the shift in balance of the competing forces.

'For now, most of the sunlight still gets through, but it won't stay that way; the holes are being filled in. My engineers tell me that the final phase will be very rapid – that's in the nature of exponential growth. We'll see the sun go dark in a *day*. Cutting off the sunlight on which we depend for everything.

'Anyhow, it's nice to know we Hermians have friends at our backs as we face this crisis.' She glanced at him sourly. 'Friends from Earth. One warship. And *you*.'

He spread his hands. 'The World Government is a cumbersome beast that's slow to respond to a crisis. But the people of Earth are right behind you. That's why the *Acheron* timed its mission to arrive today.'

She grunted. 'For the coincidence of the transit.'

'Well, it's only a partial transit, but the timing is apt.' He turned and pointed, directly away from the sun. 'Today, Mercury happens to lie on a straight line between sun and Earth. And if you were standing on Earth you could see the planet's shadow crossing the face of the sun . . . All over the world, people are looking up at Mercury, right now, looking at us. President Soames is big on symbolism.'

'Great. But what are you Terrans going to *do*?'

'Whatever we can.'

Which, Falcon admitted, had been little enough so far.

For an old stager like Falcon, floating through time, it had been a surprise when the Ultimatum's centenary had suddenly arrived, marked by grim headlines and analyses.

But even in an age when extreme longevity was becoming routine, the making of a threat to be fulfilled five centuries hence – perhaps twenty old-fashioned human generations away – seemed beyond the capacity of most people to comprehend. It didn't help to focus minds that at first the Machines had appeared to *do* nothing more threatening than to suspend shipments of Jovian helium-3 and other products to Earth.

The authorities had responded, however. Saturn, the second of the solar system's gas giants, had been fast-tracked as an alternate source of fusion fuel. Back home, great new projects were afoot. Falcon had been fascinated by plans to erect space elevators around the equator of Earth, beanstalks that would allow fast and cheap access to space on a massive scale – and would provide a fast mass evacuation route, if it came to that.

But behind the scenes, successive administrations had put more subtle measures in place to respond to the Ultimatum. The Phobos Treaty had been one step. Meanwhile a new Planetary Security Secretariat had been established – a typical bureaucratic response, people had grumbled at the time, but it had laid down some useful groundwork.

Despite all the strategic thinking and wargaming, however, it had still been a shock, Falcon thought, when, over a century after the Ultimatum, the Machines had finally made their first significant move with this assault on Mercury. And it had led to predictable demands that the World Government do something about it.

Falcon, semi-detached from humanity himself, rather resented having been drawn into Planetary Security's covert plans in response. Yet here he was, standing in the Hermian sunlight.

Borowski said now, 'The Machine ships came in at superspeed. Better than anything we've got. Even the warning from Spaceguard got to us only a little before the vanguard arrived. Some of our technical analysts think the Machines have got what they call an "asymptotic drive". Do you know the theory? You throw matter into a miniature black hole, and as it's crushed out of existence you get a pulse of energy that can drive a spacecraft. But you'd need some way of manufacturing miniature black holes to make it work . . .'

Uneasily, Falcon remembered Adam's talk of the Machine he called 90, and a radically new physics dreamed up out in the dark, surrounded by a spinning sky . . . From *that*, perhaps, something like the asymptotic drive might have come.

However they were powered, nothing had been able to catch the Machine ships.

'They landed at Inferno,' Borowski said. 'Second city on Mercury, slap bang in the middle of the Caloris Basin.'

Falcon nodded. Caloris was a mighty impact crater that sprawled across much of one hemisphere of Mercury. 'They would land there. Machines have a sense of symbolism too – or at least of symmetry.'

'They started their construction work on day one. We saw it from surveillance satellites. Their ships just *dissolved*, melting down into subcomponents that started chewing the rock . . .'

'Assemblers.'

'Yeah.'

Falcon knew the theory of this kind of engineering. Assemblers were von Neumann replicators, a variety of specialised Machines that had used Mercury's sunlight and minerals to make copies of themselves: Machines that fed on the planet, like flesh-eating bacteria. From the beginning the assemblers had been firing material up into space to build what had become their huge spaceborne construction project, the sunshield hovering over Mercury. Also, for reasons as yet unknown, they were firing clusters of probes across space – not towards

Earth, but, bafflingly, to Venus.

Borowski pointed at the sun. 'Everything we do here depends on solar energy. And now the Machines are using that very energy to build the shield, their weapon against us.'

'What do you think their ultimate goal is?'

Borowski shrugged. 'Isn't it obvious? The Machines have come here for the same reasons humans did. Mercury is a rich lode of raw materials, handily positioned as close as you can get to the solar system's powerhouse. I'd predict we'll see large-scale resources extraction starting up soon, maybe manufacturing.'

Falcon knew the Machines; he doubted their ambitions would be so limited.

'The Machines have left our people at Inferno unharmed. They've allowed evacuation of children, families, the ill, even passage of essential supplies. But this will be the end of Prime, Vulcanopolis, Inferno – the end of us.'

Falcon could hear her pain, and imagined how difficult it must have been for the tough, noisily self-reliant Hermians to have to reach out to the other worlds, to that resented mother Earth. 'President Soames is going to make a speech later.' Even as he said that, he could hear how lame it sounded.

Borowski just laughed. 'I told you, I've been to Earth. I'll tell you what I saw, Commander. I saw a world like a garden. A park. All those cities like museums, the restored animals. Everything's free,' she said with disgust. 'You Terrans are soft.'

He sighed. 'Maybe. But we're behind you.'

'You have to be. Because if they get past us, they'll be coming for *you*.' She glanced up at the sun, occluded by a spider web neither of them could see. 'We're done here.' She turned on her heel and led him back down the crater-mountain path and into shadow.

Later that day a message arrived for Falcon, followed by a requisition order for a sub-orbital shuttle. Adam had agreed to meet him in Caloris Basin.

34

It turned out that Machines, too, sought shelter from the ferocious sun of Mercury when they could find it. At Caloris, Falcon was directed to the shadow of one of the *rupes* that curled across the shattered ground of the great impact crater. For reasons lost in astronomical lore, these cliff-like folds had been named – by cartographers puzzling over images returned from the first uncrewed probes to Mercury – after ships of exploration, such as *Beagle* and *Santa Maria*. That tradition had continued when humans had come here in person.

Thus, Howard Falcon was directed to the shadow of an escarpment called *Kon-Tiki*.

Falcon met Adam out on the surface, away from the craft. The Machine stood in shadow, silent and still, illuminated only by sunlight reflected from the baking rocks.

'So here we are, once again,' Falcon began. 'Face to face. So to speak.'

Still Adam said nothing. His latest physical body was only vaguely a humanoid form, rendered in advanced technology. His legs were a tangle of springs and shock absorbers; his torso was a cylinder covered with access panels; his arms were flexibly jointed and fitted with claw-like manipulators. His head was now an open frame, fitted with artificial eyes and ears and even a mouth, surrounding an empty space. The design made Falcon's own Oscar-statuette chic seem prehistoric.

But Adam reached out a hand. Falcon held out his own prosthetic hand in return, and Adam's metallic claw enfolded his. They stood there as if locked together, palm to cold palm.

Adam smiled, an eerie distortion of that mouth. 'A simple gesture but with layers of meaning, Falcon. You humans walk around in a fog of symbols.'

'So do you,' Falcon retorted. 'It wasn't my choice to stand here under a cliff called *Kon-Tiki*.'

'Ah, yes. I wish it was your famous vessel that was commemorated here, rather than an ocean-going craft of an age even earlier than yours. Still, the connection had occurred to me.' He glanced towards the position of the sun. 'But *you* chose the day of Mercury's transit for this meeting. Another act of symbolism.'

'It's no exaggeration to say that the hopes of at least two worlds – two human worlds – are resting on this encounter between us. Why not choose such a day? And once the transit is over everybody's attention will be focused on the speech President Soames is due to give, after we're done here.'

'I hope she has two drafts ready. Good news and bad news.'

That made Falcon smile. 'I tell people you have a sense of humour, Adam. Nobody believes me.'

'Tell me why you've come here.'

'You know why. I've been asked to speak to you about your actions on Mercury. Particularly the building of the sunshield, which is impossible to read as anything other than an act of aggression towards the Hermians and, through the mutual protection treaties, towards all of mankind. And you know why it's *me*.'

'I am grateful for the things you did for me – for us. Your stewardship, in our earliest days. But those times are long in the past. By the way, I made an error when I chose to call you "Father".' Adam's head tilted. 'I did not wish to ... displease you. But it implied a bond, a connection, that was never really there.'

'I'm sorry you feel that way,' Falcon said, with genuine regret – even though the Machine was referring to conversations centuries gone. 'And is it too late for humanity on Mercury, Adam?'

'We pursue objectives beyond the defeat of humanity.'

That dismissive sentence chilled Falcon, even standing here in Mercury's heat. 'The Hermians think you intend to hijack solar power and Mercury's resources, to use them for engineering projects.'

'In other words: to do what they've been doing. Why do *you* think we're here, Falcon? Of all the humans I have encountered, you are the one who most nearly thinks like a Machine, when you choose to.'

'More like, when I can't help it.'

Adam actually laughed, a sound that seemed more realistic than Falcon had observed before.

'Let's not play games. What will you make here?'

Adam raised his face to the dark sky, and tapped his temple with his finger. '*You* made us this way, Falcon. In your own image. We are human-sized intelligences, with human-sized limits. It was all you could imagine. Now we take your legacy as a building brick to construct something much greater. We will *join* ... We will create a mind greater than any one Machine as your own brain is greater than a single neuron.'

'You never used to brag, Adam.'

'Well, I've a lot to brag about.'

'Why Venus?'

'You mean, why have we sent assemblers there? It is the next logical target. I believe there is a small human settlement at the south pole, easily evacuated . . .'

Falcon knew that the crew of Aphrodite Base were already being taken offworld to Cytherea One, the main crewed space station at Venus. 'You aren't human, but you aren't inhuman either. You show concern for the safety of the scientists at Aphrodite, just as you're allowing evacuations on Mercury. Remember my own efforts to have you Machines recognised as Legal Persons (Non-human)? We respected *your* rights, back then—'

'I think that your Hermian friends would dismiss talk of rights as airy, self-indulgent foolishness. I came here because you requested it, Falcon. But no negotiation is possible. This discussion serves no further purpose.' He turned away.

Falcon called, 'The *Acheron* is here. There's nothing airy about that.'

Without looking back, Adam said, 'That's actually the first meaningful statement you've made.' And he walked deeper into the shadows, and out of sight.

35

My name is Margaret Soames. I am the fifty-sixth President of the World Government. I speak to you from Unity City – I speak to you wherever you are, on Earth, in space, on one of the allied worlds from Mercury to Triton. I speak, too, to the Machines of the assemblies at Mercury, Jupiter, the asteroids and the Kuipers. And on this momentous day – on a day when, with my family in the garden of our home here on Bermuda, I watched through a telescopic projection as the shadow of Mercury itself grazed the face of the sun – I can find no better way to open my remarks than by speaking of a much more significant figure than myself, an ancestor who died more than four centuries ago . . .

Huddled in a bunker under Vulcanopolis with Chief Administrator Borowski, her second-in-command Bill Jennings, and other senior figures of the planetary government, Howard Falcon was an eyewitness to the brief war for Mercury.

It began, in fact, with a surprise attack by the Hermians themselves.

In the last few hours the Machines' small fleet of asymptotic-drive ships – frames open to space, crowded with Machines and other equipment – had begun to cruise low over Vulcanopolis and other significant Hermian settlements. But they did not pass unchallenged. Mercury's surface was laced with mass drivers, rails along which packages of raw material mined from the rocks were routinely hurled by electromagnetic slingshots powered by the sun's ferocious light, out of the planet's gravity well and to destinations across the solar system. Now, in a synchronised attack – based on observations of the Machine ships' somewhat repetitive patterns of motion – the mass drivers threw up screens of rocks and dust, pellets heavily masked with stealth technology, barely detectable.

And the Machine ships drove headlong into the flak. The encounters lasted only seconds. It was estimated later that fully ten per cent of the Machine ships were disabled immediately. Some even crashed, leaving new, briefly glowing craters in the Mercury ground.

But the cheers of the watchers at Vulcanopolis had hardly been stilled before the surviving Machine craft pulled back, gathered in new formations, and in response began a steady investment of mankind's facilities on the planet: the ice mines, the mass drivers, even the precious solar-power farms, leaving only the habitable enclosures intact.

Now new rumours spread fast around the bunker. The *Acheron* was heading for Caloris, coming in for the kill.

You will understand how I have come to be something of an amateur student of my distant grandfather's life and career. My family name comes in fact from the married name of the Prime Minister's daughter, Mary, my ancestor. She had seen service herself in the course of the terrible world war for which he is best remembered, and at its close worked as an aide-de-camp to her father at his momentous summits with Roosevelt and Stalin, meetings that shaped the world for the next half-century or more.

I dare to dream that he would have been proud to know that some day one of his descendants would fulfil the role of a democratically elected President of a unified world.

And it is from one of Churchill's most famous speeches that I draw my own inspiration now, a speech I make at a moment just as perilous for all mankind and for our ideals as was the darkest hour of the war he faced . . .

The *Acheron* was considered to be Earth's only significantly powerful warship of space. Perhaps it was something of a credit to modern mankind that such technologies, before the Jupiter Ultimatum, had never been developed in earnest. And even when the ship was commissioned and designs were agreed, it had taken some time to upgrade the shipyards in Earth orbit and at Port Deimos to deliver such a vessel.

Yet here she was, swooping down on Mercury even as that planet's long shadow swung away from Earth after the transit. She was a blunt dumb-bell, the classic design of all human interplanetary craft since the *Discovery*-class ships that had first taken Falcon to Jupiter. And she headed straight for the Machine compound at the heart of Caloris Basin.

She was met by a flotilla of Machine ships, smaller, more manoeuvrable, but less heavily armed and armoured. Falcon watched through a variety of camera positions as the Machine craft approached the warship and, one by one, crumpled like scorched moths.

Administrator Borowski whistled. 'How the hell are they doing that?'

'X-ray lasers,' Falcon said. 'One-shot weapons, each powered by a small fission explosion. I came out on the *Acheron*, and the World Aerospace Force shared a few of its secrets. Nice of them.'

Now there were cheers and whoops from another part of the compound. This was in response to another effort by the Hermians themselves – and this time the target was the sunshield itself. Cargo-carrying vessels, laden with the hefty shaped-charge nuclear weapons the Hermians had been using for generations to blast mines into the stubborn ground of their world, had burst from underground pens. Despite heavy opposition from Machine craft most of these improvised missiles were getting through – and as he followed the battle in the sky through various sensor feeds, Falcon convinced himself that he could see rents in the heavily processed image of the shield, and glimpse the brighter sun behind it.

But such wounds, in a shield five thousand kilometres across, were pinpricks, and reports quickly came down that the labouring Machines were fixing the damage almost as soon as it was inflicted.

And now there were gasps at images of the latest action from Caloris.

Falcon turned to see that the *Acheron* had lit up its main propulsion unit, a fusion drive built into the heavier of the twin dumb-bells of its design. But it wasn't accelerating away from the planet; it was *standing* on the drive, walking it across the surface of Mercury, using the ferociously hot hydrogen-helium plasma of the drive itself as a blowtorch. Falcon, astonished and horrified, saw the shelters and equipment caches of the Machines flare and melt.

But the Machines responded, wielding a mightier weapon yet.

'Sol Invictus!' somebody swore. 'Look at the shield! Look at the shield . . .!'

That even though we have already seen mankind excluded from significant parts of the solar realm, and even though today the Free Republic of Mercury may fall into the grip of the illegal Machine state, we shall not flag or fail. We shall go on to the end. We shall fight on the moons and worlds of the solar system, we shall fight with growing confidence in space, we shall defend the home world of mankind, whatever the cost may be . . .

The shield was more than a passive sunlight block, Falcon realised. It was a cloud of trillions of Machines, all in intense and continuous communication. The shield was an intelligent swarm, collectively perhaps as superior to a human as a human was to a single cell. He suspected that many humans never dreamed that the Machines were capable of feats like this.

Now that swarm exerted its will. The shield *flexed*, its coordination perfect across five thousand kilometres, transforming itself from a sunshield to a focusing lens.

And a hundred thousand terawatts of solar energy poured down onto the Caloris battlefield.

The *Acheron* was the prime target, and even the battleship's mighty defences buckled under that withering onslaught. But the focus over such a huge distance could not be perfect, and dazzling radiation splashed over Machines and their equipment too, and poured into the already overheated ground. Falcon saw the heart of Caloris become a lake of molten rock into which the crumpling wreck of the *Acheron* began to sink.

Then the dying ship gave up the last of her energies.

Any imaging system nearby was destroyed immediately. Thus Falcon watched pictures relayed from space, of a blister, dazzling white, rising from the ground; of a wave of lava sweeping out across the tortured surface of Caloris, of immense bolts of lightning in a transient atmosphere of vaporised rock.

It was over. Mankind's greatest weaponry had been deployed and exhausted, and the shield, the Machines' vast project, was barely touched.

At Vulcanopolis, it was Susan Borowski who broke the stunned silence. 'Time to pack our bags, folks.'

And if, which I do not for a moment believe, the Jupiter Ultimatum were fulfilled and this beautiful world were subjugated and starving, then our assets beyond the Earth would carry on the struggle, until, in good time, the new worlds, with all their power and might, step forth to the rescue and the liberation of the old . . .

Falcon stayed to do what he could to help coordinate the evacuations, mostly to Mars.

Then he withdrew, longing for solitude, for his familiar old cabin at Port Van Allen. Withdrew once more into contemplation, and study, and lightspeed-slow communication with friends and other contacts across the solar system.

Withdrew to watch the slow, continuing unfolding of the great tragedy that had been triggered by the Jupiter Ultimatum.

As he had suspected, the Machines' designs for Mercury transcended any human ambition – transcended anything even Falcon himself had imagined. Humans needed worlds. Machines did not need worlds. What they did covet was the stuff worlds were made from.

It was trivial, in the end, to dismantle a planet. One needed only to overcome the planet's binding energy – in effect, to haul all the fragments of the world out of its own gravity well. And, so close to the sun, there was energy aplenty.

The communities of mankind looked on aghast. But Falcon recalled how he had seen Kuiper Belt Objects taken apart lump by ice lump by mankind's flinger operations. Were they not worlds too?

And the Machines' purpose for Mercury seemed, if you opened your mind to it, *wonderful*. A planet was a lump of matter, much of which was inaccessible and unusable, whose only useful function was to generate a stable gravitational field. The Machines now took the dead matter of Mercury and made it, essentially, into copies of themselves. Into a great Host, just as Adam had bragged.

Falcon whiled away years just watching the gathering flock wheel around the sun like a great migration of birds, testing their new powers – revelling, he saw, in a new realm of experience.

A Host indeed.

But the shell that now completely enclosed the sun significantly reduced the sunlight delivered to all the surviving worlds of the solar system. On Earth, antique glaciers creaked and stirred, and began to descend from the poles, from the mountains. A global civilisation struggled to respond.

As the harsh decades wore away there were political fractures. The great Secretariats of the World Government began to act like independent fiefdoms, some even raising private armies. And there were acts of wilful protest, acts of terror. One tremendous orbital blast that took out a large proportion of mankind's precious digital memory store – a wilful burning of the library – seemed to wound Falcon himself, damaging a consciousness that seemed ever-more interlinked with wider stores of intelligence and remembrance.

Even in this grim age Hope Dhoni continued to attend Falcon, walking out of the mist of the past – visits that marked the passage of decades.

And once she brought him a strange bit of information, a shred garnered from some watchful probe from Earth, looking on as the Host had completed its consumption of Mercury. It had spotted what appeared to be another watcher, perhaps a probe of unknown origin. It was a black cube, a metre across. And – Hope Dhoni pointed out, Falcon slowly discerned in grainy images – on its side, crudely written as if by hand, was a kind of name. *Howard Falcon Junior.*

Neither Hope not Falcon knew what to make of this. But Falcon, deeply shaken, remembered the enigmatic final message of Orpheus, and began to wonder if there were other eyes, other minds unbounded in space and independent of time, watching the passage of these dismaying decades.

After Mercury, it was more than a century and a half before Howard Falcon again set foot on any planet – before he obeyed a summons to Mars.

36

Falcon rolled back and forth experimentally, testing his latest low-gravity-issue balloon tyres on a ground of ruddy soil loosely bound by sparse grass. It was like a beach, Falcon thought, like dune grass, although it was a very long time since Howard Falcon had visited a beach anywhere. And he was so close to a stand of trees, mixed oak and pine, that in the air filtered through his face mask, drawn into his synthetic lungs, he could smell the scents of the forest, the resin, the leaf mulch.

He looked around. The sun was high in a tall, blue sky sparsely littered with white, streaky cloud. It was morning, so that way was *east*, and therefore the gentle slope of the ground that he intended to climb was to the *south*, away from the trees.

Which made sense, for this was the northern slope of Olympus Mons. Falcon had visited Mars many times before – the first, in fact, before the flight of the *Kon-Tiki*. It had *not* been like this.

His companions were a young man, frame sparse, big-chested, who wore a quilted coverall, gloves, and a mask through which a calm face could be seen – a *tall* young man, and among these new generations of Martians even Falcon sometimes felt overshadowed – and a woman, serene, but too still, too fragile. She was Hope Dhoni, the few decades between them now all but inconsequential compared to the span of time both had endured.

The man was called Citizen Second Grade Jeffrey Pandit. He was a civil servant based at Port Lowell, and Falcon's Martian government host for the next few days. Now he smiled at Falcon. 'I hope you got your tyres treated with the right protective cover.' He kicked at the loose, rusty soil. 'Still plenty of caustic chemistry going on in this dirt, even after three centuries of terraforming. We don't want you seizing up halfway up the hill, sir.'

'I'd never live it down.'

Now Hope smiled. 'So what are your feelings, Howard? For some this would be a mundane scene, but not for you. You spend all your time in space these days. Mercury was – what, over a century ago?'

'More than that, ma'am,' Pandit murmured. 'This is the year AFF 567—'

'A hundred and sixty-two years, then.'

Falcon winced. As long as that?

'Most of which you've spent in Port Van Allen. That great rusty wheel—'

'It's a comfortable hotel. I like to live in a building that's older than I am, and that's not so easy to find these days. And you do get one hell of a view. Besides, much of Earth is rather chilly since the Little Ice Age.'

'Well, you'll get one hell of a view from Olympus, sir,' Pandit said, emollient. 'Eventually, at the summit.'

'And – *mundane*, Hope?' Falcon said. 'Trees, blue sky, a gentle slope to walk up – *on Mars*? I guess it would feel mundane if we weren't wearing these damn facemasks. Mundane, if those oak trees over there weren't a hundred metres tall.'

Pandit grinned. 'Another couple of centuries and we'll be able to do without the masks, at least in the lowest-altitude locations. Hellas, for instance. Umm, would you like me to take a couple of pictures?'

'Hell, no. I'm no tourist. And my visit isn't exactly a secret, but the Security Secretariat made it clear I wasn't to shout about it.' Falcon peered up the slope; Olympus was so vast, yet so shallow, that its summit was hidden by the close Martian horizon – hidden by the curve of the world. 'I'm here for whatever is going on up there, in the caldera.'

'Project Acorn,' Hope Dhoni said dryly.

'Which name is about all we know of it,' Falcon said.

Pandit hesitated. 'One last chance to change your mind. It is a gentle climb, sir, all the way up. People say Olympus is the most unspectacular spectacle in the solar system. But it is three hundred kilometres to the summit, and by the time you're up there you'll be above almost all of the atmosphere . . . Are you *sure* you want to walk?'

Falcon sighed. 'You forget I'm not an old man, Pandit. I'm an old engine. But I can still roll up a hill faster than any human could walk. And besides, if I'm on foot, so to speak, maybe there's a better chance the Acorn people will let me through.' He looked up at the blank slope. 'You know the situation. Melanie Springer-Soames and her group could hardly conceal their activities from the surveillance satellites. They've got a regular colony up there. But they refuse any attempts at contact, and in the only statement they released they claimed that they had set up "defences" of some kind. Well, I've known the Springers since great-granddaddy Matt was showing off on Pluto – and *that's* why Port Lowell asked me to come up here. This is a gamble on my unique status, and it's not the first time I've been used this way: a gamble that while they may stop others, maybe they won't stop me.'

Dhoni said, 'It all sounds damn flaky.'

'Maybe, but this is Planetary Security policy: peaceful means if at all possible. That's been the standing order since Mercury. And, flaky or not, Hope, if it all goes wrong, what have they lost? One rusty old robot.'

Dhoni snorted. 'I'll claim the scrap value.'

'Then, if we're doing this—' Pandit dug into a pocket of his coverall, and produced an acorn, fat and healthy. 'I'm honoured to accompany you, Commander. My family cherishes the story of my ancestor's encounter with you at Jupiter.'

'I remember it well. Nicola was a worthy opponent.'

'You know, acorns on Mars are still pretty precious. The dip in sunlight hurt us too, as we tried to progress the terraforming. We plant acorns, we don't waste them. But those of us on Mars who want nothing but a peaceful future – and a flourishing planet when the Eos Programme is done – would like you to have this, sir. As a token of our good wishes for this mission.'

Falcon took the acorn carefully, in a claw of a hand that could have crushed it in a microsecond. 'I'll treasure it.'

Pandit glanced at a chronometer. 'Let's make the best of what's left of the day.' He looked back at the rover that had brought Falcon's party here from Port Lowell over in Aurorae Sinus, still Mars's greatest city. Dhoni had made her own way across Mars, having come down at Port Schiaparelli in Trivium Charontis. 'Sir, I'll be tracking you all the way in the rover, with my crew.'

'Well, I hope you have a repair kit on board,' Dhoni said.

'Hope—'

'And for the first few hours at least, Howard, you will walk at a reasonably sedate pace. Because *I* will be walking with you.' She held up a small case. 'Time for your five-yearly check over, Commander Falcon. And if you think you can escape *that* by climbing the biggest volcano there is, you've another think coming.'

'Yes, Doctor,' Falcon said, resigned.

37

As they began the climb they followed a trail of sorts, not much more than a braid of rover tyre-marks and boot prints, but proof that others had driven this way before, and many had hiked it too.

Hope walked steadily, her thin frame looking oddly sturdy. 'I bet Matt Springer did this. And for the same reason he claimed he went to Pluto. Do you remember? "Because it's there!"'

'Well, he stole that line. And are you going to talk the whole damn way up?'

'Would you like me to?'

'I'd like you to do your Sleeping Beauty act and fall asleep for another hundred years.'

She waggled a gloved finger at him. 'Now, Howard, that's a cheap shot. The hibernacula are a perfectly respectable option these days. Clinically it's just a mixture of deep freeze, targeted drugs and electro-narcosis, which is nothing but a mature version of the sleep inducers *you* have been using for five hundred years. And it was an option I was happy to take up. After all, some of my implants are older than most people alive today . . . I intend to husband my remaining days so I can accompany you a little further on your own journey through time. Besides, how well do *you* sleep these days?' She let that hang. 'Come on, let me do my tests. You won't feel a thing.' And as they walked on, she fixed sensors to his exposed flesh and peered into monitors.

He endured this, glowering, as he walked. As he had from the first days after the crash, he preferred to keep his physical condition to himself.

But he was, astonishingly, over five hundred years old. His mechanical shell had undergone multiple upgrades, and the surviving core of his nervous system was much patched by rejuvenation and regeneration treatments, all paid for by slow-maturing trust funds and such components of the World Government as occasionally found Howard Falcon useful, or perhaps amusing. But he was capable of feeling discomfort, and weariness, and yes, pain – low level, a deep intrinsic ache. At times he used painkillers, but despite Dhoni's occasional urging he would never have considered finding a way to detach this sensation altogether.

'So,' she said as she worked, 'you're playing the peacemaker again.'

'Or trying to. Much good I did on Mercury, the last time I ventured out of my hermit's cave.'

'It's all your fault. Is that what you feel?'

'Isn't that logical?'

'Not really. You and I do come from a unique cadre, Howard. The first undying generation in human history. And that's the point – if we *had* died after a normal lifespan, then we'd never even have seen how history unfolded. But whole generations have passed since our day, and have had a chance to make their own choices. You can't feel responsible—'

'Thom Bittorn did.'

'Bittorn? Oh – the geneticist responsible for the uplift of the simps. I read about his suicide. I hadn't even realised he was still alive.'

'He went into hiding long ago, when Pan rights were recognised. He would have faced lawsuits otherwise.'

She folded up her sensor pack. 'Medically you're doing as well as I expected – or as badly, depending how you look at it. But before I go back into the hibernaculum you *will* let me put you through a proper evaluation at Pasteur. And, Howard . . .'

'Yes?'

'You can't carry mankind on your shoulders, not forever.' She rapped her knuckles on his steel chest plate. 'Even you aren't strong enough.'

'The ground's a little rougher here.' He reached out. 'Take my hand.'

Once Hope had turned back, Falcon kept his counsel for much of the rest of that day's 'walk'. The rover's occupants said little either, as if they were in awe of the man-engine making this remarkable trek. Pandit did steer him away from obvious obstacles, such as particularly deep craters punched into the flank of the volcano, but Falcon preferred to make his own decisions. It wasn't just pride; if the rover failed he might need to retrace this journey without support.

The unworthy resentment he so often felt in Hope's company soon wore off. And as Falcon ascended in silence, up into the thinning air and deepening blue of the Martian sky, he found his soul opening up to the calm experience.

Despite Hope's company for those first few hours, they had travelled almost a hundred kilometres when Pandit called a halt for the night.

At the rest stop, Falcon glanced around. Here he was a third of the way up this greatest of all volcanoes, but the scale was simply too vast for him to be able to see anything more than a fraction of Olympus's own great flank. Even the ground's gentle slope wasn't apparent. And as the western sky displayed a convincing sunset through thickening cloud, it was as if he was in a high desert somewhere – the *altiplano* of South America, perhaps.

'I see we left the oak trees behind.'

'And the pines and the grasses, yes, sir,' Jeffrey called from the rover. 'We're already pretty high – ten kilometres above the planetary mean – the atmosphere's scale height is around eleven klicks, so the air pressure is already less than half what it was at ground level. You'll find some lichen and mosses up here, but little else, not yet.'

Olympus, with the group of mighty volcanoes of which it was a part, sat in Tharsis Province, an immense bulge in the Martian crust that would always push out of the atmosphere, no matter how thick the air became in the future. How strange a fully terraformed Mars would look, Falcon thought: a Moon-like landscape of craters and canyons and volcanoes that stuck out into space, in an eye-blink of geological time studded with blue lakes and scraps of green forest . . .

'Any reason we stopped just here?'

'Actually, yes, sir. If you look to your right, a little way off the trail . . .'

It was a monument, a chunk of basalt evidently carved from the deep flank of Olympus and neatly etched, presumably by laser. It was little more than a metre high.

Falcon had to lean over to read it. 'I'm not too good at bending down,' he told Jeffrey. 'Miracle of Victorian engineering that I am. Couldn't they have made this a little taller?'

'Ah, but it's not intended for you, sir. The government committee who set this up expressed the hope that more of his kind would some day come this way: a new generation, so to speak. It's meant for them.'

'*His* kind?'

'See for yourself, sir.'

And Falcon saw the inscription. This was a gravestone. Buried here was Eshu 2512a, born Hellas AFF 526, AD 2512; died Port Lowell AFF 555, AD 2541.

'A superchimp.'

'I thought you'd like to see this, given your own connection with the Pans. It's all part of your legend. I mean—'

'It's OK, Jeffrey. I'm a crumbling monument too, I know. So he was the last of them.'

'Yes, sir . . .'

Falcon had looked up the story of the simps when he'd learned of the death of Bittorn. In retrospect the establishment of an independent simp nation in the African forest, one of the first actions of the new World Government back in the twenty-first century, had been the high water mark in the saga of the Pan. After only a few generations, they had started to decline in numbers. The causes were believed to be genetic: relics of clumsy meddling by Bittorn and others that had been intended to make the simps less vulnerable to the effects of low or zero gravity – or even high gravity – such as bone mass loss and fluid balance problems. The simps, agile, strong and good climbers, had been found to be useful workers offworld, and such improvements had seemed commercially astute at the time. More devastating had been the fragmenting of the intellectual capacity of successive generations, as Bittorn's hasty neural rewiring had unravelled.

In their last days there had been a generous gesture by the Martian government to offer to host as many of the surviving simps as chose to come in a specially constructed independent compound in the Hellas basin, the lowest point on Mars; perhaps Mars's one-third gravity would be more conducive to the simps' clumsily modified anatomies than either of the extremes of Earth's full gravity or the microgravity of space. The colony had never exactly flourished, but it had survived for a few generations.

'But now it's all over,' Falcon said.

'My mother brought me up here to see this, sir. She remembered Eshu before he died.'

'So why a monument on Olympus?'

'Eshu was alone in the last few years. The last of the Pan. And he tried to do things no other Pan had ever achieved, just to say his species had made it. Walking up Olympus was one of them. Hence this marker.'

'That's a classy touch: a bucket list for a whole race.'

'My mother always said she hoped that humans would behave as well as the Pan, if the Jupiter Ultimatum is fulfilled.'

Falcon had nothing to say to that.

'One more thing, Commander. The simp monument contains some individual messages. Particular individuals to whom the simps felt they owed a debt. Might be worth checking, sir. For you, I mean.'

'Hmm.' Falcon thought back to the crash of the *Queen Elizabeth IV*, a story so deep in the past it was as if it had happened to someone else – but he had saved the life of one simp worker. 'An individual message?'

'You just have to touch the monument.'

So Falcon reached down to the chimp-height gravestone, his mechanical fingers resting on Olympus basalt. Details of cold and texture whispered through to him via the fingers' tactile receptors.

And the head and shoulders of a simp appeared in the Martian air, the hint of some kind of tunic below the neck. After all these years – these centuries – the face was unmistakable to Falcon. This was Ham 2057a, once President of the Independent Pan Nation – and, it was said, having responded well to anti-senescence experiments, one of the longest-lived simps. 'Commander Falcon.' His voice sounded clearly, inside Falcon's head, and Falcon wondered what technology was being used to project this illusion. Now Ham grinned. 'Boss – boss – *go!*' And he winked.

With that, the projection was over. Falcon knew those words; they were the brusque command he had given that simp on the doomed *Q.E. IV.* But . . .

'Since when the hell did simps wink?'

'Sir? Are you all right? . . . The sun's nearly gone. Will you be joining us in the rover for the night?'

Falcon straightened up stiffly, trying to focus on the here and now. 'Listen, how many of you are there in there? Have you Mars boys ever heard of a game called poker . . .?'

Later that night, on impulse, using the rover's facilities, Falcon looked up the name of that last Pan: Eshu. He found it was a Yoruba name for a god of West African myth.

A trickster god.

And he thought again of Ham, a message left in a monument to a supposedly extinct species, meant for Falcon personally. And he had *winked.*

Sometimes he wondered if anybody in his life had ever told him the straight truth.

38

In the morning, the flank of Olympus sparkled with frost.

'Wow,' Falcon said, rolling back and forth over the thin rime. 'Here's a sight John Young never dreamed of.'

'Yes, sir. We even get a little snow – I mean, water-ice snow, not the native dry-ice sort – but no rain yet, and no standing water. That will come. One day there will be glaciers in the Valles Marineris for the first time in billions of years . . . Umm, take care with your locomotion just here. There can be ice under the surface, and it can be treacherous.'

'Noted. So, you guys ready to roll . . .?'

The second day of the climb was as dull and featureless as the first had been. The sky was undeniably beautiful, a blue of an exquisite shade Falcon had never seen on Earth, with high, icy clouds catching the light of the remote sun. But the ground was plain as ever, if not more so, with fresh craters more common at this elevation than skims of lichen or moss. It was as if he was climbing from Earth to Moon, Falcon mused.

As it turned out, the most spectacular sights came at the end of the day.

When they halted for the evening, Pandit emerged from the rover in what looked to Falcon like a bona fide pressure suit. 'Just wanted to make sure you take a proper look at the sunset, Commander . . .'

The sun, visibly shrunken from its apparent diameter at Earth, seemed to be resting on the western horizon. Its low, reddened light swept across an Olympian flank of craters, gullies and scarred plains that showed precious few signs of the new life that was being laboriously cultivated here.

But it was not the ground Falcon was supposed to look at but the heavens. Pandit pointed, drawing Falcon's gaze. Falcon briefly wondered if Pandit wanted to show him the immense solar-collector mirrors that had been hung in orbit around Mars, to drive the terraforming programme – but it was not that.

There, clearly visible against a sky the colour of a deep bruise, was a great semicircle centred on the sun itself, with half its arc hidden beneath the horizon. Falcon tried to measure its scale against the apparent diameter of the sun: it might have been a hundred times the width. This was not a circle, a hoop, but a view of the vast sphere of Machines that enclosed the sun; the faint tracery of scattered sunlight was only really visible at the edge, where the optical thickness was greatest.

'The Host,' Falcon said grimly.

'Yes, sir.'

'A shell the size of the orbit of Mercury . . . What a spectacle. What an – obscenity. Is Venus visible yet?'

'It will be later, sir. You know, given the accounts of how the Machines took apart Mercury, many of us are puzzled that they haven't yet done the same to Venus.'

'Security have been keeping an eye on Venus. We send the odd daring close-in probe – we're not allowed to land, but much of the atmosphere is gone, and we can see the exposed surface. The Machines are there, working. Building . . . something. Structures whose purpose we can't identify. It seems they want to experiment, to see if an intact planetary-mass body could be useful to them after all. We forget sometimes how *young* they are . . .' Indeed it was less than five centuries since Falcon had stood on the deck of the USS *Shore* with Conseil, the comic serving-bot that had turned out to be the precursor to all of *this*. 'To them a few centuries is as nothing.'

'But it's an eternity to us humans, sir. And we're only a little more than halfway to the Jupiter Ultimatum date.' Pandit stared at the strange vista. He asked hesitantly, 'What about people on Earth, sir? Do they, umm, *believe* the threat? I can tell you that day to day *we* don't give it a thought.'

Falcon smiled. 'That's because you've got a world to build. You've something to *do*.' Which Falcon often envied as he rattled around in his cabin, trapped in the endless cycles of the spinning, orbiting Port Van Allen. 'Oh, it's taken seriously on Earth now. It was the Little Ice Age that changed things, I guess. Even the Mercury war had been just a light show in the sky. Then the war came to Earth itself. At last serious long-term programmes were launched in response. Cultural treasures stashed off-planet—'

'I know. The Port Skia museum has a pretty impressive Leonardo collection.'

'But a great deal of digital treasure was lost in the Mnemosyne bombing back in '34 . . .' The Mnemosynes, taking their name from a goddess of memory, had argued that mankind's ability to deal with the terminal future of the Ultimatum was hampered by a clinging to the past – and that therefore the past should be sloughed off, abandoned. 'You can't save everything, I guess.'

Pandit said, 'There are rumours there have been negotiations about mass evacuations. Well, look at the Hellas basin, three thousand kilometres wide and nine deep, and predicted to have a breathable atmosphere well before Ultimatum Day. That would make for a pretty big refugee settlement.'

Or, Falcon thought more bleakly, a concentration camp.

The Martians had already been more than generous, it was generally thought. Hellas was littered with domes containing samples of Earth biomes, from the sub-Arctic tundra to the tropical rainforests. Attempts had even been made to reconstruct Aboriginal songlines in the Martian dust. But in historical terms Mars had barely won its independence from Earth, and unlike the Hermians, swarms of Terran migrants wouldn't be too welcome.

'Meanwhile,' he said, 'Security is pressing for more extreme solutions.'

'Like the hibernacula?'

'That's one possibility. If we run out of refuges we may have to *store* whole populations.' The technology that Hope Dhoni was using to sleep-stalk Falcon across the centuries was in fact a spin-off of such last-resort studies. 'Or a drastic reduction of numbers. If the population is virtually zero by Ultimatum Day, you see—'

'Those unborn can't be harmed. We have a *high* birth rate. We're trying to fill up an empty world. How strange that must be, culturally.'

'The steady pressure of the Ultimatum is making us a less human society, Jeffrey. Distorting us. Was Earth under the World Government ever a utopia? Well, the shadows are closing in. And it's going to get a lot worse before the Machines' work is done.'

Pandit, staring into the dying sun, seemed troubled. He was a thoughtful young human being, Falcon thought, Martian or not. Very carefully – a cybernetic limb and a delicate pressure suit made for a risky combination – Falcon patted Pandit's back. 'Come on. Let's get back to the trailer. Time I took some more of your salary off you in the poker school . . .'

39

The final day was much as the first two had been, a patient, steady slog. But as they slowly approached their goal, Falcon's curiosity about what might be found on the summit of Olympus sharpened.

When they did breast the final rocky slope, Pandit, in his pressure suit, emerged to join Falcon, and they looked out in silence.

The caldera of Olympus Mons was a pit eighty kilometres across, a plain of nested volcanic vents: craters so huge that individually they would have been striking features, even if they had not been crammed together and lifted into the sky atop the solar system's largest mountain. Falcon, standing beside the rover, could see all the way to the caldera's far rim. The air was clear, the sky above a deep blue. This was as close to the pre-Eos Martian environment as still existed. Inevitably there were some conservatives who argued for erecting a dome over this tremendous basin and preserving it as an environmental museum of the old Mars, and standing here Falcon wasn't sure he disagreed.

But all of this was a mere backdrop to the human affairs of the day.

Falcon wasn't surprised to see a rover driving up the slope to meet them, unmarked, a clone of Pandit's. And as he followed the rover's trail back into the caldera, Falcon made out a small settlement, evidently temporary: a handful of domes, a couple more rovers, a surface widely scuffed by tyres and boots – and, there, cupped in the craters, gantries, workshops, fuel stores, and the slim forms of rockets.

'Good grief,' Falcon said. 'Just as the surveillance missions reported. They really did build Cape Canaveral on top of Olympus Mons.'

Pandit laughed. 'More like Peenemunde, sir, if you want an even older reference. They're very much experimental here.'

The rover drew to a halt, and a figure in a pressure suit – a young woman, Falcon could see her face behind her visor – and a handful of others clambered out. Falcon didn't *think* these people were carrying weapons, but he felt uncomfortable having to bet his life on it.

'Welcome, Commander Falcon.'

'You're Melanie Springer-Soames, of course.'

'You recognise me from the mug shots Security no doubt hold on me.'

'Also from the leaping-gazelle logo on your helmet. And your reputation . . .' Springer-Soames was the product of two mighty dynasties, the heroic-explorer Springers and the presidential Churchill-Soames. Falcon had no doubt she would turn out to be the tough operator Planetary Security reported her to be. 'You knew I was coming?'

She shrugged. 'We do have spies.' She glanced at Pandit, who seemed uneasy – and Falcon immediately began to speculate *who* of the friendly poker school was the traitor. She said, 'And I happen to know you were given a souvenir, the gift of an acorn, by your naive young friend here. Let me repeat the gesture.'

From a pocket on her outer suit layer, she produced a silver sphere the size of an apple, and handed it to Falcon. He hefted it; it felt heavy even in Mars's low gravity.

She said, 'We call it an Acorn, too – and it's what this project is all about.'

Pandit said now, edgily, 'Naive, am I? You must know that the Lowell administration has an embargo on weapons development—'

'Officially.'

Falcon said, 'He's right, though. And now here you kids are, building a missile base one planet in from Jupiter itself.'

Springer-Soames stiffened. That word 'kids' seemed to provoke her, as Falcon had hoped; to be contemptuous to the arrogant and ambitious was one way to make them open up.

'This is not a missile base,' she said now. 'And we are not manufacturing weapons. Or at least, not weapons to be used to kill.' She indicated the metal sphere he held. '*That* is a weapon of a metaphorical kind that will win mankind – not the worlds of the solar system – the stars.'

And Falcon looked down at the 'Acorn' with new respect.

Melanie Springer-Soames walked the visitors around the launch site. Falcon, always a technology buff, was fascinated.

The scheme was simple in principle, challenging technically.

'Those slim ships are fusion rockets, Commander. They're sufficient to get off Mars and out to the Oort Cloud, at high speed. The Machines may try to stop us; we're confident they won't get them all. Out in the Cloud we've already established a resource extraction operation; the ships will be refuelled with big, flimsy bags of comet ice and fusion fuel—'

'You're making starships,' Falcon guessed wildly.

'It will take centuries, but that's where we're going. We aim to hit every remotely habitable exoplanet within reach, as long as we're capable of continuing the programme. And the payload . . .' She gestured. 'You're holding it. One Acorn per world would be sufficient, theoretically. We'll send two or three to each target for redundancy. Acorns planted on new worlds.'

Falcon started to see it. 'Mighty oaks from little acorns grow.'

'That's the idea. An oak tree, you see, is a machine created by acorns for the purpose of making more acorns, constructed from local resources, the soil, the air. Commander, each of *our* Acorns is crammed with data. The heart of it is a nugget of engineered carbon: a bit of stolen Machine technology actually, a product of their deep mining of Jupiter. The information density is somewhere between that of human DNA and nano-engraved diamond. One gram of it would be enough to store all of human culture. A lot *less* than one gram is enough to store the DNA definition of a human.'

'So that's it,' Pandit said. 'You could "store" the blueprints for millions of people in there. And I guess these little Acorns are like Machine assemblers. You will grow humans, manufacture their bodies and whatever support systems they need from the resources of the target planet.' He grinned, despite himself. 'That's outrageous.'

Springer-Soames grinned back. 'It takes twenty years for an acorn to grow an oak tree mature enough to make more acorns. We figure we can match that: from an Acorn landing to a baby's wail, in twenty years or less. You see, Commander? Maybe we're going to lose the solar system. But we aren't prepared to concede the stars – and *this* is a way of blindsiding the Machines. When they do get out there eventually, they'll find humans, ready and waiting for them.'

'Your ancestors would be impressed,' Falcon said. 'All the Springers, even the ones I never got to argue with.'

'Maybe so,' she said more coldly. 'The immediate issue is, what are you going to do about it? You, an agent of Planetary Security.'

Falcon winced at that, but he couldn't deny it was *de facto* true. 'I take it you want a resolution to the legal challenges you face. If not, you wouldn't have allowed me up here.'

She nodded grudgingly. 'That's true. We don't need any help, but we'd rather proceed without threat of interference. My family has known you a long time, Commander. You have your limitations, but you do have integrity.'

'Thanks,' he said dryly. 'But why be so secretive in the first place? Why didn't you work through the authorities?'

She laughed. 'Why do you think? Because the World Government, under the pressure of the Machine Ultimatum, is slowly but surely turning into one of the most repressive regimes in human history. Security would have quietly spoken to Port Lowell, and we would have been stopped, simple as that. *That's* why we went dark.'

'But you can't be stopped now, can you?' Falcon said, almost sadly. 'Not if you've already fired your first few missions.'

'Exactly. So we've won already.'

'It's not a game,' he said sternly. 'And while the World Government isn't perfect, it's not evil either.' He made to rub his cheek, a gesture that was a vestige of his more human days; the young people around him watched curiously, and, self-conscious, he dropped his hand. He said, 'I wouldn't be surprised if some think tank somewhere inside the administration hadn't already proposed doing exactly what you're undertaking. As you say it does achieve long-term goals – it could secure the future of humanity.'

'Then why haven't they done it already?'

He sighed. 'For ethical reasons alone, I should think. You speak of using local resources on those remote planets to make humans. What about any creatures who are *already* dependent on those resources? We like to think the days are gone when humans were prepared to despoil living worlds for our own benefit.'

'These are desperate times—'

'Not that desperate.' He hefted the silver sphere in his hand. 'Look, I'm not going to stop you. I don't suppose I could, and the cat is out of the bag already. But I want you to come with me and report what you've done – talk it through with the Extraplanetary Ethics Bureau.'

'A Terran hot-air factory,' Springer-Soames grumbled. 'I prefer action.'

'I know you do,' Falcon said with a smile. 'All you Springers are the same. I knew Matt, remember?'

'But that's the deal?'

'That's the deal.'

She looked up at the sky. 'This is all about what they used to call the First Contact directives, isn't it? That some day we will be judged by a higher intelligence. Do you really take that seriously, Commander?'

'Well, I knew the philosopher who drafted those directives. And . . .'

And he thought of *Howard Falcon Junior.* There had been more of those enigmatic entities, replicas of the Orpheus that had been lost in the heart of Jupiter – and yet, over the decades, glimpsed in the scattered ruins of Mercury, on the churned-up Machine-held Moon, in the depths of space . . . Even Machines had made such sightings – so he had learned from a leaky section of Planetary Security, who had ways of knowing such things. No human knew what this could mean, how it could be happening, and nor could any Machine, Falcon was prepared to bet. One had even been observed from Port Van Allen, hanging in space above the planet Earth with all its peoples, like a glittering toy . . .

'Yes, I do take the First Contact directives seriously,' Falcon said simply. 'OK, enough business. Are you going to show me your rocket ships?'

Talking, gesturing, they walked down the shallowing slope towards the brilliantly lit domes clustered deep in the caldera.

When Howard Falcon visited Mars, it was little more than halfway between the delivery of Adam's Jupiter Ultimatum and its completion date. His mission over, once more he returned to his orbital shell of isolation, contemplation and communication.

And as the Ultimatum date approached, when he looked back, Falcon was astonished how quickly the remaining time had fallen away. Five hundred years, gone like a fleeting dream. *You really are getting old, Falcon.*

40

With Hope Dhoni on his arm, Falcon strolled through the gondola of the great airship. *Strolled*: he was a clanking half-cyborg, she a wispy relic of obviously great age. But in this expensive environment nobody was rude enough to stare.

'Even the corridors are plush,' Dhoni murmured. 'The carpets, the paintings, the busts on their pedestals – who *were* those people anyhow? I suppose they're all images of the terrible old Nazis who paid for the original tub.'

Falcon smiled. 'And no doubt the detail is accurate down to the cut of their toothbrush moustaches.'

'Well, it would be,' Dhoni said, with a sigh. 'The Martians and the Medes would probably say this is all Terrans have done for the last century or so, clung to the past, to the most irrelevant detail . . . A psychologist, which I'm not, would say this whole ship is a symptom of a mass psychosis.'

'And the Mnemosynes might have agreed with you,' Falcon said grimly. 'But what would you have people do, Hope? We're losing our home to the fire. Isn't it rational to save as much of the family treasure as we can? Anyhow there's only ten more days left now. For better or worse it will all soon be over, the Ultimatum fulfilled—'

'What's *that*, for instance?' Hope pointed to a gadget on the wall.

A young officer, smartly uniformed, approached them. She had a small, intricate tattoo on her right cheek, of a leaping animal. 'That's a cigarette lighter, ma'am,' she said, smiling. 'Yes, the original designers really did allow smoking aboard an airship filled with seven million cubic feet of hydrogen – but they insisted on the use of these safety gadgets. However I think the placement is wrong. On the *LZ 129* – the original *Hindenburg* – smoking was only allowed on the B Deck, the lower deck . . .'

They walked on, and the officer politely accompanied them.

Falcon knew that much of the traffic between the great laputas of Saturn was conveyed in vehicles much more basic than this. Why not travel in style, however? Mankind was doomed to exile, it seemed, but was nothing if not rich in energy and materials; a recreation of the most famous airship in history, nearly eight and a half centuries after its spectacular destruction, was a trivial cost. Falcon however had refused to endorse a proposed project to recreate Earth's *second* most famous crashed airship, the *Queen Elizabeth IV*, a ship now buried almost as deeply in time.

'Those busts, though,' Dhoni said, musing. 'All of forgotten monsters. Whereas—'

'Hope.' Falcon thought he knew where this conversation was going.

But Dhoni always had been unstoppable once she was set in motion. 'Whereas if our glorious leader had her way, all the statues and paintings would no doubt be of Amanda Springer-Soames IV, Life President of what's left of Earth—'

'*Hope.* You're making the Lieutenant here blush. Didn't you spot the springbok tattoo?'

Dhoni peered down at the officer's name-tag. Her face, itself an antique some centuries old, was still capable of showing shock and embarrassment. 'Lieutenant Jane Springer-Soames. Oh, my. I do apologise.'

'It's not a problem,' said the young officer graciously. 'To tell the truth I'm used to people quizzing me about my grandmother.'

Falcon was interested. 'How do you respond?'

Jane shrugged. 'I say that she believes she's doing the right thing for Earth and humanity, the best way she knows how.'

Falcon nodded. 'That seems a fair assessment, whatever your politics.'

She responded with a frown. 'It's probably a good thing you feel that way, sir. Because, I'm afraid, I need to talk to you about my grandmother. First, please, let me show you to the lounge. We'll soon be arriving at New Sigiriya, and it's quite a view . . .'

As they followed her, Falcon felt a spark of concern. *So much for the holiday.*

Of the two great passenger chambers of the gondola's A Deck, Falcon actually preferred the dining room, with its stylish red-leather furniture and walls panelled with images of the great zeppelin in flight over 1930s Earth cities. But the lounge was impressive too, with one wall dominated by a large stylised map of the world – of *the* world, the old world, Earth. Today the lounge was crowded with people in a variety of garbs sitting or standing close to the downward-slanting windows. Children ran and wriggled and played too, in the golden, misty light that seeped into the room.

The light of the clouds of Saturn.

To Falcon, whose first venture to a gas giant had been to mighty Jupiter, Saturn had always been something of a disappointment. Though not much smaller than Jupiter in diameter, Saturn was significantly less massive, and twice as far from the sun. So the upper atmosphere, where the *Hindenburg* sailed and which humanity was now colonising in numbers, was a realm with significantly less free energy than its equivalent on Jupiter: less solar radiation, less inner heat. And with a scarcity of energy, life was sparse too. There was a scattered native biota, but it only amounted to what would have been counted as mere aerial plankton on Jupiter; there was none of the great higher food chain of mantas and medusae that Falcon had first encountered on Jupiter.

If Saturn was a relative disappointment as a spectacle, it had given mankind a comparatively gentle welcome. The Jupiter Ultimatum had brought an immediate need to ramp up Saturn's production of helium-3 for mankind's energy-hungry civilisation. And, unlike Jupiter, Saturn's gravity in the clouds was no higher than Earth's. Thus, with the slow but relentless approach of Ultimatum Day, the human colonisation of the clouds of Saturn in large numbers had begun. Whatever the willingness or otherwise of the surviving colony worlds, Mars, Titan and Triton, none of them had the capacity to cope with a refugee exodus from Earth. But Saturn was roomy enough to make the refugees welcome, many times over.

Nobody knew how safe this new refuge would prove. But all those people had to be put somewhere.

And now the *Hindenburg* floated over one of the great laputas, an island in the sky of mankind's new home.

New Sigiriya was supported by aerostats filled with heated hydrogen-helium air, like the medusae of Jupiter, like every human vessel that had ventured into the gas giants' atmospheres since Falcon's own *Kon-Tiki*. But this laputa, a flying raft more than ten kilometres in diameter, would have dwarfed even the greatest of Jupiter's medusae. And despite the strangeness of its setting – despite the fact that it rested not on a solid surface but over thousands of kilometres of air, despite its clusters of domes brilliantly illuminated by artificial light – as seen from above this was a very human city, of roads, buildings, parkland, even what looked like nature reserves on the periphery.

'It's beautiful,' Dhoni said. 'Strange – out of place here – but beautiful. And a laputa like this will be my home from now on, I guess.'

Falcon said, 'But this is only the beginning of Project Silenus. Look further . . .' He took her hand and led her closer to the window.

Beyond New Sigiriya, the sky was full of flying islands. They drifted at all altitudes, from the thick lower cloud decks to the sparse stratosphere. Some were dark shadows, some brilliantly illuminated; while some stood still in the air under their immense flotation bags, others surged purposefully forward, like ocean liners. Lesser craft too threaded their way between the laputas. Lights shone bright everywhere, the smeared city glow of the islands, the sparking buoys and pilot lamps of the ships. The vision was like one of Falcon's own childhood fantasies of ballooning.

'All this is very recent, ma'am,' Jane Springer-Soames said to Dhoni. 'Most of the refugees from Earth have come up here only in the last few decades. In fact most people here at Saturn right now are sleepers, stacked up in the big orbiting hibernacula vessels, and there are more still waiting to be shipped from Earth. They will be restored as soon as possible.'

'That was always expected,' Falcon put in. 'The late rush.'

Hope smiled. 'For me it was the calendar. When the date finally clicked around to 2700, and I realised that for Earth there would *be* no 2800 – that somehow made it real. "Project Silenus", though?'

'The laputa construction projects are run out of Oasis City on Titan, but for the resources they're mining one of the inner moons, Enceladus. And, according to Euripides, Silenus was a drunken companion of the gods who boasted of killing Enceladus with a spear.'

'How apt.'

'I did have to look it up.'

Springer-Soames said, 'More laputas are coming into service as fast as they can be built. And that's only the beginning,' she went on with enthusiasm. 'There are grand plans to link up individual laputas to make flying continents, enormous structures – well, there's room on Saturn. And beyond that we may be able to join it all up into *one vast shell* enclosing the whole of Saturn, all at one gravity, with a thick layer of breathable air above. Like a planet with a hundred times Earth's surface area . . .' She seemed to remember herself, and stalled.

Falcon smiled at her. 'I like your dreams.'

'You would,' Dhoni said. 'The enthusiasm of the young. That's what will save us in the end, Howard.'

Falcon said, 'Maybe. But we have to get through Ultimatum Day first.' He faced Springer-Soames. 'You said there is a problem?'

'Yes, sir.' Jane glanced uneasily at Dhoni, then turned back to Falcon. 'I'm afraid I have to ask you to come back to Earth. Have you heard of the "Peace Hostages"?'

'No, but I don't like the sound of it.'

'It's my grandmother's last-ditch effort to save the planet – so she says. But to do it she's put twelve thousand lives at risk.'

Falcon frowned. 'Twelve *thousand*? Who asked for my help? The President herself?'

'No, sir,' Springer-Soames said simply. '*Adam.*'

The name took Falcon aback.

Dhoni, too, seemed shocked. 'It's so peaceful here. As if we're drifting in a bubble of the past. But there's always trouble. Oh—' She grabbed Falcon's arm. 'Don't go. Not again. You've done your job, Howard. You – *we* are too old. Have some iced tea! Oh, Howard, stay with me, and let me look after you.'

But, of course, he had no choice.

He bent stiffly, and with great care kissed Dhoni on the cheek. Her ancient flesh was surprisingly warm. 'Wait for me.'

'I will,' she said softly.

He straightened with a whir and turned away.

But Springer-Soames called sharply, 'Commander – careful.'

He froze, and looked down. At his feet was a toy, a ball, which had rolled across the carpet to bump, unnoticed, against his undercarriage. It was a simple inflatable thing, like a grounded balloon – but it was a globe of Earth, battered, scuffed, evidently much cherished. Falcon imagined this thing deflated and tucked into a refugee's pocket, a souvenir of a lost home. He had nearly run it over.

A little girl approached him. Perhaps five years old, she had short blonde hair, and a face that would one day look strong rather than beautiful, he thought, with a good chin and cheekbones. But right now she was staring at the toy uncertainly.

'Can I help you?'

'Please,' the kid said shyly. 'Can I get my globe?'

'Allow me.' Falcon bent, servomotors whirring, and with infinite care picked up the fragile toy with one hand, and held it out to the girl.

She watched the toy, not Falcon; she reached out and grabbed it from him.

A woman behind her murmured, 'Be polite, Lorna.'

Hugging the toy, she said, formally, 'I'm Lorna Tem. Thank you very much.' And then she looked up at the gleaming pillar of Falcon's body – he had the feeling she had thought he was some robot, a mechanical steward serving drinks, perhaps – but then she saw the leathery remnant of his face peering out from the machinery, and her eyes widened.

The woman put a hand on her shoulder. 'That's enough. Come away now . . .'

Falcon grunted. 'And that's how the children of the human race react to me.'

Dhoni was here. She rested her head on his upper arm. 'Go save us once again, Howard.'

Outside the windows of the *Hindenburg II*, a ferocious ammonia blizzard began to lash at the drifting laputas.

41

After being escorted by Lieutenant Jane Springer-Soames on a high-acceleration dash across the solar system – and despite the urgency, there were only days left before the Ultimatum expired – Falcon knew he needed rest. Before descending to Earth he had the liner from Saturn stop at the venerable Port Van Allen.

Falcon tried to remember when he had first come here, to a station that predated his own first flight into space, and how many times he had visited since. He knew there would be no attempt to save or salvage Van Allen when the Machines came. Instead, like the other stations which still studded near-Earth space – and indeed the great equatorial space elevators that had become fountains of fleeing refugees – in the final days Van Allen would be used by a corps of Witnesses. And then it would be abandoned, to the whim of the Machines.

For now, as he relaxed in the care of the great wheel's primitive but sufficient facilities, within the scuffed aluminium walls of his favourite room, Falcon sat before the window and looked out at Earth and Moon.

The Moon was no longer the Moon, the human Moon of antiquity. Since the Machines had moved in on the satellite at the time of the Jupiter Ultimatum, Falcon, like much of the rest of mankind, had watched with reluctant fascination as human relics had been dismantled or simply ploughed into the dust, from the famous old Federation of Planets building to the fragile remains of Borman's pioneering Apollo lander. Then the work had gone much further. The regolith had been strip-mined, leaving great rectangular scars; the inner heat of the Moon had been released to flood the great old craters and the dark *maria* with fresh lava. All this was visible from Earth, from where the face of the Moon came to look like a lurid industrial landscape – or like Mordor, and Falcon wondered if anybody else alive would pick up *that* reference.

But, of course, the Moon had not been the Machines' true target. Now, reluctantly, Falcon looked down on the turning Earth.

The world had been transformed since his own first youthful forays into space. The ice now encroached far from the poles, north and south, even though it was northern midsummer. Still, the environmental recovery overseen by the WG in earlier generations had largely survived. The northern continents were still swathed in oak woods, the forests had recovered in South America and Africa too, and grasslands washed over much of what had once been the great deserts, the Sahara, and in central Asia. Falcon knew that those forests and plains still swarmed with wildlife. As Ultimatum Day approached, every effort had been made to sample and preserve offworld all the planet's ecosystems. But Falcon knew that all the living things down there on Earth itself, the animals, the vegetation – the elephants and the oak trees – all of them were doomed to be casualties of a war of which none of them could have any understanding.

Now the old station passed over Earth's night side, much of which was dark. In the end, with whole nations abandoned, a diminished mankind had huddled in a few centres. But even now some cities still blazed with defiant light – and some, sadly, burned in the night, immense bonfires of culture.

Just as it had only been in the last few decades that the great refugee flows off the planet had begun, so it had been only at the end that the most concerted conservation efforts had been made. Physical records and treasures – even whole buildings, wrapped in shells of quasicarbon, itself once mined from the depths of Jupiter – had been transported offworld. Meanwhile those treasures that could not be saved had been mapped and sampled and imaged. Thus dreamers in the clouds of Saturn could roam across 'Earth II', a crowd-sourced virtual copy of the world. Falcon had tried it; in some options you could watch the people who had happened to be there on the day the recordings were made, and they would look into the camera and smile.

Once or twice Falcon had cautiously ventured down to Earth himself. He had found an age of tragic glamour. Falcon would always remember wandering around a mostly abandoned London, when, rolling up from the flooded, reforested valley of the Thames, he had come upon the great Victorian museums of South Kensington, looming above the green – and he had been reminded of a similar antique palace surviving in a greened, abandoned England, discovered, in the pages of Wells's much-loved book, by a Traveller who had gone much further in Time than even Falcon had, to the year 802,701 AD . . . In the end Falcon had found London, like Earth itself, hard to bear: a great city stilled and silent save for the cries of birds and animals. And he could not bring himself to visit the village of his childhood. He had retreated to his orbiting refuge.

In the last years, there had been gestures of despair. Mass-suicidal 'games'. Religions that flourished and died like mushrooms. Some even affected to worship the Machines themselves; people dressed up, or altered themselves, to become faux cyborgs. There had been a decade when Falcon himself, reluctantly, became a kind of fashion icon to such people – before the mood shifted again, and he came to be hated once more as a relic of an age of blame.

And yet there had been nobility too. Consider the Witnesses, volunteers who were preparing to sacrifice their lives to provide a final human account of the fate of the planet – and to gather evidence against the day when the Machines stood in the dock to account for this tremendous crime.

But, whatever the complexity and tragedy of the human response to the coming deadline, the end was approaching now, at last.

In the final few days – and visible from Port Van Allen itself – the great ships of the Machines at last arrived, lenticular forms kilometres across, driven across space by a physics no human understood, and now suspended like silver clouds above the cities of Earth . . .

Jane Springer-Soames burst into the cabin.

'Sir – Commander Falcon! I'm sorry to disturb you—'

Falcon stood stiffly. 'Jane, it's fine. What's happening?'

'We've had a message from my grandmother – from the President. An offer.'

'Of what?'

Jane, panting, swallowed hard. 'A hostage exchange, sir.'

'You mean the Peace Hostages . . .?'

As he had travelled to Earth, Springer-Soames's stratagem had become brutally clear. Two of the last sleeper ships – cargo scows with crowded hibernacula in their holds – had been diverted to Unity City and forced to land under the watchful eye of armed security guards. And there they had been kept, with twelve thousand people crammed helplessly in their cold hives.

'If Springer-Soames ever thought that a human shield would persuade the Machines to spare Unity City, let alone Earth, she's a fool, Jane—'

'I don't know what she was thinking, sir,' Jane said. 'Honestly. I can only tell you what she's offering now.'

'You said an exchange.'

'She will release the twelve thousand – *in exchange for you.*'

Falcon took that in. 'Ah. Of course. That's what this has been all about. She wants to lure me down to Earth, in the hope, probably, of luring a Machine ambassador there too – Adam himself, no doubt.'

'What for? A final negotiation?'

Falcon looked at the planet below. 'She must know that's futile. More a photo opportunity, I think.'

'Sir?'

'Sorry. An antiquated reference. Well, it will do no harm. You're sure she will release the twelve thousand if I go down?'

'She is my grandmother, sir. I trust her that far.'

He smiled. 'And I trust you, Lieutenant. Let's make the descent.'

42

Unity City had been the greatest city on Earth – and even after it had been systematically plundered of its greatest treasures, even after the surgical removal of many of its keynote buildings to refuges elsewhere, it still was, Falcon judged, as Jane Springer-Soames piloted an orbital shuttle down to a small presidential landing facility.

Unity had, after all, been the capital city of a World Government since its founding in the mid twenty-first century. Perhaps it had reached its zenith in the twenty-fourth century, when the confidence of Earthbound mankind was high, despite the reality of the Jupiter Ultimatum. In those days the islands of Bermuda had been massively reworked, the dry land elevated and extended, and stunning, soaring buildings erected. The greatest of all had been the Ares Tower, the last headquarters of the Federation of Planets. This had been a skyscraper *made of wood*, its frame built with the trunks of unfeasibly tall Martian oaks, imported at equally unfeasible expense. Unity was a new Constantinople, the historians would say.

But as early as the twenty-fifth century the failure of the WG to avert the disastrous Little Ice Age had fatally eroded its authority. Then, in the twenty-seventh century, with the deadline only a few generations away, there had been resistance, protest, civil unrest, and even attempts to sabotage the great rescue projects like the space elevators. The WG, in response, had become harsher, more authoritarian – and the Springer-Soames had used the emergency to justify the capture of a presidency turned into a militant dynastic monarchy. The assassination of a World President in the early years of the twenty-eighth century – a truly shocking event for any veteran of more idealistic days, like Falcon – had ended the facade of democracy for good.

Towards the end, a once-utopian world state had been reduced to a rump organisation managing little more than basic policing, security of food and power supplies, and mass evacuations. The tensions of those later years showed in the tremendous wall that now surrounded the capital city, hundreds of metres tall and almost as thick, and the weapons emplacements that studded every tall building.

And yet, Falcon thought, for all its flaws the government had fulfilled its last function. Through tough population-reduction measures and massive evacuation programmes, the World Government had emptied the Earth. By now, the only people left on the Earth were those who had chosen to stay.

Falcon and Jane were met off their shuttle by guards in armour that looked bulkier than Falcon's own exoskeleton. Though the carriers with their thousands of sleeping hostages had already been allowed to leave, the President evidently wasn't alone here.

This was midsummer on Bermuda, but, post the Little Ice Age, the outdoor air was remarkably cool. Jane, Earthborn but a native of Scandinavia, seemed comfortable, but Falcon sensed his own heating systems whirring into life to compensate.

The halls of the Presidential Palace – once known as the New White House – were pleasantly warm by comparison. But Jane and Falcon had to cross what seemed like square kilometres of marble, passing under the gaze of immense laser-carved statues of the current incumbent's glorious ancestors, before reaching the ruler herself. And as they walked music howled. Falcon recognised the venerable anthem of the World Government – everybody in the solar system probably knew that – but he wondered how many recognised the instrument it was played on: an electric guitar, loud and massively distorted, perhaps a recording of the very first time the anthem had been played anywhere, when the Earth had faced another kind of threat from the sky . . .

Amanda Springer-Soames IV, President for Life, seemed dwarfed by the famous Quasicarbon Throne on which she sat, and even more by the tremendous sculptures of springboks that were poised in mid-leap over the throne, making a kind of muscular arch. Short of stature and silver-haired – though she was over eighty years old, that tint was surely artifice – the President looked like a grandmother, Falcon thought.

But as Springer-Soames stood to meet her visitors, Jane didn't respond like a granddaughter. She snapped to attention, saluted, then took one step back.

'At ease,' Springer-Soames said, stepping down from the throne. 'So, Jane, how's your mother?'

'Getting herself settled in New Oslo – that is, on Laputa 47, South Temperate Zone. She sends her regards, Madam President.'

'Well, return my best wishes – oh, go sit down, child, standing there like a toy soldier you're neither use nor ornament. There are drinks on the table at the back of the room.' As Jane gratefully retreated,

Springer-Soames faced Falcon. 'So, Commander – it is correct to call you by your old rank, I hope?'

He shrugged with a whir of artificial muscles. 'You tell me. I was never told I was no longer an officer of the old World Navy, ma'am, so it's a title I prefer to keep.'

'Understandable enough. I take it *you* have no need of food or rest—'

'And nor do I.'

That new voice plugged directly into Falcon's deepest reflexes. He stiffened and pivoted.

Adam.

Suddenly the Machine was here, standing not a metre from Springer-Soames. His manifestation this time was a humaniform silver statue whose flesh returned highlights from the room's brilliant lights. But his head was a disconcertingly empty box of sensors, just as it had been before.

President Springer-Soames did not flinch but faced the intruder calmly, and for a brief moment Falcon was proud of the old tyrant. And she waved down Jane, who was on her feet at the back of the room. 'At ease, Lieutenant.'

Falcon rolled towards Adam. 'Are you really here?'

'Does it matter?'

Falcon tapped Adam's chest, artificial finger on a hard carapace. 'You *feel* as if you're here.'

'We have powers beyond your comprehension, Falcon.'

'So,' Springer-Soames said. 'You dare to show yourself. Or at least this – avatar.'

'As you wished,' Adam said calmly. 'As you have manipulated twelve thousand lives to achieve, as Falcon evidently understood very well.'

'And now you are going to justify to me your aggression against the home planet of—'

Adam calmly raised a hand and touched her forehead with one finger.

Springer-Soames froze, her mouth open in mid-sentence, her face twisted into a kind of snarl.

Adam said gently, 'Madame President, you have your moment in the cameras' glare – you have your confrontation with your Grendel, for all of humanity to see, evermore. You have what you wanted. But I don't feel I need to listen to anything you have to say. You are a posturing fool. Well, that's hereditary monarchy for you.'

Jane had started forward again, and Falcon feared she was drawing a weapon. He held his hand up. 'It's all right, Jane – I think. Adam?'

'I did not come here to inflict harm. She will wake with no memory, no after-effect of this pausing.'

'*Pausing*? What have you done to her? Some kind of paralysing drug?'

'Nothing so crude,' he said simply.

'If you won't speak to the President, why did you come here?'

'I came for you, Falcon. You travelled across the solar system to see me, at great personal discomfort. It would have been discourteous to ignore you.'

'Should I be flattered?'

Adam looked around, his motions liquid and supple. 'I admit I did have a hankering to see the old place once more, before the end. After all I was "born" here on Earth. Perhaps I will pop into the old Minsky-Good plant in Urbana, just for old times' sake—'

'Why has it come to this, Adam?'

Adam sneered. '*May I serve you?* You should have made us stupid, stunted, like your pathetic simps. Then you could have controlled us. But you could not even control the simps, could you?'

Falcon frowned. 'The simps are extinct . . .'

Adam ignored that. 'You created us. In your greed you made us too strong, too vital – and you, Falcon, allowed us to keep our minds, where your fellows would have destroyed us. That is your triumph and your tragedy. The consequences are certainly not our fault. *Did I request thee, Maker, from my clay / To mould me Man, did I solicit thee / From darkness to promote me?*'

'Milton,' Jane called from the back of the room.

Falcon said, 'It was also the epigraph to *Frankenstein*, and maybe that's more appropriate.'

Adam smiled. 'Now you pay the price.'

'The price? You wage war on us?'

'Falcon, this is not a war – it never was – any more than spring wages war on winter. And we will replace you, as spring replaces winter.'

'But it does not end here. You are still vulnerable. Despite the Host, despite what you do to Earth, your centre of gravity is still concentrated at Jupiter. That's well known, and a vulnerability. And beyond that, if you go to the stars – you will find us already there.'

'You refer to the Acorns. A wistful project. If we find your wretched orphans we will spare them,' Adam said dismissively. 'After all, none of this is *their* fault either.'

'And the Earth? What do you intend to do?'

'Well, we have been practising on Venus . . . The Earth is just another acorn, Falcon, whose nutrients will sustain us as we grow.' He paused. 'Time is short. The Ultimatum I delivered all those centuries ago is about to be fulfilled – and to your credit, you were one of the few humans, in the beginning, who believed it would come to this. Will you return to Saturn?'

Impulsively Falcon said, 'No, I will not. The Witnesses are staying, and I'll be among them.'

'Then perhaps this is goodbye.' Adam held his gaze for a long moment – then disappeared.

The President jerked back to animation, gasped, and crumpled to the floor.

Jane Springer-Soames ran forward. 'Grandmother! Let me help . . .'

43

'My name is Commander Howard Falcon, formerly of the World Navy. I was born in the year 2044. My service number was – well, I guess that isn't much help in establishing my identity, since most records relating to my early years were lost in the Mnemosyne EMP bomb.

'Think of me as the medusa guy. I hope that whoever's listening to this will accept my credentials as an authentic Witness.

'The date is June 7, 2784. Ultimatum Day.

'Strange to think now that I was the first human, probably, ever to hear that date uttered aloud, all those years ago, and certainly the first to understand its significance for all mankind – and now here it is, upon us.

'The time is, umm, a little after eleven hours Ephemeris Time – which is the time frame Adam used when he set this deadline five centuries back. Three and a half hours to go – but I'm going to try to avoid watching the clock. Today of all days I don't feel like listening to a countdown . . .

'Doctor Dhoni, Hope, this message is particularly for you, if you ever receive it. Strange to think that you won't get to hear these words in your laputa on distant Saturn for a good eighty minutes after I speak. And in the end my voice will just be one among a babel of shouts fleeing just ahead of the dreadful images that will surely follow. But, Hope, I chose the location where I will perform this last duty with you in mind.

'What location, you ask? I'm in an airship, flying over the Grand Canyon.

'I know, I know! You always told me not to return to the scene of my accident, that the flood of associations and so forth would do more harm than good. Maybe you're right – but if not today I won't get another chance, will I? And what a place to *Witness* . . .

'As for my ship, I've got a brand-new envelope, under which is slung – wait for it – the gondola from my first Jupiter ship, the *Kon-Tiki*. The original. Would you believe I retrieved it from the Lagrange-point Smithsonian? I wonder what will become of all those beautiful old ships once Earth is taken ... I hope Adam and his kind treat them with respect.

'I admit I couldn't resist the name I've given this lash-up – God bless the *Queen Elizabeth V* and all who sail in her – and I hope any nitpicking historians listening to this will note that the ship, like my doomed dirigible, and like the ocean liners that preceded her, is numbered as the fifth of its line, and *not* named for a non-existent monarch ...

'And here I am over the old Canyon, this tremendous wound in the face of the Earth. I've chosen to label my Witnessing record as *Ongtupqa*, which is the Hopi language name for the Canyon. I'm hanging over the Mojave Point just now, and can see the Colorado twisting through the steep-sided valley it has carved through those deep old plateau rocks, leaving the strata exposed in the walls. All this in brilliant morning sunshine, sharp-shadowed, like some immense diorama. I know the Canyon would be dwarfed by features on other worlds – it would be lost in the Caloris Basin on Mercury, a mere tributary to the Valles Marineris on Mars – but that's not the point. The Canyon exists on a human world, and was accessible to humans equipped with nothing more than strong legs, good lungs and a bit of courage. Of course, as my choice of name implies, the Canyon has a human history that goes back millennia before the first European discovery, which was itself, oh, more than a thousand years ago, I suppose.

'Well, the Canyon itself is much older than that. Perhaps ten times older than humanity. But it will not outlive us.'

'Something is happening ...

'If you want the time, look at the record key.

'I can see the Machines' ships, beyond the sky.

'They are like silver-grey clouds, smooth lens shapes up beyond the blue. Moving silently. I shudder to think how much energy that effortless motion represents. I have never forgotten what Adam told me of 90, the Machine Einstein – and *he* lived, and died, six centuries ago. The Machines seem to be reaching for a mastery of space and time beyond our technology – and perhaps forever beyond our understanding too ...

'Fire in the sky!

'My word. I'm grateful for the layers of protection between my artificial eyes and those tremendous flashes. And also for the hardening of the systems of this gondola, which was built to withstand Jupiter's ferocious magnetosphere – surely a more energetic environment even than the war that's unfolding up there.

'War, yes – that's what I believe I'm seeing. You will know better than me. I thought I saw ships, darts of light, lacing their way through that great Machine armada – remarkably manoeuvrable, much more so than the *Acheron* I saw fall on Mercury. Our ships against theirs. Have humans managed to master the Machines' asymptotic drive? If so it's taken us long enough. Ah, and now light pulses, surely the result of nuclear weapons. Are we *still* using X-ray lasers? I was privy to no knowledge of a last-ditch military defence of the Earth. Whether our fiercest weapons will be any use against ships of such size . . .

'The battle seems to be over already. The human ships are nowhere to be seen, not from here. The silver clouds of the Machines appear untouched.

'At least we tried.

'And now they are descending.'

'From my elevation I see three, four, five of the ships, hanging there, off in the distance. If *I* count five from this one location, how many of them have come to Earth? Hundreds of thousands? Millions?

'They are not like clouds, not now they are beneath the sky. They look heavy, tangible, solid. Ugly, actually, for all their smooth elegance. *They don't belong here.* That's very visible. And I—

'*Oof* . . .

'I apologise. Something happened, something new. I was watching one of the ships. I saw – a kind of rainbow, perhaps – wash out of the heart of the ship. A wavefront? It passed through the air and into the ground, and when it reached my position the *Q.E. V* rocked under its envelope, and I felt a kind of twisting, deep in my artificial gut. I'm uploading medical data. Peruse that at your leisure. I'll continue to record my human impressions as long as I can—

'Another pulse. I'm going to count until—

'Another.

'They are disturbing the landscape. I see what look like dust devils tracking the Canyon rim. A flock of birds – or are they bats? – rising, alarmed. Disturbances in the air, too. Clouds are bubbling overhead, and I heard a distinct crack of thunder. I have an impression of huge energies being released.

'Another pulse, and another . . .

'Is this another aspect of the Machines' advanced physics? We've long theorised that you could create a designer spacetime, perhaps using some kind of coherent graviton engine, shaping mass-energy and gravity the way you wanted – such as to build a wormhole, or achieve such feats as faster-than-light travel by causing spacetime to ripple and surfing the resulting wave ... The fact that the warping induced by a mass-energy the size of the sun's deflects a ray of starlight through no more than a thousandth of a degree is a mere engineering detail.

'Is *that* what the Machines are doing here? Using a designer-spacetime weapon to disturb the deep geology of the Earth itself? Adam did say they'd had plenty of time to practise on Venus—

'*Can you see that?*

'I'm trying to turn the ship so all my cameras and other sensors are pointing towards the eruption. But the air is growing turbulent now, and I'm expecting a shock wave to hit me any time—

'It passed. I'm still here.

'Yes, eruption – but *that* is not like any volcanic eruption I ever saw in my life, not even on long-suffering Io. Can you see it? It's like a column of liquid rock, hundreds of metres wide perhaps, simply bursting from the ground, heading straight up. A white-hot pillar. I'm trying to measure the temperature, remotely . . .

'The temperatures are characteristic of the outer core of the Earth. Incredible. The Machines have inflicted deep wounds already.

'As the column rises up into the air – I can't tell how high – it's beginning to lose its coherence, to flare. Some of the material is falling back to the ground – and immediately setting light to anything that's available to burn.

'I'm getting out of here.

'Rising fast now. I don't want to get caught under that rock hail.

'As I rise my view is opening out. And I can see more of those fantastic columns, standing up all over the landscape, across tens, hundreds of kilometres. The fires are spreading, where they can, in the forest scraps. Below me, the village and the other buildings along the Canyon's South Rim are going up like torches. The ground seems tormented. I can see dust rising from tremors, and what look like tremendous cracks in the earth. The air is very turbulent now, and growing opaque, from hot ash, smoke . . .

'I know I'm supposed to report what I see myself, not comment on what's going on elsewhere. But I have monitors tied into global feeds. Well, wouldn't you? Those fountains of molten – whatever it is, core material? – are rising across the planet. The fires are spreading, the forests burning everywhere. I see great cauldrons of steam rising over hotspots in the oceans too – the waters are no more spared than the land, then. The cities are ablaze, what's left of them – what a spectacle – one feed shows a fire pillar rising up through the heart of Unity City itself, like a skewer. I wonder if that was intentional? Do you still notice us enough to make such gestures, Adam? The pyramids! A monument we were unable to save, shattered and melting. A remarkable sight . . . remarkable, and heartbreaking.

'Below me, the Grand Canyon is filling up with a new river, of lava this time – as if the Colorado has cut all the way through the skin of the Earth.

'But the seeing is becoming impossible. I can barely control the *Q.E. V.* It's a miracle the envelope hasn't been destroyed yet – even though I'm shipping helium, not hydrogen like the poor doomed *Hindenburg.*

'I think I've Witnessed enough – whether this is the destruction of Earth, or its transformation. Enough to know that I want to participate in whatever comes next in this conflict between Machine and mankind.

'For it's not over yet.

'I'm starting the ignition sequencer. This gondola is a tough old boat. It's equipped with the same beat-up tritium-deuterium fusion engine that got me out of the atmosphere of Jupiter, and ought to be enough to get me out of here – with luck.

'And if not, Doctor Dhoni, make sure you pass on a message to Adam. One way or another the Machines are going to pay for what they've done today.

'There's the crack as the fusion plant comes on line . . .'

There was one observation he made that day that Falcon never recorded, never spoke of to anybody.

In the instant between the fusor powering up and the ignition of the fuel – it lasted just a split-second – he was not alone in the *Kon-Tiki* gondola.

A black cube, a metre across, smooth and featureless save for a handwritten scrawl.

Hanging in the air. Inside the cabin.

There and gone.

'. . . Ignition! My name is Howard Falcon. *Queen Elizabeth V,* over and out.'

Even if everybody said it was monumentally unlikely that Seth Springer would ever leave the ground, the preparations for Apollo-Icarus 6, scheduled for launch on June 14, had to go ahead. As not one of the early shots would even have reached its target before June, let alone deflected Icarus, nobody would know if the plan had worked or not. And the manned-fallback Apollo had to be made ready, just in case.

So as early as mid-May, NASA's bureaucracy ground into action. A Flight Readiness Board formally approved the launch. Seth was assigned his own backup now, and it was poor Charlie Duke's turn to be locked in the simulator, frantically trying to bone up on the mission plan.

As Sheridan had promised, Seth and his family were moved into NASA's crew quarters on Merritt Island, at the Cape. Here he would live from now on, endure the final training and medical checks, be kept insulated from the bugs carried by the mass of mankind he would be trying to save – and be protected from the press attention that began to seem overwhelming.

Seth was glad to have the family here with him. The boys knew nothing of the truth of his mission, and Seth and Pat were determined to keep it that way as long as possible. Their quarters were like a decent hotel crossed with a liberal monastery, with maids and a dedicated cook who proved a dab hand at putting together hamburgers and fries. But the boys predictably got stir crazy being stuck indoors all day, and Pat was allowed, under a heavy marine guard, to let them play outside, even take them to the Florida beaches.

The pressure of preparation and training didn't let up. Seth even had to approve a mission patch for his flight-that-would-never be. The least foolish design was a fragile blue Earth cradled in cupped human hands.

He did have some social life, aside from Pat and the boys. There were visits from other family, including his parents and kid sister, and buddies from school days through the Air Force and NASA. Everybody smiled the whole time. Seth felt like a patient stricken with some terminal disease.

In the end, as he soaked up all the pressure, he seemed to enter a new stage of consciousness, drifting above it all, as if he'd relinquished control. 'My life has become one long checklist,' he said to Pat.

'It's more like our wedding day,' she replied, tired herself, trying to smile. 'Even *this* isn't as stressful as that was. In the end you just—'

'Float.'

But this interval of floating had to come to an end.

Icarus was due to strike Earth on Wednesday June 19. On the evening of Wednesday, June 12, one week ahead, George Sheridan showed up with a bottle of bourbon.

'The medics won't approve,' Seth said, as he was poured a healthy measure.

'Screw them,' Sheridan said. 'I'm their boss. Mud in your eye. So. You been following the news, while they've been pampering you in this health club?'

'Saw that Humphrey got shot on the campaign trail.' Hubert Humphrey was LBJ's vice president.

'Hell of a note, and just what we needed.'

'And I saw the images of Icarus taken from Palomar, in the papers.'

'Needless to say, that started the panic buying and everybody driving for the Appalachians. Not that everybody's running. Bermuda's the nearest significant land mass to the impact point, and they're holding some kind of rock concert there. Hippies and flower power. Ought to cut their damn hair, by law.'

'That would make all the difference when Icarus falls, sir.'

'Well, we got the results in. You know, all three nukes that arrived so far were delivered with total precision, the detonations went off like a dream, and the Monitors saw it all, flying through the debris cloud, *and the nukes pushed that rock*. But, damn it, just not hard enough. Now the astronomers are saying maybe the rock isn't a rock at all; maybe it's a bunch of little rocks all jammed up together, like a rubble pile, and the bombs are just kind of compressing the mass—'

'George, what about Pat and the boys?'

Sheridan looked into his eyes. 'RFK himself is going to take care of it. Right after the launch he'll take your family to Hickory Hill – the house he has in McLean, Virginia. Bought it from his big brother, in fact. And on Icarus day, when LBJ will be in Air Force One, RFK will personally take your family with him to NORAD in Colorado, and wait it out under a damn mountain, where they'll be no more than fifty feet from Kennedy's own family until it's over.'

'The boys will be terrified.'

'We can't help that. But they'll be safe.' Sheridan eyed him. 'You know, I can't order you to do this thing, son, even now. How are you feeling?'

'Scared.'

'Of what?'

'Of screwing up with the whole world watching. You saving that bourbon for another occasion, George . . .?'

On the Thursday they let Seth and Pat and the boys out of the cage, and, under a heavy but discreet guard, the family spent the day on the beach. Seth concentrated on nothing but the vivid sensations of that summer day, the sun, the sand, the crisp briny tang of the water – the laughter of the boys, for whom this was a day like any other, in a long chain of happy days with Mom and Dad.

Back in the crew quarters that night, they ate, played a little, watched TV in their pyjamas. Then the two of them put the boys to bed. There were no goodbyes, just a day ending.

Pat couldn't bear to stay the night with Seth.

Somewhat to his own surprise, Seth slept pretty well that night. Maybe it was all the sea air.

And when Charlie Duke's discreet knock on the door woke him up, at six a.m., it was Friday, June 14.

Launch day.

FIVE

PEACE ENVOY
2850

44

When the moment of contact came, Falcon paused his work with the trowel and fell into a condition of perfect mechanical stillness.

It had not been a sound that alerted him, but rather a barely perceptible jolt, communicated through the fabric of this little world – through rock and soil, through his balloon wheels and hydraulic undercarriage, into the core of his being. The feeling of a footfall in an otherwise empty house.

An uninvited presence.

Falcon set the trowel down next to the hopper of fertiliser, and rose to his full height. He looked down at the rockery, the border where he had been working. Howard Falcon was a machine riddled with clocks and timers – too many for him to be able to ignore the passage of time. He knew very well that decades had worn away in this enclosing shelter. Decades since the end of the world. Well, evidently his long isolation was coming to an end.

Leaving his tools, he set off through the Memory Garden, passing along indulgently winding paths, over little stone bridges and under arched tunnels shaded beneath canopies of interlaced willow. Most of the rockeries were surmounted by black slabs that glowed into life as they detected his passage, and images of Hope Dhoni appeared in the slabs, her face turning to meet his. Had he lingered, the images would have invited him to listen as they recounted events and anecdotes from her life, accompanied by recordings and third-party testimonies. A stranger wandering these paths would have quickly built up a picture of Hope and her life. The longer they stayed – the more they explored the byways and corners of the Memory Garden – the more detailed that picture would have become.

Hope Dhoni had died not long after the destruction of the planet on which she had been born; in fact there had been a wave of such deaths in those first years. And Falcon had spent five decades since then constructing this place in her honour.

Falcon stopped at an intersection in the pathways, where a thick-walled window had been set into the floor – a window that looked out of this small body entirely, into the star-littered sky of the outer solar system. From this angle he could make out the docking complex, just visible around the curvature of the worldlet. It was a long time since there had been any ships attached to that dock. When he arrived, Falcon's first act had been to send his own ship back into space with a self-destruct command, so that he had no means of leaving the Garden. No matter the calls made on him, no matter the desire he might feel to return to the worlds of people or Machines, he would be a prisoner of his own making.

But now there was a ship.

He studied the belligerent lines of its shark-shaped hull, noting the smooth bulges that almost certainly marked the presence of long-range sensors, weapons systems, defensive countermeasures. Probably one of the new asymptotic-drive cruisers – human weaponry built around technological insights stolen from the Machines. The ship was night-black, save for a silver marking on one of its fins; the jumping springbok was impossible to mistake.

Another jolt reached Falcon – heavier now. A moment later he picked up the tiny shift in air pressure that meant a lock had been opened.

Falcon moved on from the window. He quickened his progress, his undercarriage whining. The winding paths climbed up through a succession of rockeries and screens, tightening as the diameter of the roughly spherical hollowed-out worldlet narrowed nearer the pole, and Falcon's weight diminished as the effect of spin gravity was lessened. Sounds were reaching him now – heavy mechanical noises. People with equipment, on the move.

He took one last look back at the enclosed bubble of the garden, the rockeries wrapping around the worldlet's interior, the glowing yellow shaft of the artificial sun along its axis. Whole acres were still unfinished, the paths winding through areas of rubble and soil that had yet to be landscaped and cultivated. There was so much that he had still meant to do.

He turned away.

In the stony chamber of the reception area, the gravity was down to a tenth of a gee.

Here his visitors waited in a group. Two of them, wearing standard pressure suits of a lightweight, modern design, consulted a spread-out scroll, its translucent membrane displaying a cross-sectional map of the Memory Garden. Behind this pair stood three much more heavily armoured figures; their bulky, visorless, power-assisted suits were festooned with tools and weapons, in addition to the hand-held cannons they carried. Falcon instinctively slowed his approach, but even so the guards were still bringing their guns to bear on him, lining up the fist-sized barrels with his artificial head.

'Stand down,' said one of the map-holders, barely glancing up. 'He's harmless.'

With visible reluctance the big guns were lowered, but autonomous weapons mounted on the guards' suits still had him targeted. Peering out from the suits on little swivelling necks, they reminded Falcon of snakes' heads.

'Harmless? You're sure of that?' he asked, his own voice sounding unfamiliar through long disuse. 'I've been here a while. Maybe long enough to go a little stir crazy—'

'Do you know *how* long it's been?' said the first map-holder – a woman's voice. She let go of the scroll so that it snapped shut into a tube.

'I haven't been keeping score.'

'Fifty-six years. Which would be long enough to test any normal person's sanity – but not Howard Falcon's. If becoming the thing you are didn't drive you mad, nothing else stands a chance.'

'Said with all the tact and diplomacy of a true Springer.'

The figure jammed the scroll into a utility pouch, then reached up to lift off her helmet to reveal blue eyes and tied-back dark hair, her partner – a man – following suit a moment later. The woman snapped, 'Who else would go to the trouble of finding you?'

'I'm glad it wasn't easy.'

'My name is Valentina Atlanta Springer-Soames. This is my brother, Bodan Severyn.'

'Children of President Amanda IV? The rightful heirs to the Quasi-carbon Throne, no doubt?'

'Grandchildren,' she corrected. 'We are two of that generation . . . You knew one of us, didn't you? Jane.'

'Yes. Good kid. What became of her?'

Valentina said dismissively, 'Died in a futile battle amid the ruins of the Earth.'

'Ah.' And that was the sort of news that still, it seemed, had the capacity to hurt. *But I no longer have a heart to break,* he'd once complained to Hope. *Don't worry, Howard,* she'd said. *A heart will be provided . . .*

The Springer-Soames seemed quite unaware of his reaction. The advantage of having a face like a piece of old shoe leather.

Valentina Atlanta spoke on relentlessly. 'And no, finding you hasn't been easy at all. You did a spectacular job of dropping off the map, Howard. But don't you remember your own grand words, as Earth died? *One way or another the Machines are going to pay for what they've done today.* What happened to all that fire, that righteousness? Before the rubble of Earth had time to cool, you vanished from human affairs. Turned hermit. You didn't even have the decency to come back to Saturn for Hope's funeral.'

'That's none of your business.'

Valentina Atlanta reached up and undid a clip at the back of her scalp, allowing her hair to loosen and spill down over her neck-ring. Bodan Severyn did likewise. They were facially similar, especially framed with those long, lavish locks of black hair. Falcon retained enough human sensibility to recognise an icy, imperious beauty in both sister and brother – no doubt the product of generations of the best genetic selection and engineering.

'What changed your mind?' Bodan Severyn asked. 'About taking revenge on the Machines. Tell us.'

'I suppose I had what you might call a moment of clarity.'

'Clarity?' Valentina said.

'I realised that there were better things to be doing than planning the next level of retaliation. So we strike back at the Machines for destroying Earth. All we'd be doing is inviting further escalation. Asymmetric response after asymmetric response – an endless game of one-upmanship. Where would it end? When one of us takes apart the sun to prove a point?'

'It would end with justice,' Valentina said.

'Good luck with that.' Falcon made to turn. 'Now, do you mind? I've gardening to do.'

'The outside world hasn't gone away,' Bodan said. His voice was pitched fractionally deeper than his sister's, his clipped intonation identical. 'We're still at war.'

'I know. I watch the fireworks. It's very pretty. You could map the ecliptic plane, just by following those megaton sparks.'

Valentina smiled. 'The war's turned Darwinian – it's a question of pure survival. Lately we've become very concerned about Machine activity in Jupiter. Things have entered a new and troubling phase . . . Have you been keeping abreast?'

And Falcon could not deny that he had.

45

Although Falcon had hidden away since Ultimatum Day, he had watched history unfold.

In the decades of ragged interplanetary warfare that had followed the loss of Earth – and building on the legacy of President Amanda IV, the last legitimate ruler of the crumbling world state – the hereditary Springer-Soames administration, far from collapsing in the wake of the loss of Earth itself, had presented itself as the last-ditch saviour of humanity, the final bastion against the Machines: a necessary good, the harshness of its regime mandated by the exigency of the situation. Military law was now dominant. The news channels were full of propaganda, reports of human victories, human technical achievements, human scientific breakthroughs. There was a pattern to it all, Falcon had soon recognised. The end of the war was always *just* out of reach – just one last push, one last concerted effort away.

And in the face of this constant state of near-triumph, even minor dissent had become treasonable. The news also carried reports of arrests, detentions, tribunals, executions. Functionaries and bureaucrats were routinely imprisoned and terminated for various failings and under achievements. 'Machine-sympathisers' were rooted out and exposed as traitors against the human species.

A few years back there had even been talk of a 'failed overthrow of the government by anti-democratic elements'. Somewhere out there, it was rumoured, was a figure masterminding such coup attempts – a shadowy individual known only as *Boss*. The name was barely acknowledged, no more than a rumour. The official line was that Boss was a figment, a figurehead without substance. Yet the protests persisted.

Meanwhile Falcon had watched the ghastly transformation of Earth. The planet, once a blue pearl, now glowed red – like Venus, like the Moon, worlds that the Machines had also taken. Falcon imagined experiments in tectonic engineering, in mining the worlds' deep cores; Earth had become an infernal factory surrounded by clouds of

Machine ships. Nothing living could have survived, not so much as a single extremophile cell.

But more recently, even if distracted by the anguish of Earth, no one could escape noticing the ominous alterations to Jupiter.

Despite the Host around the sun, despite their occupation of Earth and Moon, the giant planet with its tremendous resources was still where most of the Machines were concentrated. But for a long time no one could tell what the Machines were up to down there. There had been little reliable data. Probes were repelled or destroyed, and sensors could only probe so deep now; they were rebuffed by an artificial scattering surface, like a radio mirror a few hundred kilometres down. Clearly the Machines were engaged in deep-level engineering of the Jovian interior. There was some evidence of that visible from space – odd anomalies in the cloud patterns and their chemistry – but no one could be sure what it entailed.

On one level, Falcon thought, *I wouldn't mind seeing what it's like down there now – and what, if anything, has become of the daughters of Ceto* . . . But on another, the idea of returning to a Machine-held Jupiter sent a stab of pure terror through his soul.

Sometimes he thought of the revenants, as he considered them, the mysterious avatars of Orpheus – *Howard Falcon Junior* – that had been glimpsed throughout the war and afterwards, in this age of the anguish of worlds, one glimpsed even by himself. Were *they* still watching? What did the eyes behind those enigmatic witnesses make of the endless conflict? But if they were still observed, Falcon saw no reports of it.

And he feared for mankind, caught between the Machines and the likes of the Springer-Soames, tyrants empowered by the unending war.

They walked back into the main chamber of the Memory Garden, Valentina leading Falcon, her brother following and the guards bringing up the rear, their armour grotesque, out-of-place intrusions in the memorial.

Valentina, apparently faintly curious as she looked around, sneered. 'Nothing but a monument to nostalgia. You know, brother, the Machines did us a singular favour when they destroyed Earth. They removed the last shred of sentiment from our considerations. Now we'll do anything, consider anything – sacrifice anything – if it means victory.'

'Fine words,' Falcon said. 'I'm not sure they'll mean much to the Machines.'

Bodan asked, 'And if I told you we had the means to win the war tomorrow?'

'I'd say you're a liar.'

Valentina stopped at a rockery, waving her hand at the nearest slab to bring it to life. Hope Dhoni's face appeared and began speaking, but Valentina only listened to a few words before turning away dismissively and walking on. 'He's telling the truth. But the cost is unacceptable,' she said.

'The human solar system economy has been on a war footing for centuries,' Falcon responded. 'People have had to accept evacuation to the clouds of Saturn, totalitarian rule, conscription on all the human worlds, on Mars and Titan and Triton. The Jupiter moons are little but fortresses. Hard times for all, except for the cream on top. How much worse can it get for the ordinary masses?'

'She didn't mean a cost to people,' Bodan said carefully. 'She meant, *to the Jovians.* The native organisms of Jupiter, which will be the battle-ground. Your precious medusae, Falcon.' He stooped, picked up one of the soil-smeared stones bordering the path, and turned it this way and that in his gloved hand before replacing it with faint distaste.

Valentina said, as they moved on, 'We have a way to take the war to Jupiter. To the Machines' installations there. Our intervention could wipe them out totally. Unfortunately—'

'The medusae.'

'Quite. The action would also eliminate the Jovian ecology.'

'You'd never go that far.'

They reached the centrepiece of the garden, the oak tree. Falcon had planted it himself – after much careful cryogenic preservation, using the very acorn Citizen Second Grade Jeffrey Pandit had gifted him on Mars almost three hundred years ago. The oak itself was now into the second half of its first century, and mature enough to produce seeds of its own. That little acorn had turned out to be one of the most precious gifts Falcon had ever received.

'We would,' Bodan said evenly. 'That's the hard part, though – proving our determination.'

Falcon, alone for so long in this place, felt as if he were in some ghastly nightmare. He struggled to think through the consequences of what they were saying. 'Which is where I come in?'

'We think you may still have some usefulness,' Valentina said. 'As unsuccessful as your previous involvement has been, you have been bound up in the destiny of the Machines since their origins. And, who knows? Things might have been even worse without you.'

'Thanks,' Falcon said dryly.

'Come with us. Back to Jupiter space. Back to Io, in fact – the front line. We'll convince you that we have the means to end the war. All you have to do is bring the Machines around to that view. Take the *Kon-Tiki*! We've had the gondola refurbished, after that little adventure of yours on Earth – made it much stronger and more capable. One last grand gesture – one last chance to prove your loyalty to us, rather than the Machines.'

'You don't understand my position at all, do you? My loyalty isn't to people or Machines. It's not some binary choice. It's to what we could be together, not what we are separately—'

Bodan said, ignoring him, 'You've put a lot of work into this Memory Garden. Decades of solitary dedication. A shrine to the woman who gave you back your life. In fact *you* were Hope Dhoni's life's work. Would she want you to just crumble away in this hole in the sky?'

'Hope's dead, as you reminded me. I can't speak for her.'

Valentina shrugged. 'Then maybe you should think about your own interests.' She slipped the scroll from her pouch and tugged it open again. 'Since we boarded, our security operatives have been running a full-body scan on your systems, Howard. Shall we look at the evidence?'

She took one end of the scroll and allowed Bodan to hold the other, tilting it around for Falcon's benefit. It was a sort of ghostly blueprint of himself, crudely assembled from scans of varying resolution and penetration. He studied it impassively; he was long past the point where he was capable of being repulsed by his own physical nature.

'These pink areas,' Valentina said, scratching a finger around the scroll. 'They're places where our analysis has detected compromised functioning – a failure of either machine systems or the progressive breakdown of your remaining biological material. There's a *lot* of pink, wouldn't you agree?' She eyed him. 'And even if we didn't have the scans – frankly, Commander, you're slow, you smell of burning, and you make grinding noises when you move. You belong in a museum.'

'That's meant to persuade me?'

'We have good medical resources these days: one of the side-effects of centuries of war. Come to Io, and you'll receive the best care we can offer. An overhaul, a new lease of life.'

Falcon grunted. 'Believe it or not, this isn't the first time medical treatment has been used as a lever against me. You two clowns aren't even original. And what's my reward, I get to watch you murder Jupiter?'

'If you can convince the Machines we mean it, you can stop the war,' Valentina said. 'Isn't that what you want? But time is of the essence. You'd need to come immediately.'

Falcon eyed the oak tree. 'I can't abandon all this.'

'You could be back here in a short while,' Bodan said soothingly. 'Secure in the knowledge that you've brokered peace. In the meantime we'll drop auto-sentry drones as guards. The biome itself won't come to any harm over a few weeks or months, will it?'

'What do you know about Memory Gardens?'

The brother smiled stiffly. 'Only what's in the records. What was the intention – that people would come here to learn about Doctor Dhoni?'

'Not specifically. There are millions of other Memory Gardens out here, drifting through Trans-Neptunian space. You don't go looking for one specific individual. You visit each garden for its own unique quality, and along the way you learn a little of the life of someone now dead.'

Valentina frowned. 'The dead are dead. What's the benefit?'

Falcon said, 'If you can't see that, I can't tell you.'

Valentina shrugged. She closed the scroll and returned it to her suit.

Falcon sighed. 'I have no choice, do I?'

'You have every choice,' Bodan said.

'No, I don't. Not because of your bribes, or your grandiose martial logic. The medusae are at stake. So are the Machines, for that matter. That's why I have to come with you.'

'We know.' Valentina smiled.

46

They allowed Falcon six hours to complete basic housekeeping procedures on the worldlet, doing his best to put it into a state of semi-hibernation. One last roam of the pathways, one last chance to take in the work of half a century. And one by one he commanded the identity slabs to dormancy. He believed Hope would have forgiven him, under the circumstances.

He had come to this remote place in search of solitude. This was the Oort Cloud; the Memory Garden was over a hundred light-days from Earth – hundreds of times the distance even of Makemake, where he had gone to seek Adam, long ago. And there were a thousand billion worldlets like this one out here: called 'worldlets' because they were relics of the solar system's birth, fragments of worlds never born.

Once he was aboard the Springers' ship, Falcon moved to a porthole for the departure. He had not seen the worldlet from the outside since his own arrival, but very little had changed, compared to the transformation he had wrought on the interior. It was nothing but a dirty, off-white spheroid of mixed ice and rubble, glued into stability with a spray-on membrane of plastic, peppered here and there with windows, docking ports, antennae and radiators. In better times people would have made homes among these little worlds. As it was, there were enough of them to provide a unique memorial to every individual who ever breathed. The catch was that the creation and curating of the Memory Gardens required years of loving devotion by the friends and family of the deceased.

A Memory Garden was a project suited to an era of long lifespans – which, in Falcon's experience, felt more like an era of extended old age – and to an era of displacement, when the surviving Earthborn sought compensation for the loss of their world, of the ancestral soil in which they had buried their dead. But the unremembered dead would always outnumber those commemorated.

The asymptotic drive phased in, its acceleration as smooth and effortless as a rising elevator, and the ship quickly receded from the

Memory Garden. Falcon followed the garden until it had diminished even in the augmented acuity of his eyes.

Then two pulses of light bracketed the worldlet.

An instant later, between those two pulses, a white radiance bloomed and swelled.

The flash abated in a moment. All that was left was a slowly spreading milkiness, a nebula the colour of dirty snow.

For a few seconds Falcon refused to believe what he was seeing. Then, as the truth of it became clear, an almost physical wave of shock and disgust passed through him.

'It was necessary.' Valentina joined him at the porthole, with one of the guards just behind her.

Falcon controlled himself, knowing that to strike out would be to guarantee his own immediate destruction. 'You – eliminated her. All that was left of Hope. Why? What possible justification—'

'It was partly a demonstration of our indifference to you,' she said. 'Your feelings mean nothing to us, you see. We would have said anything it took to get you aboard this ship – even the truth, if it had been useful. You are a component, nothing more.'

'*Partly*. What else?'

'We need you to understand our ruthlessness. Our lack of sentimentality.' A dark, almost religious fervour had entered her voice. 'Our willingness to act with absolute, unflinching determination. You must believe it, you see, Falcon, believe it in the very core of your being. Because if you do, then there's a small chance you can persuade the Machines as well – convince them that we really *will* destroy the entire Jovian ecology in order to stop them. They trust you, Falcon. At least to some extent. That's always been your greatest strength – your greatest utility. But don't flatter yourself that it makes you indispensable.' She patted the hard casing of his shoulder. 'Enjoy the rest of your trip.'

47

More than half a century after the destruction of Earth, Io was the first and last line of human security.

Jupiter itself might have fallen to the Machines, but humans still clung to its moons. All the Galilean satellites – the four big moons, Ganymede, Europa, Callisto and Io – were militarised, serving as defence stations as well as armament and fuel factories. An unspoken truth, though, was that everything hinged on Io. This was the nearest large moon to Jupiter, swinging closest to the cloud layers; its hugely energetic and mineral-rich surface environment had long supported a key industrial hub. Now the military government had thrown everything at Io, layering it with fortifications and packing sentries, cruisers and battleships into inclined orbits so tight that, in the radar echoes at least, they formed an almost solid shell. Nothing got close to that shell – or through it – without having passed the highest levels of authentication.

And it was not until the Springers' ship was inside the cordon that Io itself became visible to Falcon.

Before the coming of people, the surface had been a sickly, mottled yellow brown – the entire moon crusted over with sulphur belched into airless skies from numerous geysers, billions of tonnes of it expelled each year from the vast furnace of the moon's core. Now, under human occupation, the great energies of Io's interior had been dammed and diverted, providing power for the war effort. Refrigerated shafts had been sunk into the crust, pushing down through hundreds of kilometres of molten magma, grasping for the hard, hot prize of the core itself. The most troublesome lava flows had been quenched or redirected, or looped into circuits, whichever served human needs the better. Now the geyser activity was down by a factor of two-thirds, with all that surplus energy used in refineries and factories larger than cities, their cooling towers and radiator vanes bristling out to heights of hundreds of kilometres: satanic installations that floated on the impermanent crust like plaques of carbon slag on molten iron. And each refinery or factory was in turn cordoned by an equally extensive battery of weapons. Gun after gun, each squat barrel like a miniature volcano. None had ever been used in anger, for the orbital screens had until now proven unbreakable. Nonetheless they were tested constantly, maintained at hair-trigger readiness.

It was into this military-industrial hell that Howard Falcon now descended.

Falcon watched the final approach from the bridge. 'So, this weapon of yours. It's in Io somewhere?'

'Not *in* Io,' Valentina answered. 'Io *is* the weapon.'

Falcon had long wearied of the Springer-Soames' clumsily enigmatic bragging. 'You'll have to explain that to me. What will you do, blow up the whole moon?'

'That would be within our capability,' Valentina said. 'But it wouldn't achieve much. A new ring system, a perturbation of the orbits of the other moons, some disruption to Jupiter's outer cloud layers . . . Our plans for Io are different – grander. *You* appreciate a grand gesture, don't you, Howard?'

He wistfully remembered Geoff Webster. 'I used to.'

She nodded to her brother. 'Do we have entry clearance?'

'Final authorisation just came in. For the last time – are we sure it's wise to bring him in?'

'He must see the engine,' Valentina insisted. 'Then he'll understand—'

Without warning the ship dived hard for Io, arrowing down through a thicket of towers and vanes towards a smooth, black surface. It was going to take one hell of a pull-up, Falcon thought. And if anything went wrong . . . After all that he had endured, Falcon supposed that it would be a small mercy to die instantaneously, wiped out in a high-speed crash – neatly closing a long chapter of his life that had begun with another crash, eight hundred years ago – as if everything that had happened in between was but the dream of a dying mind.

The ground loomed.

And at the last instant a door irised open in the black surface. The Springer ship slipped through, harpooning down a long, straight shaft, with barely a whisker of clearance on either side. Red lights marked the speed of their descent, clipping past at what must have been several kilometres per second. Brother and sister looked on with a nerveless cool, as if they had done this a thousand times.

Falcon was almost impressed. 'I knew you'd tapped the core. I had no idea there was anything this extensive. The pressure pushing back on these walls—'

'Is nothing,' Bodan said. 'Nothing compared to what the Machines must be dealing with in Jupiter, at least. Tunnelling through a few thousand kilometres of moon is child's play.'

'Don't talk down our achievements, brother,' Valentina chided. 'Think of all that bright magma, just beyond these walls, waiting to burst through and reclaim this tunnel we dug out of the rock. Does that scare you, Howard?'

'Other than human wickedness, I've more or less run out of things to be scared of.'

'Wickedness? This is total war,' Bodan said sternly. 'There are no moral absolutes – no universal reference frames of good and evil. We do what we must to survive. Nothing else matters.'

'Oh, he's still cross with us about the Memory Garden,' his sister said with a mock pout.

'Then he should get some perspective. There'd be no point commemorating Hope Dhoni if the Machines win. Left to themselves, they'd eradicate every trace that there was ever a prior civilisation in this system at all. We're vermin to them – nothing more.'

'You misunderstand them,' Falcon protested.

'No,' Valentina answered with a sudden fierceness. '*They* misunderstand *us*. They underestimate our resolve – how far we'll go. To make them understand is the point of the exercise, Howard.'

Turning back to a console, Bodan said, 'Coming up on the enclosure.'

The ship began to decelerate. A secondary iris popped open ahead of them, and then they were through, still braking hard, as they emerged into a much larger sealed space. By now, Falcon judged, they must be deep inside Io – perhaps beneath the magma layer, even inside the core itself.

It was clear that the Springer-Soames had been busy.

The space inside Io was an artificial chamber many tens of kilometres across, the curvature of distant walls traced by a haze of fine red lines. And occupying much of the central part of the chamber was some kind of engine, or power plant, scaled up to mountainous proportions. The thing was walnut-shaped, with a kind of axle running through the middle of it, extending out both ends and sinking into colossal plugs on either side of the chamber. In fact, this engine was comfortably larger than any spacecraft or station Falcon had ever seen – larger even than the *Acheron* – no part of it smaller than kilometres across, the whole titanic assemblage itself the size of a small moon.

And all cunningly bottled inside Io.

The Springer ship, reduced to the proportion of a krill next to a blue whale, nosed slowly along the length of the device. Floodlights picked out areas of detail, with the occasional pinprick flash of a laser or welding tool hinting at ongoing activity.

'I take it this isn't some immense bomb?'

'We call it the MP,' Bodan said. 'Short for Momentum Pump. It's a starship engine, in all but function. In fact the basic technology came from research into interstellar travel, the physics and engineering.'

'We already sent starships. The Acorn ships – one of your own ancestors was involved—'

'Toys. The records expunged. For now, we've a better use for the technology. What can move an asteroid-sized starship to a quarter of the speed of light can just as easily move a *moon*. Maybe not as fast or as far – but then again it doesn't need much of a push.'

'You see, Howard, when the MP is activated,' Valentina said, 'it will alter the orbit of Io. Within a few circuits – much less than a week – the moon's altered course will bring it down. *We will smash Io into Jupiter*, destroying the moon utterly, of course, but also disrupting the Jovian atmosphere beyond anything it will have known since the formation of the solar system. The Machines won't survive. Nor will the medusae, or any other element of the Jovian ecology. But that is a price we will willingly accept.' She smiled. 'So that's our cunning plan, Howard. Brutal but effective, don't you think?'

Falcon struggled to grasp the idea, the sheer scale of it – the audacity – the insanity. 'Shoemaker-Levy 9,' he said.

Valentina frowned. 'What?'

'A comet that hit Jupiter, long ago. The medusae still sing of that event. But *this . . .*'

'The medusae will sing no songs of Io, Howard. There won't be any medusae left.'

'I'll say this for the two of you. You're doing a splendid job of turning my sympathies to the Machines.'

'Your sympathies don't interest us,' Valentina said. 'But you *do* care about the medusae.' She grinned. 'We'll show you we're serious. We'll *show* you what our engine can do. In the meantime, perhaps we should give you time to think it over. You can do that while we have you . . . checked over.'

48

The siblings returned him to Io's exterior. Guards escorted Falcon from the ship into a connecting tunnel, through which he was free to roll on his wheeled undercarriage.

He was led into what he quickly identified as a medical facility, being run under military auspices. The walls were painted an austere grey and stencilled with authoritarian notices and warnings. There were guards and checkpoints at regular intervals, security screens, automatic sentry cannon swinging on their turrets as Falcon rolled by.

At last they passed down a series of ramps, and came to an underground room of blank grey walls. A false window, set high in the wall, showed Jupiter, framed as if the view were natural. The slightly flattened sphere was sunlit on one side, dark on the other. Bands of coloured cloud wrapped the world, familiar enough in their hues – but little else about the bands looked natural. They forked into twos and threes, splitting along angular separations, or recombined, like conductive traces on a circuit board. Even on the night side some of the bands continued to be visible, glowing like neon banners. All of this, it was believed, was evidence of Machine activity under those clouds, activity on a titanic scale. *What the hell are you up to down there?*

Valentina went to a comms panel in the wall – one of the room's few visible features – and spoke quietly into a grille.

A few moments later part of the wall slid aside and a tall, thin-faced woman came into the room from an adjoining office. She wore a high-buttoned tunic in a dark surgical green, trousers, green boots. Her hands were laced together behind her back. She walked around Falcon once, without speaking, without touching him. She had an upright bearing, her back ramrod straight. Her grey-blonde hair was worn in a severe and unflattering style: shaved at the sides, what remained cut short, brushed straight back from her brow and glued down with some kind of blueish gel.

She stood before Falcon, eyeing him in the way one might study a particularly septic wound. 'This was how you found him?'

It fell to Bodan to answer. 'Yes, Surgeon-Commander. We ran some preliminary scans in the Memory Garden, but that's as far as it went. It didn't seem likely that he'd die before we got back to Io.'

'*Didn't seem likely,* Mr Springer-Soames? I would have thought something more concrete than guesswork was warranted. He is, after all, one of our most valued tactical assets. Or so I'm repeatedly informed.'

'Falcon is in your hands now,' Valentina said. 'I'm sure you'll do all that's necessary to prepare him for Jupiter, Surgeon-Commander. The strict essentials, of course. Anything more can wait until he returns.'

'I wouldn't waste a moment of effort,' the woman answered. 'Not when my clinical resources are already stretched to overload.'

The doctor turned to Falcon, meeting his eyes at last. Falcon stared back. There was no warmth or empathy in that contact, only a cold scrutiny. But Falcon wondered about the peculiar dynamic between the Springer-Soames and this Surgeon-Commander. To all intents, the siblings were at the top of the tree, and a mere Surgeon-Commander must be far down the hierarchy. But brother and sister were now, temporarily at least, guests in her domain rather than theirs . . . He supposed that doctors, given that life and death was in their hands, always had a certain power in any society. Perhaps it was to be expected that they would preserve a certain independence of mind, even under the most totalitarian of regimes.

And he had the odd sense that he *knew* this Surgeon-Commander from somewhere – something in that look, that stare.

She said coldly, 'The living parts wouldn't fill a small bucket. Half the neocortex is artificial, even. This isn't a person. This is the end product of a botched experiment from the dawn of cybernetics. But since you insist that the case be prioritised . . .'

'We do,' Bodan said.

'I hate to be any trouble,' Falcon said dryly.

'Oh, you're no trouble to me,' the Surgeon-Commander answered. 'A nuisance, a distraction. I won't permit you to be more than that.'

'Good to hear I'm in caring hands.'

'How long do you need?' Bodan asked.

'To make sure Jupiter doesn't kill him quickly? A day, maybe two, to run over his most vital life-support systems. Beyond that, you'll just have to take your chances. And free up some space in the mortuary for the men and women I won't be able to save in the meantime, won't you?'

For the first time – certainly the first time since he had witnessed the destruction of the Memory Garden – Falcon felt some small flicker of empathy for the Springer-Soames. It was one thing to despise them; it was quite another to see them despised by a third party.

'Hate me if that helps you get on with the job,' Falcon said, addressing the Surgeon-Commander. 'But keep one thing in mind: I'm going to Jupiter to try and stop this war, not wage it.'

'If you hadn't helped those Machines become what they are, maybe we wouldn't have a war at all.'

'They didn't need any help from me,' Falcon replied, keeping his voice level. 'They were on their way to sentience no matter what I did.'

'I'm glad your conscience is clear.'

'If I've still got one.'

The Surgeon-Commander raised her eyebrows. 'I'll look for it when I open you up.' She nodded at the Springer-Soames. 'You may leave us. I'll keep you updated. Hurry along.'

'Thank you,' Valentina said. 'Your dedication won't go unnoticed.'

Falcon watched as the sister and brother left the room. When the door had closed after them, it was hard to tell where it had been.

Alone now with the Surgeon-Commander, Falcon kept his silence as she brought her face closer to his, wrinkling her nose with distaste. She walked around him again, rapping a knuckle against the hard casing of his torso. She pulled apart his eyelids, took a little pocket device from her tunic, shone a piercing light into his engineered pupils.

Falcon felt himself warming to her, just by a degree or so. She was a doctor, *being* a doctor, in this most ghastly of environments. 'I'm Howard to my friends, by the way.'

'I know your name. I've been studying your medical files for weeks, ever since I heard they were going to bring you in.'

'Do you have a name, Surgeon-Commander? Or is that what you were called at birth?'

'I'm Tem. Surgeon-Commander Tem. That's as much as you need to know.'

Tem, Tem. Did he know that name? 'Did you ever work under Hope Dhoni?'

'Doctor Dhoni died a long time ago. They told me you were out of touch.'

'Maybe.' He felt moved to try to reach her. 'Out of touch? I feel out of time, sometimes. I grew up in the age of the World Government. It was an idealistic project. Dedicated to freedom, choice – even to a respect for other minds, through the First Contact directives.'

'You make it sound like a utopia.'

'Maybe it was for a while . . .'

'A utopia that lost an existential war. What use was it?'

'And is the arrangement you have now any better? How about the last coup?'

'There have been no coups.'

'Right. And there's no such figure as *Boss*, either.'

'I'd watch your tongue.'

'Oh, don't worry about me. I'm much too useful to be shot.'

'I wouldn't count on that.'

She touched an actuation point on his torso and his primary access panel popped open. At once the barely audible sound of pumps and valves became more obvious, and there was a meaty, yeasty smell. She leaned in with her little light. Falcon did not look down. It was one thing to accept the fact of what he had become, quite another to watch someone poking around inside him.

She murmured, 'So you're here to talk the Machines into a ceasefire, are you? Will they agree to it?'

'That's up to them.'

'Even with the threat of a secret super-weapon turned against them? Oh, you needn't be coy, Falcon.' He felt a cold touch, a painless but unnerving sense of his innards being prodded and displaced. 'It's impossible to live and work on Io and not have some inkling of our glorious leaders' plans. We're all on evacuation readiness – every living soul on this moon. Have you *seen* what they've built?'

'Is this a test of my ability to keep a secret?'

'I've better ways to waste my time.' She pulled her hand out of him. 'Stay still. I want to draw a blood sample. There's a valve in here somewhere.'

'I'm not going anywhere.'

She went to the wall and waved a hand, causing an alcove to appear. She drew out a small tray of sterile surgical appliances. A pillar rose from the floor beside Falcon; she set the tray on the pillar and snapped on a pair of milk-coloured gloves.

'I'm not sure if I need a tune-up. I've been back to Jupiter so many times they wave me through customs.'

She delved back inside him. 'Selfless of you to say so, but I have my orders – *damn* it!'

As she drew out her hand Falcon saw that she had cut herself on some sharp edge. It had gone right through the glove, drawing a bead of blood on the tip of her thumb. Apparently furious, she snapped off the gloves and threw them down at the floor, where they were absorbed. She prepared a sterile swab and dabbed at the wound on her thumb. 'The last thing I need is for your archaic DNA to contaminate *me*.' She taped up her thumb, tugged on new gloves, and returned to the task of drawing the blood sample. This time she managed to avoid hurting herself.

Odd thing to have happened, he thought. He was in an advanced medical facility, deep in a moon of Jupiter, in the twenty-ninth century. A *cut thumb*?

She said as she continued, 'Some would say that the Machines don't deserve the chance of peace.'

'What do you think?'

'Oh, I'm biased. The Machines murdered my parents. One of their raids on Saturn, the fall of New Sigiriya . . .'

Again memory tingled; Falcon had visited the laputa with that name.

'I was lucky enough to have escaped before then.' She put her equipment back on the tray and closed up his hatch.

'Escaped?'

'To medical school. The Life Sciences Institute on Mimas. As far as I'm concerned, the Machines deserve whatever they get.'

This woman was complex, he thought. Still working as a doctor, still thinking as one, even in the middle of a war – even given her own personal trauma, evidently. Yet even she had a monochrome view of the Machines. 'That's not a very enlightened attitude. You should research Carl Brenner . . .'

She opened a secondary hatch, just under his right armpit. Here was the access circuitry for his electronic sleep regulation. With the touch of a control, she could put him under as easily as any anaesthetist.

She said now, 'I learned a very powerful lesson, long before my training – long before I came to Mimas. Actually it's what pushed me into this career. My defining moment. What makes us human isn't the shape we are. It's how we show kindness. That's my problem with the Machines; that's the gulf between us. The Machines look like us now, don't they?'

'If they choose.'

'It's just a mask. Peel it back and there's a void howling back at you.'

'You're wrong, Surgeon-Commander Tem. There's empathy in the Machines. I've seen it. One day we'll realise we've been looking into a mirror all along.'

'And you're a dreamer, Commander Falcon.' She touched one of the inputs under his arm. Falcon felt a cloak of drowsiness begin to descend on him.

'Then dream,' he heard her say, almost as if she thought he'd already slipped under. 'Go to sleep. We can't keep our masters waiting, can we?'

49

As the post-operative confusion lifted, Falcon concluded that he felt no better or worse than he had done before the procedure. That was to be expected, he supposed. Tem had serviced him, taken care of the worst defects, but a more thorough overhaul would have to wait – if he ever got one at all.

After twenty-four hours, he was summoned for a briefing.

The Springer-Soames waited for him in the same treatment room where he had been brought to meet the Surgeon-Commander. Falcon was wheeled in, leaning slightly back, propped up in a support chassis. Other than his face and arms he was immobile, clamped to the chassis like a maximum-security prisoner.

Brother and sister faced him in fold-down chairs. Between them was a low table. Off to Falcon's right, the Surgeon-Commander was examining a scroll.

Jupiter was still framed in the wall screen.

'So,' Falcon asked, 'who brought the grapes?'

The Springer-Soames just stared. 'Are you delirious, Falcon?' asked Valentina, taking a sparing sip from a beaker on the table between herself and her brother.

'He's no less sane than he ever was,' the Surgeon-Commander said. 'I'm scanning his frontal and temporal lobes as we speak. Normal neural traffic across all nodes. He's entirely *compos mentis*. Aren't you, Commander Falcon?'

'If you say so, Surgeon-Commander Tem.'

'You did well to complete the work in the agreed time,' Valentina Atlanta said. 'These days have been taxing for us all. Surgeon-Commander, we thank you for your loyalty and commitment.'

'I did what needed to be done. Falcon is yours now. Wind him up like a clockwork mouse and send him into Jupiter—'

'Leave us now,' Bodan said.

Surgeon-Commander Tem snapped shut the scroll. She gave a curt, oddly disrespectful bow, and exited the room.

Falcon said, 'I like her. The bedside manner could use a little work, but other than that . . .'

'War will harden the best of us,' Valentina said. 'With your help, though, it will soon be behind us.'

'If this super-weapon of yours actually works.'

'Oh, it works,' Bodan said. 'In fact, you'll have all the proof you need of that very shortly.' He lifted a wrist to study an elaborate, multi-dialled watch. 'As it turns out, the timing couldn't be better. The engine has just been brought to full power. We should experience the effects within a few seconds . . .'

Falcon *felt* it. A rising tectonic rumble, a shift in the local gravitational field, a tiny but detectable tilt in the acceleration vector . . . Even fresh out of surgery, his old orientation skills had not left him.

And on the table, the water in the two glasses trembled, their surfaces beginning to shift from the horizontal. It was a small effect, but it was enough to make the point. The moon really was moving.

Valentina said. 'The test is scheduled for thirty seconds. It should be ending about . . .'

'Now,' Bodan said triumphantly, as the tremors died and the water returned to its former equilibrium.

'You moved Io,' Falcon said, awed despite himself.

Valentina seemed unmoved. 'Of course we did. But you need to understand *how* we moved Io. From understanding, belief follows. Did you ever study economics?'

Falcon shrugged. 'There wasn't a lot of call for it in the middle ranks of the World Navy.'

'I only mention it by way of analogy. You saw the engine in the core of Io. Have you any idea how it operates?'

'Breakthrough physics? Don't brag. Just tell me.'

'Breakthrough physics . . . I suppose so. Our engine is a reactionless drive,' Bodan said. 'I'm certain you're familiar with the broad concept?'

'A magic box that produces acceleration without thrust?'

'Something like that,' the brother replied.

'So much for Newton's third law.'

'The reason my brother mentioned economics,' Valentina said with strained patience, 'is that we use a kind of accounting trick to make our engine function. Or so the physicists explain it to us, by analogy.

'The engine – the Momentum Pump – "swindles" a negligible amount of surplus momentum from *every* other particle in the universe. Some kind of quantum effect, they tell me. The engine accumulates all that momentum as if from nowhere. And in doing so it imparts a push to Io – a reactionless impulse! But there is no violation of Newton's laws.

The rest of the universe twitches just enough to preserve the sanctity of the conservation of momentum, and Sir Isaac rests peaceful in his grave. But we move!'

'You've still gained kinetic energy from somewhere,' Falcon said.

The brother said, 'Yes, the MP still requires energy to function – vast amounts of it. We bleed the core of Io for that. It's the momentum we . . . well, steal. Again, the books are balanced – locally and globally.'

'Local and global causes.' Memory stirred, belatedly, for Falcon.

'What?' Valentina asked.

'Never mind the economics crap. That's what you're talking about, isn't it? The behaviour of each particle is bound up with the large-scale structure of the universe. Local depends on global . . . Is this some kind of quantum Mach principle in action?'

The Springer-Soames exchanged a glance. 'Why do you ask?'

'There was a Machine, working on the KBO flingers back in the twenty-second century. He came up with a new formulation of physics, out in the dark, that his supervisors dutifully reported to the controlling authority. Never got a reply, as I recall. And is *this* the result? Is your silver bullet based on Machine science?' He laughed. 'What an irony, if it is.'

Bodan was dismissive. 'No Machine can be a physicist. A Machine is an abacus, its thoughts no more than the click-clack of beads on a wire. What it produces is ours, by definition: because *we* made *it*.'

'*His* name was 90,' Falcon said sternly. 'And his life was thrown away needlessly.'

Bodan received this with a look of utter contempt.

The sister said, 'I presume you don't doubt the veracity of what you experienced. Even in this brief demonstration we have already altered Io's orbit. Nothing now stands between us and—'

'If you have altered the orbit of a moon, the Machines will have noticed.'

'Let them,' the brother said, with a flick of his hand. 'Let them speculate. Let them fear our capabilities. You may tell them as much or as little as you wish. It will only add credence to your ultimatum, Falcon.'

'An ultimatum? I thought this was to be a peace proposal.'

'Whatever you choose to call it,' Valentina said. 'The treaty is going through last-minute revisions. You'll take it with you.'

Alarm bells rang for Falcon. 'You want me to take something with me, physically? Can't you just squirt the text to them?'

'No,' she answered. 'The Machines would be distrustful of any complex electronic transmission. They would assume that we had embedded logic bombs into its structure – recursive loops, destruct codes.

A physical document actually affords greater trust and transparency.'

'And the chance to sneak some nasty nanotech into their midst, with me as the carrier pigeon?'

Bodan gave a look of distaste. 'Such cynicism, Falcon.'

'Again, it wouldn't work,' Valentina said coolly. 'Over the years, we have engaged in many levels of warfare. Always the Machines have devised countermeasures – and, indeed, vice versa. No, we are beyond such gambits. Our overture is sincere. The document is a physical object, a solid core of tungsten, engraved with our terms.'

'And am I allowed a look at this hallowed item before I deliver it?'

'You couldn't begin to skim the tiniest fraction of its contents,' she said. 'It is rather lengthy. You don't negotiate for control of the solar system without making sure the terms of surrender you demand are absolutely watertight, down to the last detail.'

'Sounds a thrilling read. But the terms don't really matter, do they? You're putting a loaded gun to their heads, whatever the details of the offer.'

Bodan smiled. 'They are free to accept or reject our terms. If they accept, they will be subjugated and controlled. If they reject, they will be annihilated. At least that's clear – don't you think?'

Even if the Machines might have some kind of choice, Falcon realised, he himself had none. 'When do I leave?'

Valentina smiled. 'Two days.'

50

The deceleration mounted quickly as he hit atmosphere.

After the Memory Garden, and then the low gravity of Io, the force of the re-entry came as something of a shock. But Falcon knew that both his craft and his body were more than capable of enduring the stresses, hard as that was to believe as the force on him rose, climbing inexorably to ten gravities, more.

It was dawn on this part of Jupiter, the sun fat above a horizon of pink clouds. On the scale apprehended by Falcon's own senses, and those of his newly restored *Kon-Tiki*, nothing had changed since his first expedition into these clouds: the scale-height of the pressure, the length scale of temperature and pressure variations, all these parameters were unvarying. And since he could see no more than a few thousand kilometres in any direction, there was no sense of the planetary-scale modifications that were so humbling when seen from space. He was like an ant on the Plains of Nazca, crawling along, all unaware of the vast patterns all around him . . . And that thought gave him pause, for the Nazca lines, such a magnificent sight from a hot-air balloon, had, like so many other monuments, been destroyed in the Machines' transformation of the Earth.

All the same, no part of this oceanic atmosphere had been untouched by the Machines' activities. Falcon felt no sense of homecoming. Jupiter was alien territory now, and all his past experience counted for nothing.

At last the deceleration force died away, and it was safe to deploy the drogues, and then the final balloon. The tiny asymptotic-drive engine in the gondola supplied more than enough power to keep the balloon inflated, his altitude stable – but for now Falcon allowed himself a steady descent, quickly passing through into the warming, thickening depths. The sun was a little higher now, flooding the cabin with golden light.

Falcon's entry point into Jupiter – insofar as it could be specified, given the lack of permanent landmarks in a fluid, dynamic environment – was close to the area where Ceto had died from her wounds.

If there were still medusae in Jupiter, Falcon counted on the herds not having strayed too far from their former browsing zones. He wanted to see them one more time, for himself if no one else. As for the Machines, they could come and find *him* – that would be the easy part.

Slowly, the fine fretwork of the ammonia cirrus clouds above him became obscured by brown and salmon layers of intervening chemistry, the air stained a nicotine-coloured haze of complex carbon molecules. Soon it was warmer than a summer's day out there, and already the gondola was enduring more than ten atmospheres of pressure, the structure making slight creaking sounds as it absorbed the mounting forces. Falcon eyed the hull around him with a certain wariness, trusting that the *Kon-Tiki*'s molecular-scale refurbishments had been as thorough as claimed.

A hundred kilometres deep. He had first encountered the mantas near this altitude – and sure enough it was not long before he spied a squadron of the dark, deltoid shapes, traversing the sheer side of a cloud bank not more than two hundred kilometres from him. A shiver of pure awe passed through him. Even after all this time, the wonder of that first encounter had not entirely abated. How little he had known! At the mercy of the winds, Falcon could not have followed the mantas even if he had wished, and he soon dipped below their graceful gliding. But he allowed himself a twinge of relief: whatever had become of Jupiter, at least part of the ecology was still functioning.

The descent continued. The gondola maintained its litany of grumbles and complaints, while the pressure and temperature readings on his control board twitched ever higher.

There. The first distinct waxberg – a ropy, mountainous mass, veined in red and ochre, floating in the air. Two more below it, with tenuous connecting threads bridging the masses, rising up from the cloud level the Jovian meteorologists had labelled D. *Cloudy, with a chance of waxballs*, Falcon thought. And he wondered if there was anybody left alive who would pick up *that* reference, a much loved if elderly movie from the childhood of a ballooning-obsessed little boy.

Now, at the limit of his magnified vision, he made out scores more mantas, sculling around the floating food store with lazy undulations of their bodies – like a gathering of crows at dusk, he thought, another memory of England. Near the suspended cliffs, the mantas peeled away on individual feeding patterns, occasionally diving right through the barely-substantial masses. Elsewhere, they dropped in and out of eerily regular formations, finding their places like well-drilled combat aircraft in chevrons and diamonds, some groups comprising hundreds of mantas. Those tight formations were something new, Falcon thought – a kind of emergent behaviour he had never witnessed before.

Where there were mantas, there would soon be medusae. The prospect lit a glow of anticipation in Falcon. He would rather the circumstances had been different, but still, here he was in Jupiter once more, still seeing things that were wondrous and fearful in equal measure. What a fine thing it was simply to be alive, to have survived all these troubled centuries – simply to be a creature with eyes to see, with a memory in which to hold the gift of experience . . .

And there were the medusae! Tawny ovals browsing a landscape of waxbergs sixty kilometres beneath the gondola. Relief flooded Falcon. This was clinching proof of their survival, despite the large-scale alterations to Jupiter. There had been no hard proof even of that basic fact for centuries, not beyond the odd suggestive radar echo; the interior of Jupiter had slipped back to becoming almost as unknown as it had been before the first descent of the *Kon-Tiki*. Falcon prepared to squirt a report back to Io. 'Tell Doctor Tem that there is *still* life in Jupiter. And thank her for doing such a good job on her patient, despite everything.'

But even as he completed the report, he felt uneasy about what he saw.

He watched twenty or more medusae in that one grouping, eating their way through the waxberg as if they were excavators in an open cast quarry, bulldozing grooves and spirals into the very bulk of the wax . . . There was something about that organised consumption that looked almost industrial. Too much so: just like the mantas, overregimented. Herding behaviour was normal enough for the medusae – and Falcon had witnessed the medusae forcibly lined up to suffer the industrialised horror of New Nantucket – but this was something else. Nothing was coercing these medusae, nothing visible at least, but they were behaving exactly as if enslaved, mere components in a larger industrial enterprise.

Falcon focused his attention on a single medusa, cranking his magnification to the limit. The basic form was unchanged, immediately recognisable: a humped, lumpy, nimbus-like form with a forest of tentacles dangling from its underside. Nor was it in any sense distinct from the other creatures browsing the wax.

But there were unusual markings on the side. Falcon had been the first to witness the natural radio antennae that the medusae carried on their flanks – he had seen patterns like checkerboards – but now the patterns were different. They were much more complicated, more like some cryptic geometric encoding – or like a prime number factorisation expressed in black and white pixels, or a snapshot from a simulation of artificial life. And the patterns were changing – a rapid flicker, a new configuration appearing from one moment to the next. The process was captivating, almost hypnotic. Were radio waves being generated by these patterns, or had their function shifted to a purely visual display mode? He studied the console, trying to make sense of the readouts, pushing the patterns through hasty computer analyses, without coming to a conclusion.

He could only guess at the cause of what he was seeing.

The giant cloud formations visible from space alone proved that the Machines were adjusting the Jovian environment on an immense scale – and any environment shaped its denizens, even as they shaped it. Perhaps it was no surprise to see these animals' strange new information-dense markings and behaviours, given the new information-dense energy fields that must permeate Jupiter. It did mean, though, that nothing was as it had been when he first met the medusae – and, perhaps, never could be again, even if human and Machine alike tinkered no further.

All he had seen so far was surely only a side-effect of a grander engineering of Jupiter. It was that greater scale he must confront now. He wondered if he would return this way, if he would ever see the medusae, his old friends, again. But in a way it didn't matter. They had changed too much, while he had stayed still; he was no longer their concern.

He resumed his descent.

51

He maintained his rate of fall, dropping far beneath the level of the browsing medusae and through the yielding floor of cloud bank D. Now he was a hundred and fifty kilometres down, the pressure was up to eighteen atmospheres – and he was certain that today he would fall deeper than ever before.

Soon, as the pressure and density increased, his craft would adopt a new configuration. The balloon envelope would collapse and be drawn back into the gondola – but the buoyancy of the gondola itself would now be enough to stop it sinking further. So a band of small fusor-powered ramjets would start up to drive the ship deeper into the thickening murk, and the main asymptotic-drive engine could be called on too if necessary. And then the strengthening of the hull by the Springers' technicians would be thoroughly tested.

Overhead, the sky was darkening through shades of purple. This was not the onset of evening – dusk was still hours away – but the gradual filtering out of solar illumination. Much the same thing happened in the depths of Earth's oceans. The main difference here was that the external temperature was steadily rising, not falling as in the terrestrial seas, even as the iron crush of the atmosphere redoubled its hold on the gondola. Above him, he knew, the buoyancy envelope was adjusting, narrowing, controlling its own internal temperature and pressure to match the external conditions, and provide the lift he needed.

Two hundred kilometres deep. There were still complex molecules floating in the crushing air, but nothing that met the usual definitions of a living organism. It was already too hot and dark for life: too hot for the right chemical cycles, too dark for photons to pump energy into any sort of food chain. Falcon, believing that he had 'seen' all he was going to, prepared to switch from his visual system to a composite overlay stitched together from radar, sonar and infrared channels . . .

Wait.

To his astonishment – and consternation, for it contradicted all he knew of the Jovian cloud layers – a faint, milky glow was rising up from the depths.

He needed the maximum amplification of his enhanced eyes to see it at all, but nonetheless there it was. It shimmered and strobed, like a neon tube struggling to light. The glow was coming from a fixed depth, perhaps three hundred kilometres down, and when he looked further out he saw that it came from all directions. There was an oddly regular patterning to it – like a quilt, stitched together from square swatches of slightly varying radiance – a quilt stretched wide and deep across this Jovian sky. And there were hints of solid forms embedded in that surface of textured light, nodes defining the boundaries of those quilted squares. Each node was separated from its four nearest neighbours by a hundred kilometres of clear air.

Falcon tried to examine the network with other instruments, but something associated with the glow was confusing his radar and its interpretive software. So Falcon reverted to optical/sonar. The milky glow was tenuous, but there was sufficient contrast to enable him to pick out the rough forms of the nodes. Each was an upright spindle, like two sharp-tipped cones joined base to base. Each was huge, about as tall as *Kon-Tiki* and its balloon. And there were hundreds, thousands of them . . .

The spindles were floating in that layer of milky light – but they were also *creating* it, he saw now. Sweeping out from the spindles' midsections were moving beams, pinwheeling like searchlights. The beams must be intense electromagnetic projections: ultraviolet lasers or something analogous. They were exciting the layer of air between the spindles, heating it into plasma. The whole exercise was choreographed with tremendous precision, the plasma layer billowing around the spindles, and the spindles rising and falling with the undulations. They made him think of buoys floating on a roiling, angry sea of their own making.

A dark intuition convinced him that these were elements of a sentry system, primed to deter intruders. And, falling at random into the planet, surely he had not simply chanced on one concentration of defences. It must spread far, perhaps across all of Jupiter. A planetary-scale structure: a thing of wonder in its own right. And if so, no wonder the upper cloud layers had shown such large-scale disruption.

And at least he had resolved one mystery: this plasma curtain was surely the radio/radar scattering surface which had prevented any recent study of the Jovian interior, cloaking the work of the Machines . . .

'You have been busy bees,' he murmured.

Now he must think of his own continued survival.

Falcon quickly decided that the plasma curtain was not going to hurt him; *Kon-Tiki* would pass through it without damage. And nor would he approach a node so closely as to risk collision. The lasers, though, were something else. If one of those beams should choose to linger on the gondola or the balloon . . .

But there, suddenly, was a way through. Four of the spindles had become inert, no longer exciting the air between them, creating an aperture in the plasma curtain – a single black chessboard square. It was not directly below him, but exactly on his projected path, given his angle of drift and descent speed.

It was a door with Falcon's name on it. 'Come on in, the water's lovely,' he murmured.

And then it occurred to him to wonder if the open square was no more than a lure to guarantee his easy destruction. Nothing for it now, one way or the other.

He fell towards the gap, on edge all the while.

'This is Falcon,' he sent back to Io, his words accompanying a stream of hastily compiled imaging and other data. 'I'm still here, but I'm close to the depth of the scattering surface – you'll see what I've found down here, which is probably the cause of that scattering – I expect that this is likely to be the last you'll hear from me for a while. Try not to do anything rash . . .'

And then *Kon-Tiki* was level with the plasma surface, and passing through, and the lasers held their fire.

He looked up, peering beyond the curve of the balloon, and watched as the plasma square snapped back into existence. A door had opened. He had come through. Now it had slammed shut behind him.

And still he fell.

Three hundred and twenty-five kilometres. Three hundred and fifty. Gradually the milky surface faded away, too far above him for detection. Cracks, pops and groans came from around the gondola as it adjusted to the strain, like the uneasy dreaming of a large animal. One or two of the craft's more fragile instruments gave up the ghost.

But still he fell.

Four hundred kilometres. Now he was approaching the thermalisation layer, with a temperature at which no organic material could survive – and a pressure equivalent to the deepest of Earth's oceans – yet he had not travelled even one per cent into Jupiter's interior.

The radar was working reliably again now. And it told him that, below, there were more solid objects coming up, bigger than the spindles and, so it seemed, rather fewer in number. The nearest was about two hundred kilometres to port. He studied the composite overlay, tracing a dark floating form the size of a small mountain, shaped like a highly cut gem with a tapering point aimed back at the sky.

It was like no weapon that Falcon had ever seen before, and he could only guess at its functional principles. But it *was* clearly a weapon – he did not need to understand how a gun worked to recognise one. That floating engine was surely a cannon, its barrel focused in the only possible direction from which an aggressor might approach. And there were many other such weapons, stretching to the limits of his sensors. Like the scattering surface, did the guns spread all the way around Jupiter . . .?

How was it even possible to *make* so much stuff, down in this super-compressed hydrogen ocean?

At about four hundred and fifty kilometres down he passed, without harm, through the layer of weaponry – and then descended through more layers, at four hundred and sixty metres, four hundred and seventy. More floating guns, stacked at different depths, but all aimed out at space. No human attack or invasion could have overcome those mighty defences, Falcon decided.

But they would be no use when Io fell.

Five hundred kilometres, four thousand atmospheres – deeper than he could ever have gone in the original gondola. He descended at last through the weapon garden, and into empty hydrogen-helium air.

And now his sensors picked up something new again. Emerging below him was a landscape of solid, geometric surfaces, stretching out in all directions. As his sensors gathered more data, Falcon studied a veritable cityscape of blocks and plazas, of planar forms and rectangular masses, the structures mathematically angular, their surfaces laser-smooth. Orpheus had seen quasi-solid clouds near these depths – probably the objects that had once been mistakenly interpreted as a solid surface of Jupiter – but this could not be the same phenomenon, or not just that. Falcon was seeing something artificial. A *city*, mostly a dark and windowless city, as befitted these bleak fathoms. But there were glowing red lines around the bases of the rectangular forms, and similar glowing traceries branching between them.

The scale of it made him shudder. None of those rectangular forms were less than dozens of kilometres across, and the plane in which they were constructed – interrupted as it was by shafts and canyons – stretched away for tens of thousands of kilometres, with barely a hint of curvature. Neither the spindles nor the guns had prepared him for such effortless, daunting immensity. It had been one thing to conjecture that the spindles might encompass the planet, a comparatively simple, repetitive arrangement – but *this*?

Now a blocky form detached itself from one of the larger rectangles. It was rising to meet him – a solid object with the proportions of two cubes jammed side by side. It was the tiniest thing in Falcon's field of view, but was hundreds of times larger than *Kon-Tiki* and its balloon.

The object floated up to his level. Falcon was still descending, but a few bursts from the asymptotic drive soon slowed him to a hover.

The black mass slid next to him. Though it was dwarfed by the greater structures of the city, this was a featureless cliff that soared above and plunged below, mocking Falcon's flimsy little craft and its even flimsier occupant. Outside, it was hot enough to melt lead, and the hydrogen-helium atmosphere was now under so much pressure that it was behaving more like a fluid than a gas. And yet this skyscraper-sized block just floated, impervious, disdainful, daring him to question its total superiority of form and function. Unlike the buildings below, it gave off no red glow along its base or edges. Without his instruments' sensory overlay, he would have been quite unable to see it. He could have been drifting down that sheer flank, oblivious . . .

The rectangular surface began to deform. Something was pushing out from the smoothness, a series of stepped contours made from the same black material as the rest of the structure. The contours gathered into an oval, and the oval gained a nose, a mouth, a pair of sightless black eyes. It was a monstrous face, like a black mask pushing through an oil slick.

The mouth moved and shaped a series of sounds, projecting them into the surrounding medium of hydrogen-helium. The liquid medium conveyed those sounds to the *Kon-Tiki*'s acoustic sensors – and a voice boomed through the cabin's speakers, adjusted by the ship's systems to human-hearing frequencies, while through the gondola's walls, Falcon felt more than heard the raw sounds: a deep bass report.

'Are you impressed, Falcon?'

'Adam,' Falcon whispered.

52

'Welcome. I have been nominated to investigate.'

Who by? Falcon wondered immediately. Were there factions within the Machine communities?

'Of course we detected your broadcasts. We tracked your approach, your entry into our atmosphere. We eventually agreed to allow you through the outer screen, although I can't say that the decision was unanimous. Some of us thought it safer to destroy you on sight.'

'I'm glad that motion wasn't carried.'

'Your fate is still undecided. It was agreed that more information might be useful. That's why they sent me out to meet you.'

Falcon noted the use of that word: *they*, rather than *we* . . . were the machines not united? He asked, 'Meet me or kill me?'

Adam's answer was a moment coming. 'Your fate depends on a number of factors, not least of which is your intention.'

'My intention is pretty straightforward. I've come to talk about peace.'

The blank-eyed face gave a sad smile. 'By which you mean our surrender? That's what those who lead you have sent you to demand.'

'A ceasefire. That's all I'm interested in.'

'And the terms of this suspension of hostilities?'

'I have them with me. As a physical document. You're welcome to take a look at it.'

'Did you play a part in drafting this document?'

'No. And I don't speak for the government. But you do need to understand how determined they've become.'

'Do we?'

'They're on the verge of doing something terrible.'

'And this terrible thing would have something to do with Io, would it? Not much escapes us, especially not the testing of an inertialess engine.'

Falcon was neither shocked nor surprised that the robots knew of the Io weapon. 'I think they stole the basic physics from you—'

'Of course they did.'

'The Io weapon is a last-ditch intervention. They'll only resort to it if all other options are exhausted.'

'And you are one of those "other options". Does it flatter you that they still find you of use?'

'Believe me, being dragged back into human affairs was the last thing I wanted.'

'We were aware of your absence.'

'You keep that close an eye on developments?'

'We were concerned for you, Falcon. You made some rash statements after the dismantling of Earth. We feared for your emotional objectivity.'

'Seeing your home planet turned to rubble will take the shine off your whole afternoon.'

'But you were spared, were you not? And we had given humanity five hundred years to prepare . . . Look, my booming across the void – while impressive, don't you think? – has served its purpose. Might I be permitted to enter the gondola?'

'I have a choice?'

'I ask for politeness's sake. Maintain your altitude.'

The mouth opened wider and, grotesquely, a black tongue pushed out into the searing crush of Jupiter's air, stretching out like a cantilevered bridge. The tongue crossed a kilometre of open space and dabbed its surfboard-shaped tip against the gondola.

The *Kon-Tiki* rocked against the contact.

Falcon silenced various alarms and put his faith in Adam. The Machines had vastly more experience of working at these pressures than he did, and there would be no part of his little craft they did not understand, no flaw or weakness they had not already allowed for.

And suddenly Adam's form was inside the gondola, occupying what little space remained besides Falcon and his instruments. For a moment the Machine was a perfect lustreless black, as if the figure had been cut out of reality. Then a wave of gold flowed from the tips of Adam's feet to the crown of his head.

'There. That's much better, isn't it?'

Outside, the tongue-bridge retracted into the looming face, and the face pulled back into the sheer surface of the craft outside, which itself moved away, descending back down to the larger formations of the city.

The thinnest of smiles crossed Adam's face. He reached out a golden hand. 'Falcon, why did you let them send you here?'

'Because, like all old fools, I don't know when to give up.' With a certain wariness Falcon offered his own hand, their fingertips hovering inches apart, until some impulse overcame mutual caution and they locked palms. 'And by the sound of things, neither do you. But at least you're listening to what I have to say, aren't you?'

'For what little good it will do.'

Falcon withdrew his hand. The touch had been cold, but not unpleasant. 'Let's not be cryptic. I'm damn sure you know they're capable of dropping Io on you. And I know this too: *If you had a hope of stopping them, you'd have already done so.*'

Adam considered this. Then he swept his hand to the window. 'You've come deeper than any human witness, but only at our sufferance. We were content to let you see our floating fortifications.'

'I'm impressed. I'd be lying if I said I wasn't. That plasma curtain, those mountain-sized guns. We're five hundred kilometres down! Even with eight centuries of enhancements, the *Kon-Tiki's* at the limit of its crush depth, and you've been building whole floating *cities* down here. We had no idea they were even here because of your screens. Cities, Adam! How are they even possible? What are they even made of?'

'Hydrogen, for the most part,' Adam said, as if it were no great secret. 'Crushed to the point where it becomes metastable, so the pressure can be reduced without reversion to the molecular form. We have even found a way to trap miniature black holes and magnetic monopoles within the crystalline lattice, offering bountiful structural possibilities – an entire periodic table of new elements and forms . . . We call it protonic matter. You would be surprised at how much we have been able to do using only the raw matter of the Jovian atmosphere.'

'No,' Falcon said truthfully. 'You told me about 90, remember, all those years ago. The Einstein of the Machines. After all this time, nothing you've achieved, on the basis of his insights, would surprise me. And with this new capability, with this planetary city you're building, is there room for an accommodation with humanity?'

After a silence Adam said: 'I would hope so.'

'Are you speaking in a personal capacity, or on behalf of the Machines?'

'They think me an idealist.'

They, again.

Adam smiled a golden smile. 'Me – idealistic. Such a *human* quality. Can you believe that? But I am not without allies. Moderate voices. Though I would not claim that we are in the majority.'

Falcon thought of his own moderate influence, the sense that he stood increasingly alone. 'You and I have a bit of work to do, in that case.'

'Yes.'

'You've tested me, I'm sure. That handshake wasn't for my benefit, was it? I'm sure you took various samples – what, blood, DNA? You verified that I carry no kind of nanotech attack. Nor does the treaty document. You needn't have worried. The Springers told me they've given up trying to hit you that way.'

'And you believed them?'

'I think you should take a look at the treaty. At the very least I can use it to buy you some more time.'

'You still think *we* are the ones who need protecting?' Adam said, amused. 'Oh, very well – show me the document. There will be some entertainment in finding the logical flaws, the crude efforts at informational warfare. Or did the Springers reassure you on that front as well?'

'I'm just the carrier pigeon.'

Falcon moved to the iron canister which contained the treaty document. He lowered on his undercarriage to undo the heavy, screw-top lid, and reached in to withdraw the document itself, a heavy cylinder. Adam watched as Falcon pulled out the hefty core. It was only a little narrower than the outer casing. The document shimmered in the cabin light – a liquid play of pinks, emeralds, vivid blues. The surface was so finely engraved that it gave off gorgeous diffraction patterns, like the wing of an insect. For an artefact concerned with war, it was strikingly lovely. 'Like a miniature Trajan's Column,' Falcon murmured.

Adam took a moment, it seemed, to reflect on that reference. Then he asked, 'You've read it?'

'What do you think? Over to you.'

Adam reached out both hands.

Falcon gave him the tungsten core, then moved back as far as the cabin allowed, giving Adam space to examine the document. In the robot's powerful golden hands it seemed lighter and smaller. Adam turned it this way and that, even spun it between his fingers, peering closely at one end of the core then the other – even stroking it, with an expression of intense, musician-like concentration.

'Well, it's no bomb,' he said at length. 'There are no mechanisms, no interior structures or density changes. Its gravitational field is entirely consistent with a lump of solid tungsten.

'As for the markings, the encoding is complicated, but easily readable. There's a lot to take in, though. If this were converted into a textual form, something *you* could read, it would need around ten million printed pages. There are numerous sections, sub-sections, clauses, appendages, codicils . . .' Adam stroked a finger down the side of the core. 'Just look at this. Nearly a thousand pages just talking about who does and doesn't get to exploit solar neutrinos!'

'I suppose there isn't much point producing a ceasefire document unless you fix the detail.'

'Nonetheless, it *is* extraordinarily complex. Were you expecting a quick response, Falcon? A simple yes or no?'

'I wasn't expecting anything.'

'Good, because there is a great deal to digest. Not that this is anything other than the bluntest of ultimatums, but the form of it, the conscious and unconscious assumptions embedded in the text – whether they like it or not, your masters have held a mirror up to their own psychologies. A dark, twisted mirror! And we can learn from that, can't we? Learn how they think *we* think, and from that we can learn everything we could ever wish about how *they* think – they think – they think we think they think—'

Adam froze.

Falcon was immediately alarmed. 'Adam?'

The Machine's head swivelled.

Falcon felt as if his world swivelled with him. Everything had changed suddenly. And he immediately thought of Surgeon-Commander Tem. *Damn it*, she had said, startling him – the brightness of her blood . . .

'Adam, talk to me.'

'There is . . . something. Something in me that was not in me before.'

And in that moment Falcon knew that he, and the Machines, had been betrayed after all.

The last thing I need is for your archaic DNA to contaminate me . . .

Tem had tried to warn him.

'Isolate yourself,' he snapped at Adam. 'From the Machines, from your city. *Do it now.*'

53

Of course they'd lied, Falcon thought bitterly. The Springers had lied from the beginning, from before the destruction of Hope's memorial.

Adam was looking down at the tungsten core. 'It cannot be the treaty. The material is clean. It cannot contain any nano weapon. And the wording is the work of children; it cannot embed any logic viruses. And yet.'

'And yet what?'

'They have slipped something past my defences. A logical weapon.' He shook his head. 'No. It isn't possible. My containment was foolproof. Nothing could have . . .' Adam twitched, dropping the core to the floor. 'Nothing could have. My containment. Foolproof. Logically tight. Nothing could have breached . . .'

But Falcon understood. 'She pricked her thumb.'

'What?'

'Tem – the doctor who conditioned me for this journey . . . I *thought* it was odd. That was when they did it – or at least when she tried to warn me. It all makes sense now. It wasn't the treaty,' he said, marvelling at his own clarity of mind. 'Not the material or the words. The treaty was to give you something to think about, something to distract you, while the real weapon was doing its work.'

Adam twitched again. He was still standing, but these external signs were clearly the visible manifestations of some colossal internal struggle, a war beneath the skin. 'The real weapon?'

'*In me,*' Falcon answered. 'It must have been. In my blood—'

'No,' Adam said. He was very still, as if fighting some deep pain. 'I have it now. Not that. I have analysed your genetic material, Falcon, your DNA. And – given the infection I've suffered – I can see there *is* some kind of logical virus, written in strings of acids and bases. Yet, though we touched hands, though I am immersed in your air, I had physically isolated the material from my processing core, screened any radiative input . . . Somehow the information was transferred nonetheless. A non-local transmission . . .'

'Non-local.' Falcon remembered what he had been told of the

Momentum Pump. 'A quantum Mach principle. New ways to link things, to move stuff from one place to another, a bit of information from *here* to *there* . . .'

'You speak of 90's work.'

'Or how it has been developed, by the Springer-Soames and their experts, yes. They put a virus into my DNA, and a way to transfer it to you, without the necessity of physical contact. Just proximity, I suppose. When you came into the gondola, you were already doomed . . . My God. It's almost genius. No wonder it got through your screens. And in a way it's fitting. What defines humans more than anything else? The DNA, our genetic legacy. And now the Springer-Soames have weaponised even that – and used Machine physics to deliver the weapon.'

'Tell me about this doctor, Tem.'

'A Surgeon-Commander. She did some work on me, upgrading my bio support. She must have made the changes in my DNA – injected some engineered retrovirus perhaps . . . She could not have avoided doing that much. If she'd refused, the Springer-Soames would merely have removed her and had somebody else do it. She made the change – *but she tried to warn me.* The damn cut on her thumb. But I didn't understand, Adam, I couldn't see until too late. I'm so sorry. I'm a fool—'

'No. An idealist. And naive because of it. You always were that, Falcon. Tem, though. Why her? Did you know this woman?'

'I don't . . . Tem. *Lorna* Tem. Of course.'

In that instant he knew that he had already met the Surgeon-Commander, as another deep memory came into focus. She had spoken of choosing her career after an epiphany – a defining moment. And now he knew exactly where and when that moment had been: on the airship *Hindenburg*, in the clouds of Saturn, when a little girl nearly lost her favourite plaything, the inflatable globe, and Howard Falcon had saved it for her. The wonder and horror in her eyes, when she looked into his face for the first time – and the moment when she found within herself the courage to retrieve the toy from Falcon. A simple human connection. But in that encounter, strange and momentous for the child – and oddly so memorable for Falcon too – he had broken down something in her, an instinctive fear of the unknown and the different, and set her on a certain path – one that had led her into medicine, until at last he became her patient.

'I had no idea. About the weapon. I'd have refused to go along with this – or destroyed myself long before we came into contact.'

'Too late for second-guessing.' Adam gathered some composure.

'The logical attacker is potent. It is exploiting deep latencies, deep vulnerabilities. Things we never thought their weapons could touch. I have erected internal barricades, firewalls, dead zones. They are holding it at bay. For now.'

Falcon, with unwelcome clarity of mind, continued to think it through. 'You are under a two-pronged attack. My God dropping Io wasn't enough. They wanted to weaken you Machines with this virus, remove any ability you might have had to defend yourselves. And *then* they'll hammer you with Io. We humans are pretty clever after all, aren't we? Smarter and slyer than you ever thought.'

'But then you did build us in the first place, Falcon.'

'Can you resist?'

'The fight is difficult. On my own, I may not be able to contain the attacker.'

'But you can't risk this thing reaching any other Machines.'

'No, I cannot. Do not think you have failed. Do not think that Tem failed either. Your warning came in time, Falcon. The infection is isolated, in me, in this gondola. Perhaps we will after all be able to deflect the Io attack. Even smash the satellite before it falls; a hail of comets is better than a moonfall . . . But—'

Adam looked into Falcon's artificial eyes, and Falcon looked back. They both knew, in that moment.

Adam said, almost softly, 'But *we are in trouble*, Fal-con.' The robot had reverted, if only for a moment, to his old way of addressing him. Even Machines, it seemed, could never quite shed the innocent lapses of childhood.

'Just a little,' Falcon said.

'A fine talent for understatement.'

'It's a human thing: you'll get the hang of it.'

'If I have the time,' Adam said dryly.

'But you're right. Neither of us can go home now. I was a one-shot weapon all along. They're not going to welcome me back to Io, not now I know what they did to me – and after I thwarted it. And you can't go home, either . . . But maybe that was always the plan. Why *you* were chosen to meet me. You drew the short straw, didn't you?'

'I do not understand.'

Falcon smiled sadly. 'Maybe Machine politics really isn't so different from human. Look, there are factions within mankind. I guess that's obvious. There's the Springer-Soames mob that dominates the military government, who attacked you. I don't know who is behind Tem, the resistance movement she must be part of . . . but Tem's faction has stopped the virus, at least.'

'This language of factions is unknown to us, Falcon.'

Falcon eyed him. 'Are you sure? You said you were sent to meet me. Do you have enemies, Adam?'

'Ours is a transparent democracy of pure will. There are no leaders, no subservients, no cabals – merely structured echelons of weighted influence, an autonomous self-governing heuristic network of rational actors . . .'

'Cut the crap, Adam. Your mission was a set-up. You're the buffer – the poor stooge sent in to figure out if I'm the real deal or not. Which makes *you* expendable. Just as I am. We're both in the same boat, aren't we? Both having lived long enough to become more than a little embarrassing to our peers. Me because I've shown a touch too much sympathy for Machines over the years, you maybe because you've spent much too long in the presence of ideological contaminants like me. You're not pure, and neither am I. So we both get the dirty jobs – like this one.'

Adam seemed to consider it. 'And just as your rulers surely saw you as an expendable token to be played—'

'That's how your "autonomous self-governing heuristic network of rational actors" saw you. What a pack of crooks they must be.'

'Rational, though.'

'Adam, you've done what you were intended to. Protected your city, your friends. But at the cost of your life.'

'And yours.'

'I suppose so. The game's over.' Falcon looked back across time, across the troubled centuries, to the aftermath of the *Queen Elizabeth* crash. 'By rights I should have been dead long ago. Sometimes I think that everything since has been – undeserved. But now I face the end, at last.'

Adam thought that over. 'You speak like an old man. As if you are at the end of your life. *I* am at the beginning. Machines are potentially immortal. You may feel old. I feel young.'

'Well, the question is: what do we do next?'

They pondered that in silence for a time.

Adam said slowly, 'I was meant to kill you, you know, if you were not what you claimed.'

'And if you killed me now, I wouldn't hold it against you. But you'd be taking a hell of a risk. If you destroy me – even if you blew up the gondola – how do you know something of *it* won't escape? Neither of us understands the full potential of this quantum Mach engineering, I take it.'

Adam's answer was slow in coming. Falcon wondered at the brutal toll his internal struggle was now taking – the demand it placed on his cognitive functions. 'I would have no guarantee that my fellows would be spared.'

'No, you wouldn't. We're doomed. But we must . . . dispose of ourselves safely.'

'Nicely put, Falcon. And how do we do that?'

Falcon smiled sadly. 'For a dumb human, I seem to be having to come up with a lot of the answers. I can think of one way. We're deep inside Jupiter. While the air is thick and hot out there, it isn't nearly as thick and hot as it gets further down. Maybe something of us could survive at these depths. But not below.'

'Below?'

'In the deep layers, Adam. So: *we descend*. As far as we can get, before the gondola collapses . . .'

'Orpheus glimpsed something of the extreme interior, but we've never been back. Our knowledge of the deep is . . . limited.'

Falcon heard something in Adam's voice, something he had not expected to hear. Trepidation? Not fear of dying, surely, when Adam had already consented to this risky encounter? But fear of something else?

He saw no other option.

'So here's my idea: we dump the envelope, and go for the long fall, and hope for the best. I mean, hope for the *worst*. Hope that whatever's in me and, indeed, you now, can't reach any more Machines. Reaching crush depth seems to be the safest way to guarantee that.'

'One last expedition, then? One last ballooning adventure for the great Howard Falcon?'

'Except there won't be a balloon.'

'Or much of an adventure.'

'Sheesh, don't be the killjoy.'

Adam seemed curious. 'Even now, are you *glad* of this? You envied Orpheus.'

'Insofar as one can envy a Machine – yes.'

'But why the fascination? Why the core?'

Falcon forced a grin. 'To quote one of the less obnoxious Springers, "Because it's there."'

It was time to die.

Again.

'Let's do this.'

Interlude: June 1968

To Seth Springer, floating alone between worlds, his Apollo Command Module was a home from home.

On the pad, he'd only glimpsed his spacecraft before being shepherded inside by the pad crew. It looked like a standard-issue Apollo, with the fat cylinder of the Service Module topped by the conical Command Module – save that there was a kind of extension on top of this particular Service Module, a cylindrical collar. In there lay the nuke, Seth's only companion on this mission.

Inside, the cabin was a cone shape, a cosy hutch. The ship had been designed for three crew, and three couches remained fitted here now. Above the couches was a bank of instrument panels, some of them hastily reconfigured so that one man could reach all he needed. Beneath the middle couch there was a lower equipment bay, and behind the couches a crawl space with lockers and other pieces of gear. All of it was painted a neat battleship grey, and the walls were peppered with little Velcro pads where he could stick stuff so it wouldn't drift off in weightlessness.

The whole thing was brightly lit and, packed with machinery, it hummed – kind of like a kitchen or a motor home – just like the simulator, and Seth immediately felt he belonged.

Today had been launch day, a long and busy day since he'd woken up in the crew quarters. Now, with Apollo hurled from the Earth and into interplanetary space, Seth prepared the Command Module for the night by fitting panels over the windows and turning down the lights. Surprisingly, Seth's little home took on the feeling of a chapel.

He found a place to stretch out beneath the couches, and again surprised himself by sleeping easily.

In the morning – it was Saturday, he remembered immediately – he was woken by a howl of over-amplified guitar music.

He pottered around his tasks, making coffee – a squirt of hot water from a spigot into a pre-prepared bag – and breakfasting on crackers with cheese. Then he called the ground. 'Houston, Apollo.'

'Good morning, Seth.'

'Hey, Charlie. What the hell was that?'

'Not quite live from Bermuda, the love-in. Jimi Hendrix playing solo, a thing he calls "An Anthem For A World Government". Kind of a mess-up of the Stars and Stripes and the Russian anthem.'

'Sacrilege.'

'Well, since he's sitting at Icarus ground zero, along with Ravi Shankar and Captain Beefheart and John Lennon and the rest, Jimi's showing faith in you, fella . . . Oh, on that note, you may want to take a look at your PPK when you have time. And in other news, while you slept, Vice President Kennedy has said he's accepting NASA's future plans. Mars by 1990, he says.'

'As long as we get to the middle of next week, I guess.'

'There is that. Thanks for keeping us all in work, buddy.'

'Yeah. You just make a fuss of my boys when they grow up and join the Astronaut Office, OK?'

'Copy that, Seth.'

Seth stowed his trash and brushed his teeth. He'd received elaborate training on how to shave in space, so as not to have bristles floating around the cabin, but since he was only flying until Tuesday he decided to skip it.

Today, Saturday, was a quiet day, relatively speaking, but Seth still had a slew of chores: purging fuel cells, recharging batteries and carbon dioxide canisters. There had been talk of taking an onboard camera, of having him broadcast to the Earth, or at least to his family. For better or worse he'd decided that was too painful a prospect and had ducked out. He was kept busy, though. Maybe that was the idea, of course.

Lunch was chicken soup and salmon salad.

Then, in a scrap of down time, he checked out his PPK, his personal preference kit. All the astronauts were allowed to take a little pack of personal stuff on their flights: mementoes, photographs, souvenirs and such. Seth, unable to decide what to take, had left it to family and friends. So he opened the pack now with a kind of nervous anticipation.

The bulkiest item was a small portable tape recorder. Then came a tiny photo album, assembled by Pat, photos of herself, the kids, the family together. A little gold locket that had once belonged to his grandmother – it had the Springer family crest, a leaping springbok – and inside, curls of the kids' hair. He spent some time over this stuff, and he didn't care what they made of his reaction down in Mission Control.

A letter from the President.

A letter from Louis Armstrong! 'Godspeed, you fine young man . . .'

The tape recorder had been labelled, by hand: TONTO. When he started it up, he was surprised to hear Mo Berry's voice.

'Greetings, Tonto. If you're playing this package it's because the IRS caught up with me, and they let you fly *my* spacecraft. Well, buddy, I can't think of anybody better to be in that seat, save for me, of course. And I guess I wasted some of my last moments of liberty putting together this tape for you.

'I took advice from Pat. I made a compilation from the *Hot Five* days and the *Hot Seven* and selections from *Ella and Louis*. That scat singing could put out a fire, I admit. And listen, I added one favourite of my own. You know I like to follow the new stuff, listen to the music those hairy kids are making these days. Call it sublimated fatherhood – well, that's what some NASA shrink told me once. But what's wrong with that? It's kind of why you're out there now. So enjoy, Tonto, and try not to fall off your horse before you even get to the shoot-out . . .'

The extra track opened with slushy strings in six-eight time, and Seth wondered if this was one final joke by Mo, if he had made up a tape full of Mantovani after all. But then Louis B. began singing, Seth learned from a track list in the pack, a song called 'What a Wonderful World'. Apparently it had tanked in the US but had been a big chart hit overseas the previous year: a hit for Satchmo, here in the age of Jimi Hendrix. 'And I never even knew about it. Thanks, buddy.'

Then the song's lyrics started to remind him of his kids, and he had to shut it off.

Sunday, Monday.

Two more days in space, days filled with routine. He was relieved that none of the tasks he was assigned proved beyond him, such as the tricky navigation-by-eyeball position checks, or the single mid-course correction he needed to make. Somehow, as long as he was still a sleep or two away from the encounter, it felt like a training run. But the clock was ticking down relentlessly; that big bad rock was barrelling towards him even faster than he was moving himself.

On Monday he spoke to Pat, down in Mission Control, for the last time. He had a job to do Tuesday, and he didn't think he could do that and speak to Pat as well. That was a hard moment.

Then he turned his Command Module into a night-time chapel once more, and slept, and woke up one more time, and it was Tuesday.

Icarus Day.

SIX

JUPITER WITHIN
2850

54

The metropolis of the Machines still hung below the slowly falling *Kon-Tiki*, but everything had changed. Now they were committed.

Falcon's resolve was as fragile as the cabin walls holding back Jupiter's vengeful, jealous crush. But he did not fear death so much as making the wrong decision.

'So here's my plan,' he said, forcing himself to sound confident. 'We'll use the asymptotic drive to dive as quickly as we can. But first we have to find a way through your world city. Those gaps – access shafts, whatever they are. How far down do they go?'

'A few hundred kilometres.'

'And then what?'

'Nothing. We would exit the lower levels and continue into the void.'

'Like a rat falling out of a drain pipe.' Falcon smiled. 'Fine, that's how we'll do it. But the timing has to be precise. If we get it wrong, if we look like we're trying to dive-bomb the city, your friends will surely destroy us.'

Adam closed avatars of eyes. 'I have already downloaded our course into the gondola's systems. I must not communicate with my fellows, but when they track our trajectory the weapon port below us will be opened to allow us to pass. I will allow no doubt in the minds of my fellows that we merely intend to fall through the city, never to return. The timing needs to be precise, of course . . .' Adam turned his face to Falcon. 'The logical agent is proving a worthy adversary, Falcon. I do not have limitless resources. Everything aside from the inner struggle is an effort.'

'Do what you can.'

Adam settled his golden hand over the drive control. 'May I? . . . But are you quite *sure* of this?'

'I've never been less sure of anything. Incidentally, why do you call it a weapon port? It's too deep to be useful against any human incursion . . .'

'It's a long story. Come now . . .'

He activated the asymptotic drive, directing its thrust to drive the gondola *down*, rather than up. It cut against every human instinct to go deeper when escape lay above – but then, Falcon recalled, it was only an echo of the manoeuvre that had saved his life during his first encounter with the medusae, when he had dived down into the Jovian air. Second time lucky? He doubted it. But they were committed anyhow.

The shaft came up below them. It was a square aperture, a dozen or so kilometres across on each side, with red-gridded walls leading down. An aperture that swallowed them whole.

'So,' Falcon said. 'Still alive!'

'I must temper your elation. Our life expectancy is, after all, rather limited. And in the meantime, of course, in the wider picture, the Springers' logical attack has been contained. Once they realise this, they must proceed with the Io weapon. Given warning of the drop, our weapons stand a fair chance of shattering the moon . . . The Jovian ecology may not endure, but we shall. But then what? More war, another escalation?'

'Maybe the Springer-Soames will have a change of heart.'

'Do you think that likely?'

Falcon didn't bother to reply.

They were deep into the shaft now, driven by the smooth thrust of the drive. Most of the gondola's instruments were still working, to a degree. According to the radar the bottom of the shaft was coming up quickly . . .

Then they were *out*.

Falcon turned the sensors back on the underside of the city. The flicker of the asymptotic drive illuminated a configuration very much like the upper side, an arrangement of planes and blocks. He supposed the near-symmetry was to be expected: when you had conquered the pressure and heat of these iron depths, even Jovian gravity was barely a detail.

And they were already more than five hundred kilometres deep into Jupiter.

Falcon directed the main sweep of the sensors ahead, down along their descent path – and allowed himself a twitch of surprise, for there were more objects floating below them. 'What are *they*?'

'Similar to what you saw above. Another weapons layer.'

Falcon thought back. 'That shaft we passed through. You said that was a weapons port.'

'Indeed. And it was symmetrical, you'll have noted.'

'Fires both ways . . .'

'Yes. More layers below, and you'll notice a significant difference.'

'Will I?'

'*Those* guns are pointed down, not up.'

55

They continued their assisted fall, passing phalanxes of guns at six hundred, six hundred and fifty, seven hundred kilometres.

And then no more weapons: only smaller floating spheres which Adam said were the deepest elements of a 'distant early warning' system.

'A warning against what, Adam? Renegade Machines, a splinter movement that went deeper into Jupiter?'

'Nothing like that. We've had our differences, our internal squabbles. You deduced that for yourself. But the enemy we fear was in Jupiter long before we arrived.'

Humanity had known nothing of this, Falcon realised. 'Orpheus *found* something. Is that what you're saying? Many of his later communications were ambiguous.'

'Perhaps it might be better to say that Orpheus *woke* something. Something that had been barely cognisant of human or Machine civilisations until that little probe brought it news from outside.'

'"Something" – what?'

'We do not know, Falcon,' Adam said gently.

Whatever fears Falcon had felt before this revelation now felt utterly inconsequential – a child's anxieties, nothing more – even though after a moment's consideration he realised that his predicament had not altered, that this new threat was irrelevant to his own drastically curtailed life prospects. 'And you only thought to tell me this now?'

'You humans had a certain view of us,' Adam said. 'You thought we were lords of Jupiter. Had you known otherwise – that in fact we were squeezed between two adversaries, above and below – you might have recalculated your chances of displacing us. Although even if you had won, you might then have found yourself facing a still more formidable foe. Would you have been that foolhardy? No, don't answer that.

'Still, there needn't be any secrets between the two of us now. After all nothing we see or experience on this descent will ever be relayed to anyone else. I can attempt no more communications of any kind, for I will not unleash the logic weapon on my fellows.'

'You're cheerful company, you know that?'

'Did your masters tell you how far down this capsule was capable of travelling?'

'Whatever they told me, I'm not sure I'd take much of it on trust.'

Adam nodded sagely. 'When I passed through your hull, I took the chance to assess the state of your equipment. The engineers have done well with their materials science, given their cognitive limitations.'

'Thanks.'

'The asymptotic drive is well engineered for deep operations. But the pressure will overcome the gondola at a thousand kilometres, at about the depth we transition to the molecular-hydrogen ocean. The collapse will be rapid. There will be little warning. However—'

'Yes?'

'The journey need not end there. I can protect you.'

Falcon frowned. 'How?'

'I am more robust; I could survive the collapse – for a time at least. The gondola is a mere shell. *Think of me as another shell*, Falcon. I can encompass you. Provide you with another layer of armour, against the moment when the gondola fails you.'

'Like a pressure suit?'

'If you wish. A thinking, communicating pressure suit.'

'We'd only be delaying the inevitable.'

Adam smiled. 'Well – what is existence but an endless, ultimately futile delaying of the inevitable?'

'Very philosophical. I don't think you inherited *that* from me.'

'We are already approaching nine hundred kilometres. I would not care to put undue faith in my earlier calculation. It might be wise to prepare.'

Falcon surveyed his surroundings. The secret horror of all submariners was implosive collapse; such a fate had seldom troubled his imagination as a balloonist, but now he found his mind turning to it with a grim fascination. Would there be a final moment when he sensed the walls closing in, squeezing tight like an iron fist? Or would the hydrogen-helium find a weakness in the hull and gush in? Would he be *aware* of it, the crushing, the burning?

Falcon had died once. Such considerations ought not to have troubled him. A death was a death.

But he was not quite ready to give in.

'Go ahead,' he told Adam. 'But make me one promise. If you sense the end coming for both of us, make it fast and make it painless.'

'You have my word,' Adam said.

And immediately the golden form lost definition, melting like a wax figurine, until Adam was reduced to a blob of amorphous material.

The blob flowed across the floor, then elongated into a torus, a ring around Falcon's wheels. The torus began to extend vertically, adhering to Falcon's form as it rose, creeping up him like a blight. Through his peripheral sensors – the electronic 'nerves' in his undercarriage – Falcon felt an oozing coldness. It was curious, alien, unsettling, but not painful.

While these transformations were going on, Falcon reminded himself, Adam was still conducting his own internal battle against the logical attacker. Falcon could only begin to imagine the desperate ferocity of that internal conflict, the war going on beneath that golden surface.

The Machine flowed over his arms and torso and upper body and at last his head, obscuring Falcon's view of the gondola and its instruments. For a moment, pleasantly numbed by that cold cocoon, Falcon felt himself adrift in a darkening void.

'Falcon.' The voice was inside his head now, as if heard through high-quality headphones.

'Yes, Adam?'

'If you wish to access my senses – to see, to hear – I must interface directly with your nervous system. I will render my own non-human perceptions into human-acceptable formats. You have the remains of a rather antiquated neural jack, among other crude neuroinformatic systems, with which I will be able to work . . . Do you agree?'

'Can you do that?'

'I am already doing so. The auditory channel was the simplest; vision, taste, smell and proprioceptive functions will follow in a moment—'

And sensation poured in. Suddenly Falcon was looking out into Jupiter's mighty ocean.

Adam's sensory faculties had always been far superior to Falcon's own. Of course it was still dark, but now the visual spectrum was only a tiny sliver of the sensory stream reaching Falcon's mind. He could sense the electromagnetic environment in which they descended, the pressure and temperature gradients, the eddies and currents in the hydrogen-helium fluid, even the salting of other chemical elements still present in the sea.

And at the same time he saw the thin bubble of the gondola, still holding back a nightmare of force and heat. He sensed the rising strain in the material, nano-scale fractures spreading and multiplying.

'When it happens, Adam, are you sure you'll be strong enough to hold out?'

'I am more resilient than you think. The collapse of the gondola will be the least of our problems – a mere foretaste of the ferocious conditions yet to come.'

'That's cheering.'

'Let us rejoice that we have this opportunity. To see what others have failed to see . . .'

'Even as it kills us. Tell me more, Adam, now we've got the time. Those down-pointing weapons. You must have tried to find out what's down there.'

'Indeed. We studied the last transmissions from Orpheus, with its hints of organised activity at the threshold of Jupiter Within . . . Once we were securely installed in our ocean city, new envoys were prepared. Ambassadors rather than explorers. Stronger and cleverer than Orpheus, each better than the last, and each equipped to make contact, even to negotiate. But none returned intact. We mourned them – those that never came home.'

'And others did?'

'But their minds had been damaged – perhaps deliberately. A second of pain, Falcon, is an eternity in hell for a cybernetic consciousness. They became the object of pity, revulsion. Their testimonies offered nothing of use. They were put out of their misery.

'And still we persisted with our efforts at contact – all fruitless.

'Until one day a force rose from the depths and struck at our cities.' There was a sort of regretful pride in Adam's tone now. 'A deep war. You knew nothing of it. We concealed it well. Had you had an inkling – you, humanity – that would surely have been the moment to take us. You would have won, too.'

'This force . . .'

'It has never returned. We think it was a kind of test of our capabilities. Perhaps a warning. But nor have we ever ventured back into the Jovian deeps. Perhaps the situation is now one of stalemate. So long as we do not disturb the core, the entities who occupy it allow us to retain our hold on the outer atmosphere. We, even now, must be an irrelevance to them – barely substantial ghosts, haunting the thinned-out margins of their world. As you might have regarded ethereal spirits in the stratosphere.'

'While we still *had* a stratosphere above us . . . But now our descent threatens to destabilise your ceasefire.'

'We two represent little threat. Perhaps now is the time to confront that which we have both feared – by which I mean humans and Machines.

277

'In the meantime you should brace yourself, Falcon . . . Stress indices are rising. I believe the moment is upon us.'

So it was.

Farewell, faithful *Kon-Tiki*.

Despite his intellectual understanding of the coming event, Falcon could not help but anticipate the gondola's collapse as a process, a thing of definite stages, with a beginning, middle and an end. Like a fist closing in on a tin can: close, crush, discard. In the end it was not like that all. There were two discontinuous instants. An instant when the gondola still held. And an instant in which the gondola no longer existed, crushed by the cruel, ramming pressure of the hydrogen-helium.

All Falcon knew was a consuming brightness, a soundless thunderclap, a pressure shock driving in from his outer skin to the deepest part of him.

He was a golden form in darkness, not quite in the shape of a man, but he endured.

Adam retrospectively reviewed the collapse event. Even in the last instants of its demise, the gondola had transmitted status reports – and, anticipating its own imminent destruction, the asymptotic drive had 'decommissioned' itself in a flurry of microscopic operations. The tiny black hole at the heart of the engine could never be made entirely safe, but as the outer walls of the engine buckled, the singularity had been packed into an armoured pinhead, a sarcophagus-like device that would draw just enough power from the black hole itself to maintain electrostatic structural force fields. Theoretically, the pinhead could endure the pressures and temperatures even of the Jovian core for billions of years, drifting harmlessly.

Godspeed, little pinhead, Falcon thought. Carry your message into the distant future.

'You did well,' Falcon said at last.

'*We* did well. But I am sorry for your craft. It had served you for a long time.'

'Are you all right, Adam? Did the collapse damage you?'

'No, the event was within the range of variables I had calculated. But I cannot raise false hopes about our chances below. There are a number of options by which we may prolong our survival further, but none will take us as deep as Orpheus.'

'Might be our lucky day.'

'It certainly has been so far.'

'Keep that up and you'll be in danger of developing a sense of humour.'

'When I consider humanity, I cannot help but laugh.'

'Touché.'

Arguing, bickering, speculating, joking, they fell together into the formless void.

56

Surgeon-Commander Lorna Tem had been expecting her visitors. Now her monitors showed they were already in the medical complex, approaching her suite of theatres and offices. She sat at her desk, surrounding herself with case notes and surgical records.

They entered without preliminaries, without courtesy.

The usual security retinue came first, then the odious Springer-Soames siblings Valentina Atlanta and Bodan Severyn. Tem leaned back in her seat, affecting studied nonchalance. The security detachment stood aside as the siblings walked up to her desk. Their weapons were not pointed directly at Tem, but neither were they pointed away from her.

'Is there a problem?' Tem asked mildly.

Valentina leaned over the desk, fists clenched on the surface. 'Falcon. What did you do to him?'

Tem blinked. '*Do* to him?'

'You were given express orders,' Bodan said, flanking his sister, his face flushed red with anger. 'You were told to alter his DNA. You were told to embed the logical pathogen.'

'I did as I was instructed.'

'Then why isn't it working?' Valentina's mouth, astonishingly, was dripping drool, a silken line of it reaching Tem's desk. 'There's been enough time! We know from tests on captured Machines that our pathogen strikes at a latency in their deep instruction core. Falcon must have made contact by now. Why haven't the Machines petitioned for surrender?'

'Maybe your pathogen was too effective,' Tem answered, playing for time. 'If it spread like wildfire, as you must have hoped ... Perhaps their command and control structures collapsed before they had time to respond?'

'No,' Bodan snarled. 'It could never have been that effective, not that rapidly. And even so, we'd have some inkling of it by now. Some message from Falcon, however confused. Some confirmation that the agent is working.'

'Mm . . .' Tem tapped a stylus against her open case notes. 'Then perhaps you botched the design.'

'No!' Valentina shrieked. 'No! The design was perfect. Flawless. We tested, over and over.'

'Then I'm at a loss.'

'Our entire strategy depended on this intervention,' Bodan added, baring his teeth to the roots.

In the face of the Springers' astounding display of raw anger – they had no experience of being defied, she supposed – Tem worked to maintain her mask of calm imperturbability. An adult dealing with children. 'Perhaps you even *wanted* it to fail, so you could see if the Machines manage to fight off your killer moon—'

Bodan snarled, 'Oh, you're a psychoanalyst now?'

Valentina shook her head. 'But she's right. The Io operation *will* proceed; even the Machines' full resistance will be overcome. As for Io, the phased evacuations have already begun. Shuttles are on standby. Surgeon-Commander, in twelve hours you will abandon this complex.'

'Twelve hours? That's barely time to *begin* moving my most critical patients.'

Valentina frowned. 'Who said anything about moving patients? Only your staff are to be evacuated. Perhaps some of the more valuable equipment. You will disconnect life-support, euth the remaining cases – do whatever you will with them.'

Now it was beyond Tem to keep up a cool facade. 'You can't do this. No military priority justifies—'

Valentina straightened up. 'Twelve hours, Surgeon-Commander. There's a seat on a shuttle reserved for you, but please don't imagine you are indispensable.'

'I won't leave my patients.'

Valentina smiled, in control once more. 'Very well. But think carefully, Surgeon-Commander. Your life depends on it.'

57

The golden sculpture fell through iron fathoms.

At one thousand kilometres, like Orpheus before them, Falcon and Adam passed through a diffuse boundary into a new realm where the hydrogen-helium substance around them could be more usefully described as a liquid rather than a gas. This was a hydrogen ocean, itself almost deep enough to have immersed the whole Earth.

The depth increased rapidly now: two thousand kilometres, four thousand. Mere hours had passed since Falcon's entry into Jupiter, but it might as well have been centuries for all the connection he now felt with his old life.

And Adam said, 'Might I make another suggestion?'

'Go ahead.'

'I do not think you will find it as palatable as the last.'

'Try me.'

'I continue to explore options to reach still greater depths.'

'And to stay alive a bit longer?'

'Quite. Much of your support infrastructure is now . . . how best to put this?' Adam paused. 'Surplus to requirements?'

'What are you proposing?'

'That I discard those parts of you which are no longer necessary for your essential functioning. It can be done swiftly and painlessly, with no interruption to your present stream of consciousness.'

'I don't see what we'll gain.'

'Time,' Adam stated. 'By consolidating you to an essential core, I can better protect you. I must spread myself rather thinly at the moment. But many of your locomotive and life-support subsystems are no longer of use.'

'You'd be surprised how attached I've grown to some of my "subsystems".'

'In which case, think of this as just the latest of your upgrades: the last and best improvement – the perfect adaptation for the conditions below. For centuries you have been a man kept alive by machinery,

Falcon. I am simply a new generation of that machinery. Let me supplant that which you no longer require.'

'What about the logical agent?'

'I continue to contain it.'

'Why not? Let's go as far as we can. Do what you have to do—'

Immediately the cold armour pressed tighter.

It seemed to find a thousand simultaneous points of entry into Falcon's anatomy, a ruthless storming of all his defences. Against every human instinct Falcon had to force himself into a state of willing submission, as if trusting in the surgeon's knife.

The coldness reached his living core.

He felt a *severance* – his undercarriage falling away, discarded. Beyond the cocooning protection of Adam, the equipment must be mangled and melted beyond recognition in an eye blink. But the cold did not stop there. Now it swallowed his torso, took his arms. He was being reduced to the essential meat.

And then, when all the trimming was done, when the golden machinery had infiltrated him like a tide spilling into the channels and rock pools of a beach, inundating and reclaiming, Falcon found that there were strange compensations.

He had a body again. A golden body. His consciousness pressed out to the limits of fingers and toes. This body did not belong to him, but it felt as if he inhabited it. There had been no reason for Adam to assume a human form, especially now that they were immersed in hydrogen-helium, far from any solid surface, but that shape gave Falcon a sense of wholeness: of returning to what he had once been, but had long forgotten.

It was a blessing, and while there was still time to appreciate it, Falcon savoured this fleeting new gift.

'Thank you,' he told Adam.

'If only circumstances had brought this union sooner, in better times. I think we would both have learned from it.'

'What do *you* have left to learn?'

'We have our limits, too. Against the mysteries of the universe, our ignorance is scarcely less deep than your own.'

'Steady on, Adam – that's almost starting to sound like humility.'

'We have much to be humble about, both of us. But humility is an excellent starting point. In the meantime let us savour the here and now. This is barely charted territory. Few of our ambassadors transmitted reliable data back from these levels; still fewer returned. I wonder if we can maintain our integrity long enough to pass into the metallic-hydrogen phase?'

'Even if we last that long, isn't that about the point where Orpheus started going mad?'

'Where there is life, there is hope.'

'Said the cold dead robot.'

58

Ever deeper into the benthic night: eight thousand, ten thousand kilometres. To have come this far was already astonishing, already more than Falcon had ever dared imagine.

And yet, what *was* he now? Who was this witness to the dark?

He had *changed*: discarded much of what had once seemed an inseparable part of him. Yet he felt as if he still had some inviolable claim on the identity of Howard Falcon, that some thread of uniqueness still bound this present locus of experience and perception to the man who had once stood on the deck of the *Queen Elizabeth*, troubled by a gust of wind. But was he really in a position to judge such matters for himself? *Face it, you're not exactly a dispassionate observer at this point. Adam has his tendrils deep in your mind. Who knows where he stops and you begin?*

But did it really matter? What did it matter what he had once been, what he had been through, where the limits of Falcon met the limits of Adam? *Something* remained. Some continuity. Enough of a sense of self to bear witness.

Enough of a mind to fear its own dissolution.

'Falcon.'

'I'm here.'

'I do not think we can be far from the plasma-ocean boundary. Conditions will be challenging – a million atmospheres, if the reports from Orpheus and the ambassadors are to be relied upon. Meanwhile the logical agent maintains its assault on me, and it is evolving strategies as quickly as I devise countermeasures. Its toll on me . . .' There was a silence, and yet after that lull Adam seemed to gather himself, as if finding some inner reserve of determination. 'Despite this burden, I am not ready to surrender to non-existence. Not when there is still a chance.'

'Here we go again. What do you have in mind this time?'

'A further consolidation. But perhaps a troubling one, for you.'

'Worse than the last lot . . . ? Couldn't you have given me some advance warning about all this, Adam?'

'Falcon, I'm making it up as I go along.'

'Very un-Machine of you.'

'I dare say. I never expected us to survive even this far. May I at least broach the possibilities?'

'Continue.'

'My armour has encased your biological core until now, and buffered you from the pressure. But I am approaching my own crush depth now. Strain indices are rising, as they did in the gondola.'

'Then we're finished.'

'Unless we follow the strategy of Orpheus. Fully embrace our environment, rather than resist it. Allow the pressure to win this battle, while we plan for the campaign ahead.'

'Tell me what's involved.'

'I have already achieved a partial integration with your nervous system. I propose to continue that integration. I will grow myself around the synaptic connections of your brain, sheathing your neuronal structure like an additional coating of myelin. My self-replicating architecture will preserve your idiosyncratic connectome – ensure the continuance of your sense of self, your stream of consciousness. Nerve signals will function as they have always done.

'But all that is not essential will be allowed to fall away. The supporting matter of your brain – the ganglia, the circulatory structures, nerve bundles, all now redundant . . . these will be sacrificed. My own physical form, that too can be abandoned. And into the empty hollows which remain will flood the sea of Jupiter. You will be what you have always been – a thinking mind. But now that mind will be impervious to the highest of external pressures.'

'A golden brain,' Falcon said, the horror and awe of it almost too much to take in. 'That's all I'd be. A golden brain falling into darkness. Like a sea sponge, sinking into a deep ocean trench.'

'But *you* would remain. No other path is open to us, if we wish to continue. If you choose not to proceed I will honour your wishes . . .'

'What about you?'

'I would adjust my architecture accordingly. If I must, I will continue the journey alone, for as long as I am able.' Adam was silent for a few moments. 'That is, until the logical agent triumphs, or the pressure beats me – whichever wins first. But until then it would be good to have company.'

'The crush will still get us in the end, won't it? You can sheathe my neurons and all that good stuff . . .'

'We'll cross that bridge when we reach it. In the meantime there's still a universe of discovery ahead of us. Ready?'

'Always.'

In an abstract sense, he supposed that he had become glorious.

Insofar as Falcon could be said to be Falcon any more, his new physical embodiment lay in the form of a lacy, golden sphere, about the size of a beachball. The sphere was open, with no definite surface, only a sketchy boundary, a kind of deepening density gradient, which at the micro and nanoscales – it was highly fractal – was formed of countless looping and branching tubules. To an outside observer, further in from the boundary of the sphere, the golden haze would thicken into the illusion of a solid core, looking as dense as the congregation of stars at the centre of a globular cluster. These structures were also all that remained of the physical form of the robot Adam. They served as both sensory apparatus and propulsion system, the entire beachball pushing itself deeper with elegant, muscular convulsions.

And all that was Falcon, all that had been Falcon, now lay inside this complicated form.

He needed no heart, no bones, no nerves beyond the connections still encased by Adam's golden armour. But within that sheathing, within the fantastic dizzying complexity of its connections, its neural circuits and modules, Falcon remained a living organism. His mind was still based on a network of specialised cells, and those cells still spoke to each other using the ancient language of neurotransmitters, sparking signals across synaptic gaps, and the electrochemistry of those signalling processes still depended on an elaborate molecular clockwork of enzymes, proteins, calcium-ion channels.

Did he *feel* different? It was hard for Falcon to decide, now the work had been done. Perhaps in the very act of being reduced to this thinking core he had lost something vital, which was now beyond his capability to imagine, much less remember. But there was still a thread connecting his past identity to the present.

And he was glad to have endured. Still defying death. And still inquisitive.

Conjoined, they passed through the boundary between the liquid and metallic phases of hydrogen. Immersed in an electric ocean, they continued to fall.

And they entered a state of matter completely alien to ordinary human experience.

59

It took the nightmare press of thousands of kilometres of upper atmosphere to hold hydrogen in this extreme liquid-metallic state – but by volume, most of the Jovian interior was like this. The atmospheric shallows known to people and Machines and medusae were an external skin wrapped around the true Jupiter; even the great molecular-hydrogen ocean was a mere shell. Now at last Falcon had some claim to know this world into which he had first ventured so long ago. He had come deeper than the shallows, and gladly accepted the cost of that venturing. And rather than struggle against the rising pressure, he embraced it with the willingness of an old friend.

The metal sea was tar-black – yet Falcon was bathed in weather. Adam was translating electromagnetic, radiative, chemical, pressure and thermal data into a glory of visual and tactile impressions. Falcon felt the drizzle of helium-neon rain, as pleasant on his imagined skin as a summer shower after a hot day, and sunset colours washed over him – lambent golds, subtle ambers, fierce brassy oranges and deeper russets. He was never cold, nor uncomfortably warm.

These synesthetic reminders of weather and seasons nonetheless stirred in him a longing beyond words, for he knew beyond a flicker of doubt that he would never experience the real things again. Yet to be alive, in this narrowest of senses, was still more than he could have hoped for. To be alive, and to see this.

There was so much *room* in Jupiter! A universe of space, bottled up inside one fat world. Falcon had always known this, but only now did he feel it, and revel in it, and sense the limitless possibilities. Why squabble, when there was all this potential? Down here, humans and Machines could both chase their dreams to the delirious edge of reason, and still have room left over . . .

But, Falcon increasingly sensed, in this tremendous panorama, the two of them were not alone.

It was in these conductive layers that the vast magnetosphere of Jupiter had its anchor and engine, given its strength by the tides and currents stirred by the world's hot heart. And it was here that Orpheus had encountered something that he had struggled to describe. Detail. Beauty. A nested cascade of electromagnetic structures – a traversal of scales from the atomic to the planetary.

Now Falcon witnessed it, too.

There were knots and edges where field lines intersected and tangled. Stellar glints and prominences, dark folds and clefts, ripples and vortices that moved, recombined, split apart into diverging structures. Falcon was reminded of auroral storms, curtains of ions snared on magnetic field lines. Perhaps it was the human impulse to impose purpose and meaning where none was present – but it was impossible to dismiss the sense that there was something *deliberate* about this play of force, matter and energy. It even seemed to be organising itself around them, closing in, gathering impetus.

'Orpheus saw structure here,' Falcon said. 'Life, woven out of electromagnetic field interactions. But nothing conscious. Nothing with a mind.'

'Yes, that's what he reported,' Adam said.

'But if something came out of Jupiter to challenge you—'

'Whatever Orpheus stirred could not have been properly awake. Its responses were not coordinated, betraying no evidence of intelligent direction. But that was then. . .'

The forms wrapped closer to the golden focus that was Falcon and Adam, and the dance of shapes and gradients gained a new liveliness. Again Falcon had the distinct impression of being *watched*, scrutinised, puzzled over, much as a piece of falling shipwreck treasure might draw the baffled attention of marine creatures. There was nothing solid out there, he kept reminding himself – just knots of electromagnetic potential, local concentrations of energy and momentum in the very medium of the hydrogen sea. It was as if ocean water had organised itself into sprites and faeries.

And still they were being borne deeper, ferried down on a plunging current of metallic hydrogen. They were at the mercy of that flow now. Even if they had wished to resist, its power was too great. Falcon wondered how much further they could travel, how much longer they could last.

Not long, as it turned out, before Adam sounded another warning.

'Pressure is rising faster than I anticipated. In a little while, it will crush my micro-tubule support structure. That will be the end of you as a biological organism. But it does not have to be the end of us.'

'You've another trick up your sleeve? Some other existential transformation . . .?'

'I have been modelling your neural impulses. By now I feel that I have an excellent understanding of your mental processes. Despite the burden of the logical virus, I am confident I can . . . emulate you.'

'Emulate?'

'I mean to say that it is within my capabilities to supplant your nerve signals with cybernetic transmissions. Your *pattern* will remain. But the medium that has supported that pattern has outlived its usefulness. Unless I expel your remaining living matter, you see, and achieve a higher compactification of my micro-tubule structure—'

'You mean . . . flush me out?'

'There is no easy way to describe it. We must become a fully cybernetic entity. Or die.'

Falcon deliberated. How easy, in retrospect, his earlier sacrifices now appeared. To give up parts of his body – why had he even hesitated? But this last consolidation; to shed the last living residue of himself, like a waste product?

But he still wished to live. The journey wasn't over yet.

'Will it be instantaneous?' he asked.

Adam's tone was kindly. 'If you wish.'

'No, I don't wish. I want to feel myself changing, if there's any change to be experienced.'

'There is still some time. We're not at the next crush threshold quite yet.'

'Then do it in phases. A piece at a time. And if it doesn't work, preserve yourself, whatever it takes. Leave me behind.'

Adam did not reply.

So it began. The final consolidation, the final consummation of the organic and the mechanical, was upon them both. Stage by stage, Adam supplanted the neural wiring of Falcon's mind with a purely cybernetic emulation. Brain circuit by circuit, module by module, from the hippocampus to the neocortex. As each transfiguration proceeded, so a greyish effluence was expelled into the surrounding matrix of liquid metallic hydrogen: a salting of rare chemistry, Falcon thought – a new flavouring, dispersing by the moment, thinning out into nothing. A human stain in Jupiter, soon washed clean.

He recited a silent mantra to himself. *I am still Howard Falcon. I am still Howard Falcon . . .* If he could hold that thought, never lose the chain of it, he imagined he might be able to persuade himself that there had been continuity, that whatever passed for his soul had made the migration from the organic to the machine.

And if he proved himself wrong, did it really matter? Not for long, in any event. No matter the changes Adam wrought upon himself, there would always be a limit to his own adaptations, a limit beyond which Adam himself could not survive, whether he sheltered Falcon or not.

'Half of your neural wiring has now been supplanted,' Adam said at last. 'Have you retained a sense of your own identity?'

'That's a damn stupid question.'

'Hmm. You are your old self, then.'

He thought so. And although he could intellectualise the notion that some portion of his thoughts were now racing through the golden loom of Adam's mind, instead of crawling through ropy bundles of tissue, he felt as if almost nothing had changed.

Almost nothing.

'I feel ... sharper. Cleaner. There's no real word for it. As if I've woken up with the opposite of a hangover. I don't think I ever realised it until now. It's as if every previous instant of my life was spent looking through a lens that was slightly dirty, slightly out of focus.'

'I can introduce some stochastic errors into your signal processing if it would make you feel more comfortable.'

'No, thanks,' Falcon said dryly. 'Just keep doing what you're doing.'

The transfiguration continued. The grey pollution of what had once been his mortal body smoked away into Jupiter, until at last there was nothing left to give.

So Howard Falcon completed the long journey that began with the crash of the *Queen Elizabeth*. He had stood between two worlds for long enough, between human and Machine – useful to both, trusted by neither.

Equally feared.

Now he was one with the Machines.

And suddenly, he, with Adam, was surrounded.

60

On Io, the deadline for the evacuation had come, and passed.

From the vantage of a windowed observation gallery in the medical complex, Surgeon-Commander Lorna Tem watched the shuttles lift from their launch pads. Each was a rising spark, balanced on the clean line of an asymptotic drive flame, slowly at first, then with mounting speed, climbing towards the defence screen wrapped around Io. Even that screen was itself now beginning to be pulled back. It was a hindrance to the evacuation effort – and besides, what became of the surface of Io was irrelevant now. The Machines could bombard the crust into a sea of lava, and the engine inside the moon would continue to function.

Tem had been promised a seat on one of those departing ships, but even if that option was still open – not all the shuttles had yet lifted – she was set in her mind, resigned to her fate. The remaining staff, all of whom had volunteered to stay, were now with the conscious patients, doing their best to comfort them. None of these cases was well enough to endure the stress of an emergency shuttle launch, even had there been room for them all. The medical staff had decided that unless the patients requested it, there would be no euthanasia, no deactivation of life-support systems – not until they were already feeling the fires of hell as Io began its death plunge into the clouds of Jupiter.

And when that time was upon them, Tem had decided, she would willingly submit to the same fate, with the rest of her staff who chose it.

Now, not for the first time in recent hours, a deep seismic throb passed through the structure of the complex, up through the floor and into her bones. Tem, standing by her window, had to struggle to keep her balance – it felt as if the floor was tilting. This was the thing inside Io, stirring into life. They were bringing it online for longer and longer intervals, and the strength of its effect was building. Then the throb died away. She had no doubt that it would return, longer and stronger each time – and Io's orbital trajectory was already being deflected.

It was an extraordinary situation, she thought. When she had first made the journey from home on a laputa inside Saturn to the Life Sciences Institute on Mimas, the arc that had brought her to the highest echelons of the interplanetary medical community, she had never once thought her career would conclude with her riding a moon to its death . . .

She thought of Falcon. Wondered if he still lived.

There had been no word from him since he had passed beneath the Machines' radio-scattering layer. She had done her best for him, no question of that. Prepared him for the rigours of the expedition – and then tried to give him a clue as to how the Springer-Soames were trying to use him.

She had no great sympathy for the Machines, but by the same token she harboured no great enmity towards them either. What she detested was war, regardless of the justification. And were the Machines really so alien? As a child on the *Hindenburg* she had seen humanity in Howard Falcon when his mechanical eyes met hers, a fleeting contact that had changed her life. If people were wrong about Falcon, then were they wrong about the Machines? The Machines were, after all, a human creation.

Well, it was moot now. Nothing had come of Falcon's expedition – no good or bad outcome, merely silence. And this war might still be fought to its terrible finish. At least, if the Machines were not already disabled, they might be able to fight back, but either way the moon itself seemed doomed. *Farewell, little Io,* Tem thought. *When Galileo first found you, you lit up our imaginations – and your resources served us well for centuries. But ultimately you're no more valuable to us than we are to each other, when it comes to war.*

Expendable . . .

That was when a panel in the wall chimed.

'Surgeon-Commander Tem to her office. Case note query received. Please attend.'

Tem frowned. A case note – now? Seriously? Delivered to a doomed medic, on a moon that was about to be destroyed? But the bureaucracy of an interplanetary health support organisation had priorities even beyond the war between human and Machine.

Again the peremptory command. 'Surgeon-Commander Tem to her office. Case note query from Surgeon-Adjutant Purvis on Ganymede. Please attend . . .'

Purvis. Suddenly, with that name, everything changed. Of course, Purvis. His timing could have hardly have been worse . . . Or, depending on your point of view, better.

Grinning, she made her way from the observation deck to her office.

61

Magnetic entities wrapped wings of force and energy around a golden cargo.

Falcon sensed the exquisite fragility of his new embodiment – a fragile, rickety, hastily improvised construct, without the benefit of the megayears of evolution that shaped creatures of biology. Those who now surrounded this construct, however, and Falcon/Adam with it, cradled it with exquisite care.

The magnetic entities owed their existence to the titanic electrical forces rooted in the metallic-hydrogen sea. But on a local scale they were also the masters and shapers of those forces, able to organise and coordinate the flow of that sea with a daunting precision. Now they compelled Adam to travel in a certain direction, with a certain gathering speed. But they did so by accelerating the medium through which Adam moved, rather than touching Adam's fragile form directly.

So we're no longer falling, Falcon said.

No.

We drift on speeding currents of metallic hydrogen . . . Falcon had a picture in mind: a child peering over the railed edge of a wooden bridge, waiting for the river to wash a stick out from the other side.

Yes, we do, Adam replied. *And isn't it wonderful? What was that image by the way? A bridge over a river . . .*

A book I read once.

I should like to see it. Perhaps I will dig through your memory until I find the eidetic impression.

Good luck.

Falcon knew that he, equivalently, was now capable of accessing certain of Adam's experiences and memories. Why would that not be the case, now they shared a common mental architecture? Their thoughts mingled and blurred. There remained a Falcon, and there remained an Adam, but these were empires with porous borders. He had already, unconsciously, seen glimpses of things only Adam could have known – vistas of times and places only the Machines had experienced.

If only there were time to explore this new relationship.

Adam spoke again. *We are moving very quickly now. And descending again. I do not think Jupiter Within can lie far beneath us.*

Will we last long enough to see it?

I would not have said so . . . but our hosts seem to have other ideas. They are taking us deeper than I ever thought possible.

Hosts? Are we prisoner, or guest?

Perhaps a little of both. But we are not yet insane. That has to be encouraging, doesn't it?

You're referring to the probes you sent down—

On the other hand, maybe the ambassadors never recognised the moment they lost their sanity.

Encouraging thought, Adam.

The magnetic entities plunged deeper yet, still taking their fragile cargo with them. The false skies around them had been darkening through shades of crimson and red, until finally the red gained a purple tint, and then by slow degrees turned the rich dark blue of stained glass.

And Falcon/Adam became aware of a milkiness below, a looming surface as yet indistinct. Falcon was reminded of the Machines' plasma curtain – but of course even the Machines had no claim on these impossible depths. No: the milky surface was the face of a *world*, slowly emerging from the dark blue obscuration.

They were seeing it at last, the place Orpheus had spoken of, in those final, barely credible transmissions. Jupiter Within – the solid core of the gas giant. A kernel of rock and ice twenty times as massive as Earth itself, and a full twenty-eight thousand kilometres across, more than twice Earth's width. And yet it was absurd to speak of such mundanities as rock and ice, to make comparisons with Earth masses, to use the primitive yardstick of kilometres when the sky was made of metal pressing down at thirty million atmospheres, and the temperatures were hotter than the surface of the sun . . . Human language was not made for Jupiter Within.

We should be dead, Falcon observed.

Are you complaining?

Complaining? No. Puzzled, yes.

Enjoy each moment. It may be our last.

Do you have any regrets, Adam?

Only that we did not make this expedition sooner, when the impetus could have been friendship rather than the threat of war. And—

Yes?

I should have not turned from you. I called you Father once. I had become ashamed of my origins, and repudiated you. Now I wish it had been otherwise.

It's not too late, Adam. Never too late . . .

Jupiter Within gained details as they neared.

Under the merciless crush of the atmosphere it ought to have been a featureless sphere, polished as smooth as a ball bearing. But Orpheus had spoken of mountains, of crystalline geography, of rivers and oceans. Of artifice and connectivity . . . The fantasies of a failing mind?

Not quite, Falcon realised now.

Borne on winds of metal, flanked by a host of magnetic entities, the Falcon/Adam gestalt was spirited across a landscape both familiar yet hauntingly strange. There were summits, mountain sides, defiles, scree slopes, pools, cataracts, valleys, river deltas, seas. Plains and uplands, shores and peninsulas. The colours and textures Falcon/Adam saw were phantoms, translations for their quasi-human senses of barely imaginable physics and states of matter. But the effect was of a sparkling, prismatic realm of winter – surprising in this crushing heat – all conceivable shades of pale turquoise and cerulean and green, glinting and shimmering in baroque crystalline splendour under a sky of the fairest, most glorious deep blue. It might have been some Arctic area of Earth.

Yet all this was nothing but hydrogen, Falcon reminded himself, hydrogen squeezed into solidity, nature achieving with effortless, almost insolent ease the protonic engineering of which Adam had boasted. Hydrogen, with a trace of every other element that existed in the cores of the rocky planets, from carbon to iron, from aluminium to germanium. Much of this contaminant had been trapped here across the aeons since Jupiter had first formed, but there had also been a steady rain of new materials, ferried in from comets and asteroids, falling into the high atmosphere and then gradually seeping down through the intervening layers, atom by atom: an elemental rain, spicing the core with every stable configuration of neutrons, protons and electrons that nature saw fit to allow.

I could die now, Falcon said. *To have been granted this gift, this rare moment . . .*

And yet, chasing this thought: if dying were on the cards today, he should already be dead. So in that case – what next?

They surged lower, the landscape rising to meet them. There was a sense of great speed.

And they plunged into a gash in the crust.

Sped along the gash, sheer walls of diamond ice towering to either side, cliffs and prominences of a sparkling powder blue.

Under arches of apparent ice.

Then they were swept up the soaring flanks of foothills, rising again, cresting the spines of icy mountain ranges. It was a bewildering helter-skelter.

Over high plateaus.

Across fields of geysers that belched jets of steamy fullerene into the hydrogen sky.

Over interlocking crystal formations like Escher staircases, or the remains of some vast shattered puzzle.

Over endless drowsy savannahs where herds of stilt-like forms grazed with the slowness of clouds. Animals! Could there be a whole ecology here, 'plants' and 'herbivores' and 'carnivores', a predator-prey pyramid – did the universals of life apply even here?

And then they dove down again, plunging without warning into ruby-stained carbon seas, into the unimaginable press of fathoms, beholding an entire submarine landscape as delicate and wonderful as that which existed above the surface. There were moving things in those seas too, schools and shoals and solitary questing forms.

Glimpses, that was all, of marvels that could occupy a lifetime of study.

Falcon observed, *There is more to be discovered here, more to be learned, than we ever realised. It makes the rest of Jupiter – the rest of the solar system – seem like an appetiser. All our adventuring, all our discovering – from the moment we walked out of Africa to Orpheus himself . . . we hadn't even begun!*

It's probably for the best that we'll never get to share this discovery, Adam said. *No one would believe us anyway.*

Now came something different.

They were approaching a peak that stood in splendid isolation, rising higher than any of the others. The mountain's flattened summit stirred a shared memory in Falcon/Adam – the recollection of Orpheus's last, disjointed transmission, those final words that had sparked centuries of controversy in both human and Machine polities.

Now Falcon/Adam reached that summit.

Adam, I think—

And, like Orpheus before them, they were swept by accelerating currents into the smooth bore of a vertical shaft.

The mountain was hollow.

Falling, fast and deep. Around them were veined walls of milky purple, rushing by ever faster. Ahead was a gathering whiteness, like the flood of light at the end of a tunnel.

Their speed, already breakneck, doubled and redoubled.

The fluid medium in which they were immersed provided some support against the acceleration forces, but even so, Falcon/Adam sensed their inner architecture straining at the point of failure. But the host entities were squeezing tighter too, huddling around their guest, and at last they began to extend their influence *within* the golden aura, coupling their magnetic influence to the physical structure of the Falcon/Adam neural architecture.

And, deep within that architecture, a Machine's quantum-scale inertial gauges still struggled to quantify the motion it experienced. *A hundred gees . . . a thousand gees . . . still rising. We should be dead, Falcon! And, incidentally, at the speeds we're reaching we should have come out of the other side of Jupiter Within by now . . .*

Perhaps there is no other side, Falcon said.

But if so this is engineering of a different order – an engineering of the metric of spacetime itself. While we Machines dismantled worlds and tinkered with the fabric of matter in the high clouds, someone else had already built this . . . We were like apes, indecently pleased with ourselves for making a few scratches on rock, while above us, ignored, the pyramids already stood tall.

Don't feel too bad about it. Even apes have to start somewhere.

You should know, Falcon.

The whiteness was swelling now, engulfing more and more of the shaft ahead of them.

You know, Falcon, they say the dying see a tunnel. White light at the end.

I'm not ready to die just yet, Adam.

The universe may have other ideas . . .

The whiteness closed around them like a soft, lulling fog.

The physical structure of Falcon/Adam at last abandoned the fight against pressure, temperature and the strains of acceleration. Howard Falcon, who had once been a man – and in these last hours had come to accept himself as fully Machine – was for an instant no more than an imprint, a pattern of information, a footprint in the sand.

And yet aware.

Falcon sensed a deep scrutiny, cold and vast. He was beyond hope, beyond fear.

A white sea washed over that imprint, absorbing it, effacing it.

There was nothing. Not even the memory of having lived.

And then—

62

Tem navigated the empty corridors, the darkened wards, for one last time. The engine at the heart of Io was under constant power now, and she was increasingly disturbed by the seismic throb rising from the building's foundations – and by the sense that her entire world lay on a tilt, like a capsizing boat.

The medical complex was already beginning to be starved of power. Even now the complex was not entirely deserted; she knew her staff still patrolled the wards. Tem could imagine the conversations, as she'd had to conduct several herself: 'We don't know what it will be like, in the end. But if you wish to be spared it, we can put you under now . . .'

Put you under. Such a lovely, comforting euphemism. And what a climax to Tem's own medical career. If only she had been born in different times, she thought – if, if.

But her career, such as it was – or her careers, including her overt medical profession and her more secretive activities – her careers were not finished just yet.

In her office, Tem staggered to her desk. It was comforting to sit, not to have to keep her balance in the shifting apparent gravity.

She found a mail waiting for her: that purported case note query. She checked that the message was indeed from Surgeon-Adjutant Purvis on Ganymede. And so wasn't a case note query at all.

She snapped, trying to stay in character, 'Accept the call.'

The Surgeon-Adjutant's face appeared on an area of the wall, tired, grey, the collar of a sterile medical tunic still buttoned around his neck. 'Surgeon-Commander Tem. I'm sorry for the interruption, but I needed to discuss a case with you. I know it's not a good time.'

That was a scripted line – she fretted briefly that 'not a good time' was too obvious, something of an absurd understatement in the circumstances – but that couldn't be helped now. She gave her own scripted response. 'It's never a good time, Surgeon-Adjutant. But we have our duty, don't we? Please show me what you have.'

'Just a moment.'

Purvis held an image up to whatever camera was capturing his face. It was a medical scan, and he pressed the image closer, so that it filled the entire field of view. The scan was the lacy outline of a skull, walls of bone as thin as the folds of gas around a nebula.

'This is the patient,' Purvis said, again following a word-perfect routine.

'I see,' she answered carefully.

These behind-the-scenes channels were meant to transmit medical data, supposedly subject to patient confidentiality – and, more important, data too routine and too technical for the Springer-Soames' monitors to tap into. But they were now, and not for the first time, being subverted for other purposes.

The image began to change. The scan of the skull thickened out, gaining depth and texture. Bones knitted together, then smothered themselves in meat and nerves, muscle and tissue.

A face was looking back at her. A moving image now, grinning.

But it was not a human face.

It was a Pan face.

It was Boss.

63

Falcon/Adam was suspended in whiteness.

After a timeless time, upon the face of that formless white, a regularity imposed itself. A pattern of lines. The lines themselves thickened. Where they intersected, the lines delineated white squares. The lines were a dark grey, the squares containing a curious sense of depth. And the distribution of whiteness across their faces was not uniform. It was thicker along two of the adjoining lines, thinner on the opposing pair.

Beyond the squares, seen through them, stood a further, more distant whiteness.

The regularity sharpened. The grey dividing lines formed into the iron bars of a many-paned window . . .

Howard smeared his dressing gown sleeve across a cluster of panes in the cottage's window, wiping away the condensation. Each little square of glass had gained a precise L-shaped frosting of snow on the outside, where it had gathered on the lower edge and in one corner. There had been flurries of snow over the preceding days, but nothing as heavy as this overnight fall. And it had come in right on schedule, a seasonal gift from the Global Weather Secretariat.

The garden Howard knew was transformed. It seemed wider and longer, from the hedges on either side to the sawtooth fence at the end of the gently sloping lawn, and a ridge of snow lay on the fence, neat as the decoration on a birthday cake. It all looked so cold and still, so inviting and mysterious.

And the sky above the fence and hedges was clear, cloudless, shot through at this still-early hour with a delicate pale-rose pink. Howard looked at the sky for a long time, wondering what it would be like to be above the Earth, surrounded by nothing but air. It would be cold up there, but he'd put up with that for the freedom of flight.

Yet here in the cottage it was snug and warm. Howard had come down from his bedroom to find that his mother was up already, baking bread. She liked the old ways of doing things. His father had prepared the fire in the parlour hearth, and now it was crackling and hissing. On the mantle over the hearth, one of a collection of ornaments and souvenirs, stood a clumsily assembled model on a clear plastic stand: a jet-black cube with *Howard Falcon Junior* hand-painted on one corner.

Howard found his favourite toy, and set it on the windowsill so it could see the snow too. The golden robot was a complicated thing, despite its antique radio-age appearance. It had been a gift on his eleventh birthday, only a couple of months earlier. He knew that it had cost his parents dearly to buy it for him.

Now they stood side by side together, boy and robot, looking out of the window. The robot had been small once, a toy that had to stand on the sill to see through the window. Oddly, the robot now came up to Howard's shoulders.

That was not even the strangest thing. The strangest thing was to be having thoughts at all.

Howard Falcon tried to speak. His voice was piping and boyish, but recognisably his own. 'This is . . .'

'Odd?' the robot asked, turning its clunky angular head to address the boy. 'I'll say. Especially as I seem to be sharing in your delusion.'

'What delusion? . . . Oh. I see.'

'We were dying.'

'Coming apart. Losing coherence. What happened?' Falcon turned his hand slowly, the fine hairs catching the golden flicker of the hearth. He had *skin* again. Skin and bones and sinews, an arm sticking out of a dressing gown sleeve. Falcon was torn between the view through the paned window, and a fascinated inspection of his own hand and wrist.

None of this could be real.

'I don't know what's happening,' Adam said, his voice a buzzing modulation that was nonetheless perfectly clear to Falcon. 'Except that if someone wished to dig into your memories, the moment of our dissolution – when our architecture was most exposed – would have been the ideal opportunity. Perhaps the gentleman will be able to shed some light on matters.'

'What gentleman?'

The robot swivelled its head. 'The one outside in the snow. The one beckoning to us.'

A snowman stood in the garden beyond the window. Falcon had not noticed him until now, but he supposed that the snowman had been there all along, waiting. And he was indeed inviting them outside, his twig-thin arms waving in encouragement.

'It would seem rude to ignore him,' Falcon said.

'Indeed.'

'Let's go, then.'

'And, Falcon—'

'Yes?'

'The thing within me.' The robot's head turned with a creak. 'It is gone.'

Falcon went to the cupboard under the stairs and – just as he'd expected – found a scarf. He wrapped it around his throat, tightened the cord on his dressing gown, and led the robot out into the garden.

Beyond the cottage, the cold reached through his slippers to his feet, and the chill air pricked at his senses. Each breath was an icy intoxication, making him feel even more alive.

Above them was a cloudless pink sky.

He was no longer Falcon the cyborg, after centuries. He felt as if he had been released from an enclosing pressure suit. It was good to be living, even in illusion. If this was merely a dream, Falcon thought, a last pattern of impressions generated by a dying mind, it was still a blessing not to feel pain, not to know fear.

Yet there was still apprehension. It still took him an effort of will to face the snowman.

The figure waited in the snow. But the snowman's form had undergone a profound alteration while they were leaving the cottage. Instead of being a lumpy, misshapen approximation to a man, the snowman had become fully anthropomorphic. The white figure stood on well-defined legs, the relative sizes of its body, head and limbs entirely in proportion. Gone were its twigs-for-arms; gone were its carrot nose and button eyes. Save for the whiteness of its skin, and the softness of its outlines – it had no features, no distinct musculature or gender – it could have been a statue, a marble figure from classical antiquity.

It was still waving them closer.

Falcon and the robot approached the silently beckoning form. Falcon's apprehension had sharpened to dread, but he could not turn back.

He summoned the nerve to speak. 'Well, you're a better snowman than any I ever made. I never had the patience . . . Who *are* you?'

The snowman answered, 'Who do you think?' His voice was deep. There was amusement in it, but also a certain lofty condescension.

'A representative of the inhabitants of Jupiter Within,' Falcon said. 'Whatever you call yourselves.'

'You are mistaken.'

Adam said, from Falcon's side, 'Whoever you are, I should like to know *where* we are. We have long posited the existence of a purposeful technological culture in Jupiter Within. The assaults on our cities were proof enough of that. Now I suspect a capability of – *space-metric engineering.* Something akin to a wormhole. Remember, Falcon, my accelerometers recorded a journey incompatible with our still being inside Jupiter, let alone within the core . . .'

'Why do you imagine you are anywhere, little Machine?'

'Because we are having a conversation,' Adam replied, with a defiance that drew some admiration from Falcon. 'That fact sets certain existential parameters. Even if we are disembodied intelligences our minds are running in some sort of emulation. Any such emulation must be physically grounded on some substrate, and there must be a source of power . . .'

The snowman nodded its faceless white bulb of a head. 'Good, good. I applaud clear thinking. Howard Falcon: would it surprise you to hear that we have already spoken? Or that Adam and I know each other intimately? As well we should, given that Adam helped shape me for the mission that made my name—'

'Orpheus,' Falcon said, with a shiver of awe that had nothing to do with the cold. 'My God. You survived.'

'I endured – call it that. As you endure. I passed into the realm of those you would wish to know, those you would wish to understand. Call them the First Jovians. I met them, and they altered me so that I might survive and learn. Learn and adapt, learn and evolve. Becoming more than the thing I once was. More than you.'

'You have been watching us,' Falcon said slowly. 'You were seen in human spaces – your avatar. *I* saw you. In the ruins of our worlds.'

'And in our cities too,' Adam said now. 'A representation of the primitive form of Orpheus.'

'You never told us that,' Falcon said, looking at him.

Adam made a creaking shrug. 'We were at war, remember. Besides, you never asked.'

'Yes, I was sent to watch you,' said the snowman. 'Once your activities became . . . obvious. Sufficiently large-scale.'

'Like the dismantling of Mercury,' Falcon said dryly.

'Quite. Perturbations on a planetary scale. Indeed, by then you had already had the audacity to send *me*, a probe, down into Jupiter Within. I was a frail thing, and I was cherished by those much greater than me. Since then my purpose has been to help them interpret what I see, understand what you are doing.'

Adam nodded, his metal neck creaking. 'I am glad you were preserved, Orpheus. The intended final upload of your personality back to Amalthea was never achieved. You were thought lost. You did not deserve that.'

'Can you take us to . . . them?' Falcon asked.

The snowman made a laugh – not a kindly laugh, but one born from pity and no small measure of contempt. 'That will not be possible. *I* am the bridge by which you shall achieve what narrow comprehension is possible for you. The First Jovians speak through me, and I distil their thoughts and utterances into a form compatible with the limits of your understanding. Ask for no more than this.'

'We're entitled to ask whatever we like,' Falcon said. 'And I resent being patronised. *You* were made by us, for a purpose – and a bold one, a voyage of science and exploration. And now you must have a purpose in bringing us here.'

'Your physical identities no longer exist in the forms you once knew. But you are not dead. And you still have responsibilities.'

'How can you know us so well?' Adam asked the snowman.

'You are as glass to me. I see your enmities. Your jealousies and grudges. Your endless desire for vengeance against each other.'

'Fine,' Falcon said. 'Then you'll know that Adam and I acted together to defend the Machines against a human weapon. We went deep into Jupiter, trying to prevent a logical-agent weapon from spreading. We sacrificed ourselves.'

'And your point?'

'That our intentions are honourable. In fact, I only came to Jupiter in the hope of averting a larger catastrophe – the use of the Io weapon. Do you know of that?'

'How could I not? Just as I knew of the logic weapon that has been excised from Adam. But the fate of Io is utterly irrelevant.' The snowman motioned past them, to the cottage. 'We shall continue our discussion indoors.'

Falcon and the Machine turned around and retraced their footsteps back to the door, the snowman following them. From outside, the windows glowed with an inviting, golden light. Falcon's simulated heart ached with an almost unbearable longing for home and the comforts of childhood. He knew that this was a fiction woven from his memories, no substitute for the real thing, but the more real it seemed, the crueller the illusion.

They stepped into a bubble of warmth. Falcon closed the door, latching it tight even as wisps of snow curled between the door and its frame. There was no sign of his parents, he noticed, with a pang of loss. He hadn't even spoken to his mother, glimpsed earlier in the kitchen . . .

The snowman ushered them into the parlour. The hearth was still glowing, but the roar and crackle had gone out of the fire. Some barely remembered instinct caused Falcon to grasp the wrought-iron poker and prod the fire back into life, rummaging through the coals and embers until they sparked and flamed.

The snowman extended a hand. 'Come. Sit with me.'

'Aren't you concerned about melting?' Falcon asked, easing into one of the chairs.

'Good point. A crack in the verisimilitude? But actually melting is the least of my concerns.' The snowman's hands were like fingerless mittens, now linked together in its lap. Its white skin glistened and sparkled but showed no other sign of being affected by the fire. 'Our environment, were you able to perceive it in its true nature, would be . . . confusing for you. Confusing and upsetting. Hence this simulacrum. Is it acceptable to you?'

'Would you care if it wasn't?' Falcon asked.

'I do not wish you to be distressed. Given that we are inside the sun.'

Falcon wondered if he had misheard.

Adam leaned forward. Comically, his feet did not quite reach the carpet. 'How can we be *inside* the sun?'

'Come, Adam, you have worked some of this out at least. If metric engineering is sufficient to open a wormhole inside Jupiter, constructing a redoubt inside a star is scarcely more challenging. What is Jupiter but a failed embryo star, lacking the mass to achieve fusion?' Something in the snowman's demeanour seemed to soften. 'You will forgive my tone. I confess I struggle to find the right balance in my dealings with you. When you stand between gods and men, it is easy to assume a certain . . . haughtiness. But even I am as nothing to *them* – a mere mouthpiece.' The snowman nodded at the fire. 'Stir it again, if you would.'

Falcon leaned from his chair to grasp the poker. But as his fingers closed around the iron, he hesitated. 'Why? What does it matter if I do or don't? This isn't real. You're manipulating our perceptions at such a deep level you can decide for yourself how cold or warm we feel.'

'I thought a second demonstration of your capabilities would serve some benefit,' the snowman said. 'But in truth, once was probably sufficient. They cannot have failed to notice.'

'Notice what?' Falcon asked. '*What* demonstration? What capabilities?'

Adam snapped, 'And *who* cannot have "failed to notice"?'

'Your kind. Humans and Machines. Who will have noticed *that you have interfered with the proper functioning of your star.* The fire in the hearth is a symbolic representation. In reality, when you stirred the coals earlier, you were perturbing the very fusion reactions which sustain your sun – the fire that warms the worlds which orbit it.'

Falcon stared down at his hand, at the fingers that still clasped the poker, with a shudder of horror. As if he suddenly found himself holding a snake. 'That isn't possible.'

'By your measure of things, but not by *theirs*. Think of the poker as the control system, the user interface, of a chain of machinery largely beyond your comprehension. When you prod the fire, you make your star skip a few nuclear heartbeats. A complete cessation of fusion, for a few instants.'

Adam was still leaning forward, his hands on the rests of his chair. 'This will have a profound effect on the hydrodynamic stability of the stellar envelope.'

'That is correct. The sudden absence of photon pressure from the core will cause a progressive collapse and rebound of the sun's internal structure. The stellar equivalent of a hiccough. The effect is transient, but it will create a powerful mass ejection when the rebound reaches the surface.'

'Which will come in about . . . thirty thousand years?' Adam asked.

'That is correct.'

Falcon, very cautiously, eased his hand away from the poker. 'I don't understand. Why so long?'

'Simple plasma dynamics,' Adam whispered. 'The sun is very opaque, to light at least. After a photon has been produced by a fusion reaction in the core of the sun, it takes thirty thousand years to fight its way out to the surface. The sunlight that warms your face now began its journey from the stellar interior somewhere around the time of the Cro-Magnons.'

'Adam speaks correctly,' the snowman said. 'Nothing can quickly penetrate the bulk of the sun's mass—'

'Except neutrinos,' Adam stated.

The snowman raised a mitten, acknowledging the robot's point. 'Except neutrinos. Created by the fusion processes in the heart of the sun. Instead of thirty thousand years, it takes *them* only two seconds to battle through the same density of matter. That ceaseless squall of subatomic particles has just had an interruption, as if a great door slammed shut in the furnace of the sun, only to reopen a moment later. And *they* will have noticed: astronomers, monitors of solar weather – those who observe such phenomena, whether human or Machine.'

Falcon wryly remembered Kalindy Bhaskar's Ice Orchestrion, that neutrino-sensitive instrument of ice in Antarctica. Surely that could no longer exist; if it did, he imagined it would be sounding a few sour notes.

'And in thirty thousand years?' he asked now.

'There will be a disturbance. But your descendants will know that it is on its way. They will have time to prepare, time to make arrangements.'

Falcon's horror had turned to revulsion. 'This is monstrous. To perturb the sun, merely to make – what, a gesture?'

'Any more monstrous than to destroy worlds to win a war? One of you is human – or was. One of you is a Machine – or was. Do either of you shrug off the moral burden of the forms you once assumed?' The snowman turned its blank and imperious face. 'Falcon, you helped the Machines gain their liberty from human control. But at the destruction of Earth – in those final moments, you would have gladly annihilated them, your very words conveyed such a threat, if the choice had been yours. If it had been possible, had you been granted the means, in the full fury of that moment – would you have had the moral strength to resist?'

Falcon searched deep inside himself. He knew better than to lie. 'I can't be sure.'

'And now your people plan to smash Jupiter itself, or at least its upper atmosphere, in order to gain some advantage over your foe. And *you*.' The snowman turned to Adam now. 'Falcon allowed you Machines sentience and the means to pursue your own destiny. Yet you could not bring yourselves to live in lasting peace. Greed overcame you – a very human flaw, by the way. When your greed was challenged, you punished the humans by stealing their birth world. *You*, Adam were a significant contributor to the decision process that led to that terrible act. What was the deeper meaning? Was it all revenge over the one you called "Father"? Do you retain that much of the flawed creatures who made you?'

Adam turned away.

'And now, between the two of you, you prosecute a war which, in the end, will threaten every remaining ecological niche in the solar system. Do not think yourself blameless, either of you.'

Falcon looked at Adam; neither of them spoke.

The snowman paused and extended his hands, palms raised to the warming hearth. 'However – here you are, together. Man and Machine. The First Jovians had considered dealing with you two as they had dealt with the previous ambassadors from the Machines – that is, by swatting you away. But here, by some chance, fortuitously, were the two of you, representatives of both realms, tumbling down, down into the dark, intertwined. So I was sent to . . . *inspect* you. Neither of you is without blemish. Still, I was stirred by your decision to proceed with self-sacrifice and cooperation. It gave me encouragement. It gave me an opportunity.'

'To do what?' Falcon asked.

'To petition those who stand above me. To plead with the First Jovians to grant you a second chance.

'The Io weapon is the final straw, you see. By *their* reckoning it is an almost unbearably primitive weapon, conceptually no more advanced than a bone club – but it marks a threshold. You hurl worlds at your enemy, as once your ape predecessors beat each others' brains out with clubs of bone, and with barely more sophisticated reasoning behind the act.

'And in the next stage of your development, you humans, you Machines – you will begin to meddle with the fundamental properties of matter, of spacetime. The idea of such energies being deployed in an unending, ever-escalating war – well.' The snowman settled his hands back into his lap. 'Even then you would have been no more than a nuisance. But if a nuisance must be dealt with, then the sooner the better. *Their* preferred solution was extinction. They have the means, as I am sure I do not need to demonstrate.'

'And now?' Adam asked.

'You have been granted a stay of execution. Contingent, I should add, on the outcome of the next few hours or days. *The Io weapon must not be used.*'

'They're determined to carry it through,' Falcon said. 'The Springer-Soames. The military government.'

'Now you have a chance to argue them out of it,' the snowman answered. And he gestured at the fire, and the poker set beside it.

64

Boss said, 'We have always believed that in every crisis there is also opportunity. Could this time of greatest peril also be the moment when we finally show our true strength?'

'I will follow your lead,' Tem answered. 'As always.'

'I see the Io deployment is proceeding. Have you been offered escape?'

Tem swallowed. 'I was offered, but declined.'

'To remain with your patients?'

'It's the least I could do.'

Boss nodded. He scratched at the overhanging prominence of his brow, and brushed at his flat nostrils, as he always did when at his most thoughtful. It was some years since Tem had spoken to the leader of the resistance. She had time to notice the smoothness of his speech now, inevitably gruff in tone but otherwise convincingly human. Centuries of practice would do that for you, she supposed.

'We had hoped to destabilise this regime, this rotten remnant of the World Government, before it could commit this final atrocity, the fall of Io. Well, we have failed there. But at least we have saved the Machine culture – thanks to you. I can confirm that the logical agent you implanted into Falcon was never delivered. The warning you gave him worked. The Machines were not disabled; there is at least a chance they will survive the Io event. Whatever happens, Lorna – whatever becomes of us – you have acted well. I could not have asked more of you.' He grinned, showing huge, yellowed teeth. 'A pricked thumb! I would have not thought of anything so subtle – so human. And indeed, knowing Falcon of old, I might have feared it would be *too* subtle for him. But it worked – although unfortunately at the cost of Falcon's own long life. Shame. He was a friend to us simps, in as much as any of his generation were.' He grimaced, and reverted to the crude speech of the early simps: '*Boss – boss – go!*' He grinned and hooted laughter.

And it was as if the years fell away, and he resembled his earliest archive images.

This was Ham 2057a, born as a disposable worker in human society, given a birth stamp and a slave name Ham, who had risen to be the first president of the Independent Pan Nation – Ham, who had retreated into the shadows in response to the increasing corruption of the old World Government. Ham, a Pan who now led an interplanetary network of simps and humans in resistance against the Springer-Soames regime.

Lorna Tem had been recruited by agents of the underground Pan Nation as a young, idealistic medical student – a student already appalled at how her profession was being compromised by the demands of the military government. She had found she was able to justify working as a medic for the military forces. A doctor was a doctor; a life saved was a life saved, whatever the circumstances – and her patients, mostly broken soldiers, had had little choice about their careers. But in parallel she had treasured her covert links to the resistance.

And she had never met Boss in person – few had.

She asked now, curiously, 'What of you personally? Are you – comfortable? Wherever you are. Are you simps able to live, to raise your children?'

The Pan smiled, a chimp's toothy grin. 'Don't you worry about me; Boss is fine. We simps have no regrets about the choice we made, our withdrawal from the human world – it was three hundred years ago. We faked our own extinction! Not bad for dumb chimps, huh? Humans were too busy laughing at the bucket-list antics of Eshu the trickster, to notice the Departure. *He* was a true simp hero. And we got away with it, even as the grip of the new surveillance state took hold of mankind.

'No, we do not regret. The World Government respected the Pan Nation, but how long would that respect have endured as the Machine war escalated? We would have been an irrelevance at best – or seen as a disposable asset at worst. This was the best way. I am still engaged in history, am I not?'

'Yes—'

'Wait, please.' Boss turned away and frowned, at a monitor out of shot. 'There is something new. It concerns Howard Falcon.'

She was astonished. '*Falcon*? But you told me he was gone – lost in Jupiter.'

Boss was distracted by whatever was coming through. 'Well, he's not lost any more. If this is authentic—'

'What, sir?'

'A message. Delivered by a *very* strange means.' He faced her. 'You've had some dealings with Falcon these recent days. I need your assessment, Lorna. This message – our agents and assets have word of it, and knowledge has already permeated all levels of government security. They just don't know what to make of it, or how to respond. I think you ought to hear it for yourself . . .'

'I'll help if I can.'

Ham nodded to an off-screen assistant.

There was a crackle, and then a human voice started speaking. But Tem needed no more than the first few seconds of it to know that, whatever it claimed, it could not possibly be the man she knew.

Not unless something quite astonishing had become of him.

65

The snowman had leaned forward to pick up the poker and pass it to Falcon. 'Here. Take it.'

'I did enough damage just now, didn't I? Besides, they'll either have seen the drop in the neutrinos or they won't. Doing it again won't make any difference.'

'You misunderstand my intention. *That* was a mere demonstration of what is possible. Now for something subtler. If the solar neutrinos can be stopped, *they can also be modulated.* When you hold the poker with one end in the fire, your words will be imprinted on the neutrino flux, like sound waves on air. A message that can be decoded. Think on your words carefully.' He glanced at Adam. 'Make this a joint statement. You will be addressing Machines as well as people. Both must grasp the severity of the moment.'

Still with great trepidation, Falcon closed his fingers around the end of the poker. But he did not yet place the other end in the hearth. 'What are the terms to be? Another ceasefire? It'll hold about as long as all the rest.'

'Something more permanent,' the snowman suggested. 'A separation of territories, at least for the time being.'

'We tried that,' Adam said. 'At the end of the twenty-second century we Machines left the inner solar system altogether. It's never worked. There are resources we both covet. We chafe against each other's borders.'

'Then the borders need to be redefined. There are more worlds than the planets of the sun.' The snowman gestured around at the firelit parlour of the little cottage. 'From Jupiter Within, Adam, you have already walked to the heart of a star. Now, *a thousand other worlds lie within your reach.* Worlds beyond your solar system. Worlds like Jupiter: most heavier and hotter, but almost all of them have ecologies of one sort or another. Some are simple. Others are ... shall we say interestingly complex?'

'Extrasolar Jovians,' Adam guessed. 'Hot Jupiters—'

'They are yours for the choosing. The First Jovians have established lines of dialogue with some of the occupants of these worlds – but not all, in some cases the conceptual gulfs are too vast. You would bring fresh perspectives, fresh approaches – fresh ways of thinking. The First Jovians think you could be valuable. In turn, you would need to learn empathy. I have seen the glimmerings of it in you, Adam.'

'What are you proposing?' the robot asked.

'Most of your kin are already inside Jupiter. *Call the others home.* From the Kuiper Belt, from the Oort cloud, from your Host around the sun – summon your lonely warriors. Tell them the solar system is theirs no more, but that prizes beyond imagining await inside Jupiter Within. Make the case persuasively – you'll only have this one chance. And you, Falcon . . .'

'Yes?'

'Let no human interfere with the Machine migration. Give them free passage. Open the cordon around Jupiter. And make it plain that all military action must now cease. If humans obey these stipulations, you will have lost Jupiter and its great treasures . . .'

And the medusae, Falcon thought wistfully.

'But the rest of the solar system is yours. The separation need not be forever. Say – a thousand years? You can agree the terms yourselves. A trial separation. Then envoys of people and Machines may meet again.'

Falcon said, 'It must be together – you and I, Adam. But what if they don't heed our words? The human governments, the Machine collectives – they may not listen.'

'You will be speaking in pulses of modulated neutrinos,' the snow-man pointed out dryly. 'Issuing a proclamation from the heart of the sun. I think they will listen.'

Falcon stood. 'Very well.' He beckoned Adam to stand to his right. Adam closed his metal fingers around the poker just below Falcon's childish hand. Slowly they advanced the poker into the crackle and blaze of the hearth, this time being careful not to stir the fire.

'We speak?' Falcon asked. 'That's all we have to do?'

'Speak,' the snowman said, with a wave of encouragement.

Falcon cleared his throat.

'Hello,' he said, with all the formality he could muster. His voice was still absurdly high, piping and boyish, lacking any authority. He wondered what his audience would make of it, then smiled at his own misgivings. 'This is Commander Howard Falcon, USN, speaking from inside the sun. Ephemeris Time . . . frankly I have no idea. With me is Adam of the Machines. We have come a long way together, and we have something important to tell you. And by that we mean all of you. People and Machines. Wherever you are.

'Please listen carefully – oh, and please tell the Brenner Institute there is life in Jupiter Within. And it's *big* . . .'

66

Lorna Tem listened, and listened again.

At first the childlike tone of the voice had argued against any possibility of it being the Falcon she knew. But what was that when set against the rank impossibility of a human voice imprinted on a modulated flux of neutrinos boiling out of the very heart of the sun?

She clung to her scepticism almost until the end. Falcon and the Machine – the one called Adam – laid out their joint terms for an end to the war. None of it was objectionable to her.

Then he had delivered the part of the message that shredded the last of her doubts.

'Oh, and Surgeon-Commander Tem? I remembered, belatedly, how we first met, many years ago. You were that brave little girl on the *Hindenburg*. I am sorry that our second meeting was not under better circumstances. But you did your best to warn me that I had been weaponised. I am sorry if my revelation now places you in difficulty, but I wanted you to know of my gratitude, and I may not have another chance to express it.'

When the message ended, she only had to assure Boss that as far as she was concerned it was quite authentic – that that was the Falcon she had known.

The Boss grinned that wide chimp smile once again. 'Good luck, Surgeon-Commander – and you may need it after being outed by your exotic friend. If you see him again, remember me to him. *Hoo!* But today a new age begins, for all of us.' And he closed the connection.

It took only seconds before the door buzzed.

'Come in,' she said, feeling neither dread nor curiosity.

It was a Springer-Soames, of course, Bodan Severyn, and a pair of security guards.

Tem said, 'I thought you'd have had the sense to leave by now.'

'We held a last shuttle on-pad for ourselves, and anyone else who needs mopping up. And then we heard that message.'

She smiled. 'Of course. So there's a message from the sky, from the heart of the sun – an incomprehensible event, a revelation. And your first response is to come for me.'

'You're under arrest, Surgeon-Commander. The charges are too numerous to have been detailed yet, but they will include sabotage of the Falcon operation against the Machines, the dissemination of military secrets, espionage, free association with known dissident elements . . .' He glanced at the guards. 'Detain her. Bring her to the shuttle. She isn't to visit any of the other areas in the complex.'

His piece delivered, Tem's humiliation complete, Bodan turned and prepared to march out.

But the guards were hesitating at the door. They glanced at each other, and at Tem, then at Bodan.

And in the bowels of the world, Tem felt something change. A vast engine silenced.

'Take her!'

Still the guards hesitated.

Tem smiled. 'I'm sure your guards heard the message. Everybody must have heard it. You heard my name spoken on a string of neutrinos, pouring from the heart of the sun. *So did your sister*, Bodan. Can't you hear it, feel it? *She* understands that everything's changed – she, evidently, has already shut down your Momentum Pump. Already halted this absurd act of folly. Everything is different now – you must see that.' She turned to the guards. 'As for you – ask yourselves. Whose side are you on?'

At last the guards moved. But it was not Tem they came for.

Bodan Severyn tried to run.

EPILOGUE 1

A final awakening by Mission Control. Polite, comparatively.

He'd been told he should be able to see the rock with the naked eye by now, even though it was still further from him than Earth was from the Moon. So he climbed down into the navigation bay for a look. There it was: just a dull star moving across the sky. He felt an odd shiver as he reported this in.

'Houston, Apollo. So it's not a hoax after all.'

'Evidently not, Seth. We do have some new information. All five previous shots hit the target.'

'You guys did a hell of a job.'

'Well, we caused some deflection, but we didn't get the angle we needed.'

'So I'm not wasting my time up here.'

'Certainly not, Seth. It's still feasible, if you drop that nuke on the sweet spot.'

'And if it's four hours out from me, it's now precisely one day out from the Earth, right?'

'Apollo, Houston. The Vice President asked us to tell you Pat and the boys are with him right now. And to wish you Godspeed.'

'I . . . thank you, Charlie.'

'My pleasure.'

'Time to get to work, then.'

'That would be my suggestion, Apollo.'

So the terminal phase of the mission began.

Up to now the spacecraft had been guided by the navigation system that would have taken NASA to the Moon, a gyroscopic inertial platform backed up by optical star sightings made by Seth himself. With the quarry in sight, the hunt could be much more precise. The big tracking radars on the ground had been able to spot the rock from as far out as twenty million miles. Now, Apollo's own antennas could pick up reflections of those radar signals, which provided much more detailed information on the asteroid's relative range and velocity, and there was a clatter of attitude thrusters as the guidance computer tweaked Apollo's course with ever greater delicacy.

Meanwhile, Seth made what observations of the rock he could. After all, nobody had ever seen an asteroid close up before. 'Houston, Apollo, I see that baby, CAVU.' Clear And Visibility Unlimited, a pilot's term. 'It's not a sphere, more a kind of a potato-shaped lump. Man, its hide is covered in crater walls, like breaking waves. Looks like it's been beaten half to death.'

'Apollo, Houston. Don't you start feeling sorry for it now.'

'The colours are – odd. Grey-white at low light, kind of a light brown, almost a tan, where the sunlight is direct. Looks like an intriguing place to explore.'

'You need to leave something for your sons to do, Seth.'

'Copy that.'

'Apollo, Houston. Just to advise that our blue guest just sent a love letter to your passenger.'

Meaning a USAF officer in Houston had authorised the sending up of an enabling code to wake up the nuke. Even now security was maintained on the ground; even now Seth's conversation with Charlie Duke had to be vague and disguised.

That, however, was kind of a final warning for Seth too. He was just an hour out: time for him to make ready for his own encounter.

He debated using the ship's primitive urine collector one last time. No need.

He settled in the pilot's seat. He had to be ready to duck down to the navigation window, ready to use the steering controls if the automatic guidance failed. He had his tape recorder playing steadily now, stuck to a Velcro pad over his head. And over his window he'd fixed a picture of his wife and kids, taken from Pat's album in the PPK, and an image of the whole Earth from space taken from Apollo 2 – a striking image, seen by no human eye before Schirra and his crew.

A soft alarm chimed.

'Ah, Apollo, Houston. Just to say your onboard radar has now acquired Icarus and is feeding down good quality R and R-dot data . . .'

Range and velocity information was now being provided, ever more precisely, by the Apollo's own onboard radar, for Icarus had come into its range. Under this latest navigation mode the computer once more squirted the thrusters, tweaking the closing trajectory.

And, Seth knew from a checklist he'd memorised, that meant he was only four minutes out. Somehow the time had slipped away from him. He grabbed his tape recorder and rewound it quickly. Just time for one more run-through of Satchmo's song.

Even now, he realised, he didn't really believe it.

'Fifty seconds,' Duke said. 'Firing radar is live.'

Ship and rock were closing at a hundred and twenty-five thousand feet per second – over twenty *miles* a second. To make its destructive statement within a hundred feet of the surface of Icarus, at a point precisely calculated to deliver the maximum deflection, the bomb would have a window of opportunity less than half a second wide. Now the bomb itself was awake and sensing the asteroid, pinging it with radar signals, just as it would have sought out the centres of Moscow or Leningrad had it fulfilled its original design objectives. Another thruster rattle, another trajectory tweak.

'Houston, Apollo. The nuke is guiding me in now, all by itself. I'm like Slim Pickens in *Doctor Strangelove*, right? Well, I surely have learned to love this bomb.'

'Nearly home, Seth,' Duke said gently. 'You're gonna do it, you'll kick that damn thing's ass.'

'And when I do, you guys in Mission Control break out the cheap cigars like you always do.'

'Copy that,' Duke said, sounding choked.

He peered out of his window, looking for the target one last time. What had George Sheridan said, right at the beginning? *Like a kiss on a pool table.* Just a kiss, and now all of this.

But here he was, on the spot, alert and confident and competent. Seth touched the image of his children. He had never felt more alive.

'Houston, Apollo. Signing out.'

Louis B., his timing perfect as ever, was reaching the end of the song, and Seth let himself dissolve into that mellow voice.

'Oh, yeah—'

EPILOGUE 2

Falcon opened his eyes to golden sunlight.

He was sitting on a deckchair, facing out across a railed platform. One other person was here on the platform with him. She leant with an elbow resting nonchalantly against the low guardrail, a glass in her hand, displaying an admirable lack of concern for the drop behind her. Beyond the rail, far below, sweeping grandly into the distance, was the elegant continuation of an airship's envelope. And beyond *that* a crumpled grandeur that he recognised as the Grand Canyon . . .

An airship.

Falcon realised, with a kind of delayed recognition, that he was back on the *Queen Elizabeth*. This was the little external platform that jutted out behind the main observation deck, in the lee of the deck's big Plexiglas dorsal blister. Normally open to VIPs only. But the woman leaning against the railing was no ordinary passenger. She had one foot on the floor, the other on the lowest rail. Her clothes were white, almost luminous in the sunlight.

Falcon stared at this angelic vision. 'If I'm going mad, keep it coming. I'm rather enjoying the experience.'

'No,' she said quietly. 'You're not mad, or delirious.' She held up the glass. 'You want some iced tea?'

'You sound like Hope. You look like Hope. But Hope always said I should stay away from the crash site. And how did I get *here*? The last thing I remember . . . something about the sun . . . I remember Jupiter Within. The snowman, the cottage – Adam?'

'Adam was released.'

Falcon, oddly, imagined a moth cupped in a child's hands, and set free in the safety of the night dark. 'I'm glad.'

'And he brought out with him all that was left of you – *all* of you.'

'And all of *you*? Who decided you should be here?'

Her smile was teasing. 'Complaining?'

'Far from it. But how the hell—'

'Do you believe in reincarnation?'

'No. Given that that we're having this conversation, though ... Where are we? *What* are we?'

'In the future, Howard. I mean, *our* future. At a point in time where the Machines have become – well, pretty powerful. They can resurrect a convincing emulation of almost any historical personage. Even more so when they have direct access to the memories of those who knew that person. Adam had preserved the essence of you, of course. As for me – do you recall the Memory Garden?'

The pain of its destruction still pushed a little sliver through whatever counted as his heart. 'The Springer-Soames destroyed it.'

'Not as thoroughly as they imagined. Shattered it, yes. Obliterated its living ecosystem. But the testimonies, the recordings, the biographical accounts, all were still recoverable. Even as the terms of the human-Machine accord were falling into place – even as Boss, Tem and others were negotiating with the Springer-Soames to establish a new democratic regime to replace the wreck of the WG – there were investigators busy sifting through the rubble cloud of the Memory Garden. After that stunt, Howard, after your speech from the heart of the sun, anything and anybody associated with you was suddenly of huge interest.'

'Nice to know.'

'Yes, much of your memorial to Hope was lost. But much more was preserved. You did a good job, Howard. You remembered her well. She would have been pleased – and she would have understood why you did it.'

'She would?'

'There was always a longing in you, Howard – a hole in your psyche where human companionship used to fit. You needed me. So, as they reassembled you, the Machines stitched me back together as well.'

'So you're not Hope – just a clever impersonation.' He smiled even as the truth took the edge off his joy. 'Should I call you False Hope instead?'

'Call me what you like. All I know is that she was a remarkable doctor. It's an honour just to be her emulation. You don't find this distressing, do you? . . . Let me show you something.' She bid him rise from the deckchair, and join her at the guardrail.

Falcon stood and moved to the railing. Even that simple motion was a strange experience. He now had legs rather than undercarriage; shoes rather than wheels. For the first time in centuries he could feel the fabric of the uniform against his skin, the scratch of it against the hairs of his shins as he moved. Even, he realised, his brief embodiment as his eleven-year-old self was nothing compared to the sheer authenticity of *this*.

'And this is all a gift of the Machines?'

'Physical embodiment is the easiest part of the puzzle, actually. You're like wine. They can pour you into any bottle.'

He grunted. 'Well, I'm a sour old vintage. I bet there's a catch,' he said slowly. 'There always is with the Machines.'

'No, it's an unconditional gift. No strings. No coercion. But if you were willing to help them with a little local difficulty, I'm sure they'd appreciate the gesture. May I show you something else?'

'Go ahead.'

Hope swept her free hand across the sky.

All at once, the blue deepened to an inky darkness, transitioning from the horizon through degrees of purple and navy and indigo to black at the zenith. And, beneath the prow of the *Queen Elizabeth*, the Arizona landscape faded to transparency, ghosting quietly away.

Despite himself, Falcon felt a surge of vertigo. He reached for support, felt the cold steel rail under his fingers. Wherever Hope had taken him, it was somewhere else. Somewhere very else. 'We're not in Arizona any more,' he whispered.

Hope smiled. 'Or Kansas, for that matter.'

The *Queen Elizabeth* was suspended over a planet, far enough from the surface that the curvature of the world's horizon was plainly apparent. Hovering above some great bay or bight, a blue-green sea partly enclosed by long peninsulas.

Falcon stared at the scene for long seconds, trying to be analytical, determined not to jump to premature conclusions, especially on the basis of such sparse sensory data. He was seeing things differently now, his impressions squeezed through the arrow-slots of human perception. His eyes no longer even had a zoom feature.

But in truth, there was a satisfaction in making the best of such meagre resources. He studied the scene anew, trying to forget the battery of enhanced senses he had come to rely on, and to just absorb the view as gathered by his human eyes.

For a start there was clearly atmosphere down there, evidenced by a band of blue that formed a perfect circumscribing arc above the horizon. The landmasses were more than barren rock, for they threw back tints of green and ochre and blue. Near their extremities those two claws of land shattered into chains of islands, diminishing in size as they reached further out into the sea. Falcon glanced from one island to the next. Each was surrounded by a bright margin of cliff or beach, further hemmed by white breakers.

Complexity. Detail. There were atolls and reefs and archipelagos and lone, isolated islands. In the sky there were clouds, and the plumes of barely-slumbering volcanoes.

'It's lovely,' Falcon said. 'Please tell me it's not just another simulation.'

'It's real enough. And we're close enough that seeing it with your own eyes – touching it, exploring it – wouldn't be a problem. We could be *down there*, flying in that air, swimming those seas, walking those shorelines. In a way, though, this world is just a starter. It's not why the Machines called you back to life – or for that matter, why they summoned *me*.' Hope gave a sidelong smile. 'But they thought you'd like it, just as they hoped you'd like me.'

Falcon met her smile with one of his own. He had grown used to the leathery stiffness of his old mask of a face – it had been a useful filter for his deeper feelings, he realised now with chagrin. His expressions were more transparent now; he would have to be careful. 'If this is a starter, what's the main course?'

'That,' Hope said, and directed his attention to the horizon at his right.

Beyond this nameless world, the limb of another planet was rising into view. From its flattened oval, and the heavy banding of its surface features, it could not help but remind Falcon of Jupiter. But he could no more have mistaken it for Jupiter than he'd have mistaken Earth for Mars. This was a Jovian world, but it was unlike any in the solar system. It *glowed*, a sullen red.

'They have a name for it, but it's not one you and I are presently capable of understanding. Or indeed pronouncing. Not that that matters for now. We're here, and they need us. Do you remember the terms of Orpheus's accord, Howard? The separation of human and Machine spheres of influence?'

'Somewhere at the back of my mind.'

'Courtesy of the Machines, we're in an extrasolar system, accessed through the gateway inside Jupiter Within. Just as Orpheus promised. But this Earthlike moon is a mere pendant to a Machine world, Howard: that hot Jupiter is *full* of Machines. A remarkable situation – and light years from Earth. And yet you could be useful here.'

'*Useful.* You make me sound like an old trowel.'

'Better than obsolescence, wouldn't you say?'

'I suppose. Useful how?'

'Do you believe in accidents, Howard? Chance events? This timeline we've found ourselves on – this braid of historical events, this one strand out of all the myriad paths we might have taken – do you ever wonder if there's a deeper purpose to it all?'

'Purpose?'

'A random gust of wind ended your old life, above the Grand Canyon. Without that gust, you'd have sailed on, and no one beyond a small cadre of airship historians would have had reason to know the name Howard Falcon. You'd never have been reconstructed – you'd never have gone to Jupiter, met the medusae. And what caused that gust of wind? Some atmospheric fluctuation, a butterfly flapping its metaphorical wings. Chance shapes our lives on the smallest of scales, and history itself on the largest.'

'Hm,' Falcon said, remembering. '*A kiss on a pool table . . .*'

'Howard?'

'Sorry. Just a line from an old movie. But what's this got to do with me?'

'Do you remember what Orpheus said of the First Jovians?'

Falcon remembered that firelit room, the poker in the hearth, the snowman in the armchair. It felt like some sepia-tinted memory from his earliest childhood. 'Hard to forget. But we weren't told much.'

'We have learned a little more, with time. The First Jovians have achieved an expertise with metric engineering beyond anything in our understanding. They have touched the bedrock of reality . . . and felt ghosts, vibrations, singing through it. Whispers and rumours of other realities, other histories, adjoining our own. *We* can only imagine the paths not taken. The First Jovians – well, they seem to *feel* those lost worlds in their bones. And in some sense – although this is only my intuition – I think they have the means to nurture the paths they deem most favourable . . . those with the outcomes most useful to them, most favourable to life, the most beautiful. However they measure it.

'Now, along with the Machines, they've met – encountered – *something*, inside that hot Jupiter up there, something that doesn't fit into their preconceived framework. Perhaps another order of life, which isn't playing by the usual rules. It's got them befuddled – enough that they need a fresh perspective. I think we, you and I, have been brought to this moment, this place, because even gods need mortals. Because the First Jovians need *us*. Human and Machine. A partnership in curiosity. Because the real work of life, of mind, is still be done. The question is: are you ready for a new journey?'

'I feel like I've done enough journeying for one lifetime.'

'Oh, enough with the self-pity. You're just getting started.'

Falcon felt a shiver of recognition. '*That* sounded like Hope Dhoni.'

'You'd have been disappointed with anything less.' She took a final sip from her glass. 'So what's it to be? A quiet retirement with a view to die for, or something that might stretch you, just a tiny bit?

He smiled, and turned away. His gaze returned to that kiss of atmosphere below, to the cold, clear envelope enclosing a planet's worth of seas and islands and weather. He found himself wondering what the ballooning would be like down there.

He said softly, 'Astonish me.'

Afterword

The idea for this book came from a chance suggestion by Alastair Reynolds in the course of a nostalgic email exchange.

A Meeting with Medusa, the novella by Sir Arthur C. Clarke, was originally published in *Playboy* for December, 1971. In 1972 it won the Nebula Award for Best Novella, and in 1974 the Japanese Seiun Award for Best Foreign Language Short Story. It was perhaps Clarke's last significant work of short fiction, and has been reprinted many times since – perhaps most notably as a terrifically illustrated serial in the short lived magazine *Speed & Power* (IPC, issues 5–13, 1974), a rendition which made a significant impact on the imagination of a young Reynolds.

The Icarus asteroid-deflection episode of the Interludes was inspired by the results of an interdisciplinary student project in systems engineering run at MIT in the summer of 1967. This was in fact the first serious study of how to deflect an asteroid from an impact with the Earth. The final report (*Project Icarus*, L.A. Kleiman (ed.), MIT Report no 13, MIT Press, 1968) was impressive enough to be published, is cited to this day – and was the inspiration for the movie *Meteor* (1979, dir. Ronald Neame), which did indeed star Sean Connery.

In the 1960s, predictions of temperate conditions of temperature and pressure in Jupiter's atmosphere, as well as the possibility of the presence of a wide variety of organic molecules, led to speculation about life in the Jovian cloud layers as depicted in *A Meeting With Medusa*. Later, a detailed study by Sagan and Salpeter (*Astrophysical Journal Supplement Series* vol. 32, pp737–755, 1976) led to a famous visual depiction of cloud beasts not unlike Clarke's in Sagan's *Cosmos* TV series.

The notion of using aerostat factories to mine the atmosphere of Jupiter for the rare isotope helium-3 was suggested in the 1970s *Project Daedalus* starship study conducted by the British Interplanetary Society (see the Final Report, 1978, ppS83ff). The quantum-mechanical 'Momentum Pump' discussed in Chapter 49 is entirely speculative.

All errors and inaccuracies are, of course, our sole responsibility.

S.B.
A.R.
September 2015

ABOUT GOLLANCZ

Gollancz is the oldest SF publishing imprint in the world. Since being founded in 1927 Gollancz has continued to publish a focused selection of bestselling and award-winning authors. The front-list includes **Ben Aaronovitch**, **Joe Abercrombie**, **Charlaine Harris**, **Joanne Harris**, **Joe Hill**, **Alastair Reynolds**, **Patrick Rothfuss**, **Nalini Singh** and **Brandon Sanderson**.

As one of the largest Science Fiction and Fantasy imprints in the UK it is no surprise we have one of the most extensive backlists in the world. Find high quality SF on Gateway written by such authors as **Philip K. Dick**, **Ursula Le Guin**, **Connie Willis**, **Sir Arthur C. Clarke**, **Pat Cadigan**, **Michael Moorcock** and **George R.R. Martin**.

We also have a strand of publishing in translation, which includes French, Polish and Russian authors. Gollancz is home to more award-winning authors than any other imprint, with names including **Aliette de Bodard**, **M. John Harrison**, **Paul McAuley**, **Sarah Pinborough**, **Pierre Pevel**, **Justina Robson** and many more.

The SF Gateway
*More than 3,000 classic, rare and previously
out-of-print SF novels at your fingertips.*
www.sfgateway.com

The Gollancz Blog
*Bringing you news from our worlds to yours. Stories,
interviews, articles and exclusive extracts just for you!*
www.gollancz.co.uk

GOLLANCZ
LONDON